Praise for Marie-Nicole Ryan's
HOLDING HER OWN

"I was surprised at how much depth the story had written into it and delighted that the cover fulfilled its promise of a steamy read." Reviewer: The Jeep Diva Blog

"Fast-paced and with interesting characters, this intricate novel has red herrings in abundance. The ambiance of New Orleans enhances the story by contributing to several threads. Witty verbal sparring leads to several hot and explicit sex scenes." Reviewer: RT Book Reviews

Top Pick! "Marie Nicole Ryan has a hit with this beautiful book. I loved that you have two hardheaded people and workaholics to boot put closely together. Jake and Caitlin are great from their fiery tempers to their passionate interludes. *Holding Her Own* is just an overall awesome read. Marie definitely knows how to create memorable characters and a loved that keeps the storyline plunging along. There is never a dull moment as the excitement keeps your nose glued to the pages." Reviewer: Night Owl Romance

"As a romance and suspense, Holding Her Own is a delectably perfect blend of both genres, standing out for me as top-notch in both areas." Reviewer: Madame Butterfly's Blog

"Holding Her Own...is wonderfully written, the action in this book flows like the Louisiana bayou. Caitlin, Jake and all the other characters meld together in a plot that just keeps firing in all directions." Reviewer: ParaNormal Romance

The writing is excellent, the plot believable and fast-paced, and the primary characters sexy, likable, and dedicated. The secondary characters...well, they fall into several categories: dedicated fellow agents, quirky casino workers, voodoo practitioners, dangerous and malevolent villains, and a high-functioning autistic child. Add all these together and you have a unique and well-constructed plot that keeps you guessing from beginning to end. This book is well worth the read, and an excellent example of the genre that I wish other authors would strive to emulate." Reviewer: Literary Nymphs Reviews

Other Books by Marie-Nicole Ryan

Hill Country Lawmen
Threatened, 2
Hunted, 1

Loving the Lawman Series
(Historical Western Romance)
Mastering the Marshal, 3
Taming Talia, 2
Seducing the Sheriff, 1

Music City Heat Series
(Romantic Suspense)
Measure of a Man, 3
Because of You, 2
Love Me if You Can, 1
Beginnings, Short Story Prequel

David and Miranda French Stories
One Too Many (Mystery/Suspense)
Love on the Run (Romantic Suspense)

FBI Guys
(Romantic Suspense)
Broken Promises, 2
Holding Her Own, 1

Stand Alone Romantic Suspense
Too Good to be True
The Man for the Job
See You in My Dreams

Holiday Themed Short Stories
Valentine's Gift, 3
Pillow Talk, 2
Mistletoe and Mario, 1

HOLDING HER OWN
FBI Guys 1

By

Marie-Nicole Ryan

RYANDALE PUBLISHING

Copyright

Copyright © 2008 by Mary Varble
Edited by Linda Ingmanson
Cover design by Mary Varble
Cover photo © Les Byerley/iStockPhoto.com

First Ryandale Publishing Electronic & Print Publication: 2015
Second Ryandale Publishing Print Publication: 2020
All rights reserved.

Previous electronic publication, Samhain Publishing, Ltd, July 2008
Previous print publication, Samhain Publishing, Ltd, May 2009

Library of Congress Registration Number: TX 6-975-152

Dedication

To my editor, Linda Ingmanson, for her careful and thoughtful combing out the knots of this story.

Chapter One

Today was the day. About time, too. Finally, she'd show everyone who considered her rapid advance through the ranks of the FBI was the result of her father's influence.

Special Agent in Charge of a high-profile undercover operation. Damn. She'd more than earned it. Her father be damned.

Caitlin glanced at her watch. Eight-forty-five. And the Assistant Director of Special Ops, Gutierrez, wanted her in his office at nine. With morning DC traffic, she'd never make it.

She whipped around the corner into the kitchen. Her housekeeper and ersatz mother, Bonnie, stood in front of the stove, her spatula raised at the ready.

"Don't you try pulling that I-don't-have-time-for-anything-but-a-cup-of-coffee business with me. Today you're going to sit down and have a decent breakfast if I have to cuff you to the table." The good woman folded her arms across her ample chest. "What's it going to be?"

"I don't even have time for coffee. I'm already late."

"Being late one time isn't gonna get you kicked out of the FBI."

"Not today. I can't be late. It's special. Jose just called and assigned me to an undercover operation, and I'm the SAC."

"I don't see anything so all-fired important about going undercover wearing nothing but a sack." Setting her spatula down with a whack, Bonnie frowned and huffed.

"Don't act uninformed with me. You've been around DC a lot longer than I have. You know what a SAC is as well as I do."

"Yes, child, it's Special Agent in Charge, and I don't want my girl going off doing such foolishness. You're an accountant, for Pete's sake. Number cruncher. Bean counter; isn't that what they call you?"

"Yes, but this is a big deal, and—"

"It's the same old story. You don't have to prove anything to anyone but yourself, child. There's no need for you to go out and mix it up with the bad guys. Stick to those fancy spreadsheets."

"It's a big deal to me, Bon-bon." Caitlin glanced at her watch again, then leaned over and kissed the woman who'd taken care of her since childhood. "As much as I'd like to stay and argue, I have ten minutes to get to the A.D.'s office."

Without giving the older woman a chance to object, Caitlin grabbed the thermal cup of coffee Bonnie handed her. "Thanks, you're a doll." She snatched her briefcase off the hall table and sprinted for the door.

"I'll see you tonight," she called and slammed the door of the Georgetown row house behind her.

Jake LeFevre strode down the brightly painted halls of the Shadow Pines Nursing Home to his father's room. He forced himself to stop at the door and sucked in a deep breath. It seemed with every visit, Ed deteriorated a little more. How much longer could he last?

A rock 'n' roll tune jarred him from his thoughts. Dread centered in his gut whenever his cell phone rang. It was never good.

"LeFevre," he answered.

"How do you feel about a long trip to New Orleans?" his boss Jose asked.

"Not interested. Ed's not doing so hot. I'm at the nursing home now."

"I wasn't asking. You're needed on an undercover operation in a casino. You're the one for the job. You know casinos inside and out."

"I know 'em a little too well...or have you forgotten?"

"You'll be in Security, not dealing."

"Let me think about it. I'll give you a shout after I see Ed." That'd give him time to come up with a way to get out of it without shooting himself in the foot with the Bureau.

"Get in here ASAP. I'll give you the details."

"I haven't said I'll do it."

"I didn't say you had a choice."

"No shit." He snapped the phone shut.

An undercover op in New Orleans? That was the last thing in the world he needed. Besides, undercover assignments were supposed to be voluntary.

He stepped into Ed's room and found a nurse suctioning the older man. When she finished and Ed was breathing easier, Jake raised an eyebrow. "'Bout the same?"

She shrugged and gave him a regretful smile. "A little weaker each day." She brushed the salt and pepper hair back from Ed's forehead. "But he has a strong heart. And he's a fighter."

"Ma'am, you have no idea. He took me off the streets and turned me into a real human being. And it nearly killed both of us."

"He was a cop, wasn't he?"

"Yeah. A good one, too."

"You're his only visitor. It's sad."

"We're originally from New Orleans. I'm assigned here in DC, so when the rehab doctor said he wouldn't make any more progress and was ready to ship him off to a nursing home, I had him flown up here, where I could keep an eye on him."

The nurse smoothed and tucked the sheets. "You must really care about him."

"I do. I owe him a lot."

Delaying the inevitable, Jake walked to the window and noted the cleanliness of the panes. The winter sun shone through, making the first-floor room bright and almost cheerful. He looked out at the front parking lot. Bare trees formed a sketchy pattern of lines against the clear sky.

Too bad Ed was oblivious to the sunshine.

He returned to Ed's bedside and saw his father's eyes were open but unseeing. He took his mentor's hand in his. "Ed. It's Jake." How the man had aged.

Six months ago, fifty-four-year-old Ed Hoolihan was a big, hearty Irish NOPD detective, and in line for Chief of Detectives. But a car chase that ended in a disastrous crash left him in a coma. Now he was a fragile shell of a man holding up a sheet.

"They say you might be able to hear me, so I'll keep rattling on as if you can. Jose called me today. He's got an undercover op that'll take me to New Orleans for a while. I told him, no, but it doesn't sound like he's going to take no for an answer."

Jake swallowed hard. "I hate to leave you in the lurch like this, but I know they'll take good care of you for me. I just wish I could pay you back for all you did. I didn't make it easy."

His throat tightened. He could barely get out the words. "I don't know how long I'll be gone. You know how it is with ops. It's a casino, too. Now don't worry, I'll be in Security. I won't have to touch a deck of cards or a pair of dice. I can handle it okay."

No response. Not a flicker of an eyelid. Nothing.

In the space of sixty seconds, Jake's day slid from minor irritation to going-to-hell-in-a-handbasket, to dumping him on his ass.

"Dammit! I don't want her on my team." He paced up and down the Assistant Director of Special Ops' office. "No way am I gonna put up with some stuck-up prima donna screwing up my operation."

"She's not on your team, LeFevre. You're on hers."

Jake stopped mid-stride and threw up his hands. "No way, Jose."

Jose Gutierrez's face flushed. "Cheap shots will get you nowhere. Caitlin Chaney has an accounting background. She can spot a money-laundering scheme quicker than you can load a nine mil."

"She's never been undercover."

"She has...and performed damned well."

"Hardly think posing as the wife of a diplomat at a dinner party was much of a stretch." Hands fisted at his sides, he stopped and eyeballed his boss. As calmly as he could manage, he took a deep breath and began again. "Her lack of undercover experience will jeopardize this operation. I need an experienced partner, one I won't have to clean up after—one who can hold her own."

"Dammit, Jake. She's brilliant, the best the money laundering team has to offer...and she's in charge. Now you can opt-out. I'm sure we can find another assignment appropriate to your talents— somewhere like Armpit, Nebraska."

"But—"

"But nothing. See here, your specialized knowledge and talents are needed on this op. You have the casino background, but you're not the only game in town." The A.D. shrugged. "The Palais Pontchartrain needs a new guy in Security, and you fit the bill. You'll be vetted by our contacts in Vegas."

Jake shrugged, knowing he was on thin ice. "New Orleans is risky. And there's my gambling addiction." As much as he hated reminding the boss of his weakness, he didn't have a choice.

Jose gave a dismissive wave. "You haven't been in The Big Easy since you were eighteen and left for college. You've changed a lot. As for the other, I have faith you have it under control. You do have it under control, don't you?"

"Yeah, but that's avoiding anything resembling a casino."

"Jake, it can't be helped."

"You're right." Jake rubbed his jaw while he considered the truth of Jose's words. "As for my addiction, I've had a lot of experience controlling the old itch. What's one more casino gig?" He stuck his hands in his pockets and shrugged. "If it weren't for Ed and the prima donna you're giving me for a SAC, I wouldn't balk at the op."

"Tell me about Ed. How is he...really?"

A bitter taste flooded Jake's mouth. "Not good. He's in a nursing home in Cheverly. He lies in bed, breathing through a tube, being fed through one tube and pissing through another. He doesn't know me or anything else, for that matter. And the nurse tells me he's getting weaker every day."

"Tough luck. He was a good cop."

"The best. I hate leaving him. He doesn't have anyone else—I'm it."

Jose sighed. "What if I promise to look in on him every week and let you know if anything happens? I'll make sure he's getting the best of care—just like you would."

Guilt wracked Jake. Jose wasn't playing fair, but at least he was offering an alternative. "Okay, but...about Her Highness Agent Chaney..."

"Special Agent in Charge Chaney."

The odious sound of a certain female voice brought Jake sharply around. Glittering green eyes stared back at him, and they said the lady wasn't amused. Well, neither was he. "Like to sneak up on people, do ya, Special Agent in Charge Chaney?"

"I was announced, not sneaking in, but you're so in love with the sound of your own voice, you weren't listening."

Jose stood and extended a hand to the redhead. "Caitlin, welcome. I'd just started briefing Jake on your operation." He glanced at Jake. "Have you two met?"

"Nope." Damn. He'd heard she was dynamite, but the woman in front of him was a quantum leap over TNT. She was more in the class of C. Her tits alone were an adolescent boy's wet dream.

She smiled. "I know Special Agent LeFevre by reputation only. From what I've just heard, he's a man of few words and obviously jumps to conclusions."

"It doesn't take *War and Peace* or an in-depth profile for an experienced agent to size up another." God, had he really alluded to *War and Peace*? How long before he started drooling?

Still, he couldn't keep his gaze from roaming down her trim hips. When he returned to her direct stare, her jaw was clenched, and her eyes had glazed over like a skim of ice over those green depths. Her hair was the color of a new penny, pulled back tight and screwed up in some kind of twist. So why was this uptight accountant so hot to mix it up in an undercover operation?

Chaney folded her arms across her chest, never allowing her gaze to leave his. "Ditto. You've made your feelings clear. I could hear you in the outer office."

"Good. Then we won't have any misunderstandings, will we?"

"No. We won't...as long as you remember I'm in charge."

"Oh, yeah, like that's something I'm gonna forget."

"I've heard all about you, Agent LeFevre. You're a bit of a rogue. Like to do things your way." Her full lips twisted into a sardonic grimace. "I'll have you know upfront: this operation will be by the book or you're out the door."

"Okay." Jose threw up his hands in mock surrender. "Now that we know who's who, let's get down to business."

"Fine with me." Jake motioned for Chaney to be seated. "After you, ma'am."

Caitlin sat with a huff, wishing like hell she'd not let LeFevre get to her. She'd been warned about his lone wolf attitude, and still, she'd let him push her buttons. But what no one had bothered to tell her was he exuded an aura of bad-boy sexuality. He'd undressed her with his slow, insolent gaze and hadn't even tried to hide it.

"Caitlin, you already know most of this. You and Jake are going in as an accountant and security."

"Won't they be suspicious of two new employees at one time?" LeFevre asked with a frown.

"No. You'll be properly vetted and besides," The A.D. cast his gaze downward and adjusted a stack of files on his desk, "you're—uh, married."

"Married!" Caitlin and Jake rose from their chairs simultaneously. In his earlier brief, the A.D. had omitted that singular point.

"Yes, Caitlin's background will be confirmed by one of our contacts in the Delateo family in Jersey. And Jake's from the Bellagio in Vegas. The head of security there is retired from the

Bureau. He's vouching for you. The two of you have been married for six months. Your contact at the Palais Pontchartrain is Agent Alex MacGregor. We sent him ahead four weeks ago. He's been undercover in Security. He's expecting you on Thursday. You have forty-eight hours to perfect your covers."

"Why this particular casino?" Jake asked.

"We were contracted by a whistleblower, but before we could arrange a meet, she disappeared, which told us we were on the right track. The casino is owned by a consortium out of Miami called Rivera Corporation, so drug interests are a good bet. Once the money is laundered, there's no telling where it'll end up. We need to shut these folks down. I don't need to remind either of you..."

Unforgettable images of the flaming towers, the terrible collapse of the first and then the other. The lives lost, the incalculable human toll. Caitlin spoke first. "No, sir, you don't. We'll clean out this bunch."

"Don't underestimate them. Our whistle blower's never been found, and you're taking her place. These folks aren't playing tiddlywinks."

LeFevre leaned forward. "That's why I need someone with more experience, boss."

Gutierrez frowned. "Jake, right now, you're more replaceable than Chaney here. Get used to it. Caitlin, here you go."

He handed her a disc file. She took it. Luckily her hand didn't tremble, but her insides rumbled as if the Metro had made a scheduled round. Was she really up to the job?

"Fine." Jake grabbed his file and turned for the door. "When will the paperwork be ready?"

"Pick it up at nine. In the meantime, become Kate and Jack Girard."

"Fine. See you in the morning, Special Agent in Charge Chaney."

The arrogant jerk was trying to run out on her. "Don't you think we should spend the next forty-eight hours working on our covers?"

Her new partner's scowl deepened and transformed his face into the Crypt Keeper. "Don't know about you, but I'm a quick study. I've got better things to do if I'm going to be stuck with you for the next God-only-knows-how-many months."

"Look here, LeFevre, I'm not any happier about this situation than you are, but it's our job. It's what we do. So get over yourself." So, he thought he was stuck with her? Then he'd better keep his eyes directed somewhere besides her breasts.

As if he could read her mind, a smirk spread across his sensual mouth, erasing the frown. "Maybe a six-pack of tallboys will make this assignment look a lot better in the morning. I'm gonna find out. Join me, if you want."

"As if." Kate watched him swagger from the office. She turned to Gutierrez. "He's the most despicable man I've ever come across. I'll show him."

The A.D. sighed. "He's not as bad as he seems. He's a top-notch agent and his experience with casinos is unparalleled. You're tough enough to keep him in line. Your father will be proud of you."

Her father?

"My father has nothing to do with this operation. You've given me this assignment because I'm the best person for the job. You said so yourself. And whether or not my father is proud of me is totally irrelevant."

"Now, Caitlin."

"If that's all, I have to chase down my reluctant partner and figure out how to convince everyone else I'm a newlywed who's madly in love with her husband."

"Good luck."

Jose's wry tone told her what she already knew. "Luck? With Agent LeFevre, I'll need the patience of a saint and wine coolers on tap."

The A.D.'s laughter followed her out the door. Let him laugh. She'd show them all. She was in charge because she'd earned the position, and her father's being Secretary of the Interior had nothing to do with it. Nothing at all.

*

Jose waited until Caitlin cleared the outer office and buzzed his assistant. "Get me Secretary Chaney on the phone." Then he sat back and waited.

"It's done, but I don't like it."

"You owed me, Jose."

"Well, now I don't."

"The end justifies the means. I want my daughter to get the idea of being an FBI agent out of her head."

"Have you ever considered she'll succeed?"

"Considering who she has on her team—no, the assignment will be a disaster."

"It's a big risk. Her life's at risk as on any other undercover assignment."

"LeFevre better not let anything happen."

"There're no guarantees, Dexter. What makes you so sure Jake can screw up the assignment and still keep your daughter's skin intact?"

"I've had a run-in with him. He's the kind of man she hates. They're oil and water; they'll never make an effective team. Therefore, the mission will fail before it gets started. She won't have time to get into real trouble."

"You underestimate Caitlin. You always did. She's a grown woman, a qualified agent and damned smart. If she finds out—"

"She won't...will she?"

"Not from me. But understand this: I don't owe you anything else. No more favors."

"Understood."

"I just hope you don't regret it."

"My daughter. My problem."

Jake shook his head in disbelief. It certainly was a small world, and DC was a damn village. Caitlin Chaney, daughter of Secretary of the Interior, Dexter Chaney. The man was a political suck-up who owed his position to his long friendship with the president and history of hefty donations to all his campaigns through the last fifteen years.

What irony. Only two short years earlier, Jake's ex-wife, Melissa, had been Chaney's law clerk...and his lover. When Chaney tired of her, he recommended her for an associate's position with a prestigious firm on the west coast.

Once Melissa had cleared out, he'd discovered her diary on the PC. He showed up at Chaney's condo and took out his anger by slugging the Secretary of the Interior.

It wasn't Chaney's fault Melissa'd decided to sleep her way to the top but slugging him still left Jake with a great feeling of satisfaction.

But having Chaney's daughter in charge of what should be his undercover op still sucked big time.

Caitlin stood outside Aaron's Retreat. The bar possessed all the prerequisites for a local hangout for FBI agents—plenty of mirrors for covert surveillance, dark oak paneling, comfortable booths and discrete potted plants where any number of handy listening devices could be hidden. And it had the benefit of being LeFevre's local hangout.

It was now or never. She gripped the handle and opened the door to a din of noise and laughter. She threaded her way to a table in the bar section and ordered a glass of chardonnay. Luckily it was still early.

But not too early for one particular agent.

She smiled into her chilled glass of wine and took a tiny sip. Agent LeFevre had just bellied up to the bar and ordered a Bud Light. How cautious of him.

When he'd swaggered arrogantly from the meeting, she made up her mind to show him just how undercover she could go. She changed clothes and formed her plan.

Right about now.

She caught him watching her in the mirror behind the bar and smiled at him over her glass of wine. *Come hither* wasn't exactly her usual style, but she'd show him.

Ah... He eased off the barstool and made his way to her table. He arched a dark eyebrow. "May I?"

"Sure." She took another tiny sip of wine and stifled the rush of glee rippling through her.

Piece of cake. Like the spider said to the fly. Yeah!

"Haven't seen you here before."

"Haven't been here before." She batted her mascaraed lashes at him. Was she overdoing it? "Just sublet a condo from my cousin. Great place, more than I could ever afford on my own. He's with the American Embassy in Mali."

The about-to-be-suckered agent rolled his eyes. "I don't need your life history. Do you wanna get laid or not?"

What a Neanderthal pig. And this was the agent with whom she'd have to spend weeks, possibly months? She bit back her anger and took a deep breath.

LeFevre looked at his watch. "This is how it is. I'm not interested in a relationship. I need to get laid. If you're not interested, I'll move on. I have to spend the next two or three months working with a broad who acts as if she'd rather suck rust through a straw than smile."

Caitlin gritted her teeth, then forced a smile. "I don't need your life story either. Let's go." She stood, threw down a twenty and jerked her purse onto her shoulder.

How far was she willing to go to show him up? Well, not quite *that* far.

She shoved her way through the crowded bar. He was right behind her. The scent of his aftershave tickled her nose, something woodsy with a hint of the outdoors. What conceit. Agent LeFevre wouldn't know a cord of wood from a pinecone.

The door opened and a cold blast of air hit her face and chilled her cheeks. She pulled her faux leopard coat around her shoulders. "I have my own car. Better you follow me."

"Fine." He pulled her into the shelter of his arm. "Let's keep you warmed up."

"Oh, I'm warmed up all right. Don't you worry 'bout me."

She let him keep her cuddled up until they reached her black Acura. He backed her against the car. "My cousin's place—it's not too far. Georgetown."

"Georgetown it is, little gal."

Little gal. Who did LeFevre think he was? John Wayne?

"See that you keep up with me. I wouldn't want you to get lost." She affected the breathy tone of a femme fatale and batted her lashes while hoping lust would blind him to her real identity a little longer.

"No chance of that." He reached around and gave her butt a squeeze.

She flinched. "Oh…" She'd get even with him for that. Yes, she would.

"Later." He turned and tossed her a smile and waggled his fingers in a see-ya-toots kind of wave.

Caitlin gritted her teeth. This was a mission close-to-impossible. And she couldn't wait to kick his arrogant butt.

In truth, her row house wasn't far. After finding parking places, they reached the front door of her three-story, brick townhouse.

Think fast. Or he'd be inside, and frankly, she wasn't sure what he'd do when he discovered he'd been had. She didn't trust this no-nonsense, do-you-want-to-get-laid-or-not jerk.

She fumbled for her keys. "Silly me. I know they're here somewhere. She glanced back toward the direction they'd come. "God. I hope I didn't drop them—"

"These?" LeFevre jiggled her keys right in her face.

"How? Uh—" she sputtered.

"Picking pockets—one of my many talents…Cait."

Damn. "But—"

Jake pulled her to him. "You can't kid a kidder." He slanted his lips across hers and kissed her soundly. Without meaning to, she responded. His kiss was surprisingly tender, not demanding or rough like she'd expected. Not that she'd ever really expected…

She liked his lips on hers…a lot.

But reason returned quickly, and she shoved him away.

"Dammit. Stop."

Jake stepped back, hands up in surrender. "All you have to say is 'no'." A lazy grin kicked up the corner of his mouth and a strand of black hair fell across his forehead. He flicked it back, shrugged and said softly, "'Night, Cait."

"Wait! When did you know? What gave me away?"

"At first glance, your fake leopard jacket said working girl. Then I saw your Rolex. The two images just didn't jive. That piqued my curiosity."

"So when you came over and said...what you said, you already knew?"

He bit his bottom lip to keep from laughing. "Yeah, I figured if you didn't slap my face right then, I could have some fun before I called you on it."

"Fine." She huffed and held out her hand. "My keys, please."

"Yes, ma'am, Special Agent in Charge Chaney." Jake ignored her outstretched hand and unlocked the door.

"Good night." Her tone was firm. Was it firm enough? She placed her hand on the doorknob, but he covered it with his own. In spite of the frigid temperature, he'd kept her warm. Too warm. He opened the door and the nervy bastard followed her inside.

She turned and blocked him. "Just what do you think you're doing? If you think I'm letting you—"

"We need to work on our covers, don't we?" His dark brown eyes glittered as his bad-boy smile widened. "It was your idea."

"Yes, well...I thought..." She shrugged as if it made no difference what he did.

"Thought what?"

"Never mind. Come on in."

Chapter Two

Jake stepped into a softly lit foyer. A flight of stairs led directly to the second level like a lot of townhouses in the area. Hardwood floors shone with a soft glow where they weren't covered by an oriental rug. On one wall a large gold-framed mirror was flanked by ornate wall-mounted candlesticks. Way too high-tone and girly for his tastes. "Your cousin has nice digs."

"About that cousin thing..."

"So that was part of your con? This is *your* place?"

"Yeah." She held out her hand for his coat. "Would you like some coffee? Then we can get to work."

Jake shrugged. "You're the boss."

At the far end of the foyer a door opened, and a silver-haired woman peeked through. "Miss Chaney? Back so soon?"

"We decided to work here. Is there some fresh coffee?"

The woman grinned, a web of wrinkles wreathing her full face. She patted her hair; it was so fine it reminded Jake of a pile of white cotton candy. "You know I always keep a fresh pot on. I'll have it for you in a jiffy. Dining room or..."

"The study will be fine, Bonnie."

"Yes, ma'am." The door closed.

"Old family retainer? *Yes, ma'am,*" he muttered. Clearly, Caitlin Chaney was used to the finer things in life. Probably thought being in charge of an operation was her due just because she was the Interior Secretary's daughter. She wouldn't have lasted twenty-four hours on the streets of the French Quarter.

"Bonnie isn't just an employee to me. She's a dear friend and the closest thing to a mother I've ever had."

"Sorry. How was I supposed to know? Gives us something in common."

"*My* mother didn't run off. She died when I was two days old." As if realizing how harsh she sounded, she stopped. "I'm sorry. I didn't mean for it to come out like that."

Hurt rose in his chest, but it was an old hurt. He shrugged it away like an out-grown jacket. "Don't be. Shows you've done your homework."

She leveled her gaze on him. What now? he wondered.

"You have a way of pushing my buttons."

"You'll have to get used to it. We're joined at the hip..."

Her eyes widened at the word "joined". "If you think—"

"Until this op is over," he finished, in a vain attempt to hide his amusement. God only knew what Jose was thinking of sending this neophyte into an undercover situation. If they both came out with all body parts in working order, it would be a damned miracle.

"Let's get to it then. The study's this way."

A lamb to the slaughter, he followed. Kate's disguise for the evening included a short skirt that cupped her bottom like a second skin. He sucked in a breath. The rear view of her toned thighs...inspiring.

Down, boy. There'll be no joining—at the hip or otherwise—tonight.

The study turned out to be a comfortable, almost masculine room. Two leather couches faced each other in the middle of the room, and a massive old desk was placed in front of the bay window. Books lined the walls and there was an oil portrait over the fireplace. He glanced around, half expecting to see a bewigged Thomas Jefferson penning the Declaration of Independence with a quill.

Caitlin plopped down on the closest sofa and motioned for him to take the other. "Get comfortable. It's going to be a long night. Jake? Earth-to-Agent LeFevre."

He gave a bark of laughter and sat. "This is a great room. For a minute there, I thought I'd stepped into another century."

"It's been like this ever since I can remember. It was my mother's family home. She left it to me in her will. I guess she must've known she was dying and made it out right before she died. I was still a baby."

He stretched out a leg and tested his long frame against the length of the couch. "Sorry about your mother. Must've been rough growing up without her."

Kate's gaze grew steely. "That's my mother...up there, the portrait."

"Beautiful woman. You're very like her."

"Yes, she was. Thank you. It's odd. I've looked at her portrait so many times, but I've no clue what she was really like. Was she terribly in love with my father—difficult for me to imagine—was she afraid at the end? Her portrait tells me nothing."

"But I'm sure your father must've told you stories about her. He must've been grateful to still have you."

She glared back and ignored his comment about her father—why?

"We need to focus on the operation. This trip down memory lane is an unnecessary diversion."

"Yes, ma'am, Special Agent—"

"And can the SAC crap, too. If we're going to function as a team, we have to pull together and watch each other's backs."

Jake laughed. "You sound like you almost know what you're talking about. I'm impressed."

Her gaze narrowed. "I went through the same training at Quantico as you, LeFevre."

"Let's see if I've done my homework. You completed your training five years ago. All you've done since then is sit on your very attractive ass and crunch numbers. Tell me if I'm getting warm?"

An angry flush spread up Kate's neck, splotches appeared, marring the soft, pale skin. "Go to hell."

"That's warm."

"I'm as qualified physically and mentally as the day I left Quantico—if not more. I maintain a firing range and a gym in my basement." She raised her chin a notch. "Care to test me?"

He shook his head. "I'd rather have you in one piece for the op."

"Maybe *you'll* be the one at risk."

"Me? Chèr, have you lost your mind?" Amused, he stood. At six-feet, one-inch, he towered over her. "You're five-six at most." He paused and eyeballed her trim figure. "And at two-fifteen, I outweigh you what—a hundred pounds?"

"Not quite." The muscle in her jaw worked, demonstrating to his experienced eyes just how pissed she was. What was she trying to prove and why?

"I'm solid muscle. No excess."

Jake laughed. He knew full well she possessed one area that wasn't solid muscle. He'd pulled her against his chest at the front door. Her breasts were full against him, and no set of pecs were anything like as sweet.

She stood, then gave him a mock uppercut to the chin. "You'd do well to keep your gaze on my *face*, LeFevre. You're treading a fine line here."

He grasped her wrist and held it firmly but gently. "I'm guilty of being all male. Can I help it if I'm easily distracted?"

Caitlin shook her head, then jerked her wrist from his grasp. He couldn't get by with treating her like a sex object. "This is never going to work. I'll call Jose now and ask for a replacement."

"Hold on a damn minute. *You need me.*"

She gazed into his dark, impenetrable eyes. What kind of man was he really? "How's that? Jose said you were *replaceable*."

"He was blowing smoke, trying to mollify you. Listen, babe, I know casinos. I've worked in Security. I've worked as a pit boss on a half dozen undercover ops. You need me, Chaney. And you don't have enough experience to know how much."

"Then get this straight. You will treat me with respect. I'm supposed to be your *wife* for Pete's sake. We've only been married for six months. We're going to be living in the same small apartment. What's your problem anyway? Do you hate all women agents, or is it just me?"

"I don't hate women agents. I've worked with some—"

"So it's me?"

"Yeah, it's you. I don't know how you made it through Quantico, but I suspect your father's position in the government had something to do with it."

Caitlin clenched her fists, her nails digging into her palms. She took a deep breath and willed her hands to relax. "I don't care what you've heard or what you think. My father has nothing to do with any of my accomplishments. As far as I'm concerned, he paid my school bills. I owe him my education and not another damned thing."

"So, my father was a shit, too." Jake shrugged.

Anger ripped through her as though LeFevre had waved a red flag in her face. "Never mention him again."

"Translation: sore point."

Another word and she'd have to shoot him. And how would she dispose of his body? "Excuse me," she said through clenched teeth. "I'll see what's keeping the coffee."

A tap at the door filled her with relief. She let out a sigh. There was good-as-gold Bonnie rolling in a tea cart set with the Limoges which was only used for special guests. Whatever possessed her to do that?

"I thought you all might get hungry." Bonnie smiled at LeFevre. "Most big men I know have big appetites, so I fixed some ham sandwiches for you, and Cait, darlin', just for you, fresh brownies."

A small moan escaped before Caitlin could hold it back. "Brownies." The word came out as a sigh. Her weakness.

"Miss Bonnie." Jake beamed widely and bowed over the housekeeper's hand. "I'm so delighted to make your acquaintance."

"Are my ears playing tricks on me? Do I hear a hint of the Big Easy in your voice?"

"Born and bred there, don't ya know?"

"Very nice to meet you, too." She glanced at Caitlin and winked.

The traitor—she'd already succumbed to LeFevre's dubious charm. "Sorry, Bonnie, this is Agent LeFevre. We'll be out of town for...indefinitely."

"Oh, my." Bonnie beamed right back—actually fluttered her lashes. Well, she could flutter away because his charms were lost on Caitlin.

"Sugar girl, you do have all the luck." Bonnie batted her lashes again. "Agent LeFevre, you take good care of my girl now."

The cheeky bastard cut his gaze toward Caitlin, and an unmistakable "I told you so" was there for her to see.

"Yes, ma'am."

Bonnie placed her hands on her hips. "Don't get me wrong. She's the toughest young woman I've ever known. You'll see. She'll hold her own." As if aware of the undercurrent buzzing in the room, Bonnie shot Caitlin a shy smile, then ducked her head. "I'll leave you to it then."

"Thanks," Caitlin said. "We have an early meeting and a flight at eleven. I'll pack tonight—the few things I can take with me. Don't bother getting up early."

"Hmph." Bonnie shook her head. "No way my girl's going off without a good breakfast."

"G'night, Bonnie." Her tone was pointed, but Bonita Hazard wouldn't hold it against her. Their relationship was deep, forged by thirty years of ups and downs, and a brusque word or two from Caitlin wouldn't faze the woman who'd raised and given her the love her father denied.

After Caitlin's housekeeper left the room, Jake nodded. "She takes good care of you."

"She's a genuinely good person all the way down to her cross-trainers."

Jake grabbed a croissant from the tray and chomped half of it in one bite. "She makes a great sandwich, too."

His hostess had calmed while her housekeeper was in the room.

He hoped her new mood would hold.

Caitlin reached for the coffee pot and poured a cup. She paused. "How do you take it?"

"Black." So the manners she'd probably been born with were in place, for now anyway. He accepted it. "Thank you."

"Might as well start calling me Kate. That's who I'll be from now on."

It's good they kept your name phonetically identical. You won't—"

"I know the drill. Let's get down to business."

"It's the little things that'll trip you up. Like what kind of toothpaste I use. Where we went on our first date."

She leaned back and took a sip of coffee, her fingers long and elegant, curved round the fragile cup. He could just imagine them caressing—

Stop. He couldn't keep thinking like that and get through this mission. She mystified him. Maybe she was tougher than she looked—if attitude counted for anything.

"Okay, tell me all about yourself."

She glared at him and let out a heavy sigh. "All right. I'm Kate Girard. I'm thirty-two, birthday..."

Jake waited until she finished reciting her rote memory work. She was good, he had to admit. "Now tell me about me."

"You're thirty-five. We met in Vegas while I was at a convention. My associates and I had a problem with one of the blackjack dealers. You intervened. We fell in love, got drunk and got married. I came back to Jersey to close up my apartment and give notice. Then I moved to Vegas, but you wanted to come back home to New Orleans. So here we are."

"Wrong. For the record, I'm thirty-six. What else?"

She glared before continuing. "You were brought up by your mother, graduated from Ste. Helene's High School. Quit going to church when you were twelve. Started playing craps and moved to Vegas right after you graduated in..."

"1989," he prompted. "What's my favorite color?"

"Black."

"What side of the bed do I sleep on?"

"The side next to the door."

"First place we made love?"

"My room at the Bellagio."

"Our favorite way to make love?"

A pink flush crept up her neck. She glanced down at the papers. "I don't think that particular piece of information is in here or pertinent."

"Like hell! We're newlyweds. You're hot for me—just like I am for you. Now, where's the kinkiest place we've ever done it?"

"I don't know about you, but I don't plan on discussing my sex life with anyone at work."

"You never know when the subject might come up." He grinned, knowing he was pushing her buttons big time.

She glared. "That's the most juvenile response I've ever heard." She started gathering the scattered papers, her movements jerky. "I can study better alone." She stood. "I'll see you at nine. Good night."

"Okay. I'll leave, but you have to know this. It's one thing to recite facts. It's something else to convince everyone you come in contact with you're an entirely different person with a totally different set of emotions and values."

"I can do it."

"Then kiss me."

Her gaze widened in surprise. "What?"

"You love me—Jack Girard. I want to look at you and see Kate-with-a-K, my sweet-lovin' wife who can't wait to get me all hot and sweaty. That's who I need to see when I look into your eyes."

He took a step toward her. She took one back, a hint of disdain curling her upper full upper lip.

Jake roared with laughter. "See here, chèr, that ain't it." He took another step toward her. This time, she didn't budge but glared at him from beneath thick, spiky lashes.

"I need to know how you feel in my arms, the taste of your skin, the way your body molds against mine. There's only one way to know something like that. Kiss me, Kate-with-a-K."

"I suppose it's inevitable. All right," she groaned and closed her eyes, her lips puckered like those of a kissing gourami.

When he didn't take the bait, she peeped at him from one eye. "Well?"

"You're so cute. But I think this is more what I had in mind." He took one more step, closing the distance between them. He held out his hand, palm upward.

And waited.

Her lips parted. Would she protest or...?

Caitlin took his hand. Could he feel her trembling? The thought of kissing him, being held by him—could she?

He wasn't rushing her. He was waiting for her to prove herself. There it was, the skeptical glimmer in his dark gaze. Her mouth grew dry; she licked her lips and swallowed.

The glimmer grew to a glitter. So he liked that. Mischief shouldn't be denied; she licked her lips again.

His fingers curled around hers. They were strong and warm...and surprisingly gentle.

"I won't hurt you."

"I know." Her voice a bare whisper, she stepped into his embrace, unable to pull her gaze from his, as if some form of magnetic attraction had captured her and wouldn't release.

No. She stiffened, ready to retreat.

"Don't," he said. "Just take it slow. You're in control. I won't do anything you don't want."

She tore her gaze from his. "I feel so silly."

"Not to me."

The rise and fall of his chest increased. Was the role-playing getting to him, too? She relaxed in his arms; they closed around her, comforting her, protecting her. He ran a finger down the back of her arm. Every cell in her body sparked awake to his simple touch and cried for more, but she forced back the moan that rippled deep inside.

His hand eased its way to her neck and fiddled with her hair.

"Beautiful...like silk."

He leaned closer. His breath was warm against her skin.

"In the bar...did you really think a different hairdo would fool me in the bar?"

"Mm. Guess I was wrong...." Being in his arms...it was nice... Okay, better than nice. She could pretend to be enamored of him, but could she pretend well enough to convince anyone she was in love with him?

He wove his fingers through her hair, pulled her head back and kissed the hollow of her neck. She molded to him. His chest was hard with muscles that tapered to a trim waist. "You're very healthy," was all she said when she wanted to say so much more.

He let out a low rumble of laughter. "You could say that. Uh, you feel healthy, too. Very nice triceps...for a girl."

She grinned and poked his chest. "You! 'For a girl'?"

"I know. I'm just a prime example of your average chauvinist pig, but you feel really good in my arms. But I don't think we've done the kiss part yet. We really need to do that—just once."

He really was kind of sweet, in a seductive bad-boy kind of way. What was one kiss?

"Come on, Kate-with-a-K. Just one."

Her breath escaped as a sigh. She nodded. "No tongue," she whispered.

Jake grinned and slanted his lips across hers. He tasted her, licking just the inside of her lips. The tip of her tongue met his. Tentatively at first, then with enthusiasm.

His body jolted into arousal. God. He wanted her.

No. He'd made his point. She could pretend to be hot for him. Oh, yeah.

Reluctantly he let her go, then took a step backward. He couldn't risk falling into the honeyed trap of her mouth and skin.

Her eyes widened in surprise. "What?"

"You'll do." He nodded approvingly. "You made me believe. Good job." He wiped his mouth with a handkerchief. If she had any idea how much she'd affected him, she'd wipe the floor with him.

"Good job?" She arched an angry brow, but then shrugged and told him in a tone so cold he'd have to check his body parts for frostbite, "I told you so."

"So you did." He turned. "G'night, Agent Chaney. Thank Miss Bonnie for the coffee and the sandwiches." He grinned, giving her the full blast of his Cajun charm. "And you, chèr—thank you for the kiss. It rates right near the top as kisses go."

"Hmph."

"Now you get a good night's sleep, what's left of it." He strolled to the door, then turned back. "We're going to make a great team." He and one Mata Hari-wannabe who had no idea just how complicated an undercover op could be.

Like hell. His bad-boy self was in deepest—as in up to his eyeballs—shit.

And after that kiss—tops—no matter what he'd said, all he could think about was getting her into his bed. What was it about her that pushed his buttons? Made him reckless enough to kiss her... Reckless enough to want her.

Chapter Three

At eight the next morning Jake sat in his Bureau cubicle, leaning back with one ankle propped on the opposite knee. His determinedly casual posture belied the misgivings that ripped through his gut. Caitlin was letter-perfect with her cover, but could she maintain it under the stress of a long-term mission?

She'd made it clear last night she'd heard more than enough about his doubts.

All right. He'd keep his mouth shut...and eyes and ears open.

Behind him, the door opened, and a transformed Agent Chaney entered. Her coppery hair had been freed from her usual uptight whatchamacallit—a bun thing—cut and carefully styled into a tousled, just-crawled-out-of-bed look that would've made Meg Ryan proud. And tinted bright red.

All pretenses aside, Jake stared. "Good God, woman. That's a change."

"I'll take your comment as positive."

"You certainly look less like an uptight accountant than you did before." He dope-slapped his forehead. "Forgot. You *are* an accountant."

She rolled her eyes and huffed. "I don't think I need to look quite so formal in a casino setting."

"Good point." Jake shrugged. "No one would ever mistake you for the Interior Secretary's daughter now."

An angry red flush mottled Kate's ivory skin. "That's enough about my father." Jaw clenched, she started pacing. If he wasn't mistaken, she was about to give him another of her tongue lashings. Then he remembered...the kiss.

She whirled on him, obliterating the sweet memory. "Not another word about my father." Her gaze darkened. "I've—"

"I won't mention it again."

"Fine," Caitlin said. "Let's go over our notes again. Main suspect—one Heaton Boyle, controller at the Palais Pontchartrain. Our missing whistleblower fingered him as acting suspicious," she glanced down at her notes, "starting in October. His wife's terminally ill. Medical bills have exceeded his insurance coverage. Could be he's augmenting his income to cover them. But that would be simple embezzling, not corporate money laundering."

"Sad about his wife, though."

"I'd have more sympathy if our whistleblower hadn't disappeared. Agent MacGregor has been with security since that happened, but due to restrictions of not being able to associate with the other staff, he hasn't turned up anything."

Jake frowned and let out a groan. "Give me a break. I know about gambling protocol, especially the one about security not fraternizing with the rest of the help. Alex is a good man to have inside security. I'll have his back and he'll have mine."

"Look, Jake, if you'll put a hold on the pissing and moaning, I'll stop belaboring the obvious. Now, this is how it's going down."

"You! You are so much like her."

"Who?"

"My ex, Melissa,"

"So you're partial to redheads? That's scary."

"I don't mean in looks—in disposition. She's an attorney and took a job that was more than a couple of steps up the career ladder without so much as telling me."

"My, my, what a terrible thing to do. She accepted a job promotion. Yes, I can see you've every right to be upset with her." She flashed him an insincere smile.

"The job was in fucking L.A. And she served me with divorce papers before I even knew what was going on."

"Poor baby. An FBI agent and yet so clueless."

"I'd been deep undercover for six months—oh, hell! I don't know why I'm explaining all this to you of all people." Damn the woman. She possessed a distinct talent when it came to getting under his skin.

Her hands set on her hips, Caitlin huffed. "Don't think I'm not on to your type, either. You're a bad boy, used to having your own way. Used to operating on your own. This time the situation is different. *I'm* in charge—"

"How could I forget? You've reminded me at least ten times since we met less than twenty-four hours ago."

"Furthermore, if you think sucking up to me will help your career, forget it. The only thing which will help your somewhat pathetic career is following protocol and my lead."

"Your lead? You don't have a clue, chèr, how to develop an undercover identity. Your experience in undercover work consists of spending one evening pretending to be a diplomat's wife at an embassy party."

"Well…"

"Well, what?"

"*Well*, you are correct. I don't deny it, but I'll be doing what I do best. There's no real danger in a spreadsheet."

"Tell that to your predecessor. Oh, that's right. You can't. She's missing. And odds are on dead."

"It's too soon to say. They haven't found her body."

"There will be."

"You are the most arrogant male with whom I've ever had the misfortune to work. You remind me of *my* ex-boyfriend."

"Boyfriend? You mean you've cuddled up to something besides your spreadsheets?"

"Briefly. He was a user…interested in furthering his diplomatic career. Although no one in their right mind would ever suspect you of having diplomatic aspirations."

"Ya got that right."

The idea of her old boyfriend intrigued him. What was she like in bed? Did she ever let go of her uptight ways long enough to hit the sheets with the dude? No doubt she presented him with a chart detailing her favorite positions and stats on which ones were most effective in achieving climax.

"Come on." Caitlin nudged his foot with the toe of her shoe. "It's getting late. And we have a flight to catch."

New Orleans

Rain...and lots of it. Caitlin shivered and pulled her trench coat tighter around her body. "Somehow I thought New Orleans would be warmer."

"It usually is, but this is winter, and this is a thunderstorm." He tried to keep the patronizing tone from his voice and failed. Okay, he didn't try that hard. "You know, hot air from the south meets cold air sweeping down from Canada and this is what you get. Beats a hurricane any day."

"No argument here," she said.

"For once." He nodded at their rental car. "Come on. This isn't a spring shower. It won't let up."

"You know the area. You can drive."

Thank heaven for small favors. "Where to, boss?"

"Local field office." She dug in her shoulder bag for the map. "I know it's here somewhere."

"I know where it is."

"The new building?"

"Yeah, made a few quick trips to see Ed after his accident before I moved him to DC Never spent more than one night, but I still know the local layout."

"Where's our apartment? Know anything about the area?"

"Yeah. The Warehouse District is an up-and-coming area and it wasn't flooded after Katrina, but the Bureau's not going to put us up in one of those fancy converted condos. We're newly married, so we'll draw a small place."

"In other words, minimal warehouse." Her withering tone sent a shiver down his back.

"Well, chèr, if you're as smart as Jose says, we won't be here long enough to redecorate."

Would there be more than one bed? Of course, there would. If not, then he'd just better get used to sleeping on the floor.

After they checked in at the local field office, Jake headed for the warehouse district and their apartment.

He turned onto Wharf Avenue. Signs of gentrification were readily visible. At least they wouldn't have to worry about rats. Fronts of old buildings had been sandblasted, and in front of some of them, young trees had been planted between the sidewalk and the streets.

Nothing like the Wharf Avenue of twenty years ago. Parking would be a nightmare, but then it wouldn't be New Orleans if it weren't.

Situated on the edge of the Warehouse District, their building was comfortably far from the hotels and convention center, but still close enough to walk. Lots of restaurants were nearby, but not so close the rents would be as high as those next doors to the restaurants.

"There it is. Used to be a bakery."

"How interesting. How safe is this area?"

Jake snickered. "So, the SAC's concerned about her safety? Damn it. I was right all along. This op's going to hell in a handbasket. Only thing worse would be an ice storm."

Instead of his remark pissing her off, a tight little smile appeared on her lush lips. "Well, it *has* been a warm winter."

"You can wipe that smirk off your face. I bet dollars to beignets you've never ridden out a hurricane of any kind."

"Well, you'd be correct on that point."

"Most of New Orleans is below sea level. A hurricane anytime is a bad proposition—

"I watched the news, Jake. I don't need a refresher course."

"—but one in winter would be a total freak of nature. Anyway, you don't have to worry. Hurricane season ended in November."

"What are the percentages? Come on. Give me some stats."

Jake shot her a steely glare. "You want stats? Call an accountant." He smacked the steering wheel with the butt of his hand. "Stupid me. I keep forgetting *you're* the accountant."

"Actually a statistician would be more appropriate."

"Great. Now you're giving me a vocabulary lesson."

"Now wait a minute. You're the one who was giving me lessons on weather and all that B.S.?"

"B.S.? Can't you even curse without abbreviating it?"

"Hell, yes, I can! Now, if the pissing contest is over..."

He ignored her comment and went on as if they hadn't engaged in verbal fisticuffs. "This area's pretty safe. Lot better than twenty years ago. Soho South, they call it now. Very trendy."

He wiped off the fog forming on the inside of the window. "There's supposed to be a garage in the next block where we can park."

"And we're supposed to walk a block in this rain—with our bags?"

Jake grinned. "Guess so, unless you want me to drop your highness off at the front door."

"It's pouring. And as your *wife*, I would appreciate your consideration—just as any normal wife would." She gave a theatrical sniff. "Besides, I can take our bags and check out the condo."

"Fine. You do that."

"I will."

After his ersatz wife flirted unashamedly with the building super who awarded her two sets of keys for their new digs along with a wide smile, Jake hefted their luggage and stepped onto the freight-style elevator. "You coming?"

"No, I thought I'd take up residence down here. I love all the old brickwork. And just look at those timber supports along the side. They're massive."

"Kate, darlin', aren't you anxious to see our new home?"

A sudden frown shadowed her expression. "Henry said not to expect too much."

"Henry?" She was already on a first-name basis with the super?

"The concierge."

Jake groaned. "You say, concierge. I say super."

"Whatever." His newlywed wife took her sweet time but eventually sashayed onto the elevator.

"Finally."

She plastered on a fake smile. "Are you always this charming?"

"Only when I'm soaked to the skin and you're holding up the show."

"Good to know."

When they reached the fifth floor, the elevator shuddered to a stop. Jake yanked on the metal gate, raising it with a clang that reverberated through the open space of the loft. He whistled. "Ol' Henry sure knew what he was talking about."

The space could barely be called an apartment. Sure as hell hadn't had any fancy-schmancy conversion work done on it. A couch, a card table with two chairs and a bare mattress, resting on a pathetic excuse for a bed made up the furnishings. A sink and tiny stove occupied the far wall. The commode and a shower stall were situated in the rear far corner.

All open. No walls. No privacy. But plenty of brickwork and beamed ceilings. Kate-with-a-K ought to be thrilled.

He heard Caitlin let out a gasp. "This is unacceptable." She waved her hands. "Someone's made a terrible mistake. We can't live here. I'll just call..." She glanced around. "No phone." She reached into her purse and retrieved her cell phone.

"Hold on." Arms outstretched, he walked farther into the room. "It has everything. Couch, bed, stove, and john. What more do you need?"

Her face flushed, and the deep breath she took said a lot. The loft apparently didn't meet her high-toned Georgetown standards. Hell. It didn't meet his either, but he'd never admit it aloud. "Okay, okay. So, it needs a little work."

"Granted, I'm not used to long-term undercover operations, but this is truly grim. Why?"

"Okay, let's look at it like newlyweds. Our first loft and it's an adventure. As part of our cover, we'll shop and furnish it. We have no idea how long this will take, so we might as well be comfortable."

"I don't understand. We're here to do a job, not shop for furniture."

Jake smiled, spread his arms. "See, it's perfect. As the shopper of the family, you can bond with your fellow worker-bees. They'll tell you all the best places to shop. Maybe you'll even find out what happened to our whistleblower."

"Your patronizing attitude really stinks." She took two steps into the loft but left her luggage behind. "We can't possibly stay here tonight. We don't even have a sheet for the bed. No privacy. How am I supposed to change clothes?"

"Kate-with-a-K, we're *married.* Don't be shy with me, chèr." He awarded her his best leer. "Although I do find your shyness very touching."

"Get over yourself! We're in private, and we sure as hell aren't married. And make no mistake, you won't be touching anything of mine."

"Then for tonight, you'll just have to trust I'll be a gentleman and look the other way when you have to change and—uh, you know..."

"You're enjoying this entirely too much. I wasn't expecting luxury, but I assumed—wrongly—our apartment would be minimally furnished."

"This is minimal all right." He reached out and turned her around. "I know it's not what you're used to, but in this very city, there are people who are lucky to be alive and would kiss these grimy floors just to have a roof over their heads. We have electricity, and somewhere there's bound to be a phone line or two for our computers."

His faux wife bit her upper lip—and what a sweet lip it was. Wouldn't he just like to bite it himself?

"I'm such an idiot. I'm sounding like the poor little rich girl, aren't I?"

He gazed up at the exposed pipes. "Ya think?"

"All right. I am. At least we should go out to dinner. We can do that as newlyweds, can't we?"

"Definitely. In fact, we're supposed to meet Alex."

"We are? How is it *you've* already set up a meet with our mole?"

"Oh, God. Let it go. I know Alex from our last op together. And I know the city, so I set the meet first thing. We can get an update and..."

"And just when were you going to let me in on your plan?"

"I just did."

"This is never going to work. You're verging on insubordination. I was warned about you, and against my better judgment, I agreed I'd work with you."

"Against *your* better judgment? Lady, you don't know the half of it. Given your inexperience in the field, I'd lay odds they wouldn't agree to your being on the team unless *I* was there to cover *your* backside." Make that a *lovely* backside. He was beginning to realize how much he wouldn't mind watching it at all.

Chapter Four

Caitlin relaxed her shoulders and sighed. What a pain in the butt he was. Time to smooth his ruffled feathers or he'd grow more impossible than ever. "Calm down, LeFevre. It's just this damned apartment." Despair washed over her. She sank down on the sofa.

Big mistake. A cloud of dust emanated from the cushions. She gasped and sucked a lungful of the noxious, musty mess into her lungs which sent her into a fit of coughing.

Another big mistake.

When she could finally draw a clear breath, she shook her head. "This is disgusting. That does it. I'm going to a hotel. I don't care what you do."

"'That does it'?" A sneer twisted his handsome face into a mask of disdain. "May I remind you at this very moment, there are men in Iraq defending our freedom who are sleeping in sand dunes, dodging bullets and suicide bombers. And you're whining about a lumpy couch that needs a good vacuuming."

The truth of his words jabbed her like a knife. "You're right. I'm selfish and more than a little spoiled. But I can do this." She stood, squared her shoulders and raised her chin a notch, meeting his level gaze. "I'll show you and everyone else. I'm the right person to head this team."

"I sure as hell hope you're right because failure isn't an option in an operation like this. Doing the job and being alive when it's over is all I care about. I don't have anything to prove or anybody to impress."

He probably couldn't hear the pathos of his reply, but she could. "I'm sorry." She meant it, too. As much as her father had neglected her, at least she had him, and most of all Bonnie, who'd been as good a mother as anyone could ever want. All Jake had was a comatose father who couldn't recognize anyone, much less Jake.

Jake's expression grew confused. "I accept your apology. If you don't mind, clue me in. Just exactly why are you apologizing?"

"I meant I'm sorry you don't have anyone to impress, not that I'm sorry for the other—I'm not."

"Hmph." He shrugged and a slow half-grin flickered for a moment before morphing into a full-fledged frown. "You're confusing me. Not sure I like it."

"How's that?" At least she was doing something right, even if she didn't know what.

"Most of the time, you're a by-the-book hard-ass with a chip on your shoulder the size of a blackjack table, and sometimes—like now—you go all girly. And for the record, not having anyone doesn't bother me. Except for Ed and the two years I was married to Melissa, I've been alone most of my life. No big deal." He shrugged again. "I like it."

He was confused? Well, dammit, so was she. She didn't want to like him, but there was something damaged deep inside him. Something which drew her in and held her back at the same time, and yet made her want to wrap her arms around him and give him the love he needed and had never had.

Bright yellow neon spelled out "Bar Bayou" in a loopy script. The light emitted a faint flicker as if the electrical connection was on the verge of shorting out. Jake opened the heavy weather-beaten door and held it. "After you."

Caitlin shouldered her way inside the bar. Dimly lit and crowded, it reeked of stale beer and unrealized dreams lost in the bottom of a bottle.

She rolled her eyes and sighed. "Nice place."

He nodded, then a wry smile warmed his expression a tad. "I learned the facts of life in this bar."

A shudder shot through her. "Really? And who was she—a waitress or a bartender?"

He shook his head and gave her a gentle nudge. "Neither. After my mom ran off, I ran off, too. I swept floors so I'd have money for food. You can learn a lot by sweeping floors."

"I thought your father was a cop."

"My *adopted* father was. Not everything's in my file."

"Fascinating."

"Go on." He nodded toward the back of the bar. "Alex is in that corner booth. Let's hear what he has to say."

She headed to the booth he'd indicated while wondering what he'd meant about everything not being in his file. What secrets could he have from the Bureau? Or was it something on a need-to-know basis that she didn't need to know?

As they approached their Security contact, agent Alex MacGregor, he unfolded his long legs and got to his feet. Caitlin looked up. He was at least six-three and didn't look as if he were a day over twenty. Dark blond, mousse-spiked hair made him look more like a club deejay than a member of security personnel, much less an FBI agent.

He grinned and deep dimples appeared in his cheeks. "How you all are, chèr?" he drawled, then leaned down and kissed both her cheeks.

Her mouth dropped open. "Uh—"

"Close ya mouth, chèr. I can't be French kissing you right now." Alex winked at Jake. "Ain't she just the cutest little gal?"

Jake glared at the younger agent as if waiting for her next response.

Caitlin gave them both a smug smile. "Now that's a damned shame," she drawled. "'Cause I think you're the cutest thang *I've* seen in a long time."

"Just 'cause I am, chèr." Then dropping his New Orleans accent, he added, "Jake, you lucky dog, you get to play house, too."

"Yeah, well. That's not quite how it works."

"Come on, sit yourselves down." Alex grabbed Caitlin around the waist. "And that's why she's sitting with me instead of you."

Jake's gaze narrowed. "Fine." He nodded and slid into the booth.

"Hold on." She raised her chin a notch. "And I suppose I don't have a choice?"

"No, ma'am." Alex winked at her. "You see, I need to get to know the SAC on this operation. And I can't exactly do that at work."

Glaring up at the two of them, Jake motioned for them to sit. "Cut the Cajun charm." His tone sharp enough to cut glass. "You're no more Cajun than Caitlin."

She shook her head. Typical male posturing—what had she gotten herself into? Here she was with one agent who resented her and another who didn't look old enough to buy condoms.

She slid into the booth. Time she took control. After all, she was in charge. "Alex, tell us what you've learned in Security. Has there been any mention of the whistleblower? And do you know for certain who she is?"

The young agent picked up a menu and pretended to study it. "This is what I've heard. Only one person decamped and matched the timeline with the whistle blower's stopping contact. Terri Thibedoux from Accounting. I managed to meet her best friend on the outside. She said flat-out she didn't believe what she was being told."

Alex continued quietly, "Head of Security, Bud Harris, says she sent an e-mail resignation and ran off to work in Vegas.

Jake nodded. "We'll put in a request to check the Vegas casinos. All casino employees have to have background checks. If she's relocated, an inquiry with the gaming commission ought to tell us her whereabouts."

"Has anyone else heard from her?" Caitlin asked.

"Not a peep—at least that's what her friend Annie says."

Caitlin drummed her forefinger on the slightly sticky table. "This Annie works in security, too?"

"No, she works in the cashier section; Terri worked in

Accounting."

"But I thought you couldn't fraternize with anyone outside Security?" Alex obviously did whatever the hell he pleased whether he was on or off assignment. Caitlin would've bet her retirement pension on it if she thought she'd live to earn it.

"True, but..." Alex showed his deep dimples again. "...where there's a will, there's a way to get around most rules."

Caitlin snorted. An agent with Alex MacGregor's charm could find plenty of ways of bending the rules. Too bad Jake didn't have a quarter of Alex's charm. Not that it would keep her partner from pushing the legal limits either.

"Good. So what does Annie think happened to Terri?"

"She's worried. Terri had told Annie she thought something was going on in the casino or Accounting. Too much money going through the cage—more than typical on some days. Money that wasn't showing up on the books. Annie said she warned Terri to be careful, and the next evening, Terri didn't show up for work. Then the e-mail resignation came, supposedly from Terri."

"If her friend was suspicious, why didn't she report it to the locals?"

"She did, but they said with the e-mail, they couldn't do anything. Annie checked Terri's apartment the day after she disappeared, and all her belongings were still there. But here's the clincher. Two days later, when she checked again, the building super said Terri's brother paid off her lease and packed up her belongings. But Annie says Terri never mentioned having a brother."

A frown creased Jake's face. "Not good. You better cool this friend of hers. She's going to be in hot water or worse."

"Man, I've tried. But she's a little on the stubborn side. Sweet as can be, but definitely determined to find Terri."

"Since you're already in contact with her, you have to convince her not to make waves. Somehow without breaking cover, you have to let her know it's being handled," Caitlin said.

"I'll do my best. She's already scared. That might keep her from doing anything risky."

"Sound okay to you, Jake?"

Her unwilling partner glanced around the bar as if looking for a waitress. "You're in charge, chèr."

She forced her lips into an approximation of a sweet smile. "True, but being in charge doesn't mean I don't respect your experience and opinion."

"Woo hoo." Alex let out a low hoot. "Dude, she's tough." Dimples deepening, he grinned down at her. "I don't mind a woman being in charge."

Caitlin glanced around at the Friday night bar crowd. Given the fact an impromptu wet T-shirt contest was starting, no one was paying the three agents any attention.

A frown creased Jake's forehead. "Reel it in, Alex. Our boss is by-the-book, and if you're not careful, she'll have you up on sexual harassment charges, and you'll have the shortest career in Bureau history."

"Jake, he's just needling you. Surely you can tell the difference." Caitlin gave a pleased sniff. Alex was a charmer and a pleaser—too bad he was so damned young.

Jake curled his upper lip. "Did you go to convent school or something? Is that why you can't tell when you're being hit on?"

"Enough," she said, her tone going raspy with frustration. "We're here for Alex's update." She turned to the young agent and smiled. "Anything else?"

"Nah." He glanced down at his watch. "We done?"

"Got a date?" Jake asked with a curled lip.

Alex's grin widened. "You know it, dude."

Caitlin watched the lanky agent disappear into the crowd and out the door, then looked at Jake where he sat glowering like someone who'd had lost his k. "How's the food?"

Jake's lip curled again. "You want to eat here? Isn't this dump a little low-class for you?"

"Drop the Elvis impression. This place has food. I can smell it, and I've seen plates heaped with French fries going by to other tables for the last fifteen minutes. Translation: Yes, I want to eat here."

"All right, chèr." He lifted two fingers to his mouth and whistled. When the waitress came to take their order, he waved away the menu. "Two house specials."

"That's fine." Caitlin glared. How dare he order for her? "As long as the house special includes fries."

"Sorry, chèr, but they have the best popcorn shrimp in New Orleans."

The waitress fluttered her lashes at Jake, then directed her gaze to his left hand and wedding ring. Her smile faded a touch. "O'course it includes fries, but I guess since you already got your man, you don't mind a few extra calories."

Bitch. But Caitlin smiled, reached across the table and squeezed Jake's hand. "That's right, and he likes me just the way I am. Don't you, honey?"

"For a fact, I do." His smile turned into a glassy-eyed stare directed at her breasts.

Damn him.

"We'd like to eat sometime tonight if you don't mind?"

The waitress sniffed. "That's it then?"

Caitlin nodded. "It sure is." The waitress gave a slight shrug and left.

Her supposed husband frowned. "You were rude."

"No, not at all. She was the one who was rude...or don't you recognize it when you're being hit on?"

"What? You mean the waitress?"

"I'm simply amazed at your deductive skills. I'm sure this operation will be a breeze."

"Sarcasm is an unattractive trait in a wife, and it sucks when it comes from the SAC."

So he didn't like his pronouncements turned back on him.

Tough.

Back in the apartment, Caitlin looked around and sighed. "It wasn't my imagination. This place is even worse than I remembered."

"I'll take the couch," her partner offered and gamely plopped on the sofa raising another minor dust storm.

"No. I'll take the sofa and you can take the mattress. You're too long for the sofa anyway." She glanced down at her watch. "It's eleven. I'm going to bed—such as it is."

"It's early, chèr. This is the Big Easy."

"Spare me the Dennis Quaid imitation. I've had enough."

"Oh, but old Dennis imitated me, not the other way 'round."

"Whatever. Now, will you leave?"

"Leave?"

"So I can get ready for bed. I don't trust you to not peek."

"I'm wounded." He placed both hands over his heart. "You know trust is the most essential ingredient between partners in an undercover op. This attitude of yours doesn't bode well for our success."

"Out!" She stamped her foot. Damn it, what was it about Jake LeFevre that made her act like a spoiled brat?

She tried again. "Sorry. Please, just for a couple of minutes."

"Magic words. That's all I needed. I'm already on my way out." He bowed, then swaggered out, clearly pleased with himself from the confident swing of his broad shoulders.

She waited for the door to slam, then quickly stripped off her clothes and took advantage of the minimal facilities. She slipped into a nylon jogging suit. No way would she allow her bare skin to come in contact with who knew what had last touched the sofa.

She was brushing her teeth over the rusty sink when she heard Jake's polite tapping. "Okay to come back in?"

She rinsed and spit into the sink. "Yeah." She ran her fingers through her tousled curls. "It's all yours."

LeFevre grinned. "I won't take long. Come back in about ten minutes."

"What do you mean? I'm not going anywhere."

"I expect the same courtesy in return."

"See here! I've had enough of this. I'm going to bed. Believe me, I have no desire to peek. I'll be asleep before my head hits whatever passes for a pillow."

"Are you *sure* I can trust you?" he asked, a crooked grin lifting the corner of his mouth.

"You said it yourself. Trust is essential." She grinned back at him, more than pleased she could turn his words back on him again. "Trust me, Jake."

After Jake plopped down on the bare mattress, he admitted to himself—not that he would ever admit it to her—Caitlin was right. No telling what was on the mattress. He just hoped there weren't any critters of the biting persuasion. His sweatpants and T-shirt wouldn't protect his hide from fleas or bedbugs.

Sleep? Who was he kidding? How could he? As aggravating as she was sexy, Caitlin Chaney was, ounce for ounce, the biggest damn temptation he'd run across since his ex left...and way out of his league.

She'd grown up with the finest of everything, and he'd grown up on the streets of New Orleans. Sixteen years ago, if he hadn't stumbled onto a nightmare of blood, he'd be in prison or pushing up daisies like the other street rats he knew at the time.

He punched the lumpy mattress, then sat up and looked around. The rain had finally stopped. Feeble rays of moonlight streamed through the tall windows. Caitlin was right—the loft was a dump. The undercover work could go on for months. First chance, he'd do something about their surroundings. Then Miss High Maintenance could climb down from her high horse. At least *he* could cook, so they wouldn't starve.

Not that there was any danger of their starving in New Orleans.

He reached over, grabbed the shirt he'd worn earlier, wadded it up and stuck it under his head. For what seemed like hours, he stared at the ceiling and watched a spider spin a slender filament of silver that glinted in the moonlight as it made its way down.

"Kate-with-a-K?" he asked quietly. No point in waking her if she had managed to fall asleep.

He waited.

Caitlin sat up and turned around on the sofa to look at Jake.

"I'm awake. The sofa's musty and—" She took a deep breath in a vain attempt to control the building tickle. "—ah choo!"

"Jeez, I felt the spray all the way over here."

"No, you didn't." She stood and placed her hands on her hips. "I get it now. You're being silly."

"Anything wrong with that?"

Caitlin stood, then walked over to one of the windows. She rubbed a clear spot through the grime of years and watched the citizens of New Orleans go about their business. She went up on tiptoe to reach the latch. Afterward, she tugged on the window, trying to raise the damned thing. "Some fresh air might actually help."

"Need some help?"

"You mind? It's been painted shut."

He strolled toward her, wearing a smug grin. "I'm impressed."

"Why? It's not like I—"

"No, chèr, you admitted you needed help. The SAC admitted she needed my help. There's hope for you—make that us—yet."

Caitlin rolled her eyes. "Us?"

"As a team."

"That's all there is—a team." As they struggled together to raise the stuck window, she breathed in the scent of the man and sandalwood. He was way too close.

Without warning, the paint-stuck window gave way, and Caitlin pitched forward and dislodged the screen. His strong arms snaked around her and jerked her away from the yawning opening. Held close against his muscled chest, her body absorbed his warmth. She was secure...for now. His rapidly beating heart told her something else, too.

"Are you all right? I didn't hurt you?" he asked in a voice roughened with emotion.

"Think so." She let out a sigh. Her heart was beating even faster than his, but when she gazed into his shuttered eyes, his emotions were unreadable. "Thank you."

"Couldn't let the SAC fall on her pretty ass, now could I?"

She pulled back a little. He grinned down at her, but his

expression told her nothing. "Wouldn't look good on your report if I fell five stories and—actually, I'd be more likely to land on my head if I fell from this height."

"Yes, ma'am, you sure would."

Lips parted, he leaned closer.

Her breath caught in her throat, but nerve deserted her. "Jake, we have an early day tomorrow. It's time we went to bed."

"Chèr, I thought you'd never ask."

Her heart turned a somersault in her chest, but he was teasing. At least she knew that much. "Yours is over there." She pointed at the bare mattress.

"I know. I know," he responded, then pouted as if he were a spoiled child deprived of his favorite toy.

Caitlin gave herself a mental shake. In spite of his testiness and their constant bickering back and forth, there was something so appealing about him. His dark brown eyes were unreadable most of the time, but in unguarded moments they held pain and vulnerability.

"G'night, Jake."

"'Night, chèr."

Chapter Five

It's now or never. This is your chance to prove you can do the job.

Caitlin took a couple of deep breaths to steady her ragged nerves, gripped her purse tightly and opened the door.

Accounting. What a drab contrast to the gaudy lights of the casino proper. Beige walls, beige loop carpeting with a worn path that left the pile pressed down as flat as if ironed. The furnishings appeared fairly new, but definitely low-end from the local office supply.

She stopped at the first desk occupied by a very non-beige young woman. She wore a frilly magenta blouse and had apparently taken great pains to match the blouse with her lipstick and glittery eye shadow.

"I'm Kate Girard. Mr. Boyle is expecting me."

The woman in magenta sighed, slipped a bookmark into her murder mystery and only then acknowledged Caitlin's presence. "He's at the hospital with his wife, but he told me to expect you. I'm Lisette." She jerked her head in the direction of a cubicle. "That's yours. Procedure manual is on the desk. You can read over it until ten. Orientation's at ten. You'll sign up for your benefits and get your key card and photo badge there. Don't lose 'em. You're gonna need 'em every day."

"Yes. I understand." She walked back to the small cubicle. "Thank you, Lisette."

Lisette didn't respond. She'd already gone back to reading her paperback.

Clearly, Caitlin was as welcome as a big dip in the stock market.

Heaton Boyle slumped in at nine-thirty. Caitlin's new boss and her prime suspect was a man in his mid-fifties with male-pattern baldness. Fortunately, he didn't try to cover it with one of those long sweeps of temporal hair. He was unabashedly bald, fairly trim and wore a cheap suit. If he was her embezzler/money launderer, he wasn't spending it at Armani.

"Mrs. Girard, I'm Heaton. We're a small office and pretty informal. I hope you don't mind if I call you Kate?"

"No, that's fine."

He spent fifteen minutes explaining her duties in one long recitation as if he'd done it more times than he could count. "Anyway, you come highly recommended, and we're glad to have you. Our last accountant left us quite suddenly...without notice." He pulled out a handkerchief and mopped his shiny forehead. "Most inconvenient. I-I hope you won't do anything like that."

"Of course, not." She glanced at her watch. "I think I'm supposed to be in orientation in a few minutes."

He waved his hand in the air in a dismissive gesture. "Yeah, go on."

Caitlin gathered her purse and headed out the door. She'd certainly run into Jake at orientation, and later they could compare notes on what they'd learned so far.

The hurdy-gurdy cacophony of the slots, the buzzing undertone of conversation, punctuated by excited shrieks and squeals when someone scored—all of it slammed Jake's gut like a jackhammer, set his blood afire and his head to spinning like a roulette wheel. He could control the old urge. He would. "It's larger than I thought."

The Head of Security and Operations, Bud Harris, was tall and lanky with sandy hair and about forty. He nodded as if he understood. "First time in a New Orleans casino?"

"Yeah, I'm used to sand and the strip. Thought working a smaller casino would be claustrophobic. But it's not."

"The Bellagio it ain't," Harris admitted.

"No, but it's a great opportunity."

"Newly married, I understand."

"Yeah. 'Bout six months. My wife's starting in Accounting."

Harris shook his head sadly. "Yeah, I heard they had a sudden opening there."

"Perfect timing for the two of us. Kate's a CPA. She can get a job anywhere, but casinos are all I know."

"You're in the right place then. Still doesn't explain why you left the Bellagio."

"N'awlins is home. Grew up here...wanted to come back. O'course, it's changed a lot."

"Yeah. You already got a place to live?"

"Just beyond the Warehouse District. Needs a lot of DIY. The wife just about freaked when she saw it. She wanted to move to a hotel until she could shop...and redecorate."

Harris chuckled. "Women are like that. She'll be happy as a clam while she's doing it up."

Jake followed his new boss, as they passed row after row of slot machines. He'd never wasted much time on slots. Damn things brought in eighty percent of a casino's revenue. Blackjack and craps had always been his weakness...and the reason for his spiraling descent into addiction.

Even now the itch was there in his fingers. He clenched his fists. This op would test him even more than his partner. Still, he was a long way from the Indian casino on the UP of Michigan.

Jose, I hope you know what you've done.

Harris showed Jake to the locker room. "You'll work day shifts with Sellars this week. After that, you'll start on nights. Ten-hour shifts, four days a week. But I expect you'll hit the deck running."

Jake nodded. "No problem. Looking forward to it."

Yeah, just like he'd look forward to a run of snake eyes at the craps table.

After the employee orientation session, which Jake had missed, Caitlin returned to Accounting. Apparently, there were two sessions, and Jake was scheduled for one at eleven. She slid into her cubicle and quickly hacked into Heaton's network files. One spreadsheet after another and nothing. The figures didn't lie. Nothing was out of place. The solution must be staring back at her. Why couldn't she see it?

Before she could investigate further, a flurry of footsteps stopped her. Heaton Boyle stood at the entrance to her cube. She minimized the spreadsheet. Technically she didn't have proper access. Not that she cared.

"Snap to, Kate. The Chief Financial Officer from Corporate is on her way." Heaton mopped his forehead with the sleeve of his jacket.

"Scary, is she?" She gave a snort. "A bean counter from corporate? What fun."

Her boss's eyes grew wide. "Hush. Don't talk like that. She'll hear you."

Caitlin rolled her eyes and folded her hands in her lap just like a proper lady of the Fifties. "I'll behave."

A tall blonde glided into the room. Her pale hair was short and cut in an asymmetric style. Her skin was as pale as her hair, as were her gray eyes, which were so light the irises appeared almost transparent. A designer suit graced her model-thin frame. She held out a languid hand. "Angelique André. So you're Heaton's new assistant. I've seen your résumé. Quite impressive."

Caitlin shook the CFO's hand. Languid the other woman might appear, but she possessed strength and great energy in her grip. "Thank you."

"I'm sure Heaton has already shown you the ropes. Welcome to the Rivera Corporation family." She turned to Heaton. "I want to go over those last figures. I'm not convinced we're utilizing the revenues appropriately."

The CFO slithered away with poor Heaton in tow.

Family—oh yeah, like I'm buying that one.

Jake headed to Accounting, anxious to see how Caitlin had fared so far. A tall blonde emerged from the secured area...a tall, familiar blonde. Dammit, he knew her.

He stopped. "Angie? Angie Andrews."

The blonde blinked at the mention of her name. "No, sorry. You must be mistaken." Her eyes widened, then a slight frown drew her lips into a pout. "Jack-man?" she asked, her tone low and sensual.

He grinned. "None other." He registered the changes in her appearance. Very smart and sophisticated. Nothing at all like the fifteen-year-old hooker he'd known.

"You've done all right for yourself, chèr." He dropped his tone. "Still in the business? If you are, you've really done well."

One corner of her mouth twitched, the only clue he'd upset her. She'd always been a cool customer, but now she was icy.

"No. If fact, it might be wise if we got together very soon and did some catch-up." Her gaze darted from side to side. "I'm known as Angelique André now. I'm Rivera Corp.'s CFO. In fact, meet me tonight. Nine-ish at—what's wrong?"

"I'm married. It'll be a little difficult to leave my bride all alone our second night in town."

Annoyance flashed across her face. "Married? Too bad." She lifted her slender shoulders in an elegant shrug. "Lunch then, at The Pier—one?"

"If I can. First day on the job, you know?"

"Doing what?"

"Security. My wife just started in Accounting."

"Don't tell me." Angie's pale eyes rolled back a bit. "The little redhead?"

"That's my Kate." He gave old Angie a wide, besotted-newlywed husband smile.

"How sweet. Never thought you'd settle for the cute type."

"An-gie…" he warned. Caitlin would hate being called cute.

The restaurant Angelique had named was an upscale one specializing in Creole cuisine. Jake followed the maitre d' to her table.

She grinned and gave him an appraising up and down glance.

"Have a seat, Jack-man."

Misgivings be damned, Jake sat. By what winding road had a fifteen year-old-prostitute known as the Albino Virgin ended up as CFO of a large corporation?

"Angie." He nodded. "Scotch rocks," he told the waiter.

"You grew up nice." She took a tiny sip from her cocktail. "Last I heard, some cop took you in."

"Yeah, swore he'd kick me out the first time I screwed up, too. Old coot thought he could reform me. I saved him the trouble. I ran off the first chance I got." His father would forgive the lie. "Headed west, ended up in Vegas. By then I looked older, lied about my age, worked the casinos."

Angie leaned forward. "I'd just as soon my employers didn't know about our...colorful history."

The waiter brought Jake's drink. He took a sip, never taking his gaze from hers. "So chèr, what's your story? I know for sure it's bound to be more interestin' than mine." The soft New Orleans drawl had already begun creeping back into his voice.

She took another sip of her drink before answering him with a slight smile. "Yes, I have managed to capitalize on my assets...some more than others. And like you, there's a great deal I've managed to leave behind, along with my old name."

"I'm more impressed, chèr than I ever thought possible. And all I am is one of the security geeks."

"You can do better than that, and I can make it happen." She reached across the table and ran a manicured talon along the back of his hand. "Unless your little wife objects to having a successful husband."

"I think she'd object to anything to do with you, chèr."

"Then we'll have to be careful."

"Come on, give me a break. I'm a newlywed, and I'm not looking for a divorce."

"Oh, it doesn't have to be *that* complicated."

Jake shook his head. God. Of all people to run into his first day on the job.

"You've got to forget we ever knew each other, Angie. I'm Jack

Girard. I spent some time inside...in Arizona. Had to change my name so I could get past the Gaming Commission."

"I understand." A smile played around her lips. "We're both creatures of our own devices. New and improved, so to speak."

"It's important—the life I have now. Kate doesn't know about that part of my past."

"Gently brought up, was she?" A smug satisfaction played over her perfect features.

Unease filtered through him, bubbling like an old-time coffee pot. "Not exactly. Her family's connected, but she's sworn to leave it all behind."

"Really?" Angie's eyebrows spiked. "What family?"

"Delateo. Jersey."

"Now I'm the one impressed. Not a bad family to fall back on."

"You've had dealings with them?"

Son of a bitch. Little Angie had gotten around in the last sixteen years.

She gave a dismissive wave. "Read about them. Some trial or other."

"Yeah, that would be them."

As soon as the waiter placed their lunches in front of them, Angie's cell phone chirped. She gave it a hurried glance and scowled. "Sorry, I have to take this. I'll just be a minute."

A salad for Angie, green with who knew what in it? For him, a smothered andouille po'boy served with slaw. He breathed in the spicy aromas of the sausage, green pepper, and onion. "Mmm."

"It looks just wonderful. I'm sorry." Angie smiled at him. "There's a problem at the office. I have to go. Finish your lunch."

Jake rose briefly and watched her leave, her hips undulating and reminding him of a sidewinder snake slithering along the desert floor. After a mental shiver, he sank back down in his chair and smiled.

Now he could eat in peace.

Angelique opened the door to her condo, then walked over to

the window. Her wall-to-wall view of the marina never failed to thrill her. The boats, sails furled, masts spiking like a forest of exclamation points in the dreary winter sky. It was her view as much as anyone. She'd paid for it with her blood and soul, and she would never allow anyone to take it from her.

She kicked off her Manolo Blahniks and walked into the kitchen. After pouring a glass of merlot, she walked back to the window. The heady taste lingered on her tongue.

New Orleans was her city, her life. And now fate had brought Jake back home, and his new wife would just have to step aside...or she could have an accident.

So unfortunate really. So young. Too bad.

Jake LeFevre had been the only bright spot in her young teenage life. He'd treated her with respect and never judged her for selling her body. After all, a girl had to do what a girl had to do.

She still did.

For nearly a year Jake had been there for her, then suddenly he was gone. Rumor had it he was pulled in by the cops who liked him for a murder, then the grapevine said he'd been taken in by one of the cops. According to Jake, it hadn't worked out. Why hadn't he come back for her?

Maybe he had. She'd moved on by then.

Next time, she and Jake would move on together. Spain. Italy. Morocco.

Yes, travel. She'd spent a lot of time clawing her way to her present position; it had taken education and more effort than a young hooker could ever have imagined. And it hadn't all been on her back either.

Angelique picked up the telephone and punched in the familiar number.

"Tulip Cottage." She recognized the soft, sweet voice of the house mother.

"Aurelia. It's Angelique. Did she have a good day?"

"'Bout the same as always. Miss Angelique—sorry, but they say the payment's late for this term. She's doing so well here."

"I know. I know. Look, I'll have it—soon—by the end of the

week."

"I'll tell the headmistress, but it'd be better if you call her directly." The housemother paused. "She—uh, says you don't return her calls."

"I'm busy all day with meetings. You know how it is."

"Yes, ma'am, I do. I just don't want Charlie to lose her place here. Her progress is somethin' to behold. When you gonna come see her? She asks 'bout you every day."

"After Mardi Gras, I'll try to take off a few days, but then, it'll be tax time. Tell her I love her, okay? And I'll see her soon."

"Yes, ma'am, you know I'll tell her."

She thanked Aurelia and replaced the phone. She walked over to the window and stared at the marina until the sunset, turning the sky and water a deep indigo. The flickering lights appeared one by one and illuminated the floating city below. She turned from the familiar scene with a sense of anticipation.

It was time.

Chapter Six

A little after seven, Jake finally made it home to the loft. Bless her little home-making heart. Just like the new bride, she was supposed to be, Caitlin had already started working on the loft. The trash was gone. The floors were shining, as were the tall, arched windows. And there were two new sofas, an assortment of tables and lamps. A partner desk and—of course—a bed.

How in hell had she managed it all?

"I could've sworn you went to work today."

She glanced up from chopping a large stalk of celery. "I did."

"But—" He made a sweeping gesture. "All this?"

"It's called a telephone. I ordered everything on my lunch hour, paid extra for delivery today, and called the concierge so he could let everyone in. I also called a cleaning service." She pulled a platter from a cabinet, which hadn't been there that morning, and started arranging the vegetables into what, if she kept it up, would be a round work of art. "What did you do at lunch? I looked for you like a good little wife."

Jake grinned. "I had a date."

She wrinkled her cute nose. "Well, that's pretty quick. Unfaithful already."

He wondered just how much he ought to tell her. If all else failed, the truth?

"There's a little complication—but I think it'll be okay."

A quick flush spread from Caitlin's neck to her face. Her gaze narrowed. "A *little* complication?"

"I ran into someone I used to know." He winced as he said it, knowing just how lame and unprofessional he sounded.

"In other words, you've been compromised." She spat the words at him, quick and deadly like bullets from a semi-automatic.

"That's who I had lunch with, but she'll keep quiet."

"Oh, I'm sure you worked your manly charms on her." She shook her head. "No. No. This is off to a bad start. What makes you think you can trust her?"

Okay, his SAC was pissed, but he couldn't resist. "You think I'm charming?"

"Your charm's not the point. This mission is already at risk. I'll have to notify Jose. He'll pull us out for sure." She glared around at the apartment. "Not that I'll be sorry to leave this place," she muttered, but not low enough. He still heard her.

"Hold on. I maintained cover. I told her I spent some time in prison, so she understands my reasons for using a different name. She's not using the name I knew her by either."

"So she's some low-life you knew before you were adopted?"

"Yeah, but she's no low-life now."

"I don't care if she's the Vice-President of the United States, I'm calling Jose right now. This is his decision."

Jake swallowed, then chose his words carefully. "What's the matter? Can't make a decision on your own without calling an older male counterpart—sort of like checking in with *Daddy*, isn't it?"

"It's procedure!" She drew her arm back and threw—

Jake ducked. The spear of celery missed him by a good two inches, but he bet she wouldn't be calling Jose to pull them off the operation anytime soon.

"Mm. Something really smells good. Did you really find time to cook, too?"

"Catered. I *can* cook, but—"

"Hey, I met your cook, Bonnie. Translation: Don't expect a home-cooked meal every night."

"Bonnie is more than my cook. She's a dear friend and the closest thing to a mother I had."

"I know. At least you had someone when you were a kid." The words came out more bitterly than he'd intended.

Expression contrite, she looked up from chopping a fresh stalk of celery. "I didn't mean to bring up what must be unpleasant memories."

"You didn't. Hell, I don't blame my mother for running off. My father liked to smack her around."

"But she left you behind with an abusive man. I don't understand. How could she?"

"I guess she had a chance to blow town, so she took it. Like I said, I don't blame her." But in truth he did. How could his mother have left him with the SOB who was his father? Caitlin's tender tone cut through his armor. Cut him to the quick.

"Was he abusive...after she left?"

Why couldn't she just let it go? Jake scratched his head and said. "He gave it a try, but I was big for my age. I fought back and lit out, too. I spent the next two years living on the streets."

"That's when you swept floors at the Bar Bayou?" A frown of concern formed across her forehead; she set the chef's knife on the counter. "Who took care of you?"

Enough of this crap. He jumped up and walked to the refrigerator. "Got any beer?"

She nodded toward the fridge. "Second shelf. Don't avoid the question."

He turned to face her. Lovely face she had, too. "I took care of myself. Wasn't hard. Pan-handled, swept floors, played three-card Monte on the streets, and ran numbers for Fatso Martinelli. Good work if you can get it."

"Very industrious."

"Hunger makes you that way."

"Was that the first time you gambled?"

"No, chèr. My daddy taught me how to shoot craps as soon as I was old enough to count."

Setting the salad masterpiece aside, she cocked her head to the side and gazed at him with puzzlement. "Where did you sleep?"

If she only knew. "I said I was big for my age. I didn't have any trouble finding a bed."

She sniffed and picked up her knife again. "I guess not."

And he'd only told her the abridged version of his life on the streets.

During the dinner of Cajun beef and vegetable stew, Jake hunched over his plate. Crisp French bread, green leafy salad—hell, he could get used to having a *wife*. "Sorry, my manners are on the rusty side, but the grub is great. You do great take-out."

She huffed and gave him another one of her eye rolls. "I'll have you know I did the salad myself."

"I saw. You nearly speared me with a stalk of celery." He buttered a piece of bread then took a bite. "Mm, honest to gosh butter," he said with his mouth full. After washing the bite down with iced tea, he said, "For future reference, the dressing isn't bad, but I prefer Thousand Island."

An expression of disdain spread across her well-bred features. "That's the purest virgin olive oil and the best balsamic vinaigrette you're turning your nose up at. Tell you what. I'll be sure to put Thousand Island on my next grocery list."

"Enough already. Let's debrief." He snatched another piece of bread from the basket. "So what about your day? I guess you already have it all figured out and we can go home?"

She lifted her shoulders in a slight shrug as she buttered a piece of bread no bigger than a poker chip with a dot of butter. "Not quite. First person I met was Lisette, the receptionist. She's quite colorful, not a major player, but if she can get over her surly attitude, she might be a good background source. Then there's my boss, Heaton Boyle. He's a poor slob of a guy. Looks desperate enough to embezzle, but I don't see him as a killer or behind the money laundering."

She stopped her recitation long enough to take a small bite of her prissy salad.

"I also met the CFO, one very cool iceberg of a woman, one Angelique Andre. She hounds Boyle. He absolutely cringes whenever he sees her, so if any money laundering is going on, it's with her knowledge. Fear rolls off Boyle in waves. Sweaty palms and nervous tics—all the signs. Something's going on in that office."

"Uh, about the CFO. Guess you need to know, she's the person who recognized me from the old days. But believe me, we both have secrets. She bought my version of where I'd been and who you were and your family connections."

Caitlin's fork poised midair. "You're sure?"

"Yeah, we're cool." Better change the subject before she asked more questions. "Game plan on your end?"

She set her fork down beside her salad. "I've already hacked into some of Boyle's private files."

"You *have* been busy today."

"I don't want this to last any longer than you do."

"You wound me. Being back in town feels right. Besides, you can't go in like gangbusters. It'll raise suspicions...and that's dangerous. Developing a deep cover isn't an overnight deal."

"Anyway, nothing jumped out at me, so as soon as I can, I'll copy what's there and bring it home. I would have today, but I was interrupted. We can go over it together. What's your game plan?"

"Basically, doing my job, keeping my ears open and making connections wherever I can. Alex is pretty observant, but he needs a little reining in. He's come up with some good intel, but he's a little on the reckless side."

"You're going to rein *him* in? And I'm here to ride herd on *you*." A smug expression crossed her face.

"We all have our crosses to bear."

"Look, I know what you think of my being SAC."

"So? I've made it pretty clear."

"You have. But this is the very opportunity I need to prove you and everyone else are all wrong."

"As long as it's not over my dead body, I don't give a hang about your career advancement."

"Hm. Your dead body." She smiled but it wasn't meant to warm his heart. "I must admit that has a singular appeal—at times anyway."

"Ouch."

Once her partner's stomach was full and his mood mellowed, Caitlin started to clear the table. Jake pushed his chair back and helped her load the dishes into the new stainless-steel dishwasher, then glanced around the loft.

"I notice you only bought one bed. I knew it. I'm growing on you. You're hot for me, aren't you?"

Her chin dropped. "Don't be ridiculous."

"You are. A guy can tell."

Caitlin rolled her eyes. "I refuse to admit to anything that'll make your already inflated ego any larger."

"So you're going to pine for me in secret?'

She waved away his last comment. What a jerk she'd been paired with. Not only was he an off-profile kind of guy, but he was also a typical male who only thought of his effect on the female population. "The sofa pulls out and makes a very nice bed for you. The bed is mine."

"I'm crushed. How can you expect me to perform at my peak if I'm sleeping with a metal bar in the middle of my back every night?"

"Your performance depends on your brain. I hardly think sleeping on a sofa bed will affect that particular part of your anatomy."

"Sleep deprivation *will* affect my brain. Have you ever read the studies done by—"

She banged the counter with a wooden spoon. "Enough! I don't care about studies. You're an adult. I'm an adult. I'm taking the bed. *You're* on the sofa."

"It has nothing to do with being an adult. You're pulling rank. You're the boss, so you get the bed."

"Fine. I'm pulling rank."

"Fine. You know, I'll be working some nights and sleeping days, at least part of the time. I could use the bed when you're at work."

Strangely arousing—the thought of his sleeping in her bed when she wasn't there, his male scent lingering after he left for work and enveloping her with his presence. "No. The arrangements stay just as I've outlined them."

"Okay, boss lady."

Later that night, Jake tried not to watch as Caitlin took her jammies into the bathroom which, while not "decorated", was clean and screened off from the rest of the loft. Too bad she hadn't chosen a shoji screen; that way he could've seen her shapely body though the rice paper which would only run a close second to seeing her naked.

Oh well, can't have everything.

The homey sounds of Caitlin brushing her teeth were strangely comforting.

She returned from the bathroom minty-fresh and all prim and proper in a pair of pajamas which must've been tailored with Shaquille O'Neal in mind and rendered her body completely asexual.

But her PJs really didn't do the job. He wouldn't be losing sleep because of a metal bar in his back. Her prim presence tricked out in those over-sized jammies was more of a turn-on than he could ever have imagined. Visions of her ivory skin and lithe body danced in his fevered imagination. The chances of ever seeing her in anything except his imagination were slim to none. In fact, the odds were more in his favor of breaking the bank at the Palais Ponchartrain.

Dammit! Why couldn't he just keep his mind on the operation and forget about Kate? Not good odds on that happening, either, with her sleeping not fifteen feet from him.

Chapter Seven

Outside it was raining...again. Far beyond tired after a long, boring day at the casino and absolutely nothing accomplished, Caitlin rubbed her eyes, re-read the e-mail, then printed it. The news was bad and effectively set their investigation back by weeks, if not months. "Jake."

He glanced at her from the other side of their partner's desk. "Yeah?"

She slid the email over to him. "We've heard back from the gaming commission, Terri Thibedoux hasn't applied for a job in any of the casinos in Vegas or Atlantic City."

"Official, then. We have a missing person. My guess, she's floating in Lake Pontchartrain or if they were really mad, they dumped her in the nearest bayou. Which makes her gator bait, and we'll never find her."

"You're that certain?"

"Yep. Felt it in my gut that first night...when we talked to Alex."

"You did?"

"Didn't you? What's the matter?" He arched an eyebrow in her direction. "Don't accountants have gut instincts?"

Jerk thinks he's so smart.

Through gritted teeth, she began, "Statistically, I considered it a very real possibility—"

"Crap!" He wadded the e-mail into a ball and lobbed it in her direction. "Spoken like a true accountant."

His words grated just like he'd meant them to. She looked at him and sighed. "Frankly I'm too tired to argue the point."

"How 'bout a massage?" He held up his hands and waggled his fingers. "These are good for what ails you."

A deep shiver shook her, but she straightened in her chair. "Wh-what?"

"I rub your back." He shot her wicked grin. "You rub mine?"

Did she dare?

Every muscle in her neck and back ached for his touch. His offer was too tempting... Caitlin nodded. "Okay. But just watch it. Just my neck and back."

"Yes, dahlin'." He walked toward her, his wide grin more wicked than usual. "But of course, the same goes for you."

"I—?" Did Jake really expect her to massage him, too?

"That's the deal." He reached into his pocket and pulled out a coin, flipped it, and then caught it on the back of his hand, covering it. "Call it."

"Heads."

He peeked at the coin. "Tails it is. I go first."

The insufferable man ripped off his shirt as if he were a hero in a romance novel. "I'm ready."

"Fine." The man just didn't know how close she was to strangling him. On the other hand, his physique was as buff as any male model. The muscles rippled across his chest and six-pack abs.

"What's wrong? 'Fraid you'll find me irresistible?" he asked with a cocky grin.

"Irresistible? I find the thought of touching you *quite* resistible."

"Way too harsh. But you're not getting get out of this. I won the toss. You lost."

"Fine. Just stretch out across the foot of the bed." She extended her arms and wiggled her fingers just to show him how ready she was.

"What? No soothing music, no smelly candles you girls—excuse me, women—are so fond of?"

"Don't push it, Jake."

"Okay. I get it. One bargain-basement massage coming up." He smiled, lay down...on his back, folded his arms across his chest. "I'm waiting."

"Look here, buster, I don't know where you're used to getting your massages—no, I'm not going there—but if you don't turn over on your stomach pretty damned quickly, I'm going to wring your neck and all bets are off."

A hearty, satisfying chuckle echoed through the loft, but he turned over just the same.

"Thank you." She leaned over and gave his shoulder a tentative nudge. "You don't feel very tense to me."

"Kate, come on. Where's the oil?"

"Picky, picky. I'm fresh out of massage oil. How about some nice lotion?"

"Better than nothing."

Caitlin walked over to the bathroom and returned with a bottle of lotion. Instead of pouring it into her hands, she trickled the lotion directly onto his back.

"Aw, come on. You're supposed to warm it with your hands first."

She giggled. "Sorry, this is the first massage I've ever given." She took a tentative swipe at the lotion on his heavily muscled back.

"I'll show you."

Before she could respond, Jake flipped over, grabbed her shoulders and she was underneath him. "Whoa, fella."

His face was so close to hers, his dark eyes glittered and bored into hers. "I'll show you."

He shifted his weight, and for a brief moment, his hard erection pressed against her thigh. God. He was aroused.

Even worse, so was she. No, she couldn't give in to what her body wanted. A warmth grew in her face and spread downward. "Y-you're getting lotion on the duvet."

"Screw the duvet. I'm going to show you a real massage."

She averted her face from his and scooted up on her elbows. "I'm no longer tired."

"But you have a lot to learn."

"So do you, but if you don't get off me, you're not going to live long enough to graduate kindergarten."

He rolled off her with a laugh. "Sorry, but you were just too tempting. I couldn't resist."

"Resist what? Committing attempted rape?"

"You were in no danger. Besides, I didn't hear you say no."

"Well, no!"

"Heard it loud and clear that time." He slid his feet to the floor, stood, then gazed down at her. Why did she have the irresistible urge to pull him back down?

No. No way.

She sat up, rearranged her clothes and—

The intercom buzzed.

Jake headed for the door but stopped short. "This isn't over, chèr."

"This? What this?" she hissed.

He shook his head and laughed the rest of the way to the door. "Better be good," He said into the intercom.

"Hey, man. It's Alex. Buzz me in."

"Better be damn good," Jake growled into the speaker before buzzing in the younger agent and unlocking the door.

Alex ambled into the loft with a wide grin across his face. "Dude, what's up?"

Caitlin let out a quiet sigh. At least with Alex here, she wouldn't be alone with Jake. The massage situation was too close to getting entirely out of hand.

The younger agent sniffed. "You smell like a girl." His eyes widened and a wicked grin flashed across his handsome face. "I didn't interrupt the honeymoon, did I?"

"No!" Caitlin and Jake answered together.

"Then why do you smell like a refugee from Victoria's Secret?"

Jake folded his arms across his chest. "Never mind all that. What're you doing here?"

"Just thought I'd drop by and..." Alex shrugged, but the devilish grin never left his face. "I brought you a housewarming present."

He produced a *Times-Picayune* from behind his back.

"Very thoughtful of you," Caitlin gushed with relief and then grabbed him by the hand, pulling him into the living area. "Come on in. It's good to see you again. Would you like something to drink?" She headed to the kitchen and set the newspaper on the counter.

"Wife, aren't you the polite one?" Jake smirked, his arms folded across his chest.

"I know how to treat a guest."

A wide grin spread across Alex's face. He sat, then leaned back against the sofa with his fingers linked behind his head. "Yes, ma'am, whatever you have."

She turned to fetch the fruit tea when her guest's next words stopped her.

"Man, you have it made. I'd love to have someone like Caitlin puttering around attending to my every whim." He high-fived in Jake's direction.

Jake gave a snort. "Lower your voice, man, or you might lose some valuable body parts. You're a guest. I don't get this kind of treatment."

"No, he most assuredly does not," Caitlin said. "Do not, I repeat, do not confuse what we're doing here with a relationship."

"Oh, no, ma'am. I won't make that mistake." An expression of pure mischief spread across Alex's handsome face.

Her point made, Caitlin quickly returned with a tall, frosty glass of fruit tea. "There's more if you want some, Jake."

Jake grinned at Alex. "Translation: get it yourself. It's just like being married, for real...without the benefits."

Caitlin ignored his smart-ass remark and leaned forward. "Now, then, Alex, why don't you tell us what's on your mind."

"The rumor mill was working overtime today. Seems the head of Security and Operations, Harris, was close, as in personal, to our missing Terri Thibedoux."

Caitlin leaned forward. "I thought Security employees didn't..."

"Hey, it's the Big Easy, nobody pays any attention to those rules."

"Is such a blatant disregard of regulations typical of casino employees, Jake?"

"Kinda difficult to enforce in real life," Jake said.

"So any indications he's all cut up about her not being around?"

"Nah, that's just it. My source says Harris and Terri were real tight, and some folks are curious why he's not."

"Maybe they broke up before she left."

"Don't think so. Before Terri disappeared, she'd started spreading the news she and the boss man were getting hitched."

"Hmm. I think I'll do some follow-up with the receptionist in my office."

"Good point," Jake said. "They worked together so she'd know the scoop. Don't come at her with a bunch of questions. Give her time. Let her open up to you."

"I *know* how to talk to another woman, Jake."

"I can see you now. You'll go in there like gangbusters and put her on notice, and you won't find out a damn thing."

"There's a very set way to go about interrogating someone without their knowledge. If you would just stop treating me like some kind of damned rookie."

"Kate, interrogation's an instinctual thing...an art. You can't do it by following instructions from Interrogation. There's no real guidebook."

"You studied the same techniques I did at Quantico," she insisted. Why did he have to make everything so semi-mystical when interrogation was a matter of common sense, observation and following the rules?

"Given more experience, you'll learn things that aren't in books. And there comes a time you have to throw the books away and work from your gut, from your knowledge of what makes people tick."

"I'm not a rookie."

"No, you're not a rookie when it comes to spreadsheets or money scams, but I know people. I *know* them. Their fears and hopes...and the dirty secrets they hide."

She shot Jake a knowing grin. "I might just surprise you."

Shaking his head, Alex stood and headed for the door. "Don't mind me, folks. You two can work this out without me."

"Oh, Alex..." Caitlin wrinkled her nose in Jake's direction. The man had no business acting so smug. "I'm so sorry. I completely forgot you were here."

"That's all right. I'm forgettable like that."

"No, really we were unspeakably rude."

"Nah. I came at a bad time. And, dude, if I were you—" He broke off and laughed. "You still smell like a girl."

"Yeah. I heard you the first time."

"It's a very nice lotion...expensive, I'll have you both know."

"Right. So, I'll let y'all get back to whatever you were doing...honeymooners." Alex started laughing and didn't stop until the metal gate clanged shut and Caitlin could no longer hear him.

"I'm heading for the shower." Jake rose; his long legs unfolded slowly. "If you have no objections, that is?"

"Gonna wash the girly smell off?"

"You bet." He wiggled his dark eyebrows up and down. "Want to join me? Saves water."

"Not on your life."

"Don't know what this world's coming to when a man's wife won't get in the shower with him for a little honeymooning."

She huffed. His teasing and games were getting to her...along with his hot body.

"Why can't you just take a shower without involving me? You lack a sense of professionalism and..."

"What? You're gonna put something in my permanent record?" He stuck out his bottom lip in a pout. "Aw, please don't give me a black mark. My career—what will I do?"

She huffed. "I refuse to respond to such childishness." Okay, it wasn't his childishness she found irritating. His playfulness was far too appealing.

"Refusing to respond is a response."

"If you wish to be argumentative, we can always debate the number of angels who can dance on the head of a pin."

He grinned and took a step forward, closing the distance

between them. "I love it when you get all hoity-toity. Your eyes flash and your cheeks turn pink. And red splotches pop up on your chest and neck."

By reflex, her hand went to her neck. Damn the man—he noticed everything. Why didn't he just go on and take his damned shower?

"And right now, there's a touch of steam escaping from each of your pretty little ears." He bent over and laughed. "You're so cute when you're mad."

"If you're taking a shower, take it...and don't use all the hot water!" She stopped, remembering his earlier suggestion. "And *no*, I'm not sharing the shower with you."

Jake frowned and assumed an expression of feigned disappointment, then followed with a wink. "You don't know what you're missin', chèr. I'm mighty good at washing backs."

The thought of hot steam and his strong hands washing, caressing her back sent a wave of heat flooding to her lower belly. She bit her bottom lip.

Pain. Good—anything to keep from thinking about washing his strong, muscled back in return.

Apparently tired of being an absolute ass, he shrugged and headed for the shower.

"The screen. Don't forget the screen."

"'Fraid you won't be able to keep from lookin'?"

"You are the most absurdly arrogant man I've ever—"

"Been married to?"

"I have work to do," she said with a huff, then marched back to the laptop, then sat. With her back to the bathroom, there'd be no temptation—not that she was tempted—not at all.

Liar.

The next morning Caitlin breezed into the office fifteen minutes earlier than usual. It had become the highlight of her day to see what outlandish costume Lisette would deem appropriate for office wear. And she wasn't disappointed. Her style-challenged co-worker was reading an Anne Rice novel and attired in a somewhat Gothic flowing gown. Black lipstick and fingernail polish added to the effect as did the gold upper arm bracelet in the form of a serpent. Perhaps the local author was having a book signing and Lisette was going.

Caitlin stifled a sigh and headed to the already empty coffee pot.

Empty. Wouldn't it be nice if Lisette were a little more passive-aggressive? She bit back the snarky comment she was sorely tempted to make. "I'm going to make a fresh pot. You ready for another cup?"

Her co-worker's face contorted into a puzzled mask. "Uh, yeah, sure." Then as if remembering her manners, added, "Thanks."

"No problem." When the coffee finished its noisy snap, crackle and pop routine, Caitlin poured two cups and set one of them on her co-worker's desk. Then she pulled her chair from her cubicle and settled down by Lisette. "So who was my predecessor? Did she get a better job or get married?"

With a frown, Lisette placed her book face down on her desk and glared pointedly at Caitlin. "What do you care? You're not in any danger of her coming back."

"How so?"

"Well, they'd never rehire anyone who quit with only an email notice," Lisette replied with the manner of a duchess.

"How long did she work here?"

"Five years."

"That's a long time for her to just up and leave."

Lisette slammed the desk with her fist. "She didn't even say good-bye, either. I don't have any use for folks like that."

"Is that why you won't even give me a chance?"

"No point in making friends with you. You're on your way up. I've heard about your family."

"My family?"

"Yeah, mob princess."

"That's nothing to do with me. That's why I left Jersey. I don't want anything to do with *the life* or their dirty money."

"Sure." Her tone was filled with skepticism.

"I left my family, met my husband Jack, and never looked back. Maybe that's what—what's her name—did, too."

Lisette fixed her gaze on the desk and gave her head a tiny shake. "No, Terri was involved with someone—someone here at the casino."

Another confirmation of what Alex had already related. Still, Lisette might know more—like who. "Oh?"

"Don't ask me who. I'm not telling. But he was seeing someone besides her."

"Really?" Caitlin leaned forward on her elbows. Maybe this was just the lead she needed.

"I know something else, too." Lisette glowered at Caitlin. "You're mighty damn nosy. I'm not spilling my guts. I know better. I'd like to keep working here for a few more years." Lisette averted her gaze, picked up her paperback and resumed reading.

Caitlin hid her disappointment and shrugged. "Just trying to make conversation, Lisette. That's all."

Dammit. Jake was right. She'd come on too strong like the greenest rookie. The more she tried to prove her worth, the more she proved was she was cut out for riding herd on spreadsheets.

Chapter Eight

The sun was low in the evening sky and the mist had already started to gather and hang over the water of the bayou. Jesse Doucet shuffled through the damp leaves and kicked an empty bird's nest while his dog Teon pranced ahead. Dang it. His cousin was trying to ditch him. "Remy! Where you headed?"

His cousin stopped and turned up his nose. "None your bid'ness, you sorry piece of gator shit. Got things to do, and last thin' I need what some whiney kid slowin' me down—dat be you."

Jesse set his hands on his hips like his maman did when she was blessing him out. "You Cajun shithead! I'm not a kid. We're da same age."

"Not so. I'm three months older. My birthday's Sat'day, and I ain't running around wid eight-year-ole babies. And don't be callin' me a Cajun anything, you dickhead."

"Dickhead!" Jesse kicked at something in the matted leaves. "Lookee here, some gal done lost her dress."

"Teon!" Jesse hollered at his dippy dog. "Come on. Let's go on back home. "Teon!" Dang dog had no business running off into the bayou, anyhow.

"Gator'll get 'im. Good 'nuff for de mangy mutt."

"Dat dog of mine ain't no mutt. Teon's a pure-bred blue ticker hound."

A low warbling howl rose in an eerie crescendo, sounding through the bayou. The hair rose on Jesse's neck. "Dang it! Where you are?"

He picked up his pace until the sweat ran down his neck. The winter damp stuck his clothes to his back like flypaper.

"Dere you are." His dog was snuffling at the root of a big old cypress tree. "What de heck's de matter wit you?"

He drew closer; his nose wrinkled. Spoilt meat. That's what. He tripped and landed at the base of the cypress. The twisted roots rising from the wet were bigger around than his arm.

He scrabbled back, trying to get away from it. Unable to catch his breath, Jesse pointed.

Twisted in a chain...a hand, clinging for life. Nothing but two hands. Finally, his breath returned. A whimper, then a scream ripped from his throat.

Caitlin's cell phone rang. She rubbed the sleep from her eyes and fumbled around the top of the bedside table.

"Chaney."

"Agent Lascassas here. You might want to make a call at the medical examiner's office. They might've located your whistleblower."

"The M.E.'s office? Any chance she's working there?"

"Nope."

"Thanks."

From the sofa bed, Jake sat up and groaned. "What?"

"Get up. We're going to the M.E.'s office. Local office has a tip they've found the Thibedoux woman."

"Can't it wait until tomorrow?"

"No. We'll keep our presence low-profile if we go down there now."

"Yes, ma'am, boss lady." He flipped a cheeky two-fingered salute in her direction.

"I know you truly can't help it but try not to be such a jerk."

Her partner yawned and stretched.

And don't think she didn't notice his chest was bare and the muscles gleamed in the moonlight shining through the tall windows. Her breath caught in her throat.

"Kate. Turn your head. I'm sleeping in the—"

"You're naked?" She swallowed the lump forming in her throat.

Sleeping nude was definitely something that should've been mentioned in his dossier.

"Yeah." He pulled the sheet tight. "So turn your head, woman."

"I have no desire whatsoever to see your naked ass."

"I'm told it's mighty fine." He waggled his eyebrows in imitation of Groucho Marx.

"I'm sure. But in spite of what I'm sure is a great volume of anonymous recommendations, I'm not interested."

Not much.

"Right. Now, are you gonna turn around or not?" He whipped back the sheet and...

Without meaning to, she let out a gasp, but then quickly recovered, hid her eyes and raced for the bathroom.

The sound of his laughter echoed through the loft. She leaned against the sink and splashed cold water on her burning cheeks.

Why did she let him get to her this way? She certainly couldn't threaten him in kind. No, he'd just stand back and enjoy the view.

"Kate." He rapped on the screen. "You coming out any time soon?"

"Just a minute." She snatched up a comb and ran it through her short, curly hair. Bedhead—the worst.

"Come on, Kate."

"Are you dressed?"

"Halfway."

"Better be the right half."

"What was that? Come on. I don't like yelling through the screen."

With an air of calm that was totally bogus, she walked around the screen and gazed up into his dark brown eyes. "You don't have to yell. It's all yours."

"I knew you'd come to your senses sooner or later." He grinned and opened his arms wide.

As if... "The *bathroom*, you jerk."

The low rumble of Jake's laughter echoed throughout the loft. Damn the man. He had to turn everything into a double entendre.

*

In the crypt, the odor of death pervaded the air. Would she ever get used to the stench?

Terri Thibedoux's remains, what little there were, were arranged in anatomical order. Two hands, the fingers long and bare. The wrist bones with shreds of tendons still in place, a complete radius and ulna on the left, but on the right, they ended in jagged shards of bone.

"That's all?"

The Medical Examiner nodded. She was an elegant woman of Asian heritage in her mid-thirties. Mini glasses perched on her nose. She gazed over the rims at Caitlin and nodded. "They're still dragging the bayou where she was found for additional remains, but this is it for now."

"Any idea how she died?" Caitlin asked.

"The victim was chained by the wrists to the roots of a cypress tree in Petit Pierre Bayou. Alligator got most of her. Insects the rest."

"But how did she die? When?"

"According to the insect life and state of decomposition, I estimate she's been dead three to four weeks."

"And the method?" The images which came to mind weren't pretty.

"The method." The M.E. sighed. "Normally when this is all we have, there's not much chance of knowing. However, the crime scene investigators found deep scarring from the chains, as well as blood, in the root where she was chained."

"She was chained alive and left..." Caitlin's voice gave out.

No.

"Exactly. Left as bait for the alligators." The M.E. walked over to the table and picked up an evidence envelope. "One of her co-workers identified the victim's ring left on her right hand. DNA tests from the bone marrow are pending. We have Ms. Thibedoux's sister and mother to check the alleles against. That'll make the final determination."

Jake spoke for the first time. "Petit Pierre isn't that far off the track. So basically this was damn near a public execution."

The M.E. nodded. "A warning to anyone else who might have any ideas of doing whatever she was doing that pissed off the killer."

The horrifying image of being chained to a tree and helpless... Struggling, pleading for her life, until she bled, and the scent drew...

Oh, God. The room started spinning, Caitlin's knees grew weak, and spots danced in front of her eyes. She flailed for support.

Jake grabbed her before she could fall. Safe and secure in his arms, and more than a little bit flustered by the body contact, she tried to push him away. "Let me go. I'm all right."

"Sure you are." His arm still around her waist, he guided her toward the door. "Except your complexion is a nice shade of green but it clashes with your eyes."

"I'm not green."

"You're fooling yourself, chèr. Come on. Let's get away from the smell."

"No. It's not the smell. It's knowing what horror...what she must have suffered. Waiting. And then... It flashed through me—as if I were there."

"Best not think about it."

"Too late." Still supported by his strong arms, Caitlin stopped at the door and turned in the M.E.'s direction. "Thank you, Dr. Pacion."

"Any time."

Outside the autopsy room, the smell of death lingered.

"Glass of water? Coffee? Why don't you sit yourself down—'til you get your bearings?"

Already stronger, Caitlin shook her head. "Thanks, I'm better."

"Dammit. I knew you'd go all girly. You're not cut out for this."

"Don't be ridiculous. My imagination kicked into overdrive for a couple of seconds—that's all."

Suddenly awkward, Jake loosened his grip on her. "All right. You're on your own."

Without his support, she started sliding...

He grabbed her once again. "You *will* sit yourself down, chèr. Either that or I'm going to carry you outta here."

"I'll sit." Truthfully, she didn't mind him holding her—not at all. He was warm, even comforting in a weird way. She inhaled the scent of him, a mingling of the soap from his early morning shower and a hint of light sandalwood.

Jake was so...alive. So incongruous...in the hallway outside an autopsy room. God. Was she pathetic or what?

All through the day, the casino grapevine had buzzed with the news of Terri Thibedoux's body being found. Was it Terri, for sure? Did they really find only her hands?

The most persistent rumor was that she'd been involved with the head of Security, Bud Harris. If true, she could've had inside information about any money laundering operations.

Like the rest of the casino employees, Jake had his own set of questions. What had she been about to tell the Bureau? Who had left her for the gators? Was it really Terri? Was her death related to the casino at all or was it something more personal?

He would've liked a chance to talk it over with Caitlin at lunch, but he'd been too busy in Security for more than a quick sandwich at his station.

More than glad his ten-hour shift was over, Jake opened the door to the loft and found Caitlin in her usual position, hunched over her laptop.

God, not again. He couldn't take another night alone with her without touching her. "Come on. I'm taking you out tonight."

"Why?"

"Because I'm going crazy cooped up in this apartment. And in spite of your great wisdom and efficiency, you haven't seen fit to furnish the loft with a TV."

"A TV? You want to watch television? What's the matter? Are you going into Monday Night Football withdrawal?"

"Look, we're here for the long haul. We've gone over those files night after night until—"

"Only two nights."

"—I'm seeing spreadsheets in my sleep."

"We're here to do a job. Not watch TV."

"We still have to have a moderately normal life. That's why we're going out."

Kate let out a resigned sigh. She watched him over her reading glasses. "All right. Where are we going?"

"It's a surprise. But I promise there's nothing like it."

"But I have to know *where*."

"Why?"

She chewed her full bottom lip, and without warning his trousers grew snug. "So I'll know what to wear, you jackass."

"Chèr, this is the Big Easy. Nobody cares about what you wear."

She frowned in protest and straightened her shoulders. "But—"

"You look fine, even divine."

"And you've morphed into a Cajun poet right in front of my eyes."

"This is gonna be fun. And you have all the symptoms of needin' a dose of fun."

"And you're the doctor to deliver it?"

"You're catchin' on now. Let's go." He held out his hand. "Come on, chèr."

Caitlin shook her head. "No, there's work to do. I'm very close to figuring out Boyle's system."

"Nope, not tonight. Until they put me on nights permanently, I'm gonna give you a taste of the real New Orleans."

"What's so special about tonight?"

"It's Thursday night, chèr. And you're in for a real treat."

Caitlin pushed back from the desk. "All right…for a little while, but I really have to get back to these files."

"You won't be sorry. I promise."

"Where are we?" Caitlin asked as soon as Jake parked.

"We're in Mid City, on Carrollton Avenue, specifically. This place flooded when the levees gave way after Katrina, but just the first floor. The owner reopened the place later that fall."

She let her eyes read the large neon sign. "Rock 'N' Bowl? Are we going dancing or bowling?"

"We can do both. They have a zydeco band here every Thursday night, and they're always great. I bet you don't even know what zydeco is."

"Then you'd lose that bet. It's like Cajun country. Very catchy stuff."

"Catchy? I don't know if I'd call it *catchy*, but it's the heart and soul of this old Cajun boy."

Once inside the second-story Fifties-era bowling alley, Caitlin couldn't believe her eyes. There were loads of people, dancing, drinking and generally having a good time. One intriguing gentleman attired from head to toe in a blue velvet suit danced by and blew her a kiss. Two women dressed in silk baby doll pajamas danced with each other. And all of them moved to the infectious beat of zydeco. Her body began to move of its own accord.

"You're a natural, chèr. Come on."

"It looks too complicated."

"No, you'll love it."

He pulled her close; she had no choice but to follow him. It had nothing to do with the foot-tapping rhythm of the band or the sexy-sounding lead singer's Cajun French lyrics which she couldn't quite make out. The warmth of Jake's body plastered to hers, and then he swung her body away from his and back again into his arms before she could catch her breath. Next, they were spinning backward.

When the music finally ended, she ended up in his arms again, breathless and laughing. The band segued into a melodic waltz in a minor key. She gazed into his warm brown eyes. "Thank you, Jake. This is the most fun I've ever had in my entire life."

He led her flawlessly around the room. "Then it's time you really lived, Kate-with-a-K."

Her heart slipped into a rhythm that bore no resemblance to the band's three-quarter time. "I think New Orleans is working some kind of spell on me."

"You wouldn't be human if it didn't. I keep telling you it's the Big Easy."

"I think you've mentioned it once or twice," she teased. Why couldn't her life be like this all the time? Why?

"Long as you're in N'awleans, you'll keep hearing it."

"Sometimes, I wish..." She stopped before she said something she couldn't call back.

"Wish what?"

She shook her head. "Nothing. Not really."

Instead of digging, he said. "I'd forgotten how much I love the city. I'm gonna hate to see our—the operation end."

"Me, too, Jake. Me, too." Even that small admission shook her.

He gazed down at her. "You thirsty yet? I got a ragin' thirst."

"Yeah, I'm thirsty." For his lips on hers. For his hands on her body. Damned thirsty. She managed to say, "The words to the waltz—what was he singing about?"

Jake smiled at her, and the skin at the corners of his eyes wrinkled in a very pleasing way. "The title is *Pa Janvier* and it's about a Cajun Romeo and Juliet."

"It's a beautiful song, but I knew it must be about something sad." She fell silent. What more could she say? It felt as if she were getting to know Jake, not Jack her supposed husband, but the man...the one who hid his pain behind dark, impenetrable eyes and off-hand quips.

"Unrequited love always is, chèr."

Now, what did he mean by that? Caitlin's mouth grew parchment dry. "How about that drink?"

With her in tow, Jake plunged through the crowd and found them a table. "Beer?"

"Yeah, one of the lite ones."

He took off for the bar, while she waited and watched the crowd. She'd never seen anything like it in all her life. At that moment the band struck up another tune. Before she knew it, she was tapping her feet and bouncing in her chair—most undignified, but she didn't care.

Jake returned with two beers and a bowl of popcorn shrimp. "You're having fun. I can tell."

Her feet stilled.

"Don't stop on my account. I like watching you squirm around in your chair. It's kinda sexy."

"I wasn't squirming."

"Mm-hmm. You most certainly were."

Her cheeks grew hot, but his wide grin pulled the admission from her. "All right. I was. It's the music. I can't help it."

"No need to feel ashamed, chèr. You're supposed to have fun tonight, let your hair down."

At the word "ashamed", she straightened her shoulders. "I'm not ashamed. Maybe I just feel a little guilty. We're here to do a job. We're not supposed to be out painting the town and having fun."

He leaned forward. "It's part of our cover. Newlyweds go out once in a while, so I'm told."

"If there's no one here from the casino to see us, what's the point?"

"You never know who you might see. This place is a tradition for a lot of locals." He scooted his chair closer to her side of the table. "In fact, since we are newlyweds, we ought to be cuddling just in case someone does see us."

"Cuddle? In public?"

"Oh, yeah." He eased an arm around her waist and pulled her close so they were hip to hip. "Kinda like this."

"It's just make-believe," she murmured. "So keep your hand above my waist."

He grinned and stroked under the curve of her breast with his thumb, and she jumped. "Not *that* high above my waist."

"Your beer's getting warm. Better have a sip."

She took a sip of the cold, tart brew. "So tell me more about your life after you were adopted."

"Translation: time to change the subject."

"I like knowing about you." She took another sip of her beer.

"That in your pretty little rule book? Get to know your team members, chapter one."

She shook her head. "No, really, I'd like to hear more."

"Ed was tough, but he was consistent and kind. Never once raised a hand to me—not even when I tested him. And I did test him every way this street kid could think up." He took a long pull on his beer. "I don't know why he didn't boot my butt back on the street. But I'm glad he didn't. I owe him everything."

"What about love?"

"Does one brief marriage count? Otherwise, I never found time for it." He took another long pull. "What about you?"

"Never found anyone who wasn't more interested in meeting my father than being with me." She nursed her beer.

"That sucks."

She studied the 's laminate tabletop and traced the design with her forefinger. "Yes, it does." Disturbed she'd revealed so much about herself, she forced a smile to her lips and met his gaze. "So, tell me about your gambling problem. When did it start?"

"See here. Why are you probing my dark past? All the better to know me?"

She shrugged. "Yes," she said primly. "That's chapter two in the rule book, under the heading of 'Know Your Team's Weaknesses'."

"You know what? You're almost funny. I didn't think you had it in you. I have a weakness or two. I don't suffer fools gladly, and I'd rather play Twenty-One than eat fresh lobster. Hell, I'd rather hit the gaming tables than breathe. And that's the God's honest truth." He held up a hand as if warning her not to jump to conclusions. "Don't worry. I have it under control. That's the truth, too."

"When did it get out of control?" Still, she couldn't help but wonder if Jose hadn't made a mistake in assigning Jake to this operation. Surely, he wasn't the only agent who knew the ins and outs of casinos. Maybe the whole operation was a test...for both of them.

"When did it get out of control?" He gave a self-deprecating chuckle. "'Bout the time I blew the money for the baby's new shoes."

"Cute. Very cute." She smiled and quickly envisioned him gingerly holding a baby with red curls.

No! What the hell was the matter with her? Focus!

"Okay." A half grin kicked up the corner of his mouth. "There's no baby going barefoot, but I woke up drunk and broke one morning outside an Indian casino in Bum-fuck, Michigan. I'd blown my entire savings account on poker slots—and I hate slots. I found I'd signed over my car—no, not *my* car, one that belonged to the Bureau—to the casino."

Caitlin choked on her beer. Once she could breathe again, she said, "You did what?"

A mischievous grin spread across his rugged and handsome face. "It's true. And that, Kate-with-a-K, is the closest I ever came to losing my job."

"I'm amazed you didn't."

"I went to GA, got some counseling—the whole nine yards."

"Was your gambling the reason your ex decided she'd better take a hike up the career ladder?"

"Nah, she'd already tired of my long absences for ops. No, wait a minute. What Melissa said was she'd gotten used to my not being around and preferred it that way."

"That's pretty cold." And here she was just getting used to having him around.

"Oh, yeah, that, too." Jake slapped the table and stood, taking her by the hand. "Enough of Ancient History 101. Come on, chèr, let's cut a rug."

Without a single thought to the contrary, she jumped to her feet. "Let's do."

Before she could catch her breath, he swung her into his arms and pulled her onto the dance floor. "Are you havin' fun?" he asked, his eyes shining with excitement. "Don't lie just to keep from hurtin' my feelings."

As if... "You know I am." And she was. Caitlin "By-the-Book" Chaney was having a damned ball and didn't want the night to end.

*

On the ride home, Caitlin fell asleep, her head resting on Jake's shoulder. The scent of her shampoo teased and tickled his nose. Kate-with-a-K was all woman, soft and prickly by turn.

Hell. What was he thinking? Caitlin Chaney was just another career-focused broad, and the sooner he put paid to stupid ideas like hooking up with her for real, the better.

Odds on, he stood a greater chance of winning the Lotto than sweeping the SAC off her feet with his non-existent brand of charm.

After waking her and parking the car for the night, Jake opened the door to the loft. "Now don't you feel better?"

"I do." Caitlin gazed up at him, not trusting the surge of emotions that set a fire burning in the pit of her stomach and weakened her knees.

"Better get some shut-eye," he said, his tone turning gruff and slightly husky.

"Right." No point in thinking about his piercing gaze or his hard body. He'd taken her out for some R and R. Pure and simple. She was getting on his nerves, and he'd taken appropriate action for some relief.

The fact he'd held her tighter than absolutely necessary when they'd danced didn't mean a thing—not in his book anyway. But in hers, well, maybe she'd just imagined it, but he'd sniffed her hair in the car. She'd pretended to be asleep while trying to process the whirligig of emotions their evening out had produced.

She'd learned a great deal about him, things his dossier didn't include. For one, he was a damned fine dancer. He had to be because he'd made her feel more than competent. Dancing wasn't one of her better events, but by the second dance, she was following his lead without a care in the world.

And the man certainly knew how to have fun and share it with one somewhat uptight bean counter. He'd been tender and respectful. Hadn't made a single pass. Not a serious one, anyway.

Dammit.

And now he was heading for the bathroom as nonchalantly as if they were mere roommates. Well, that's all they were but... "Jake?"

He whipped around, contrition written across his face. He gave a sweeping bow and motioned. "Sorry, you first. I wasn't thinking."

She shook her head. "No, I just wanted to thank you. I really needed to unwind, and the Rock 'N' Bowl was perfect."

He brushed his hair from his eyes. "You're not half bad when you unwind, chèr."

"I suppose that's the best you can do as a compliment?"

Straightening, he grinned. His dark gaze seemed to intensify, and he focused on her. "Depends. I can do better...if and when the situation calls for it."

Situation indeed. Her heated thoughts brought the blood rushing to her face. Her face must be lit up like a candle. Damn, why was she cursed with such fair skin? "I'm sure."

"'Night."

She tucked her head, hoping to hide her confusion and slid behind the screen. "G'night, Jake."

Chapter Nine

The sun was warm, and the day was mild—a perfect New Orleans winter's day. The sky was blue, and sprigs of clouds dotted the sky. Jake spotted Caitlin sitting on the promenade deck of the casino under an umbrella of green and gold, Rivera Corporation's signature colors. Her short red hair whipped in the slight breeze, and she was eating an ice cream cone.

Smiling she raised her hand in greeting like any dutiful wife meeting her husband for lunch would. He moseyed over to the table, leaned over and gave her a quick husbandly kiss. Her lips tasted of vanilla, and he would've gladly kissed her all day long.

She straightened then caught herself. "Hi, baby. I'm so glad you could meet me for a few minutes. I know how busy you are."

He grinned and slid into the chair beside her. "Me, too, chèr."

"I've been a *very* good girl today," she said, lowering her voice, then lightly ran her hand over his thigh and gave her cone another slow lick.

Keep your cool, old buddy. She's just operating within her cover and having a little fun while she's at it.

Now if his body would just listen to his head. "Tell, me. What's kept you so busy and put you in such a good mood."

Mischief sparkled in her eyes like emeralds. "I was able to install a spyware program on Heaton's computer which will record every keystroke he makes. It won't take long for me to figure out his game or games. I just wish I could do the same to the CFO's computer."

Jake thought for a moment. "Maybe there's some way we can get into her office."

"That would be too much to hope for. She's in the corporate building. You have any idea how security works over there?"

"Not yet. I'll find out what I can. These operations take time, Kate. We can't just rush—"

"I know—like gangbusters." Another sweeping lap of her ice cream.

Now if... Dang. Why couldn't she just finish the damn cone?

"Not to change the subject," he said, "but in the last two days, there's been a major increase in the buzz about Terri Thibedoux and my boss. By all accounts, Harris is definitely the one she was involved with."

"More smoke means more fire. You think he's good for having her killed?"

"More than likely. Listen, chèr, you've got to take it easy. Stay under the radar. If he'd have his bed partner killed, he wouldn't hesitate to take you out."

Caitlin gave a solemn nod, looked at her cone with disgust, then tossed it into the nearby waste receptacle. "I don't need these calories."

Before he could tell her how pleasurable it was to watch her take in those calories, his cell phone trilled. He glanced at the number and frowned. "I have to take this. It's Harris."

Rising from her chair, Caitlin nodded. "No problem. I need to get back anyway. Lisette watches the clock like she's the one paying my salary."

She started to walk away. "Hold on. Don't I get another kiss?"

"Of course, you do, you silly boy." She eased into his open arms, her eyes wary.

He pulled her closer and lowered his lips to hers. She was soft and sweet as the vanilla cone she'd just tossed away. He deepened the kiss—

"Ahem."

Jake stopped and turned.

Angelique stood, tapping the toe of her designer shoe. "Newlyweds. Go figure," she said, her tone sarcastic. "Mrs. Girard, I believe Heaton is trying to find you." She turned, dismissing

Caitlin as if she were last night's dinner.

"Now, Mr. Girard, we need to discuss that job opportunity we talked about the other day at lunch." She started walking in the opposite direction of the promenade. Jake had no choice but to follow.

He lowered his tone. "I don't know what you're up to, Angie, but it won't work. I told you I like the job I have just fine."

"I'll just have to change your mind, won't I?" she said with a husky chuckle. She ran her hand up and down his back, then sashayed off, leaving him standing there like a damn fool.

No way was he going down that particular road again.

Later that evening at the loft.

At the familiar squeal of the elevator, Caitlin glanced from the laptop screen toward the door and smiled.

Jake.

But she resisted the urge to run and meet him like the newlywed she was supposed to be. Living together had its advantages. Still, she couldn't give in to the very real attraction that was growing stronger day by day. Dammit. Her heart had no business tripping into warp speed every time he was near.

Jake stormed into the loft, his face pale. "Did Alex call? He didn't make the meet."

"No? What meet? What are the two of you up to now? Do you have any reason to think something untoward happened?"

"Don't know. He's not answering his cell."

She shrugged and gave him a dismissive wave. "Maybe he blew you off for a date."

"No. He left a message with my supervisor just before the shift ended. Asked me to meet him at the Bar Bayou. Dammit!"

Jake paced the length of the loft, and in his haste stumbled over a newly delivered ottoman in a perfect pratfall. "What the hell?" He righted himself and continued pacing in long strides from the living area to the kitchen. He stopped and stared out the window.

"I'll never forgive myself if anything's happened to him."

Caitlin's heart thundered in her chest. That dear boy—no, Alex was an agent and took an agent's risks in the name of the Bureau. She'd grown genuinely fond of him. He was so full of life. He just couldn't be...

She brushed away her negative thoughts. "You're acting like a nervous parent and blowing this completely out of proportion."

"I've got a bad feeling. This isn't like him."

"What should we do? Call the Bureau and the local authorities?"

"The first, for sure." Jake shook his head. "No, get the locals, too. We need everyone on hand for this."

Before Caitlin could pick up the phone, Jake's cell rang.

"Maybe this— Yeah?" While Jake listened, his frown faded, and he sank into the nearest chair. "Man! Don't let it happen again!" He turned off the cell and shoved it into his jacket pocket. "Alex ran outta gas, and his cell was dead. He called from the gas station. He's on his way over." He shook his head as if weary to the bone. "Can you believe that?"

She walked over and sat beside him. Without thinking, she rested her head on his shoulder. "I think I aged about twenty years," she said with a shiver. "I keep thinking about that poor girl in the bayou. These are bad guys we're dealing with."

"No shit." Jake reached over and gently brushed a strand of hair from her forehead. "You have the greenest eyes. I—" His gaze focused as if seeing her for the first time. He jerked his hand back. "Uh, I'd hate to see anything happen to them."

Caitlin straightened. What had he meant to say? Really? But instead of asking, she said, "We just have to work together. No keeping secrets from me. No secret meetings I don't know about."

No making me fall in love with you.

Silence.

"Agreed?" She nudged his ribs with her elbow.

His lids dropped half-mast as his gaze grew inward. "Agreed."

"I mean it, Jake."

Instead of answering, he rose and ambled to the kitchen and

leaned his elbows on the island. "What's for dinner?"

She frowned and gave him her evil eye expression. "I'm going to carve up some FBI agent flank steaks if you don't stop scaring me half to death.

"Now, chèr, you don't mean it. I'm just paranoid about our covers." He walked over to his laptop and booted it up. "We need some music in this joint."

"You can't drown me out with some loud music."

"You wound me, chèr. N'awlins is the world's best city for music and food. I don't see any dinner in the making, so we can at least have some music. I bet you two beignets I can find some zydeco. You remember zydeco, Kate?" His half-grin kicked up the corner of his mouth. He gazed at her with a softness and warmth that seemed genuine.

She let out a dramatic sigh. "Of course." How could she forget last night? They'd had so much fun? The night she'd almost forgotten she was on an undercover mission that had to succeed because her entire future career depended on it.

Back to business. "Did Alex say why he wanted to see you?"

"Nah." He shook his head and shrugged. "Maybe he just wanted to have a beer."

He fiddled with his computer, and soon the energetic rhythms of zydeco filled the loft. The memories of their evening at the Rock 'N' Bowl came flooding back. They'd been in tune. So much so she could almost envision a life with Jake—a life filled with great food and good music and—dare she even think it—love.

He walked over to her, his hand outstretched. "Wanna dance, chèr?"

Did she want to dance? Yes, but...

She drew away from him. "Dance with yourself, Jake. As you said, 'What's for dinner?'" She shut down her laptop, stood and waltzed over to the kitchen. Anything to get away from him and his puppy dog eyes and sexy, teasing lips.

She willed her hands to stop trembling and reached for a butcher knife. Chopping veggies might not be the safest occupation right now, but she had to focus on something besides him.

But he came behind her and took the knife from her hand and set it aside on the counter. "The agency won't let you keep working if you cut off one of your pretty little fingers," he said softly into her ear. He put his arms around her and pulled her close.

The warmth of his breath on her neck sent a chill up and down her spine. She tried not to shiver.

"I want you, Kate-with-a-K. More than I've ever wanted anyone."

Warmed by his words and the feeling behind them, she turned around in his arms and gazed up into his soft brown eyes. "We can't. It isn't possible."

"I know, but it doesn't stop me from wanting you every second I'm around you."

Her heart thudded in her chest. She wanted him, needed him but... "Jake, please, we—"

"Hello! Anybody home?"

Caitlin jumped away from Jake's embrace. "Alex."

"I buzzed," Alex said with a grin. "I guess y'all didn't hear me, so the concierge let me come up."

"Buzz a little longer next time," Jake grumbled. "What did you want anyway?"

"Just wanted to have a beer, but if dinner's ready I won't turn it down."

"Careful, buddy. Kate's already threatened to carve some agent flank steaks. She just might make good on her threat if we don't give her some room."

"Ouch! Tell you guys what. I'll spring for pizza and we can watch the ball game."

Jake let out a bark of laughter. "Look around, man. There's no TV,"

Alex frowned. "Then what do y'all do for fun? I take that back. I don't need to know," he said quickly.

"Okay, new game plan. I'll order the pizza, we'll eat, and then I'll get out of your hair."

"Sounds good," Jake said.

"Jake! Don't be rude. Alex, thank you. Pizza would be lovely, and you may stay as long as you like."

Blue eyes twinkling, Alex grinned at Jake. "Dude, she's got great...manners."

Frankly, Caitlin was relieved by Alex's appearance, and the longer he stayed the less she'd have to deal with Jake's soft words and her utter need to have his hands all over her body.

Finally, Alex left at 10:30. Jake shut the door and locked it. No more interruptions. Pizza and beer had mellowed his mood, but not his desire for Kate. She was right. Their getting involved could turn into a nightmare, and he sure as hell didn't need another career-focused woman in his life. One was enough. Thank you very much.

Kate was already in the shower. Avoiding him, no doubt.

Wonder what she'd do if he just got in the shower with her?

A knee to the groin or would she surrender?

He couldn't take the chance...or advantage. Their living together left them both vulnerable to natural urges. But dammit, he wasn't an animal. He could control his urges. And he would.

Soon enough he'd be off orientation and on the night shift rotation of four nights on and one-off. Those would be four nights he wouldn't have to worry about his urges.

After a restless night of tossing and turning and being unable to think about anything but Kate in her bed only steps away from his uncomfortable sofa bed, Jake slid into his chair only ten minutes late for the security department meeting.

Harris frowned over the podium. "Girard, glad you could join us."

"Me, too. Sorry. Traffic."

"As I was saying, we have a slots tournament coming up at the end of this week. That means an extra thousand grinders to keep track of and keep happy. I don't have to remind you that slots bring in seventy percent of our income. They may not be whales, but the tournament is our gift to them."

Poker slots. God, how he hated slots. Twenty-One, roulette, craps, anything but slots.

"Here's how it goes." Harris droned on as if no one in the room had ever heard of a slots tournament. "It's by invitation only. It only lasts twenty minutes each day, but it'll draw in every hardcore gambler in the region. They'll sign in, be randomly assigned to a particular slot. Machines are set for higher pay off frequency and machines are set to pay higher. Sunday the slots will give double points. Any questions?"

A short, stocky security analyst by the name of Diego raised his hand. "I'm gonna need to take the weekend off, boss. I got a headache."

Laughter erupted in the room, but Harris didn't smile.

"No excused absences for any reason. You'd better be dead if you miss a shift during the tournament."

Diego grinned and slid down in his chair. "Just kidding, Mr. Harris. Just kidding."

Laughter erupted again. Everyone in Security knew Diego was the owner's nephew and in no danger of ever being fired.

Outside the door to his wife's hospital room, Heaton Boyle took a deep breath. Dread filled his heart. Would today be one of her good days or a bad one?

He tapped softly and eased open the door. Her eyes were closed, her cheeks pale and sunken, her jaw slack so her mouth formed a small "O".

June was only fifty, but cancer had sucked the life from her until his darling wife looked thirty years older. "Honey?" he whispered.

Her eyelids fluttered opened. "Heaton." She tried to raise her hand in greeting, but it flopped weakly to the bed.

"It's me. Couldn't start my day without seeing my best girl."

She smiled. "You always know what to say. I love you so much."

Tears filled her eyes. "It wasn't supposed to be this way. We were going to travel and take up square dancing. Instead...I have to leave you."

He pulled the chair up close to her bed. He grasped her thin hand in his. "Now, can't be helped. I know that. We don't know what life's got in store for us. I mean, I could get hit by a bus tomorrow."

"No." June reached for his cheek, but her strength failed her. "I couldn't bear it. Don't you dare talk like that. What would happen to me then?"

"Now, June-bug, I'm not going to leave you. And we'll be together again."

She picked at the sheet. "I'm so tired. I wish I could just go on. I don't know how much all this is costing, but I know the insurance doesn't cover it all."

"Most of it," he lied. "That's my job...taking care of you."

"Y-you could help me along. I'm so tired. And you look tired, too. This is even harder for you than me."

Heaton shook his head. It wasn't the first time she'd asked him to do the unthinkable. "You know I can't."

"I know." She struggled and tried to sit, finally managing to prop herself on one elbow. "Listen here. After I'm gone, you need to marry again. You're a good-looking man. I don't want you to be alone. A man needs a wife. Only natural."

"No, darlin'. I couldn't. Only one little girl for me, and that's you, June-bug."

Her gaze went to the wall clock. "Better go on. You'll be late."

"Don't matter. I'm the boss."

"You've got a boss. I've seen her, and she doesn't look like she has much of a heart."

"She doesn't pay too much attention as long as I keep my nose to the grindstone."

"I hear you. Now you go on. I think today's going to be one of my good days."

Blinking back his tears, he rose, leaned over and kissed her forehead. "I'll see you tonight. Might be late, but I'll be here."

"I love you, Heaton."

He winked. "Same here, June-bug."

Quickly, before he could break down, he left his wife.

She wouldn't love him nearly so much if she knew what he'd done. The fact he'd done it for her wouldn't matter. His wife had principles and she expected he'd have them, too. And he always had...until that pale bitch from hell had taken over as CFO of Rivera Casinos.

Chapter Ten

Boiling mad, but in complete control, Angelique Andre walked by the receptionist who gave her a simpering smile. Where did they come up with such drudges?

"Can I get you a cup of coffee, Ms. Andre?"

"No, thanks, I'll just be a couple of minutes. Heaton in?"

Lisette nodded. "Yes, ma'am. He's expecting you."

Jake's mousy little wife occupied a cubicle in the rear of the office. No doubt the little newlywed was pouring over her precious spreadsheets. How could a bad boy like Jake LeFevre, or whatever he called himself now, marry someone as boring as an accountant? No point in wasting polite conversation on his tedious little number cruncher.

She opened the door to her patsy's office. Like his new accountant, he was also hunched over his keyboard, his right hand dancing the flamenco on the ten-key pad.

She waited for him to notice her. "Heaton..." She kept her tone honeyed and soft. He was such a nervous Nellie. Best handle him carefully.

Heaton looked up, wide-eyed and mouth open, gasping for all the world like a fish left out of water a little too long.

"Ms. Andre? I-I thought you said three."

"Is it a problem, Heaton?" She leaned over his desk and gave him a brief view down her blouse before straightening and crossing her arms under her breasts. "My Cayman account is hungry. You haven't made the deposit. I want it now. Do it."

"M-my figures aren't done yet. It's very tricky." His gaze was riveted to her breasts.

Poor slob.

"I don't want excuses. I'd hate to tell your poor sick wife what you've been up to while she's lying in a hospital bed...all eaten up with cancer."

Heaton's chin trembled. "N-no! You can't. It'd kill her. It's just—I have to be careful. You don't want to get caught, do you?" He swallowed hard.

"I won't be caught. You will."

Panic flashed across his face. He blinked.

"You have thirty minutes."

Message delivered, Angelique turned and sashayed from her underling's office. If she suddenly looked over her shoulder, she knew she his attention would be riveted to her ass and not his precious figures.

So perfect for her needs.

Caitlin watched the bitch-in-white glide by her cubicle. *By all means, don't speak. You're just after my husband.*

No. Jake wasn't her husband. They were only pretending.

A mission.

Undercover.

How many times must she remind herself? A shiver ran up her spine and shook her. No point in thinking about being under the covers with Jake. It wasn't going to happen. She couldn't *let* it happen.

Please, don't let it happen.

She forced her attention back to the hidden file she'd located before the Chief Financial Officer had paid her daily visit to Heaton Boyle. What was going on between those two? Was it something to do with the missing funds or was it more personal?

Good grief. Why would the bitch-in-white be involved personally with a loser like Boyle? It just didn't add up...like a lot of things in that office.

She could hardly wait to get home to see what her spyware had uncovered.

After lunch, Caitlin hoped to run into Jake again, but he was nowhere to be found. She settled for a walk around the casino floor and headed back to Accounting.

Heavens. Lisette's outfit du jour owed a great deal of influence to gypsy fortune tellers. A rainbow-striped skirt swirled over the sides of her desk chair. A white ruffled, off-the-shoulder blouse showed plump freckled shoulders to a not bad advantage. Bright red lipstick, turquoise eye shadow and a ton of gold jewelry completed her ensemble. How did the woman manage to use a keyboard with rings on every finger?

"Any calls, Lisette? I thought maybe my husband—"

"Nope." The administrative assistant sniffed and shrugged...just like always.

Caitlin stopped. "Is it something I've said or done?"

"Huh?"

"Have I offended you? Is that why you're unfailingly rude to me every time I walk into this office?"

"Miss High and Mighty, why should I be nice to you? You waltz in here every day like you own the place. You're almost as bad as the other one."

Angelique Andre, of course.

"But you're not rude to her."

"She's the boss, the *real* boss. I'm afraid of her. You, I can take or leave."

Caitlin tamped down her frustration. "Look, we have to share the same office space. It's counterproductive, not to mention downright unpleasant, for us to go on this way."

"For you maybe. I couldn't care less," she said with an insolent shrug.

"Fine. If you change your mind, let me know." Caitlin walked back to her desk and yanked out her chair.

A tiny makeshift doll with red silk thread for hair lay there. It was wrapped in thread and stuffed with feathers. And it had a large thorn jammed through the chest. Great!

She snatched the doll and strode to her co-worker's desk. She plopped the doll in front of Lisette. "Is this your idea of a joke?"

"What?" Lisette turned pale, screeched and shoved away from the desk. "Get that thing away from me."

"Explain."

"I'm sorry. I know I've been rude. I don't like change, but please, don't put a spell on me. I'm sorry. I really am."

"I just found it in my chair. I thought you—"

"No, no."

"Then who? Who's been here?"

"No one. Heaton's gone back to the hospital."

"Is she very ill?" Possibly a reason for Boyle's embezzling, the late morning arrivals and depressed demeanor. No wonder.

"Yeah. She has cancer, eaten up with it. Poor woman. She was always really sweet when she came in to see him."

"I'm sorry."

Lisette's gaze kept darting toward the voodoo doll.

Caitlin picked it up. "I'll get rid of it."

"No!" Lisette held up her hand. "You have to get someone to reverse the spell...or lessen it."

"Surely you don't believe—"

"This is the Big Easy, but everything ain't so easy. Voodoo's a big part of this city. Don't turn your nose up at it. It's real. I could tell you—"

"Okay, then tell me where to go to get it reversed? That's what you said I needed to do—right?"

Lisette nodded, then flipped through her Rolodex and pulled out a business card. She slid it across the desk toward Caitlin as if afraid to touch her. "Here. I-I go there...for candles sometimes."

"You go to a shop that specializes in voodoo for candles?"

"They're special candles." The woman's hands shook. "I-I got to get back to work now. Go on. It's your problem. Not mine."

Not that Caitlin had ever seen Lisette do much work except answer the phone and read her latest paperback. Maybe once

Caitlin had seen a tarot card web site pulled up on Lisette's computer. Maybe her real work was reading fortunes for folks on the Internet. Yeah, right.

"Thank you for the suggestion. I'll check into it."

Check into it? Indeed she would. If her office mate wasn't playing tricks, then who was? The Andre bitch? Why would she try to scare her? If Lisette were telling the truth, no one else had been in the office.

Outside the *Le Gris Gris* voodoo shop with the doll clutched in her hand, Caitlin hesitated. Not that she believed in voodoo. Of course, it was just for show—for the tourists. Still, she couldn't deny the prick of curiosity or the uneasiness that nagged her.

She opened the bright red door and entered the shop. The doorbell jingled, signaling a warning to the shopkeeper a customer had entered.

Caitlin looked around. The shop looked like a voodoo movie set on steroids. There wasn't an inch of counter or wall space that wasn't covered with voodoo paraphernalia. Beads, candles, and boxes of incense lined a table in front of a large poster of a dark-skinned woman. A local priestess maybe? On the walls were more candles, a collection of small cloth bags—heaven only knew what they were for. Jars of herbs and oils occupied another counter. The combined heavy smell of scented candles and heady incense almost overwhelmed her. Beneath a glass counter were jewelry, books about voodoo and educational videos.

Before she could change her mind and get the hell out of there, a low, sultry voice beckoned from the rear of the shop. "*Bonjour.*"

A tall, slender woman with a lovely café au lait complexion emerged from behind a beaded curtain. Her hair was covered with a red and gold floral print scarf. Gold hoop earrings hung from her ears, and a necklace made of what looked like gold clam shells draped from her neck. She glided along gracefully, her long red skirt rustling like silk. She made a gesture of welcome, her long scarlet nails glistened even in the dim light of the shop.

"What desire brings you to Lyontine? De cards—you want me to tell your future? Or is it a love potion you need for de dark, handsome man in your life?"

Caitlin flinched. Dark, handsome man? Too close. She shook off the unease in the back of her mind. No, it was just a lucky guess on the woman's part.

"Ah, you have trouble, no?"

"No—well, sort of." Caitlin held out the voodoo doll. "Here. Do something with this."

The voodoo woman's gaze widened. She took a step back, then held up her hands. "Someone wishes you harm. Someone powerful."

"I don't really believe this stuff, but I was advised you could reverse the spell or whatever."

The woman pointed to the counter. "Set it d'ere."

Caitlin did as directed. "Now what?"

"I cannot counteract de power of dis curse. A priestess more powerful than I prepared it. Only she can remove de spell."

"Why would she if she did it in the first place?"

"'Twould depend on de reason. If it was on de behest of a client...she might make consideration for money." She pointed at Caitlin, "But if you have personally incurred her ire, she will never reverse de spell."

"It must be someone else. I've only been in town a week, and I don't know any voodoo priestesses...personally." The entire voodoo doll thing had to be a rip-off. Consideration of money, indeed.

"Den you are most fortunate, but if you have made an enemy of one, you must take it to her under de phase of the new moon and trick her into reversing her spell."

"Trick her? Sounds risky."

"*Oui, madame.* It is."

"So you know who made this thing?"

"I fear so. Marie-Ange—her style, her aura, dey are unmistakable."

"Who is she?"

"She claims to be the reincarnation of Marie Laveau." Lyontine shrugged. "Perhaps you've heard of her?"

"Voodoo queen—or something like that?"

"Exactly like dat. Whether or not 'tis true, Marie-Ange is very powerful. Beware of her."

"Where do I find her?" Like she would really hot-foot it to some voodoo ceremony.

"Ceremony take place in two nights. It is not a ceremony staged for tourists. Dis da real t'ing. You must change your appearance, or you will—"

"Stand out like a sore thumb?"

"Like a cat in de dog pound."

Caitlin smiled, but her stomach churned. "I see what you mean. How will I know her?"

Lyontine leaned forward and lowered her voice. "You listen to me, girl. You will know her. She is unmistakable. She de center. She de queen."

"Can you just describe her? I mean, I might run into her on the street and I'd like to know who I'm dealing with."

"She is tall, light-complexion, with eyes so pale dey see de way to your soul, girl. You best stay away from her and de ceremony."

"Where is it?"

"I will not tell you. 'Not for nonbelievers. I see de fire of anger in your eyes, but she will know you are dere before you show yourself. She knows all."

"Fine." Caitlin shrugged away the unease building in her chest, grabbed the doll and stuck it in her purse. "I don't believe in this voodoo curse stuff anyway."

"You say dat now. Come back in two days. We see what you believe den. You still want to go? I take you."

Angelique glanced around her office in the Rivera Corporation building and drummed her nails against the desk. Seeing Jake again brought back too many memories. She'd started turning tricks before she got her period. Damned specialists who got off on breaking in virgins. Hell, she'd forgotten how many times she'd given up her cherry.

Unfortunately, they'd all been robbed, since one of her mother's boyfriends had seen fit to take care of that little detail when she was ten. She shook off the memory of his smarmy voice and the things he did afterward.

At least no one would ever treat her daughter like a windup sex toy; she'd seen to that. She reached for the telephone and punched in a well-known number. "Hey," she said breathlessly when he answered. "I need a favor."

"Sure, doll. Whatcha need?"

She hesitated. "It's a delicate matter."

"How delicate?"

"Extremely."

"Public or private?"

"Public, but delicate." It wasn't her first, or even second, request for his assistance; the code was pre-arranged.

"I'll need more particulars."

"As arranged before."

"Time frame?"

"ASAP."

She broke the connection and rubbed her hands together. Done. And soon she *would* have Jake to herself.

Back in the day, he'd made love to her so enthusiastically, and he'd made her laugh...and no one else had ever made her laugh.

For once, Caitlin was relieved Jake had finally started his night shifts. In spite of not believing in the power of voodoo, she was reluctant to bring the thing into the loft and left it in the glove compartment instead. Whether or not Jake needed to know about the creepy thing was a question for which she didn't have a good answer. Still, it troubled her sleep. She dreamed of snakes, chickens, and monsters wearing frightening masks chasing her into a bayou full of alligators.

Undeterred by a restless night, she set out for work as usual, more than glad the rain had stopped, and the sun was shining. She checked the glove compartment and verified the voodoo doll was still there. Satisfied it was, she flipped on the car's AC in hope of mitigating the humidity that had already turned her stylish and tousled hairdo into a cap of corkscrew curls.

Easing from the parking garage, she turned left onto South Peters Street. She fiddled with the radio until she found the local public radio station.

Her only warning—an engine revving and the screech of tires. She checked the rear-view mirror.

"Damn!" An SUV had come from nowhere and was swerving in an attempt to pass her. She forced her attention to the street ahead and whipped the steering wheel to the right. The SUV was too close and there were cars parked on her right.

Metal scraped metal as the oncoming car thudded and knocked her vehicle into another on the right.

She stomped the brake. Shaken and her heart pounding in her ears, she sucked in a deep breath.

And the son of a bitching SUV drove off without so much as a second look.

"Dammit!" Frustration mounted and a shot of adrenaline coursed through her; she slapped the steering wheel. "Dammit!"

"Lady!"

Startled, she looked to her left. A gray-haired man with a kind but a flushed face was peering through the broken window. "Are you all right, lady?"

A little confused, she glanced down. Her navy suit was covered with tiny fragments of glass. Her cheek stung. She touched the spot and her hand came away with a speck of blood.

"I-I think so." She rubbed her left elbow. "I've bruised my elbow, but I'm okay." She shoved against her door. It wouldn't budge. "My door's jammed."

"Hold on," her rescuer said. "I'm gonna see if I can pry this door open."

"Thanks." She unfastened her seatbelt and swiveled around in the seat. She kicked as the good Samaritan yanked on the mangled door.

"Good thing you were wearing your seatbelt."

"Yes." Was it just good luck? The hair on her neck rose. The accident—was it really an accident?

"Kick it again. We've almost got it."

She kicked again, and this time, the door gave way.

Her knight in not-quite-shining armor took her hand and helped her ease through the opening.

A little unsteady on her feet, she leaned against the front bumper and dragged in another deep breath. "Thank you."

"See here, you can't drive that thing. Damn foreign cars," he said, dismissing her sub-compact. "I'm gonna call the police and an ambulance."

"I don't need an ambulance." She gave her head a determined shake. "What I need is a taxi. I'm late for work." She squeezed back into the car. She reached into the glove box and retrieved the growing-more-ominous-all-the-time doll. Slipping the damned thing into her purse, she pulled out her cell phone.

Before she could call, a squad car with its blue lights flashing pulled up behind her.

It was nearly eleven when Caitlin finally made it to the office. For once, Lisette was almost normal—if you could call a cowboy shirt, boots, and a long denim skirt normal. A ten-gallon hat covered the Rolodex. Well, it was normal for Lisette.

The receptionist set her book on the desk glared. "It's about time you showed up. Heaton's been asking for you. I didn't know what to tell him."

"Sorry, my car was sideswiped. It took a while for the police to get it all sorted out and for the wrecker. Then I had to call a taxi and arrange for a rental car."

Lisette's chin fell. "What? Are you hurt?"

Caitlin shook her head. "Just a bruised elbow."

"You're cursed. It's the doll. I warned you."

"Don't be ridiculous."

"Did you go to the shop? Did you talk to Lyontine?"

"I did, but—"

"You mark my words. You're going to die. That's all there is to it." Lisette made a washing motion with her hands as if that settled everything.

Caitlin let out a sigh. Absurd, but if that's what the girl thought, let her. Voodoo and curses? No one in their right mind, well, at least no one with more than an average intelligence believed in such silliness.

But it was her first car accident...ever.

The hair rose on the nape of her neck and a cold chill shook through her entire body. "I'll be fine."

Lisette rolled her eyes and shrugged. "It's your funeral. Anyway, Heaton wants you in his office now."

Without dignifying her co-worker's pronouncement with a response, Caitlin tapped on Boyle's door and entered.

Heaton glared up from his computer. "Someone's been tampering with my files. Know anything about it?"

She assumed her most innocent expression. "I don't have access to your files. Do I?"

"No. You don't. But someone's been in here. I have my ways."

Crap. Her spyware had been detected after all.

"Maybe someone at the corporate office? The CFO would have access, wouldn't she?"

Heaton frowned at his computer screen. "Maybe. Yes, she would." He gave a somewhat artificial shrug. "Never mind. I just thought you might...no, course you wouldn't."

"No, I wouldn't," she said in as reassuring a tone as possible. What had she tripped when viewing his files? She'd certainly be on the lookout for potential triggers the next time she delved into his dealings. Old Heaton was cagier than she'd figured.

Before she sat at her desk, she checked the chair, just in case. No more unwelcome gifts.

She spent an uneventful, and unproductive as far as investigating was concerned, afternoon toiling over the weekly earnings figures.

Chapter Eleven

That evening in the loft Caitlin booted up her laptop to see what the spyware software had found. Damn. It was nothing but gobbledygook. Obviously, Heaton's files were heavily encrypted. But she had decryption software galore. She inserted the decryption CD and waited for it to do its job.

Line after line of more symbols and utter crap filled her screen. Then the screen went blank. And her system shut down. Not good. Not at all.

"No!" She banged her fist on the desk. Not that doing so would make a damned bit of difference.

"Okay. I'll reboot," she muttered. That always cured everything. Almost always.

She spent the rest of the evening restoring her system, but whatever the spyware had done with Heaton's system on her end, it was a waste of time and she was back at stage one.

She glanced down at her watch. Twelve. Was it really? Might as well give it up. If nothing else, she could ask the local Bureau techies to give it a look. Even if the information appeared to be gone, they might be able to retrieve it.

Instead of going to sleep, however, she tossed and turned for what seemed like hours. Despite her determined focus on retrieving the data, she missed Jake's presence. His jokes. His needling her about one thing or another. His constant trips to the fridge. How that man could eat. And he never gained an ounce.

Ought to be a crime against it.

Yes, he could be like an ever-present thorn in her side, but his absence left her empty and—dammit—lonely.

She felt the thrumming vibration of the elevator then heard Jake's key in the door. Her heart sped up at the familiar homey sounds.

Concerned and half expecting to find Kate missing, Jake opened the door to the loft. Her car wasn't in its usual spot in the garage. Where would she have gone without him? And why?

The loft was dark except for precious little moonlight streaming in through the tall windows.

"Jake?" The lamp beside her bed came on, bathing the loft in its soft light.

"Yeah. Where the hell's your car? I've spent the last five minutes trying to figure out where you'd go at this time of night."

She rolled over in the bed and propped herself on her elbows. Her baggy PJ top slid off her shoulder and revealed the ripe swell of her breasts. He could just make out the impression of her pebbled nipples. Pink or fawn? he wondered.

"I—uh, was sideswiped when I left the parking garage this morning."

A wreck? He dropped his keys on a table and rushed to her side and sat on the bed, scanning her body for injuries. "Are you all right? Why didn't you call me?"

"I'm fine." She sat up and held out her arms to show him. "See, just a bruise on my left elbow. That's it." She smiled, reached out and stroked his cheek. "Besides, you worked the night shift and needed your rest."

Her thoughtfulness and tender gesture surprised him. Most SACs would've hauled his ass out of bed without a second thought.

"Anyway, after the uniformed officer filled out the accident report, I called a taxi. I had it take me to the car rental place. Needless to say, I was quite late."

"Tell me exactly what happened. Did they cite the other driver?"

"No, he took off. If I didn't know better, I'd think it was on purpose or maybe it had something do to with the—"

"What?"

"Now I know you're going to think I'm silly to be concerned, but someone left a voodoo doll in my chair at work."

And who the hell would leave a voodoo doll for Kate at work? One possibility came to mind. Like a lot of the working girls, Angie had been fond of voodoo spells and candles. Her room had been awash with candles and beads and gris-gris bags.

"You sure it wasn't your co-worker Lisette who left it?"

Kate shook her head vigorously. "No, she turned six shades of white when I asked her about it. She said I needed to take it to someone and get the curse reversed."

He took a deep breath. "I'm listening."

"First I went to the voodoo shop Lisette recommended. The proprietor told me someone very powerful made it, and only she or someone more powerful could undo the spell."

A chill spread up his neck like an ice pick popsicle. Was the doll meant to unnerve Caitlin or was it meant to cause harm?

"Where's the doll now?"

"In the glove compartment of my rental car." She shrugged. "I know it's silly, but I just didn't want the thing in the condo."

"Good. Describe it."

"Black cloth in the shape of a human, stuffed with feathers, wrapped in black thread, except for the head. That thread was red." She reached up and wound a curl around her finger. "Like my hair."

"Lisette was right. We need to get the curse reversed."

"Before the wreck, I might've said you were nuts, but now...maybe we should." She smiled at him. Here he was sitting on the side of Caitlin's bed. Close enough to touch her soft skin. The tropical fruit scent of her shampoo filled his nostrils. His dick grew hard. God, he wanted her.

But keeping her safe was more important than letting the boys out to play.

To stall for time and to regain his composure, he walked over to the fridge and pulled out two bottles of water, then carried them back. "Here." He opened both and handed one of them to Kate.

"The real problem, as I see it, is who is trying to put a curse on me? Is it personal or has our operation been compromised?"

She took a long swallow then licked the moisture from her lips.

Damn. Did she have to do that? He gulped down half a bottle before he could trust himself to speak. "There are a lot of ways we could look at it First, it's a serious threat. Exactly who told you it was created by a powerful priestess?"

"A woman at the shop, named Lyontine."

"I remember her. She's been in business for a long time, but it used to be more service-oriented—if you know what I mean."

"Really? A prostitute?"

"A madam. Guess she parlayed her savings and bought the shop. We have to find this priestess first—no, correction, *I* have to find her. I want you to stay as far away from the voodoo scene as you can. I'm a native, and I'll be less conspicuous investigating her whereabouts."

"No. We do this together. I don't need to be protected like some damned civilian." She shivered and set the bottle of water on the floor. "I feel like someone just walked over my grave."

"For once, will you listen to me? Keep your nose in the spreadsheets and follow the money trail. I'll check out the ceremony and the voodoo priestess. Did Lyontine happen to mention her name?"

"Marie-Ange, I think. She's supposed to be a direct descendant of Marie Laveau."

"Aw hell, chèr. They all claim that." Marie-*Ange*? Too close to be mere coincidence. Still, he needed to see for himself. If it was Angie, he'd put a stop to her shenanigans pretty damn quick.

"Maybe it's related to the money laundering? Perhaps the one responsible wants to scare me away from the casino so someone else more amenable can take my place?"

"Can't rule it out. Not until we know for sure who ordered the curse."

"I still think this is something I need to handle myself."

He shook his head, stood and walked over to a window. The woman was reckless, stubborn and so damn sexy he could barely keep his head on straight. "You'll be the death of me yet, chèr."

"Is it my imagination," Caitlin said with a giggle, "or is your accent getting thicker the longer we stay here?"

"See here, darlin', this is my hometown. The smells, the sights, the sounds of jazz floating in the air at night..." He let out a long sigh. "I love this place with ever' bone in my body, all the way down to my little toe."

Kate's eyebrows rose at least an inch, "Left or right?" Her tone was deadpan and left him confused.

"Say what?"

"Which toe? Left or right? You didn't specify. Just for the record." A half-smile quirked the corner of her pouty lips.

He let out a bark of laughter. "Your sense of humor is improving. Keep working at it. It's like a muscle, needs a lot of practice."

Her green eyes gazed across the room at him through a fan of dark red lashes. The smile widened to include both sides of her lush mouth.

No doubt about it. She was flirting with him. He grinned back...and reined in the urge to kiss her into next Monday. No point in spoiling the hint of promise in the air.

He shifted his stance. His woody had all but cut off the circulation to his crotch. "Don't make me come over there and kiss you."

"Wh-what?" A dimple appeared in the corner of her mouth.

"Don't make me come over there and kiss you."

She stood and scowled. "You can put any thought of kissing me right out of your mind."

"Well, that settles it." With two long strides, he closed the distance between them. He cradled her face in his hands. "See what you've done. Now I have to kiss you. I have to taste those lips."

"No, you don't." Caitlin put out a hand and stepped back. The nerve of the man.

And then his mouth was on hers. Fierce, demanding and hot.

She weakened and her body molded to his. His heat infused every cell of her in waves setting off sparks of electricity that ignited and flashed.

Staggered by the ferocity of her body's response and the sheer need to touch him, to feel his bare skin against hers, she backed away.

"No."

The single word was uttered as a hoarse rasp. His hands dropped from her face, skimming slowly down her body.

"No. We can't," she said, shaking her head. "This is crazy. You're crazy. I'm crazy."

Pulling away from him hurt. A pain so real and full of loss so deep it shook her soul.

Jaw clenched, Jake stood his ground but didn't come after her.

The silence grew longer. Finally, he spoke. "Tomorrow, we go to Lyontine's together. Otherwise, you'll just go on your own and get that cute ass of yours caught in a nest of alligators...or worse."

"Agreed. Together." Back in bed, she pulled the sheet up around her neck and pretended to sleep. But, how could she? His kiss had shaken her to the core. Never had she wanted to give herself to anyone like she did Jake.

Maybe when the operation was over. He might be stubborn and convinced his way was best, but he was a good man. She could do a lot worse. She had, in fact.

But would there be anything between them after the op? Was he just focused on the mission and its success, or did he really care what happened to her?

Across the room she listened to his pacing for a while, then he pulled out the sofa bed and bedded down for the night.

Soon the sound of his soft snores reached her. He was asleep. Finally.

The next evening while Caitlin waited for Jake to make his appearance, she assembled her version of appropriate garb for attending a voodoo ceremony. As instructed by her partner in crime, she'd worn white which strangely enough signified purity—just like a traditional bride. Some bride she was.

She pulled on the full white gathered skirt and tucked in the tail of a white blouse. The sleeves were loose and comfortable. She tied a red cotton scarf around her neck. Later she would tie it around her head kerchief-style to hide her blazing red hair. She didn't have to alter her skin since Jake told her voodoo devotees were a diverse group, but she took care to make subtle changes in her appearance by darkening her eyebrows and heightening the drama of her makeup.

She stared at her reflection. A somewhat exotic creature stared back. At least there was nothing discernible of FBI Special Agent Caitlin Chaney nor Kate, the accountant. Maybe she was silly, but she felt like she was about to go trick or treating. Hopefully, the trick wouldn't be on her.

Maybe she shouldn't wait for Jake. She was the one with a voodoo curse. Not that she really believed she was cursed. On the other hand, someone must've thought she was enough of a threat to try such a scare tactic.

No. She'd spent too much time harping on how they were a team. Time she proved she meant it.

The winter sun was already low in the sky. She glanced at her watch. Dammit. What if he couldn't get off in time? He was still new on the job.

He'd call if he couldn't make it. Of course, he would. She could go on, but he wouldn't know where to meet her.

She sat at the desk, pulled out her cell phone and quickly keyed in the number of his. She drummed her nails on the desk.

No answer. Just voice mail. She left him a quick message.

The door opened. Jake.

"Finally. I was ready to leave without you."

Jake moseyed over to the desk and perched on the corner. A knowing, yet playful, grin spread across his rakish face; a shock of dark hair fell forward on his forehead. "Damn good thing you didn't, chèr."

He reached and flicked a curl off her cheek and tucked it behind her ear. "Gotta change into my voodoo duds. Wanna help?"

Caitlin glanced into his warm, dark eyes. The invitation was clear, but... "Alas, Agent LeFevre, you are a big boy and can dress yourself. Besides, we're short on time."

"Knew you'd say something like that." He hopped off the desk, then ruffled her hair. "By the way, you oughta wear some red beads around your neck. And make sure you have flowers and candles for offerings."

She stood and placed her hands on her hips. "I thought I'd pick those up when we meet Lyontine at her shop. If you get a move on, that is."

He grimaced, then snapped her a two-finger salute. "Yes, boss. Right away, boss."

She watched him head to the bathroom. He pulled the screen, but she could imagine the long lean lines of his body as he bent over to change. She couldn't deny she wanted him in the absolute worst way.

But jumping his bones could seriously affect their mission. Maybe it was different for Jake, but having casual sex wasn't her style. She still didn't know him well enough to judge if it was his.

Yet somehow, she knew deep down he was a good man, even if he did an amazing impression of a typical male jerk about fifty percent of the time.

The sun was just a hint of vermillion and gold over the horizon when Caitlin and Jake reached the voodoo shop. They walked inside, and the overpowering scents of incense and candles—and who knew what else—hit her nostrils.

"You're too late. I'm closin' de shop. Come back tomorrow," the owner said.

"I was here the other day...with the voodoo doll. You said to come back if..."

Lyontine's dark brows pulled together in a frown. She leaned across the counter. "Ah, now I recognize you. You are much different today. Dis de man who give you many problems?"

"Right," she said, hoping Jake wouldn't pick up on the "problem man" comment. "You said I should change my appearance. I thought this way I could blend in with the other congregants. I want you to take us to the ceremony tonight—the real one."

"Now why would I want to do dat?" The voodoo woman folded her arms across her chest. "He goin', too?"

"Oh, yes." Caitlin gave her best-besotted smile in Jake's direction, hoping he would play along.

Such a sweet guy, he wrapped his arm around her waist and pulled her close in a possessive gesture. "I was born here, so I know a bit about the ceremonies," he drawled. "I'll keep her from making any embarrassin' or disruptive mistakes."

Lyontine glanced from Jake to Caitlin, then shook her head. "I don' know."

"You said..." Frustrated by the woman's reluctance, Caitlin was ready to beg if necessary. "Look, we'll pay you...whatever you want."

"It'll cost you—maybe more dan you can afford."

"I have to know why someone left the doll for me at work."

"Why is *simple*," she said with a wry smile. "Dey wish you harm."

"But why? I've only been in town for a short time." The real question—had their operation already been compromised?

"'Course, any spell placed can be removed. It takes de money." The woman rubbed her thumb and first two fingers together.

"We have it," Jake said. "We're prepared to buy whatever she needs to take as offerings."

"'Tis against my better judgment, but I will take you. Five-hundred dollars is my fee. Whatever happens dere is on you. I bear no responsibility."

"Agreed," Caitlin and Jake said in unison.

Jake forked over their entire stash of petty cash while Caitlin picked out a bunch of fresh flowers and candles as her offerings.

The woman stuffed the roll of bills deep in the front of her blouse. "Den best we hurry. Gettin' late."

A sense of foreboding settled on Caitlin as she gathered her offerings and handed them to Jake. "Mind?"

"Glad to be of service, chèr," he said with a cheeky grin.

His arm went around her waist again. "We'll follow you in our car," he told the shop owner, who nodded her assent.

In spite of having only known Jake a few days, his arm made her feel secure. Whatever was about to happen in voodoo land, he'd have her back. Just like she'd have his.

Chapter Twelve

With Jake at the wheel, they followed the shop owner through neighborhoods halfway through the process of rebuilding, then through desolate areas where houses were nothing more than piles of wood and destruction. The odor of mold and rot filtered in through the car's air-conditioner.

Caitlin turned to Jake. "I can't believe it's still so bad."

He shook his head. "Some of this will never be put to rights."

Finally, deep in the forest—or was it an actual bayou—Caitlin felt the drums before she heard them. Vibrations thrummed through the soles of her sandals and up through her body until her hair felt as if it were vibrating as well. She and Jake followed Lyontine, dodging ghostly trailing strands of Spanish Moss. The humidity gathered and dampened her blouse between her shoulder blades and breasts. The ripe odor of decay underlaid everything around her.

"We're getting close, aren't we?"

Lyontine stopped short and turned, her eyes shuttered and gaze level. "'Tis not too late. You can still turn 'round."

"No," Caitlyn said. "We're almost there. The drums—I hear them. I feel them."

"Stay behind me. Don' you speak to anyone. Keep your eyes down. Don' stare at anyone. Shh. Someone comes."

A rustle of leaves, the shuffling of feet.

The feverish beat of the drums grew louder and even her heart seemed in sync with the unremitting pounding. The urge to call off the entire outing built within her chest. What was she thinking?

Voodoo wasn't real.

No, this was a chance to show Jake she wasn't just an accountant.

Hypnotic. Compelling. Driving. Sensual. The drums beckoned. She resisted the power...or tried. Curiosity—that's all it was. She wanted to see the person who'd fashioned the voodoo doll and wished her harm.

They came to a clearing of sorts where a light blue wood-framed building stood with mystical symbols painted on the sides. Not only were there symbols, but skulls and skeletons, too. Eerie to say the least.

Everywhere eyes seemed to be watching. She shivered and kept a tight grip on Jake's hand.

They reached the perimeter of a small crowd of worshipers dressed in white just like Jake had told her. Surrounded by people who danced about in convulsive, shaking movements, she ducked her head and did her damnedest to remain inconspicuous. Jake shook his head, but his feet moved to the beat as well. Just how much did he know about the ceremonies? Had he ever practiced voodoo, even as a joke?

Lyontine appeared as if she wanted to join those dancing. Her gaze swept from side to side. Her broad shoulders twitched to the beat of the drums. Her sandaled feet shifted restlessly in the undergrowth.

Caitlin leaned over to Jake. "What now?"

"Shh," Lyontine warned. "We go inside."

Inside the building were more symbols scrawled in chalk on the floor consisting of intersecting lines with circles and even more symbols inside the circles. There was a poster or painting of a woman, like an icon. Candles and flowers had already been placed in front of what was obviously an altar of sorts. A bonfire burned in a large black iron kettle, and underneath the pounding of the drums, she heard what sounded like the bleating of a goat.

Would they actually sacrifice an animal? No way was she sticking around for that.

By now most of the worshipers were inside the building. And

the drums. Would they never stop? She moved closer to Jake.

"This was your idea," he said in a low undertone but kept her close to his side with an iron grip.

"She comes," Lyontine raised a bony finger to her lips. "Sh."

On the far side of the circle, the gatherers parted. Tall and slender, draped from head to foot in a white headdress and robes, the voodoo priestess entered. Just as her guide had described, the priestess was light-skinned, no darker than a deep suntan. Gold bangles adorned each slender wrist, and a gold snake armlet decorated her upper left arm. The circle of worshipers closed behind her. She raised her arms and implored the god in some sort of mixed-French patois. Caitlin could make out a few words, but not many.

Ready to lay her offerings at the base of the makeshift altar, Caitlin started to make her way to the inner circle, shaking off Jake's attempt to restrain her. But Lyontine clamped a firm hand around her wrist and dragged her to the edge of the worshipers.

"Don' you go pushing yourself forward. She find you soon enough."

"Right." Holding tightly to the flowers and candles, Caitlin hung at the periphery of the devotees, but it seemed as if the drums compelled her feet to move. The drums pulsed and pounded with the beat of her heart. Jake had moved to her side once more, but his attention was fixed on the priestess.

Arms akimbo, the priestess danced, before the bonfire, the flames licking near but never quite touching her. She tossed her head, uttering who knew what kind of spells. It was all gibberish to Caitlin, but she fixed her gaze on the tall, slender priestess. Ignoring everything except the figure in front of her, she walked forward with her offerings...and her question.

Who are you? Who paid you to place a spell on me? Who wants to scare me away?

Pale, penetrating eyes flashed in the firelight. For a second the priestess's gaze caught Caitlin's. A hard chill ran through her body. Then a creeping sensation of hate, and a dark unknowable fury. Evil, yes. Pure evil danced along Caitlin's nerve endings and sickened her to the point of nausea.

Frantic to escape the presence of the purest evil she'd ever experienced, she retreated into the shadows. Somehow, she had to get away. For all she cared, Jake could stare at the dancing priestess until he turned to stone. Now, if she could just remember where they'd left the car.

"No, you don't." Jake snatched at her wrist, but she yanked free and ran. Outside, the painted skeletons and skulls on the blue building seemed alive and laughing. Where was that damned path? Why hadn't she brought a penlight, at least?

She hesitated long enough to toss the flowers and candles into the undergrowth. Once away from the dimly lighted building, an eerie blackness descended and settled in her mind. All but blinded by the dark shadows within and without, she walked with one arm outstretched.

A rustling behind her. Was someone was following? Jake?

She turned. No one. No one she could see anyway. She quickened her pace. Branches raked her cheeks and tore at her arms, but she kept her headlong rush.

Out of breath, she stumbled into the clearing where Jake's car was parked. She leaned against the door and sucked in long ragged breaths. Her blouse clung to her chest in damp folds.

Enough of this. She unlocked the door and scrambled inside; she glanced into the back seat. Empty.

But the sense of a presence following her remained.

Time passed and her breathing regulated. Her nausea receded.

Jake. Omigod. He was still at the ceremony. Should she go back? Gazing into the black of night... No, she couldn't.

No way. She'd never go anywhere near that voodoo mumbo-jumbo again.

She crossed her arms. She'd wait. He'd be after her soon enough...if he could tear himself away from ogling Marie-Ange.

What the hell was Caitlin up to? Coming to this ceremony was her idea. Least she could do was stick around.

He should've followed her immediately, but he couldn't help but watch for another minute or three. The high priestess was putting on a hell of a show, don't you know? Angie had always been industrious, but the voodoo priestess gig was a new one. And no doubt lucrative.

Two female worshipers had already fallen to the ground twitching and speaking in some sort of unknown tongue. It wasn't any sort of French-Creole patois he'd ever heard. More likely some native dialect brought over from Africa.

Angie was dancing around with a large snake on her shoulders. Amused, and more aroused than he would ever admit, he watched until her gaze moved in his direction. He imagined her pupils dilated. She saw him all right.

The jig was up, and she knew it. Now he had more on her than she had on him. And he'd use it to keep her away from Caitlin.

He nodded, turned and headed back to where they'd left their ride. Hopefully, his team leader hadn't lost her way in unfamiliar surroundings. Serve her right if she did.

Hell. No doubt about it. What an ass. Here he was supposed to be covering his partner's back, but he'd let Angie's sensual pull get the better of him.

Okay Agent-in Charge Chaney, I'm a-coming. He turned from the worshippers and booked it back toward the car.

When Jake reached the car, a surge of relief hit him. Caitlin was sitting inside with her arms folded. Probably mad as a hornet, but safe, nonetheless. He opened the door and slid inside, ready for her attack.

Deciding to take the offensive was a better strategic move, he demanded, "What the hell were you thinking running off like that? You could've gotten lost. Are you that anxious to be a gator's nighttime snack?"

Her eyes were wide and unfocused; her face was flushed as she gesticulated wildly. Very unlike the businesslike accountant he knew and...

No. He was not in love. No way.

"I had to get out of there. There's something very evil about that woman. It's as if she looked into my heart and soul and dispatched a posse of demons to keep me company."

"A posse of demons, huh?" He chuckled. "If you only knew."

"Knew what, smart-ass? Maybe you're used to this stuff, but it was something new for me."

"Okay. Just calm down, chèr. I recognized the priestess. You should've, too. She's your CFO."

Caitlin ripped off her head wrap and shook her short curls free. "No way."

"Damned good show she puts on, too."

"So that's why I had to stumble along...alone in the dark. You were checking out your teenage lover. Great. Just great." She exhaled with a furious huff.

"You made it just fine." He brushed a strand of hair behind her ear and wished he dared kiss her. "I only stuck around long enough to make sure it really was Angie. Knowledge is leverage. Believe me, I'll use what I know to keep her away from you."

"If she figured out who I was—because you were there, after all—then all that hate was just for little old me. She's evil, but I already suspected that."

"Nah. It's just a gig for her. She was having a whale of a time."

"*No.* She thinks we're married and she's damned jealous. My life might really be in danger, and not because of some silly doll she stuck with a pin."

"Give me the keys," he said. "You're not going to let this go, are you?"

"No. What I'd really like to do is—"

She drew back her fist, but he caught her wrist with his hand. "I said I'll take care of Angie. She'll leave you alone. I promise." Her fingers opened, and he brought them to his lips and kissed them. A sharp intake of breath was her only response. But his cock hardened.

Dammit. Only one thing on his mind, taking this sexy woman to bed and screwing her all night.

"Leave her to me," he said, as soon as he could breathe. He took the keys and started the car.

She let out a long sigh. "All right, but—"

"No buts about it."

It might not be tonight, but one night soon. He would fuck her all night all night long.

Angelique peered into the mirror at her reflection. The high priestess. The premier voodoo queen of all Louisiana. Well, at least no one could say she didn't give her devotees a damn good show.

Goat's blood notwithstanding. She flicked at a speck of the damned stuff where it was crusted on her armlet. Another tiny spot marred the hem of her gown.

She removed the head wrap and set it on the ornate rosewood fern stand, the dark curly wig with it.

She shook her head and ran her fingers through her short blond strands. She slid the gold bangles over her wrists. All the accouterments which transformed her into Marie-Ange, voodoo priestess and direct descendent of Marie Laveau.

Normally after a ceremony, energy coursed through her until she was ready to jump out of her skin.

Not tonight.

A power had made itself known. During the ceremony, a slow nudging influence crept into her awareness and nearly made her falter. She'd curtained her mind. Had she not been at the climax of the ceremony, she would have sought the power's source more directly.

Then just as suddenly, the power was gone, evaporated like a ghostly wisp of swamp mist. One of her flock was a pretender. Only at the last had she recognized Jake in the group. And what brought him to the ceremony? It could only be his milk-faced little wife. Had she come because of the little gift she'd left for her?

Angelique smiled. No doubt she had.

*

Caitlin opened the condo door with Jake who followed comfortably close behind her. The sense of uneasiness she'd experienced all evening veiled the dark interior with mysterious undercurrents. Reaching quickly for a light switch, she held her breath until light flooded their home away from home, then let out a sigh filled with relief.

"You were awful quiet on the ride home, chèr. Are you all right?" His husky tones and warm breath on her neck sent a different kind of chill, one that warmed as well as raised the hair on her neck. He brushed the short strands of hair from her neck. His lips—so close she could almost feel them.

No. She couldn't give in. How would she maintain control of the operation if they were involved? In an attempt to ignore her body's reactions, she rushed into the kitchen. "I'm still off-balance. Tonight. The ceremony in the bayou. I didn't expect to be so...affected by it. Then I ran away like some child. But I was scared. No doubt about it."

He followed into the kitchen and leaned back on the counter. "Maybe running away has become a bad habit with you? Do you always run away when a man gets too close?"

His words hit home, especially since they meant he knew her better than she'd ever admit. Her mouth dry as sand, she turned and gazed into his dark eyes "It's safer."

Thank God, he was giving her time to catch her breath. If he'd actually kissed her, what would she have done? No, it wouldn't be the first time, but they couldn't make a habit of it.

The muscle in his jaw jumped. She turned away, unwilling to watch the frustration, or was it irritation that tensed his body?

"It's all right. Caitlin. I understand. I won't rush you."

He understood? Was he psychic? Caitlin flitted nervously over to one of the windows. She stared at the street below. In the distance, she heard the low, sensual tones of a growling saxophone coming from a bar down the street.

Again he followed her and placed his hands on her shoulders. "Wish I could stay all night. We need to settle this."

She whipped around and faced him. "Where are you going?"

Did she sound like a jealous wife or what?

"Casino."

"The casino?" Was he angry with her after all and going to self-destruct by gambling? "But I thought you were off tonight." In spite of her best efforts to remain cool, the last ended with a definite whine.

He grinned. "I traded six hours with Diego so I could go with you tonight. He gets off for the night, but I have to cover his shift from midnight on. What's the matter, chèr? Afraid I'll fall into my old bad habits?" he asked, his mouth twisting into a smirk.

"What I see is someone else who's running away."

Jake chuckled and with his forefinger lifted her chin a notch. "No, I don't believe in running from a fight...or a discussion. I really have to work."

Without so much as a by-your-leave, he kissed her.

Lightly. Sweetly. "With the promise of more to come," he said, then smiled.

Then he was gone. Her lips still burned from his kiss. She reached to touch them. An ache of longing swept through her body in wave after wave. How much longer would she be able to resist him?

But she had to keep her head. They weren't at all suited. Their personalities were just too different...and their backgrounds. The investigation—now that was the only thing that mattered. An emotional involvement between agents could serve to lessen the effectiveness of both. Right from the rule book.

Quit lying to yourself. That was just so much BS. Getting involved with Jake and caring about him was just too risky...to her...to her heart.

"Dammit." Jake pounded the steering wheel, then reached over and hit the radio's scan button. Had to be something better than honky-tonk, my-love-done-me-wrong music.

He settled on a station playing zydeco. "Now that's more like it." He smacked the steering wheel with his palm in rhythm with the music, not from frustration.

He pulled into the employee parking garage and sat there until the music stopped.

"Crazy damn woman," he muttered. She had him so horny with her smooth skin and full breasts. And those eyes—sometimes they sparkled with mischief when it wasn't out and out mistrust.

If she just didn't turn him on with every step she took. Big as the loft was, it wasn't big enough for the two of them. She was driving him crazy, coming out of the bathroom at night, smelling all womanly with lotion and shampoo. What was a man supposed to do?

Kate was all woman, all right...and it'd been a damned long time since he wanted one the way he wanted her.

Hell. He must be losing his mind. Was he ready to risk everything just to touch that soft, sort of sweet woman and make her his own?

Damned if he wouldn't. A little time and persistence and she'd fall into his arms again like she had the night at the Rock 'N' Bowl.

Only the next time he'd fuck—no, be honest—he'd make *love* to her like there was no tomorrow. Yes, he was falling in love for maybe the first time in his life. Adult love. Not the lust-driven love he'd felt for Angie as a teenager or the way he'd loved Melissa as a young adult. What he was feeling for Kate was different. He'd meant it when he said he wouldn't rush her. She needed to come to him. No matter how much waiting for her trust hurt him.

Chapter Thirteen

Outside Washington, D.C.

Jose Gutierrez straightened his tie, then raised the knocker and let it fall on Dexter Chaney's door. The side door. It wouldn't do for anyone to notice his connection with the Secretary of the Interior, a man who wielded more power under the table than anyone in DC.

People thought the Head of Homeland Security had power. Bullshit. Chaney could teach him more about surveillance and skullduggery than the FBI and CIA combined.

The great man opened the door himself. Jose nodded. "Secretary Chaney."

"Welcome, Jose." Chaney motioned him inside—as if he were a welcome guest, instead of one who'd been summoned.

A pair of leather chairs were positioned on either side of a marble fireplace. Jose rubbed his hands together, warming them in front of the crackling fire. All in all, it was perfectly furnished—for a wolf's lair. "To what do I owe your gracious invitation?"

His host emitted a low chuckle. "Let's get down to business. How is my daughter's mission going? Dare I say badly? Is she ready to call it quits yet?"

"Too soon to tell. It's early days."

"Put the pressure on, man. I want results. I want that mission compromised." Chaney walked over to a lacquered Chinese chest. "Brandy?"

Jose nodded. "Great."

Chaney decanted the richly colored liquor into a large snifter, carried it across the thick oriental carpet, then held it out.

"Thank you." Jose took the heavy snifter, swirled the rich contents and gave an appreciative sniff. "Excellent." He considered his words. Wouldn't do to be rash. "You're asking me to compromise a mission which has every chance of succeeding and taking down a money-laundering setup."

"I'm not asking."

"How's this? You're shortchanging your daughter and putting her at risk."

"Nonsense. Giving her a taste of undercover with a screw-up like that LeFevre will send her packing back home to Georgetown quicker than a cat after a mouse."

"LeFevre isn't a screw up in the sense you mean. Yes, he's a loose cannon...and a rogue with the ladies, but he's a damned effective agent."

Chaney shrugged. "Anyone who distracts my misguided daughter from a career in the FBI is more than welcome. Women have no business chasing all over the country dealing with low-life criminals and serial killers. If her mother had lived, she would've seen our daughter had a proper upbringing." He took a sip of brandy. "I blame myself. I should have never left her in the care of a soft-headed housekeeper who actually encouraged my daughter's unfeminine career choices. Accountant, FBI agent. To hell with all the women libber dyke bitches!"

Jose counted to ten. "Thoughts best kept to yourself, Dexter."

Chaney's mouth twisted into a grimace. "Yes, must remember to be P.C., mustn't I?"

"It's a dangerous game you're playing."

Chaney's pale gaze leveled on Jose. "You owe me. I have a long memory."

Jose's shoulders tightened with the not-so-subtle hint of threat. "We're even now. I've done what you asked." Enough, dammit. Enough of the secretary's dirty work.

"Not until I see results. And not until she gives up these silly notions and settles down and leads a normal life."

"I can't guarantee any of that will happen."

"It better. I'm counting on it. I'd hate for the President to hear about your unsavory predilection for..."

"For God's sake, watch your tongue." Jose glanced around the room. Son of a bitch probably had it bugged.

"We're quite alone." Chaney gestured with palms upward. "See, no tape recorders."

Jose stiffened his shoulders, but his asshole puckered on its own. Damn the twist of fate that had drawn him into the secretary's duplicitous web.

"I believe we have an accord?" Chaney said.

"Yes."

Until one of us has an unfortunate accident.

Silence settled in the room. Jose steadied his hand and set the snifter on a side table. "We're done then?"

Anxious to escape, Jose rose, ready to head for the side exit.

Dexter Chaney nodded. "We're done—for now." He savored Gutierrez's apparent discomfort. Better than the finest wine it was. Better even than the Napoleon Brandy he'd just shared with his minion.

He waited until Gutierrez departed, then reached for the telephone, but stopped short and slipped a cell phone from his inner pocket. He hit the speed dial and waited.

The guttural voice of his silent business partner answered. "Speak."

"Your brusque attitude is one of your charms. I'm sure your other business associates find it...charming. However, I do not."

"Things are a little tense here. Come to the point, *el jefe*, and I promise I'll be more charming next time you call."

"I want to know how our operation is going."

"Business is great, but income is down. Our group won't be ready to deploy until I get it figured out."

"How much? Why?"

"Millions. For the last year. We haven't traced the bastard yet. Whoever it is, is damned good."

"Millions? Son of a bitch! See here, you're supposed to be the expert at handling things on that end. Put an end to it—now! Just like you did with that other problem. Anything come of that yet?"

"Nothing traceable."

"What the hell do you mean by 'nothing traceable'?"

"Paper says a couple of bayou rats found her hands. That's all the 'gators left behind."

"Find your embezzler and do a better job of disposal. I want the fund drainage stopped. *Comprende, amigo?*"

"*Comprende.*"

His business partner was a slimy but necessary fact of life. He couldn't risk anything being traced back to him—the real reason he was so adamant about assigning his inexperienced daughter and her screw up partner to the case. He had plans. His President and country needed his intervention whether they knew it or not.

And intervene he would.

Jake knocked off work around six. When he let himself into the loft, he inhaled the smell of fresh coffee. Kate was already up and hunched over her laptop. He stifled a yawn with the back of his hand, then walked over to the counter and poured a cup. "Want some?"

"Thanks. Already had a cup." Caitlin smiled, but the dark circles under her eyes said she hadn't slept well.

"Here we go," she said. "Come here. I've something cool to show you. Bring it up on your screen, too."

"Oh, yeah?" Carrying his coffee, Jake sauntered over and booted up his laptop. Angie's bank records scrolled down the screen. Easing down into his chair, he rolled his eyes and shook his head. "Okay, expert, do your thing."

Caitlin folded her arms across her breasts and shot him a wide grin. "Don't act as if you've never seen bank records before."

"Don't act so damned smug. I can read a balance sheet, but you—fantastic bean counter that you are—can spot trends and anything hinky a lot quicker."

"Thank you." She smiled, then her eyes widened. "Whoa! Take a look at this. She's paying a fortune to a private boarding school called Bridgeview Academy."

"Boarding school?"

"You didn't know she had a child?"

"The subject never came up." How many secrets did Angie have anyway? he wondered.

"Tuition is sixty thou a year."

"Ouch. Kinda steep, even for a high-salaried CFO."

"Hold on, Jake. This is a residential school for autistic children. No wonder it's pricey."

"Age range?"

"Nursery school age through—permanent residency."

"A warehouse?"

"Bit pricey for a warehouse."

"Wonder how old the kid is?"

"Why? Worried it might be yours?"

"Not beyond the realm of possibility." Holy shit. Surely not. Nah, couldn't be. Angie probably had a couple of dozen lovers, not to mention all those johns. Wouldn't hurt to know the kid's age.

"Uh, think you can hack into the school's database?"

"If I can't, I'm not much good, am I?"

Kate's green eyes sparkled with excitement. The chase was on and she was in her element. He watched her long slender fingers play the keyboard with the expertise of a Twenty-One dealer.

Intelligent. Confident. Beautiful. Everything he'd ever wanted in a woman. Not to mention sexy as hell.

"No Andersons or Andre listed. Maybe she was married, and the child is under his name."

Caitlin peered at the screen, her face drawing into a slight scowl. "All right. No record on any Angelique Andre ever marrying in the state of Louisiana. In fact, your Angelique first appears when her social security number was issued in 1994 —needed it for college enrollment. Not much else until she graduated from Tulane in 2000 with her MBA."

"She's come a long way in eight years." How *had* Angie

managed it? Did she still have a sugar daddy?

"From ex-hooker to CFO of Rivera Corporation? Oh, yeah. I'd say she's come a very long way. She's bound to be in this up to her scrawny neck. I don't know yet if she's merely embezzling, responsible for the money laundering or both." She scrolled down the spreadsheet.

"Knowing Angie, I'd say both." Jake rubbed his eyes. Damn spreadsheets made his eyes burn. He'd rather go frog-gigging in a bayou full of 'gators than stare at a computer screen all day.

"And apparently you knew her pretty well?" she asked him, her expression playful.

"We were kids...teenagers. We did what teenagers do. Hell, I was going to save her from the streets."

A tiny smile played about her luscious lips. "Hm. White Knight complex? Somehow that doesn't surprise me at all."

"I was young. I got over it. Okay?" All right that was a little too testy. God. What if the kid was his? What would he do?

She batted her lashes. "You haven't changed much."

"Aren't we all in the Bureau because we want to save the world?" He took a swallow of his coffee. "Say, Miss Hotshot Accountant, haven't you found that money trail yet?"

"Give me time. I will." She smiled, her eyes glinting with good humor.

She was in too good a mood, but she didn't have the possibility of an autistic child hanging over her head. "Sooner would be better than later," he reminded her.

Caitlin stuck out her bottom lip and pretended to pout. "Tired of me already, husband?"

Tired of her—God no. "Not you, chèr—the casino."

An expression of concern crossed her face. Frowning she stopped keying, her long fingers poised over the keyboard. "With your...problem, it must be difficult."

"It's no picnic, but I manage okay."

"Just the same."

"Chèr, I'm a Fed. If I want to stay one, I do whatever, wherever and whenever they need."

"I know. It's not much of a life."

"It's what I signed up for. If and when I meet the right person..." Before he could reveal anymore, he shrugged.

She gazed at him, her deep green eyes shining. "What would you do?"

"Hell, Kate. I don't know. I'd...figure it out then."

"Uh-huh."

Desperation to talk about anything but feelings poured through him like a storm surge. "Can we get back to Angie and her money trail?"

"If you insist." She let out a heavy sigh. "The first red flags I see is Boyle's records coincide with deposits into the CFO's account, and with payments made to the school. But—this is the important part—the funds in Angelique's account came from an offshore account. What I'm pretty sure is happening, is Boyle is transferring funds to the offshore account—hers—and then she transfers them to her personal account in the US."

"Then they're in it together."

"More than likely. This is definitely a case of embezzlement, but without access to her corporate records and accounts, we're not going to prove the money laundering."

He stood, walked around behind her, then leaned over her shoulder where the citrus scent of her shampoo filled his nostrils. "What you need is a promotion. They should've placed you in Angie's office rather than in Boyle's."

She shook her head, and he backed away. "We're here for the long haul. Considering how Angelique feels about me, I doubt very seriously she would ever approve my transfer to any department but Housekeeping." She gave a visible shiver.

"This is taking too long. If we don't make some progress soon, they'll pull us out and put someone else on the inside."

She spun around in her swivel chair. "What? No. That doesn't fit the game plan. I—we'll—close this case long before that happens. Besides, it would only delay the operation to set up new backgrounds and get new agents in place."

"Yeah, that would interfere with your climb up the Bureau

ladder, wouldn't it?"

A scowl drew her pretty face into a mask of pique. "I don't deny I'm ambitious. What's wrong with that?"

He leaned forward and placed a hand on each of her slender knees, getting right in her face. "Listen, chèr, it's not ambition that drives you. You think you have something to prove. But you're tough and smart. You'll stick it out until you hit the jackpot, no matter how long it takes."

She stared up at him, challenging him, her gaze narrowed. Her chest rose and fell rapidly. "Maybe I do have something to prove."

His heart hammered, the blood pounding in his ears as if he were on the verge of breaking the bank at Monte Carlo. "At least you can admit it. That's a clear sign of progress." He wanted to shut her up with his mouth on hers. He wanted her...now and in every way possible.

Chapter Fourteen

After Caitlin left for work, Jake did some investigating of his own. He'd keep his word about calling off Angie. He found her at her condo where no one would see them and remark on their knowing each other. He entered the building just as she was exiting the elevator.

"I was about to leave for work, but come on up, chèr," she said with a knowing self-satisfied smile.

He followed her swaying hips into the elevator. Damn, the woman was hot, as if she radiated some kind of energy.

After entering her apartment, she removed her silk jacket and laid it across the back of a chair. Her surroundings were cold. Glass. Steel. Chrome. Topped off with a million-dollar view of the marina and Lake Ponchartrain in the distance.

She poured a cup of coffee and handed it to him. "I was surprised to see you at the ceremony last evening. Did you enjoy it?"

Her pale eyes watched him, giving him the sensation of being hypnotized. Summoning his strength, he forced his gaze from hers. "I found it interesting, yes."

"But you didn't join the celebration. Why not? Were you afraid?" Her tone held an undercurrent of amusement.

"No."

"Then why did you come? Curiosity? You know what they say about curiosity." Her pale gaze grew more intense with each word.

He didn't answer. There was too much he needed to say. A drop of sweat trickled down his back. He waited. Best let her take this at her own pace.

"Jack-man. I never thought to see you at one of my little ceremonies."

"Never thought I'd see you leading one." He pulled at his collar. His breaths were short. Dammit. The woman still had some kind of effect on him.

Angelique shrugged. "A girl has to do what a girl has to do."

"Does that include leaving a voodoo doll in my wife's office?"

She threw her head back and laughed, a low sensual growl that jarred him all the way to his balls. "Was she scared? How naughty of me. I couldn't resist."

"Not scared, but very curious. I don't want my wife asking questions about my past. You're part of that past, Angie."

"You were my first love. Play your cards right and you could be my last."

She eased closer, insinuating her thigh between his. He hardened as she rubbed against him. Pure reflex. Nothing more.

"Love me, Jake. Take me right now. The ceremony leaves me so aroused. Our lovemaking will be so wonderful it'll make the gods weep."

She slid a slender finger up his chest and unbuttoned his shirt slowly, one button at a time. Her wide gaze never left his. His breath caught in his throat. God, he wanted her. His dick and balls ached to explode.

No. Not Angie. He wanted Kate.

"You want me. The little wife never has to know. Remember how it used to be with us?" Her breasts rose and fell rapidly with each breath she took. "You would come over and over until we were swimming in fluids, and I licked your cock and drank your cum until you were sucked dry. And you would eat my pussy until I couldn't walk the next day."

"No." God, yes, he remembered, but he didn't want *her*.

"It'll be even better now." She lifted her shoulders, one after the other, and let her top slip down around her waist, baring breasts that shone like ivory in the sunlight. "And I know so many more ways to pleasure you and even more ways you can pleasure me..."

She cupped her breasts and offered them to him, her small nipples already puckered, pink buds he wanted to nip. He dragged in a ragged breath and tried to push her away, but his arms were useless as overcooked pasta.

"Ways we never dreamed of, Jake—"

The ache built in his balls, the beginning of— "No!"

Her lush mouth pulled into a pout. "Then why did you come if you're not going to... come?"

"I'm warning you. Leave Kate alone. She's off-limits. No more of this voodoo curse bullshit. Hear me?"

She rolled her eyes and shrugged. "You're so tiresome. I can't imagine why I thought we could still be friends."

He clenched his fists at his sides. "Do you hear me? No more. Leave my wife alone. Forget the past. It's over. It's been over and done for years."

"You can believe that if you wish. But I know better...and so does your cock."

He stood and let out a ragged breath. "I have to get some sleep. I'm on nights." What a joke. What kind of man wimped out so much that he needed to catch his Zs? "One more thing, Angie..."

"Yes, darlin'?"

"I don't think you want the folks at HQ knowing about your extracurricular activities. A voodoo priestess CFO might just make some folks uncomfortable... so leave Kate the hell alone."

She gave a heavy sigh. "Oh, all right. I was just having a little fun."

"No more fun." He spun on his heel and headed for the door. The farther he got away from her, the easier the air moved in and out of his lungs. Strength returned to his muscles. Her presence had nearly suffocated him and almost ripped a climax from him without his ever entering her body.

She had power...beyond a sexual pull. More like she had control of his body.

He reached his car and sat there for another ten minutes, listening to the street sounds of the city. Somewhere near, he could smell beignets frying. What the hell was he going to do? If he knew anything about Angie, she wouldn't give up just because he told her to. How many more times could he resist her onslaughts of sensuality?

He glanced at his watch, nine-thirty. Time to go home.

Home. Funny, he thought of the loft with Kate as home. The only semblance to a real home he'd known since living with his adopted father.

Jake worked his evening shift and made it home by one-thirty. As usual, Kate was still up working. She gave him an absent-minded wave. "Any luck on decrypting Boyle's files?" he asked.

"Not yet, but I'm close. I can feel it."

On the famished side of hungry, he headed for the fridge in hopes of finding some kind of snack. No such luck. He opened a cupboard and pulled out a bag of barbeque chips. "Were you hoarding these for some special occasion?"

"No, go ahead, gorge yourself."

"I'm not selfish. I'm willing to share."

A quick shake of her head, then, "No, thanks. Too much sugar and salt."

Too much sugar and salt. Silly woman. He moseyed over to his office chair and pulled it around to Caitlin's side of the desk. "Am I already sweet enough?" He sat beside her and wiggled his brows.

"No, I am." She gave him a smile—one of those guaranteed to restart the heart of a dead man.

As much as he enjoyed, even welcomed, her playfulness, it was time he told her about his visit to Angie's condo. Not that he'd tell her everything. His responses to Angie's attempted seduction troubled him. Maybe she did have some kind of mystical powers. Could she have held on to anything personal of his from back in the day and used it to cast some kind of voodoo love spell over him?

"I saw Angie today. Told her in no uncertain terms to leave you—my wife—the hell alone. Told her I figured she'd rather the corporate folks not know what she was up to at night when she wasn't riding herd on spreadsheets." He grabbed a handful of chips and ate them. Salty, but sweet, too. Dang. Kate was right.

Hell. He didn't love her. His cock just thought it did.

"And what did she say to that?"

"She finally agreed she'd leave you alone. No more voodoo bullshit."

"And did you believe her?"

He shrugged. "We can always hope."

"I guess we'll know sooner or later." She glanced in his direction. "How about you? Picking up anything new about your boss and Terri Thibedoux?"

"Not much more than we've already heard from Alex. Everyone in Security is pretty mum on the subject. The owner's nephew Diego is a real jerk-off when it comes to departmental work, but he seems to be Harris' eyes and ears."

"Careful then." She stopped keying and leaned her chin on her fist and gave him a wistful smile. "Wouldn't want you to end up in the bayou."

"Dammit. We have to find whoever left that poor woman out there for the gators."

"We will, Jake. And it would be my pleasure to do the same—if it weren't illegal, that is."

"Sometimes, just no fun being on the right side of the law, is it?"

"Nope. Not in cases like this." She finished with a yawn. "I'm heading to bed. How about you?"

Shaking his head, he grinned. "I need a little more time to decompress...unless you meant...?"

"As if." She gave him an eye roll.

Still, he couldn't help but be pleased she was still in a teasing mood.

From the comfort of her bed, Caitlin heard the ring of a cell phone. She groaned and stifled a yawn. The green LED numbers on her clock said three-forty-five.

Who the hell? Then it struck her—what if something had happened to her father? She sat up, ready to grab her cell.

"Don't bother. It's mine," Jake muttered from the sofa bed. He sat up, swung long, muscular legs over the side of the bed, and fumbled for his phone.

Still, thankful the call wasn't for her, Caitlin sighed and lay down.

He spoke so softly, she couldn't hear a word. If it was about their operation, it would've been her phone, not his.

Still, who could be calling him at this hour? Better not be that blond witch of a CFO.

Better not be.

"Thanks for letting me know," she heard him say. He sat on the side of his bed, staring into the darkness. Without a word, he hurled the phone. It hit the brick wall, then fell to the floor with a clatter as the batteries rolled across the loft floor.

"Jake?" She slid from the bed and padded over to his bed and sat beside him. "What's wrong?"

Instead of acknowledging her presence, he stood and walked over to the nearest window. He shoved it upward and the faint sound of jazz drifted into the loft.

She jumped up and followed him. Without warning, Jake started pounding his fist into the wall. She placed her hand on his shoulder. "Jake, stop it! You'll hurt yourself."

He turned and stared through her; his eyes glistened, full of pain. "My father—he died." Agony contorted his face into a mask. He opened his mouth but no sound emitted. Yet the sight of his raw grief sliced through her, sharp and painful.

"I-I'm so sorry—"

In an abrupt move, he spun away from her and smacked the back of his fist into the wall. Then slowly he crumpled and slid down the wall.

What should she do? She sat beside him and slid her arm behind his back and laid her head on his shoulder. "I'm so sorry." His body shook against hers. She glanced up at his face and watched a single tear slide down his cheek.

So tough on the outside, but a man with a great heart, in pain and in need of comfort. She reached up and smoothed back a lock of hair from his forehead as if he were a child instead of a man full grown. "Tell me about him."

"I have."

"Tell me again. I want to know what he was really like."

"Tough as nails on the outside. Had a big heart, though. Must've been a little crazy, too." He gave a wry chuckle. "He took me on, didn't he?"

"Quite an undertaking, I agree," she said softly and gave him a sad smile.

"And he loved Elvis. Dragged me all the way to Graceland when I was seventeen. For Ed, it was more like a religious pilgrimage. And my going made him so happy. He kept introducing me to everybody we met as his son." He swiped away the tear. "That's when I knew for sure...he loved me." He laughed again. "God, I miss that man."

"I don't presume to know how you feel. My mother died right after I was born, so I never knew her. And as bad as my relationship with my father is, I sort of panicked when the phone rang."

"You thought something happened to him?"

"Yeah. Kinda surprised me." Somehow during their brief conversation, Jake's arm snaked around her waist, and her head rested on his shoulder. Being close to him felt good—no. No. It felt more than good; it felt *right*.

"You're not half bad, Kate-with-a-K. I saw Ed right before we started this op. I moved him to a nursing home outside DC about a month before Katrina hit. He—uh, had a stroke after he got injured on the job. He didn't know me. I was all the family he had...and he didn't know me. He could've retired five years earlier and still had his full pension, but he loved being on the job."

She nodded. "I know. The job—it gets in your blood."

Jake angled his body to hers; his gaze was soft in the night. Her heart pounded, and the rush of blood thrummed in her ears. Reining in her desire, she snuggled closer, then lay her head back on his shoulder. This wasn't the time or the place. Poor Jake was gutted by the news of his father's death. No doubt he felt guilty because he wasn't there.

His next words echoed her thoughts. "I should've been there, Kate. He needed me. And, where was I? Off playing super agent." He gave a harsh self-deprecating laugh.

"No. Listen to me. He would've understood, Jake. You know he would. You just said how he loved being a cop. I know he was proud of you. He had to be."

A wistful smile played about his lips. He nodded. "He was proud. Bragged to all his pals on the force about my being in the Bureau," Jake said, his voice hoarse with emotion. "I was so lucky to know him. No telling where I'd be if it weren't for him."

"And he was lucky, too. I'm sure he loved you as much as any father loves his biological son. You gave him a family."

He scooted away from the wall and gazed directly at her. The pain was still there and doubtless would be for a while, but he gently caressed her cheek. "Anything good you see in me, Ed's the one who put it there. He made me into a man. Gave me his values. And verbally kicked my ass when I didn't live up to his expectations."

"But you didn't disappoint him often."

"Maybe at first, but he was patient, and I couldn't stand so see the disappointment in his eyes when I screwed up."

Caitlin smiled. "Come to bed."

"T-to bed?"

"As much as I'd like to hold and comfort you all night, my ass is getting splinters from the floor." She gave a wink.

"You don't have to do that. Hold me—I mean."

"I want to. You need me, and I need to give you what you need."

With a bittersweet expression kicking up the corner of his mouth, he stood and pulled her to her feet. "You might be biting off more than you can chew, chèr."

"I'll take the chance." She kept hold of his hand and pulled him toward her bed.

"Are you sure?"

"I'm offering comfort...not a night of passion," she said, then smiled. Although she was taking a risk, he needed her arms and heart more than he needed the other parts of her body.

She eased into the cool sheets and patted the spot beside her. "Come on, hon."

He sat somewhat tensely on the side of the bed, then lay back in a stiff posture as if for sleep.

"That won't do." She turned on her side. "Put your arm around me—and no funny business," she teased. "Take a deep breath, then let it out."

"Yes, boss," he said, then inhaled.

By the time he exhaled, he was asleep.

Job well done, old girl.

Caitlin luxuriated in the warmth of his body, but sleep eluded her for a long time. There were so many questions and no good answers. Agents did fall in love and marry. It happened all the time, but...

Chapter Fifteen

Caitlin sat up with a start. She must've fallen asleep after all. The other side of the bed was empty, but the sheets were still warm from his body. Where was he? "Jake? Are you all right?" Of course, he was all right. In the air was the life-giving aroma of fresh coffee brewing.

"Better." He shuffled around in the kitchen, opened a cabinet, then set a couple of cups on the counter. "Mind if I turn on a light?"

"Go ahead." She swung her legs over the side of the bed. Her bare feet on the cold wood floors sent a shiver through her body; she pulled her PJ top tighter. "Coffee smells good."

He avoided her gaze.

She said, "There's no reason to feel awkward about our sleeping together. Nothing really happened."

"Something did happen. The connection between us—it's real, but you're right. Getting involved is a bad idea anytime and with another agent—my boss?

"I don't know if it's right or wrong. I feel too much to hide it anymore." She reached up and caressed his cheek. The stubble against her fingers, the hard plane of his face—when had he grown so dear?

He captured her hand and kissed the tips of her fingers. "Still a bad idea, Kate."

But he didn't let go. Instead, he pulled her closer into a kiss, a long senses-drugging kiss. His lips were hard and demanding. She opened her mouth to him and met his tongue, battling for dominance. The warmth in her belly flamed into a fire. All will, all resistance was for nothing. Her knees weakened. His body was hard against hers.

She'd thought to comfort him, yet his presence and his scent comforted her like nothing she'd ever known. She managed to whisper his name as he picked her up and carried her to the bed.

He paused long enough to ask, "Are you sure? Still a bad idea."

"But nothing in life is sure. I just feel..."

"Chèr, you have it right. Feelings are all that matter."

"*Now* is all that matters."

He settled her carefully on the bed, but she pulled him down with her. Poised over her, he unbuttoned her pajamas slowly, prolonging the torture. She wanted him. The backs of his hands grazed her nipples. They tightened into tiny nubs as he slipped the PJ top off her shoulders.

"You're so beautiful. Like I always imagined."

"You imagined me naked?"

"Many times. Dreamed 'bout doing this, too." He bent over and kissed her neck. "Only you didn't talk so much."

"Then shut me up, Jake."

He let out a low growl. His mouth fastened on hers and a thrill ran through her body. He tasted of chicory. His tongue swept against hers. He tugged his shirt free and whipped it over his head while sunlight played over his chiseled muscles. She reached out and caressed the hard muscles of his chest, and it was his turn to shiver.

He kissed her again, this time like a man starving with a deep abiding hunger.

A hunger as fierce as her own.

He slipped a hand between their bodies and touched the damp folds between her legs. Heat blazed again, flushing her body with fire. A whimper forced its way through her lips.

"Did I hurt you?"

"No," she gasped. "I need you. God, I need you so much."

He groaned and buried his face between her breasts. "Soft. So soft." His teeth fastened gently on her nipple and tugged.

Pain, an exquisite pain, morphed into whirlpools of pleasure and swirled from her tightened nipples to her groin. She moaned. He was too slow; she wanted him to fill her...she wanted the heat of his body against hers. Through his jeans, his rigid hard-on pressed against her thigh.

"Take 'em off." She fumbled with the button and zipper of his jeans. Levered on one elbow, he arched away from her slightly and freed his dick. She grasped his firm length; his shaft jerked and pulsed at her touch.

"Easy," he warned. "Or this will be over."

She managed a gasp. "We wouldn't want that."

"No, we wouldn't." A chuckle rose deep from his chest.

He reached back and shoved his jeans below his knees, then kicked them off.

The heat of his skin against hers sent a thrill through her entire body.

His body. Warm. Hard...and so close.

She pressed upward and gasped his name.

He stilled her with a slow, sensual kiss, then, his breath warm against her ear, he nibbled the lobe. "I've wanted you for so long...from the first moment when you walked into Jose's office."

"Hush. Show me." What was it about him that turned her into a pool of need? No man had ever stirred her emotions like Jake.

"Anything for the boss."

"You have to get over that."

"I'm gonna get over you, chèr." He nudged her thighs apart and slid two fingers deep into her wet core. "'Bout the time I break the bank at Monte Carlo."

Her inner muscles clenched tight around his fingers as he moved them in and out of her slick folds. He raked the back of her thigh with his thumb.

She bit the inside of her bottom lip as a surge of pleasure ripped through her. Why this man? Why could he touch her like no man ever had? Not just her body but her heart.

He removed his fingers, slowly, sensuously rubbing her

pleasure center. She was wet, so wet. He was driving her insane with his slow seduction. Then his mouth was on her, his tongue swirled around her clitoris. She arched against him. God, she wanted him inside her. "Please." Her fingers winnowed through his hair as she moved against his mouth.

"Sweet as honey," Jake murmured against her damp curls. Again he flicked her clit, the scent of her female musk driving him wild with desire. More than anything, he needed to feel her body around his cock. He grasped it and nudged her wet pussy with the head. Her legs widened and gave him the entrance he needed. He thrust into her silken depths and nearly lost control. Her inner muscles grasped him as firmly as a hand.

"Easy, chèr." Poised on his elbows he began to thrust slowly, filling her depths with each thrust. He kissed her neck, then nibbled on her shell-like ear. He found her lips and kissed her deeply. She opened to him and he swirled his tongue inside. Together their tongues battled in a dance as old as time.

Her fingernails pressed into his shoulders as she met him stroke for stroke. Her body heated against his; he raised his head and saw the red splotches flush across her chest.

Her inner muscles gripped him as she rode to her orgasm. She screamed and cried his name, locking her legs around his waist. Unable to hold back any longer, he quickened the pace and strength of his thrusts and drove into her wet core over and over until his balls contracted with his climax and emptied into her warm, wet depths. He groaned with the effort. Pulsation after pulsation until he was drained. Collapsing over her, their bodies wet with their loving, he brushed back a damp curl from her cheek and kissed her.

"I've never known anyone like you," he murmured against her neck. He wasn't a man to whisper meaningless words. Truly, he'd never had a woman who gave herself so completely...so wonderfully...so sensually. He'd hit a trifecta.

Caitlin opened her eyes. Damn, her vision was blurred. What kind of man could make love like a love machine and still screw her blind? She giggled and snuggled against his chest, her fingers swirling around in the fine dark fur on his chest. "Yeah, I guess that was—uh, pretty good."

He levered up on his elbow, his eyebrows furrowed in a puzzled frown. "Pretty good?"

She giggled again. "Okay, so it was basically fantastic. On a scale of one to ten—I am an accountant, as you well know—" She paused as if still considering Jake's performance.

"Well?"

"A twenty—completely off the chart." She buried her face in his shoulder. In spite of their wild exertions, Jake's scent was still clean and manly.

And she could get used to sharing a bed with him.

As Ed's executor and only heir, Jake knew most of the arrangements regarding his father's wishes. But there was still the matter of notifying all his old colleagues who'd want to say good-bye.

All of this while juggling the mission, his feelings for Kate and God only knew what else. So far, he'd controlled his urge to gamble. Ed would've certainly been proud of that.

Halfway through the long list of Ed's colleagues, his cell phone rang.

The soft sensual sound of Angie's voice startled him. "You have to come over here right away. It's important."

"Can't. I'm too busy at work," he lied. No way could she know about Ed's death and his lie about running away.

"No, you have to come. I have something important to tell you."

"Tell me now."

"No, it's too personal. I have to see you face-to-face."

"This better not be an excuse to continue your old crap. And it better be damn important."

"It is. And..." Angie paused.

"Fine. I'll come over, but I don't have much time." He let out a long sigh. Might as well get it over with. Damn woman wouldn't take "no" for an answer.

*

Caitlin made it into the office only thirty minutes late. A long shower had eased the sore muscles and the tender spots somewhat lower. Her cheeks heated every time she thought about it. And she thought about it often. How could she not?

"Any messages?" Caitlin asked, as she rushed to her cubicle and dumped her purse on the desk.

"Just one." Lisette, today in Native American garb, handed it over, her turquoise and silver bracelets jangling with the movement.

"Thanks." Caitlin glanced down at the note and frowned.

Meet me at 208 Marina Way, # 402. ASAP J—

"Is this all? Did he say what it was about?"

Lisette shook her head. "Annie from the cage took it while I was at lunch. That's it, as far as I know."

"Men. Guess I'd better see what my husband thinks so important."

Lisette giggled. "If he's like most men, whatever he wants is important...whether it is or not."

"You know where this is?"

"Oh, yeah. Some very pricey real estate, it is, too." She rattled off the directions, finishing with, "Marina Way condos are right at the end."

"Sounds easy enough.

"Can't miss 'em."

"Thanks. I'll be back as soon as I can. If it's something that will take a while, I'll call you."

Caitlin made her way to the employee parking area. Why hadn't Jake called her cell? How did she even know the message was really from him?

She pulled out her own cell and hit the speed dial for Jake.

Voice mail. He must've turned it off.

Jake jabbed the doorbell twice and gritted his teeth. Angie had better have a damned good reason for summoning him to her place.

The door opened. His jaw dropped. Angie was as near-naked as a woman could be without really being nekkid. The blue filmy thing which hung from one of her ivory shoulders didn't hide a damn thing. Her nipples peeked out like twin rosebuds already begging him to bite them. His gaze was drawn down to the dark blonde nest of curls...and to her long, slender legs. Memories of a much-younger Angie assailed him. Blood rushed to his groin. Not an unexpected response, given the situation.

"Dammit, Angie. What do you want? I told you last time we weren't hooking up again."

"You *know* what I want." Her manner was as overt as her lack of clothing. Her lashes fluttered and her smile was all-knowing. In spite of himself, his body responded with another blast of heat to his groin. His trousers grew snug, and it took all his willpower to tamp down the shakes. He remembered every sweaty second he'd spent in her arms in that tatty room off Dubonnet.

"Plain to see what you expect, but you're forgetting one little detail. Read my lips. I'm married and not in the market for some strange."

A pink flush stained her long neck and spread up to her cheeks.

"No need to be so crude, Jake. But then you always were blunt. You remember, don't you?" Her gaze zeroed in on his crotch. "Of course you do, chèr. Come on in before you bust your britches. I'm not that great with a needle."

He ignored the little voice in his head—the one that told him to run like hell—and stepped inside. Maybe she did have something important to tell him and this act was all window dressing.

She eased the door shut. Again she fixed her gaze on him like a sleek white cat ready to play with her prey before pouncing and killing.

Big mistake. He should've run. Not that he was in fear of his life. But his new bond to Caitlin was fragile, and the sexual heat radiating from Angie's sleek body wracked his with need.

She slithered a step closer and teasingly ran a long fingernail up and down his zipper. "You always were a big boy. Glad to see that hasn't changed."

"Jesus, Angie! Cut it out. Get some damn clothes on. You said you had some important information for me. So spill."

She lifted her shoulders and sighed. "You're determined to be a stick in the mud, aren't you? I'll get dressed." She turned then cast him a heated glance over her shoulder before sashaying from the room.

He jerked his gaze away from her shapely ass and walked over to the window. He sucked in a deep breath and tried to blot the old images from his mind.

Pricey digs in the marina. Yeah, she'd really done well for a teenage prostitute. Too well for completely honest means?

Was she still in the game?

"Nice, isn't it?"

At the sound of her purring tone, Jake turned—and wished he'd kept his eyes glued to the view. She'd managed to add another layer of filmy material, but everything he'd seen before was still in plain sight.

She held out a glass of wine. "Here, chèr, take a load off. I'll keep my hands to myself."

"I know you will." He reached for the glass and misjudged.

The glass tipped and splashed all over the front of his shirt and down the front of his pants.

"Oops!" Angie shrugged. "Oh, well. Guess we'll have to do something about that big bad...stain."

"Dammit." He jumped back and brushed at the large spot. "You did that on purpose."

"Now. Now. Give me your shirt before you get it all over my carpet. I'll get some club soda. It'll come out all right."

"You did it on purpose." Was there any trick she wouldn't pull to get him in her bed?

"So what? Let me treat the stain while it's wet. You wouldn't want to go home all wine-stained to your sweet little wife, now would you?"

"You conniving witch."

"Don't be tiresome. I promise I'll behave. Just hand it over."

He gritted his teeth, then forced a grudging smile. "All right." He unbuttoned his shirt. Damned thing was already sticking to his chest. He held it out gingerly. "Make it fast."

She took the stained shirt and dropped it to the floor with a graceful, cavalier gesture. "Now, that's better." With eyes the color of pale slate, she gazed up at him. "It's been such a long time. I've never forgotten what sweet love we made all those years ago." She pressed her hands against his chest. "You *do* remember, don't you?"

He stepped back. Better get some distance between them before he succumbed to his body's baser instincts.

Angie eased forward. "Now, Jake."

"Angie...the door."

"Let 'em knock. They'll get tired and go away."

Again, her hands splayed across his bare chest.

"No—"

The door opened.

Jake's gaze darted toward the sound.

God, no. Caitlin.

Chapter Sixteen

One glance at Jake and Angelique, and Caitlin's hope for the future shattered. Jake, shirtless, startled and pale. Angelique Andre, her long, slender fingers splayed seductively against his chest, her expression clearly annoyed by the interruption.

"J-Jake?"

"It's not what you think."

"I don't think anything." How she managed to sound so calm, she'd never know. "I didn't mean to intrude." She took a shaky step back then forced her body in the direction of the door.

A low, theatrical sigh from Angelique slowed Caitlin's steps.

"Surely you don't begrudge my sleeping with your husband?" Angelique's tone was as soft and seductive as a cat's purr. "It's not the first time. You see, he's the father of my child."

"Child?" Caitlin turned and glared at Jake. His chin dropped; his mouth gaped in shock.

"Child?" His pallor was quickly replaced by the flush of rage.

"What do you mean—his child?" Caitlin managed. The autistic child Angie kept in the private school was his? The emotional part of her wanted to freak, but her logical side asked for proof. And only a DNA test would suffice.

Angelique lifted her arm above her head and pulled her body into a languorous stretch. Her feline movements accentuated the slim lines of her body. "She's fifteen. You're an accountant. Do the math."

Disbelief settled in the pit of her stomach. Her mouth grew

Sahara dry—too dry to spit. "Fine," she finally mustered. All right, so he had a child. Or was Angelique just blowing smoke, trying to manipulate him? That was something to be figured out another day. But had he just made love with Angelique? That wasn't so easy to overlook.

"Kate! We didn't—" He snatched his shirt from the smug blonde and jerked it on.

Caitlin reached for the doorknob, unable to hide her trembling hands. She closed the door quietly behind her. She wouldn't let them see any more of her pain or her anger.

It doesn't matter. All we did was have comfort sex. It didn't mean anything to either one of us. Not really.

Liar.

"Kate, dammit. Wait!" His plea followed her down the hall. She reached the elevator and punched the button.

The assignment? How could she continue working, not to mention living, with him as if nothing had happened?

Close quarters. Way too close.

Somehow, she made her way to the street. For a while she walked along, self-derision lodged in her throat. How stupid she'd been. Like the most naïve of schoolgirls, she'd already planned their lives together, starting with the simple but elegant wedding, where they'd live, how they'd manage their two careers in the Bureau with the children they'd have. How could she have been so damned stupid?

How could Jake go from her bed straight to Angelique's? How could he? Men and their small brains...especially the one located at the South Pole.

If Jake had abandoned the mother of his child, he wasn't any different than her father who'd abandoned her emotionally after her mother's death. But Jake's expression was as shocked as hers must've been at Angelique's announcement. No, he wouldn't have abandoned his child...if he'd known about her.

She walked until the ripe stench of the river grew stronger. Where the hell was she?

*

Jake followed Caitlin down the hall, but she disappeared into the elevator and was gone. He returned to Angie's condo and found her lounging comfortably on a white leather sofa.

He loomed over her. "You're lying. You must be. This is nothing to joke about."

"No, it's not a joke, nor am I lying. You have a daughter."

A daughter—an autistic daughter. What in hell was he going to do? "Then where is she?" No need to let her know he already knew she had a child.

"She's away at school. She's fifteen, and her name is Charlotte, but everyone calls her Charlie."

"Why didn't you tell me?

"You disappeared off the face of the earth after you were arrested. How could I?" Angie lifted her shoulders in a casual shrug.

"Did you even try?"

"Don't act like you would've even cared. You were out for nothing but yourself then."

"If I'd known...I wouldn't have deserted you."

"You were always running some kind of a scam. And I wouldn't be surprised if you weren't pulling something now—you and your precious wife."

"Don't change the subject." He sat down on the chair opposite Angie. "I'm just trying to have a life. Kate and I—we're just starting out and springing a daughter on us could wreck our marriage, not to mention what she saw when she opened that door."

"I can't help it if she doesn't trust you and jumps to conclusions," she purred with a self-satisfied smile.

"Just how did she turn up at just the wrong time anyway?"

She shrugged. "My bad. Forgive me?"

Fists clenched at his sides, he paced back and forth. Was she the one pulling a scam or was her child really his? "Dammit, you've got some explaining to do."

"Sit down, chèr, I'll tell you all about our daughter."

"Not now. I have to go after my wife."

He strode to the door, snatched it open, and stomped outside. While he re-buttoned his shirt, he looked up and down the street. He had a daughter? No, he couldn't think about that now. Angie was bluffing and to hell with her. Caitlin was what mattered. Of course, she'd jumped to conclusions—just like Angie planned.

"Damn." After last night, he'd let his guard down with Kate. Would she believe him? More important, would she ever believe another word out of his mouth? Last night Ed's death had been so unexpected. She'd offered him the comfort he needed, then the heat that blazed between them this morning.

Unexpected didn't half cover it.

He strode down the street and looked both ways. Caitlin's rental car was still parked on the street, but no sign of Kate. As pissed off as she was, she must've taken off on foot.

The thought of Kate on foot. What if she wandered into the wrong area?

Hell. Why worry? She wasn't a delicate flower. She was an FBI agent who could toss any piece of street trash on his ass.

Where was she? Dammit. He had to explain. Somehow, he had to convince her what she'd seen was all a product of Angie's manipulations.

Desperation building, he raked his fingers through his hair and headed toward his car. He found a street person wiping the windshield. He pulled out a twenty. "Hey, buddy. You seen a redhead come this way?"

"Really built?" His soiled hands gestured in the air, forming the figure of a woman.

"Yeah, short, tousled hair, but pretty."

"Oh yeah. She had a mad on, don't cha know."

"Yeah, I know."

"She was talking to her purty self and shaking her head. You de one what made her mad?"

Jake nodded. "Don't you know."

"She went stompin' toward the boardwalk, but I don't think she gonna stop 'til she hit de Gulf."

"Thanks, fella." Jake handed over the twenty.

A wide smile wreathed the man's grimy face. "Anytime. Good luck with de redhead."

Jake nodded and shot the man a two-fingered salute.

He jumped in his car and drove slowly down Marina Way. He ought to catch up with her pretty damn quick if she hadn't changed directions. He fumbled in his pocket for his cell, then punched the speed dial for Kate's.

Voice mail. Damn. As mad as she was, she wasn't answering.

From the shadows Heaton watched Kate leave, anger written across her sweet face. Then he watched her husband come running out, his shirt half-buttoned and a wine stain down the front of his pants, talk to a homeless person, then take off in his car. Poor Kate—she was a sweet girl, a hard worker; she deserved better than a cheating husband.

Angelique Andre was a demon where men were concerned. She'd do anything with anyone to further her twisted aims. Months ago she'd seduced him so she could blackmail him into her embezzling scheme. Shame roiled through and sickened him, as always, when he thought back to that night. And now she'd seduced Jack Girard.

Now that his June had died this very day, Angelique had no power over him. As for her firing him? He was about to take care of that problem, too.

Inside his car, the air-conditioning bathed his sweat-dampened shirt in cool air. He waited another ten minutes before crossing the street to the bitch's building. He reached up and smoothed his hair, then straightened his tie. Now that he was sure Jack Girard wasn't coming back for a second round with Angelique, he'd pay her a surprise visit.

He walked into the building foyer—not too fast, not too slow. No need to attract attention.

No answer.

She had to be home. He hadn't seen her leave. He punched all the buzzers on the floor below hers.

One of them would answer. And did.

"Delivery." He altered his voice affecting a very southern drawl.

Now, time to do the job. With his calmest manner, he headed for the elevator. The doors opened and he stepped inside. New Age elevator music filled the air, but the soothing tones didn't calm the fury that roared through him. Instead, the excitement began to build and fizz. He clenched his fists at his sides.

The gloves.

He yanked the latex gloves from his pocket and pulled them on.

Better not leave any fingerprints at the scene. Thankful he was alone in the elevator, he chuckled aloud. With any luck, someone else would be blamed. He rode to the fourth floor and then headed down the hall to Angelique's door.

It was open a bare inch. He stopped, peered inside.

His mouth dropped open; he sucked in a ragged breath. The bitch was lying on the floor. The angle of her neck—unnatural.

Had Kate's husband had killed Angelique?

Good for him.

Heaton eased back from the door, closed it and removed his gloves. He wadded them into a ball and stuffed them into his pocket.

Now he could plan his wife's funeral at ease in the knowledge that the blonde bitch who'd made his life a living hell for the last eight months was dead.

He reached for his cell phone, then thought better of it. Instead, he started the car and drove to the nearest phone booth.

He wrapped the receiver in his tear dampened handkerchief and dialed 911.

"I want to report a murder," he said, then gave a description of Girard, and the address. They pressed him for more information, but he quickly set the receiver back on the hook.

Back at home, Caitlin downed the final sip of coffee then stuffed the last bite of beignet into her mouth. She swiped the powdered sugar from her upper lip and chin. Had she really just eaten three beignets? The sugar and caffeine had her body vibrating, but the carbs had given her time to calm down and think clearly. Maybe now, she could listen to his six voice mails without stomping the cell phone into smithereens.

The sound of Jake's key in the door sent her to her feet. The door opened. She set her hands on her hips and said in a Hispanic accent, "You have some splainin' to do, Jakey."

"You have to know nothing happened. It was all a set-up. One of Angie's manipulations."

"I don't call her child a setup or manipulation. Her child— maybe your child—is very real."

"But revealing it the way she did was classic Angie—maximum effect for maximum damage. Listen, chèr. The kid may be real, but there's no way to know without a DNA test if she's mine."

"And if she is?"

"Then I'll help Angie support her."

Why did men think support was all a child needed? "Is that it? She needs a father. You've already missed years of her life."

"Look, we don't know how serious her condition is. Or whether or not my sudden appearance in her life will be disruptive." He collapsed on a chair and ran his hands through his hair, leaving it standing in wild peaks. "I'm stunned. I might have a kid..."

He shook his head and one lock fell forward. She wanted to brush it back...comfort him again.

Of course, she'd jumped to the wrong conclusion. Just a knee-jerk reaction. With all her heart she wanted to believe in him, in them. Believe what they'd shared last night and this morning wasn't just a roll in the hay. It certainly hadn't been for her. She'd reached for him in comfort, but it had been more than comfort if less than love.

"It's a lot to take in," she admitted, trying to hide how much she cared.

"After last night, you had to think I was a low-down horn dog."

"To put it mildly...for a few minutes."

He took a step forward, his expression so earnest it hurt. "I'm sorry. You have to know I wouldn't do that to you."

She backed up a step. He was too close. She wasn't quite ready to…

"Maybe we made a mistake," she said. "It was the situation. You were hurting."

That's it, Caitlin. Back away like the coward you are.

He retreated a step. "Yeah—well, I appreciate your drying my tears. You're right. We need to keep this business as usual."

Before he could flee any farther, a vigorous pounding on the door startled them both. Jake glanced at the door.

What now?

"We're busy. Go away!" Jake shouted.

Her heart pounding, Kate shrugged. "You might as well open the door. We've covered it all." No, not even by half. Why was she such a coward? Afraid of confrontation? Afraid of being hurt?

"New Orleans PD. Open the door."

"What?"

Jake strolled over to the door. "Coming. Coming." He yanked open the door and stepped back.

Two plainclothes detectives flashed their badges. "Detective Sergeant Pelletier and my partner, Detective Sweeney."

Jake stepped back and motioned them inside. "What can we do for you, detectives?"

"Jack Girard?"

"Yes."

"We'd like you to come down to the precinct and help us with an inquiry."

"Related to what?"

"Angelique Andre, CFO of the Rivera Corporation. She's filed a complaint against you."

"A complaint? What the hell for?"

"When was the last time you saw her?"

"Earlier this afternoon."

"And where was that?"

"Her condo." Jake scowled at the plainclothes policemen. "What's this all about, detectives?"

"Just answer the questions. Under what circumstances?"

"She left me a message to meet her there. Now look, what did she say I did?"

"We're just trying to get your take on what happened. You know women. Sometimes they get overwrought."

Jake glanced over at Caitlin; she stood, arms folded across chest, her expression tight.

"She seemed to be under the mistaken idea that we could take up where we left off sixteen years ago."

"Which was?" Pelletier asked while Sweeney scribbled down the answers in a notebook.

"In our teens. We spent some time together."

"Intimate?"

"Yeah. We were kids."

"And now?

He nodded toward Kate. "We're newlyweds. I love my wife. I told Ms. Andre I wasn't interested."

"What happened after that?"

"I left and went after my wife."

Pelletier raised an eyebrow. "Your wife was there, too?"

"It was a setup. Kate walked in on us. Angelique was wearing almost nothing. My wife jumped to conclusions and took off, so naturally, I went after her."

"Hm. This may take some time. We'd like you both to come on down."

"Sure. Let's get this cleared up." He glanced at Caitlin. "Kate, honey?"

"Sure." Caitlin grabbed her purse and tied the arms of her sweater around her neck.

The ride to the station house passed quickly. Once there, tall, lanky Detective Sweeney whose long face bristled with more than a hint of five o'clock shadow nodded toward the back hall. "I'll talk to you there. My partner will interview your husband."

Caitlin and Jake were herded into separate interview rooms. Something was up. The divide and conquer ploy was a familiar one. She'd used it herself. It had to be more than Angelique's filing a complaint against Jake. But what?

Not for a minute did she believe Jake had assaulted Angelique. The bitch was playing games just like Jake said she was.

He might not always play by the rules, but the man she'd held in her arms last night and made love with this morning wouldn't hit a woman...even one as deserving as Angelique.

No way. He'd been too tender, too sweet.

She sat on a metal folding chair with the sergeant across from her.

"Would you like some coffee or a cold drink?"

"No, thanks. Now, what's this about? I don't believe my husband would do anything to that woman."

"Why don't you tell me how you came to be at Miss Andre's apartment?"

"At work, I was given a phone message to meet my husband at an address on Marina Way. It turned out it was Miss Andre's condo."

"So why did he want you to meet him there?"

"He didn't leave the message. It was Miss Andre who left it."

"Now why would she want to do that?"

"She and my husband knew each other when they were teenagers. I suppose that she wanted me to find him in a compromising position."

"And did you?"

"I thought so—until I calmed down."

"Describe his state of dress."

"Now, Sergeant, I don't see—"

"Please, humor me, Mrs. Girard."

"Fine. His shirt was undone. There was a wine stain—at least, I assume it was wine—there were two glasses on the table. Anyway, his shirt was undone, and she had her hands all over him."

"And you thought the worst."

"I did."

"And what happened next?"

"We exchanged words. Then I slammed the door and left."

"You go back to work?"

"No, I walked along the wharf, found a beignet shop, a Starbucks, hailed a taxi, and came home."

"What time was that?"

"Let's see, I received the message after lunch—about one-thirty. Thirty-five minutes to her place. I wasn't there for even five minutes. After I left, I walked until it started getting dark, then I called a taxi. By the time I reached home, it was around six."

"You didn't see your husband until when?"

"Well, I didn't look at the exact time, Detective, but I had enough time to eat three beignets and drink a grande cappuccino. About forty-five minutes. He hadn't been home very long when you all showed up."

"You ate three beignets?"

"I was upset." From the look of lanky Sweeney, beignets wouldn't put any extra weight on him. He probably didn't understand the need for carb consolation.

"Feelin' better now, Mrs. Girard?" Sweeney asked with a smirk.

She smirked right back. "If wired and jumpy from the sugar and caffeine is better."

"What did your husband have to say for himself?"

"That she'd engineered the entire scene. That nothing happened."

"And you believed him?"

She smiled. "I made him sweat a bit, but I finally admitted I believed him. We were on the verge of making up when you arrived." Or they would've been if she hadn't chickened out of the conversation. "Is that it? Are we done?"

Sweeney stood, yawned and rubbed his nose with the back of his hand. "That depends..."

"On—?"

"On how long it's gonna take for you to tell me the truth."

"What's going on here? What did that bitch say Jake did after I left?"

"She wasn't saying much 'because someone killed Angelique Andre not too long after you left your husband there."

"Miss Andre's dead? How was she killed?" Stunned by the

news, she leaned back and took a deep breath. She should've known. The detectives had been much too polite. "I know Jack didn't kill her. He couldn't have. Is he under arrest? Has he been read his rights?"

"Like I said. We're asking the questions, trying to figure out in our limited way which one of you did the deed."

"Which one of us?" Holy hell. They suspected her, too? Her hands started to tremble. With great effort, she folded them in her lap. What a colossal fuck-up.

"Yeah, we got you running around buying beignets and fancy coffees until six o'clock, and maybe you went back after he left and offed her yourself. So tell us how you did it?"

Her training came to the fore. She leaned forward and fixed her gaze on the sergeant. "For the record, I didn't kill Angelique Andre. Am I under arrest? If so, read me my rights. I want an attorney."

"Now hold on, this is your only chance to tell us what really happened. You went back and found he'd killed her? This is your chance to come clean. We can help you. You don't have to protect him."

"I can't be forced to testify against my husband." She folded her arms across her chest. "I've answered your questions as truthfully as I can. If I'm not under arrest, I'm leaving."

"Hold on. Let me see what's going on with your husband."

"I'd appreciate that."

She watched the detective as he left. God. What a nightmare. They actually thought she or Jake had killed Angelique. As much as Caitlin would've like to wring her boss's neck, she certainly didn't deserve to be murdered.

And that poor child, what about her? She was now without a mother. Being left motherless was something Caitlin understood too well. True, she'd had Bonnie to love and care for her, but who would see to the girl's needs? Had Angelique even had enough forethought to leave a will?

If she were Jake's child, what would he do? He wouldn't abandon the girl—she knew that much about him already. But how would the presence of an autistic daughter affect their relationship, their careers?

Jake leaned back and waited. As soon as his prints were run, the FBI honchos would shortly appear and intervene with the LEOs. Cooperation was his middle name—even volunteered his prints.

"Detective Pelletier, I've already told you. Angelique Andre was alive when I left her. There was this homeless guy who cleaned my windows. He saw me take off after my wife. Find him. He'll remember me. I gave him a twenty."

The detective sneezed, then wiped his nose with the back of his hand. "Maybe the twenty was for an alibi. Just where are we supposed to find him?"

"In front of Marina Way condos, if he hasn't been shooed away by now."

"Yeah, so describe him."

"Dirty red baseball cap, bill worn backward, wore a couple of coats. The top one was an old London Fog. Age—maybe fifty to sixty. Limped on his right side."

"That's an awful specific description, Girard."

"Happy to be of service." Jake smiled at the detective. Not exactly a social occasion, but there was no need to be nasty. His problem was getting it through his head Angie was dead. And apparently killed minutes after he'd left. No, his real problem was these bozos liked him for prime suspect.

"I ain't buying."

The door opened; another plainclothes entered. "'M'ere, Jim."

Jake drummed his fingers against the tabletop. Dollars to beignets, the Feds had arrived. 'Bout damn time. Any run on his prints or background check would flag the Bureau. And the sooner the better.

He was on the wrong side of the interrogation table. Not exactly a comfortable position, either.

Detective Jim Pelletier walked out into the hall. "What?"

"Someone thinks your guy looks familiar," Sweeney said. "The desk sergeant says he reminded him of a kid held back in the day for the murder of a working girl—by her pimp, as it turned out. Detective by name of Ed Hoolihan adopted the kid and sent him to school. Your guy's a Fed, Jim."

"A Fed? Hell, I don't care. I like him for this murder."

"Like 'em all you want. Ain't gonna happen." He looked over his shoulder. "If I ain't mistaken, they're here now."

"No wonder the fucker was so cool. All he had to do was sit there and pass the time. Shit."

Five minutes later, Pelletier joined the Feds in the Lieutenant's office. He wasn't about to give up without a fight. "See here, neither one of them has a solid alibi for the time the M.E. says Miss Andre was killed."

"You do you have evidence?" the taller Fed asked.

"Fingerprints—his in the apartment, hers on the door handle."

The second agent spoke, "If LeFevre were the killer, he'd certainly be smart enough to sanitize the crime scene."

"Maybe he was in a hurry. Someone knocked on the door and your guy panicked."

The second Fed spoke up. "And maybe you need to consider someone else killed her after he left. He's already admitted he was there."

"Which makes him my prime suspect."

"If you arrest him, you'll interfere with our investigation. Money laundering. We're sure the Rivera Corp. is laundering drug money through their casino. Our agents are in place and they need to continue their job."

"Don't think just because he's an agent that we'll overlook evidence that's not in his favor."

"Wouldn't expect you to, Detective."

The same thoughts kept whirling through Caitlin's mind. What would happen to Angelique's child? Jake Certainly didn't have the money to keep her in the special school. Someone would have to notify the school. And they would choose how to tell the poor girl her mother was dead. Would she even understand?

A scowling Detective Pelletier lumbered into the interview room. "You're free to go...for now. Sorry for any inconvenience."

"Funny, you don't look sorry."

The detective's jaw clenched. "The department appreciates your cooperation."

"What about my husband?"

"Free to go...for the time bein'."

"Thank you, Detective." She kept her response simple. No point in rubbing his face in it. Obviously, the Bureau had stepped in when Jake and her backgrounds were run.

"Look, I don't care who you are. You don't have to play nicey-nice with me. I still like your husband, if that's what he is, for this. Don't let misguided loyalty stand in the way of justice."

Ready to leave, she gripped her purse. "You're wrong on this one, Detective."

She exited the interview room and was more than relieved to find Jake standing in the hallway.

As if they were only leaving a party, she gave Jake a bright smile. "Are we ready, dear?"

He let one eyelid drop in a slow wink. "Yeah. I think our ride's here." He nodded at the two agents still hovering at the entrance of the squad room.

Detective Pelletier and his partner headed to their desks. Pelletier's beefy face was flushed, and his lips were drawn into a thin line. They'd been so certain that she'd flip on her *husband*. In his place, she'd feel much the same. No one liked having an outside agency come in and take over an investigation. Even if there was a tacit agreement they would work together, the NOPD wouldn't give up on proving Jake was guilty.

Never.

And that meant more time diverted from their undercover op.

Chapter Seventeen

Jake slammed the Bureau car door. "Thanks for the assist."

"Anytime."

Jake shot a quick glance toward Caitlin but held his tongue. Too much to think about. Angie dead? Unreal. Was her child really his? He'd call the school first thing in the morning. The police would have notified them by then, and they would know what arrangements Angie had made for her daughter.

His daughter?

What the hell did he know about being a father—especially to a child with challenges?

Once inside, he collapsed on the sofa; Caitlin sat beside him. "You're awfully quiet. What can I do?"

He shrugged. "Not much anyone can do until some questions are answered."

"Her daughter?"

"That and—God, how could I forget Ed? I have arrangements to make. That's what I was in the middle of when Angie called."

"Let me help you." Her hand rested lightly on his shoulder, but her gesture touched him on a deeper level. This crazy op had brought them together—two people so different.

"Do you want to bring him back to New Orleans? Or maybe a simple memorial service in DC?"

He forced himself to focus. "Uh, I have a list of names, officers from his old squad. Already called about half of them."

"Let me do that then. So you're bringing him home?"

"Yeah, that's what he wanted. He left instructions, long before he ever got hurt on the job."

"That settles it then. We'll do what he wanted. I'll call Jose and make the arrangements."

He nodded as gratitude wove through him; warm waves of tenderness enfolded him as surely as if she'd embraced him. No matter who her father was or what her issues were with him, she had a good heart.

"The list of officers—there's a copy on my laptop. File name's—uh, edwardh.doc. Not very original, am I?" A bark of laughter ripped from his throat, leaving it raw. He stood and shook his head. "I gotta get outta here for a bit. Clear my head."

"Sure. Do whatever. I'll take care of this."

"Thanks." He headed for the door. No way could he get involved with Kate right now. And her soft eyes, hands, hell—her whole body, said touch me, love me. And God, he wanted to, but—so much had happened. Ed's death, making love with Kate, then Angie's big surprise, and her murder. Too damn much for one simple Cajun to comprehend.

Life and death spinning faster than a roulette wheel...as always, the odds were against him.

Caitlin sighed and set the phone down. All the arrangements were completed. Ed's remains would arrive tomorrow at noon and be taken to Rotier's Mortuary. Luckily the funeral director had known Ed from his time on the job and agreed to make the arrangements after hours. Relieved that she'd been able to relieve some of Jake's burden, she looked around for something else to do. The sound of his key in the door brought a rush of blood to her face.

He entered the loft and started tugging at his damp clothes.

"What happened?"

"Aw, hell. Got caught in the rain."

"What you need is a hot shower."

And me to wash your back.

He grabbed a towel, went into the bathroom, hurriedly pulled the screen in front of the door.

"I won't watch," she said. "Besides, I've seen it all."

A slight chuckle was the only response.

"How about I pour you a cup of coffee and tell you about the arrangements for Ed's funeral?" She walked over to the kitchen.

"Go ahead," he said, his voice muffled.

"You sure you're all right?"

"I'm fine."

"Okay, here goes. Ed's body will arrive tomorrow at noon and be taken to Rotier's Mortuary. There'll be a visitation the next evening or a wake, whatever you call it down here. It'll be another day because they're booked up with burials, so the funeral will be the next day after the wake with full police department honors at the graveside. Is that okay?"

The screen moved back, and Jake emerged, his hair damp but combed. He'd put on a clean T-shirt and a pair of athletic shorts. He walked over to the counter and snaked his arm around her waist. "Thanks, chèr. I appreciate it...more than you know."

She relaxed in the warmth of his body against hers. "I'm still sorry for jumping to conclusions when I saw you with Angelique. It just hit me wrong. Even though ten minutes later I calmed down enough to know she'd stage-managed the entire episode."

"It's just so damned unnecessary. First, Ed dies and I'm not there. Then someone kills Angie. Dammit, all to hell!" His body tensed against her; he slammed his fist on the counter and rattled the cups.

She faced him. His swift change of mood startled her. His anger was evident from his frown to his furrowed brow and from the dark red flush. Could Angelique have enraged him after Caitlin left? Enough to kill her?

"You've jumped to conclusions, again." His tone was low. Deadly even. "It crossed your mind that I might've lost my temper enough to actually kill a woman...a woman who might be the mother of my child."

She shook her head. "No, I—"

"Don't deny it. I saw it as clearly on your face as any player's tell."

He pulled away from her. She took a step back, but no, she wouldn't back down. "See here, Jake."

"Some would take this disagreement as a form of foreplay."

Foreplay? She straightened her back and raised her chin. "I'm not interested in playing games."

"Right."

He advanced another step. Her heart jammed in her throat; she tried to swallow, but her mouth was too dry. "Jake..."

He drew closer, forcing her back against the counter. His breath was warm on her neck. "You want me."

She tried to shake her head, but he placed both hands on each side of her face. "Don't deny it." His voice was raspy with emotion. "Even now, when you think it's possible I killed a woman I once loved. Yes, I loved her as much as I knew how. I was a bundle of teenage hormones, and she was the most beautiful girl I'd ever seen. Unspoiled. Nothing like what she became."

His hand slid down the sides of her face to linger on her throat. "It would be simple. One snap."

His hard chest against her breasts. His eyes darkened with passion...anger? No, she didn't believe he'd killed Angelique, anymore than he'd snap her own neck now. For all his rage, she sensed the restraint and gentleness that were part and parcel of the man she'd come to know.

Caitlin shook her head. "For a second, only a second. You're a good man, a good agent. I believe it with all my heart."

"Would you bet your life on it?"

"Yes. I would." Her heart rat-a-tat-tatted against her chest. Her breath came in ragged gasps.

Jake lowered his lips to hers. His kiss was tender and long. She opened her mouth to his and deepened the kiss. His hands skimmed under her shirt and raised it over her head and threw it across the room. He unsnapped her bra with a quick twist and cupped her breasts in his strong hands. He tweaked her nipples which quickly tightened into nubs of exquisite sensation. He kissed down her belly until he reached her jeans.

"Damn," he muttered and unfastened them, inching the zipper down slowly until she thought she would scream with frustration. She wiggled her hips until they slid down to her ankles. She stepped out of them and kicked them aside.

Skin to skin, his jutting erection pressed into her belly and she rubbed her pelvis against it. An overwhelming desire to simply screw herself senseless gathered in her lower belly and centered between her thighs. Heat flooded her body until she burned with a fever, so hot she might combust.

He eased her over to their bed and gently laid her down, covering her body with his. Their fingers entwined, he pulled her arms above her head; she wrapped her legs around his waist. Somehow his athletic shorts had disappeared, dissolved—whatever, it didn't matter. All that mattered was having him inside her. She gazed into his passion-glazed eyes. "Now."

"No, not yet."

A moan ripped from her throat. Pure torture of the sweetest kind. How could she have doubted him, for even a second?

"You doubted me," he murmured into her ear.

"Never again."

"Promise?" Soft as a sigh, his plea sent a thrill through her entire body.

"Yes." The words came without volition. Never would she doubt him. Never.

Hands released, she winnowed her fingers through his hair, shoving his head to her breasts. He grasped one of her nipples in his mouth and sucked it into a tight bud. Pleasure, excruciating ripples of pleasure, grew in her breasts, swelling and threatening to send her over the edge before he so much as entered her, an offering to this man...to her man.

She groaned and stiffened, the tell-tale heat overtaking her and catapulting her into a shattering climax. While she still throbbed from coming, Jake separated her thighs and inserted one, then two fingers; his thumb circled her clitoris as she moved against his fingers.

Body burning a furnace and mind blown to the four winds, she shuddered into another climax, but then he left a trail of kisses down her belly to the apex of her thighs.

"No, I can't. Not again."

"Yes," he whispered between her thighs, his tongue flicked at her clitoris, making her legs quiver involuntarily. Then he licked her labia all around, lavishing attention to the lower edges of her slit.

A moan collected in her throat, threatening to shut off her air, but when his teeth fastened gently on her clit and pulled, she sucked in a breath and cried as her body yet again slammed into another orgasm. Her arms and legs flailed in unison with her throbbing inner muscles. Was this a convulsion?

Jake rose and cradled her in his arms. "You all right?"

Tears streamed down her cheeks, but she managed to nod. "Yes."

He grinned. "Good, 'cause we're not through."

"No, we're not." She giggled. Must be hysteria. "Because I intend to have a taste of you."

"Just a nibble."

Jake turned over on his back and pulled her with him. He was rock-hard. She lowered her mouth and licked the drop of cum at the tip.

Jake shifted beneath her. "Careful. I don't want to come yet."

"Oh, you're going to come all right." Her words were brave, but could she actually swallow it? She never had...but this was Jake.

Tentatively she circled the head of his shaft with her tongue. His musky male scent was so...uniquely his. She slid her mouth farther down his rock-hard shaft moving it in a circular motion and swirling her tongue around it as she did.

A groan tore from Jake's throat.

She stopped and raised her head. "Am I hurting you?"

"God, no."

So far. So good. Jake had remarkable control. Really, he did.

Sucking hard, she bobbed her head over his dick. With her free hand, she stroked his inner thighs and then cupped his balls gently. Jake groaned and his body tensed; his cock jerked and throbbed in her mouth. He groaned again as semen spurted over her tongue. She swallowed and swallowed again as his cum pumped until there was no more.

Finally, Jake's entire body went limp.

"Was that okay?" Damn, she was such a novice at fellatio. But at least no longer a fellatio virgin. She would improve with time, surely.

Eyes glazed, he slowly levered up on one elbow and groaned. "*Okay*? Omigod, it was fucking wonderful."

Pleased by his praise, she couldn't hold back the smile. "Good. I'm glad I did it right."

"You did it *so* right. Mm."

She snuggled into his warm embrace. Raising her head and pouting her lips for another kiss. And another.

After the briefest of naps, Caitlin startled awake and found Jake staring at her. "Hi, handsome. Ready for another go-round?" She swung a leg over his body and straddled him. She leaned forward and swung her breasts in his face, just beyond the reach of his mouth.

"I love your breasts." He cupped and weighed them in his hands. "never seen any so beautiful. Perfect."

His mere touch sent shivers down to her lower belly and the warmth pooled there. God, she was so wet, and he was hard again, pressing against the soft cheeks of her ass.

Behind her, Jake's thighs formed a backrest. She leaned back. "I think you have something happening down here." She winked and pointed at his groin.

"You're right. Lift your hips."

She obeyed and his dick sprang upward. Gingerly she elevated her hips farther and positioned the head of his dick at her opening. She slid down on his huge erection, willing her body to adjust to the thickness of his shaft and length. Filled until she could take no more, she began to rock back and forth. Jake thrust his hips upward as she moved against his erection, grinding his shaft against her G-spot.

Her body flushed, her nipples tightened into searing buds while her inner muscles grasped and released him. He caught one of her nipples between his teeth and gently raked it into even tighter nubs. She leaned forward and nipped at his flat male nipples. "Fair is fair."

Beads of moisture grew between her breasts and slid down her belly and onto Jake's. Their bellies smacked together again and again with the exertions of their passion. Warmth, then heat, then fire ripped through her as her climax ripped through her body. Damp and spent, she collapsed on his chest and moaned. Never had she ever been so fucked or loved. God, how could she ever give him up?

Jake kept moving. He wanted her again. Had to have her again. "Come on, baby. Come again. You can do it."

Again? What a man! Caitlin shook her head against his chest. "Unh-uh."

"Yes, baby." Without pulling out, he flipped her over on her back and lifted her legs over his shoulders, cupped her ass and pulled her closer. She grasped the headboard and rose to meet him thrust for thrust as he pounded into her hot, wet pussy. She gripped him so tightly with her inner muscles that he nearly came. No, he wanted this to last. He slowed the pace, inching in and out, tormenting them both with the sensual movements. Beneath him, she rotated her pelvis around his cock, driving him mad.

Finally, his entire body on fire, he relented and increased the pace, grinding against her clit with each pounding thrust.

"Now, baby. Now," he groaned.

The pressure mounted and grew in his balls and burst, sending spasm after spasm of cum, pumping into his marvelous woman's pussy.

Beautiful, beautiful woman.

A thousand times better than any jackpot.

A long low moan came rolling from Kate's throat. Her body, hot as an oven against his, shuddered and the moan escalated into a scream.

Totally spent, his dick slipped out. He gently slid her legs off his shoulders and held her in his arms. "Baby, my sweet baby."

She mewed against his chest. "Mm."

He brushed the damp hair back from her face and kissed her lightly on the forehead, eyelids and the tip of her nose.

"Mm, you're some kind of woman. I've never known anyone like you."

"That's a big ditto for me, my friend."

"I'm glad you agree, chèr, 'cause my ego couldn't take it if you had," he said and followed with a long, low chuckle.

Chapter Eighteen

Jake sat at their dining table and stared out into the night. From the bar down the street, he made out the sounds of a jazz band. In the kitchen, Kate was fixing another pot of coffee.

"I think we both need this," she said and set a cup in front of him, then sat across the table from him. "There's a beignet leftover from yesterday. Want a bite?" She took a sip of coffee and bit into a beignet. Powdered sugar-coated her upper lip and the tip of her upturned nose. How he longed to reach over and lick and kiss it away. Instead, he wiped it with the pad of his thumb.

"Tell me about Ed. What kind of trouble were you in when he found you?"

"I was arrested for murder."

"*Murder*? Whose?"

"Her name was Delilah. She was—uh, a prostitute." Jake shrugged and the years slipped from his shoulders.

"You have to realize I was tall and looked older than my age. Delilah was my first. She took me in one rainy winter day, fed me, and well, you can probably figure out the rest." Yes, she'd bathed him and rocked him to sleep between her lush thighs. She had skin like milk chocolate and her body was ripe in contrast to Angie's slender, boyish one.

Kate shot him a knowing smile. "Yes. I'm pretty sure what happened next."

"Anyway, that day I was horny as the devil—well, like any day back then."

"That hasn't changed much. Thank goodness."

His mouth pulled into a smile. "Angie had blown me off for one of her regular johns." Lord, that Angie. When she wrapped her long legs around his waist, he damn near forgot everything Delilah'd taught him about pleasuring a woman. Angie was better than Mardi Gras and the Fourth of July all rolled in one.

"I went over to her crib and headed up to the fifth floor. I'd just rounded the fourth-floor landing and started up to the fifth when this tall black dude came skittering down the stairs. I yelled at him, but he slammed me against the wall and took off."

"What happened next?"

"I didn't think too much about it. I was intent on getting laid."

"Typical male," Kate said.

"Thanks, chèr. Glad I've restored your faith in my gender." He shook his head as the next memory surged.

"I tapped on Delilah's door, then opened it. She was sprawled on the floor. There was blood. Lots. She was covered in it. Her throat gaped. And the blood. So much blood."

"How horrible."

"I'd seen lots of bad things go down on the streets, but never anything like that. A switchblade lay in the pool of blood—blood that was still spurting from her throat."

Kate paled. "Omigod. She was still alive."

"Like a fool, I told her to hold on. I'd stop the bleeding. I got down on my knees and tried to pull the edges of the skin together. Anything to make the bleeding stop. Of course, it was wasted effort."

"You poor baby." She reached across the table and covered his hand with hers. It was a small measure of comfort, but welcome.

"I think she knew me for a second. Her eyelids fluttered, then opened. Then the light in her eyes went out, and the blood stopped gushing. I reached over and closed her eyes."

"I can't imagine what you must've gone through."

"I was a kid. Don't know whatever had made me think I could do anything for her."

"You were there. She didn't die alone. In this world, Jake, that means a lot."

Angie died alone, except for her killer. But Jake kept going. "I looked around the room, picked up the knife and wiped the blade on my sleeve. I figured if I hurried, I could still catch the bastard who killed her...and return the favor. I slipped the blade into my pocket and scrambled to my feet. There wasn't anything else I could do. Maybe a priest...but that would have to come later.

"Next thing I knew, there was a cop yelling and holding his gun on me. I tried to tell them what happened...that I'd found her dying."

"But they didn't believe you."

"Hell no, they didn't believe me. I wouldn't have believed me either. I'd just put the knife in my pocket. I was covered in her blood. The cop was joined by his partner, a big beefy, red-faced guy. They laughed and said it didn't take a detective to solve that murder and how they'd be heroes or maybe make detective themselves."

"How crude and insensitive. With the poor woman lying there on the floor."

"I tried to tell them about the guy I met coming down the stairs, but they wouldn't listen. They figured they had all the evidence they needed. Man, it was a fuckin' nightmare. I'd just about decided to take my chances and bolt for the door when Ed strolled in. He was a tall, muscled guy in a wrinkled suit. His hair was buzzed short like an ex-marine. At the time I didn't know he was my savior. I figured he was just another hard-nosed cop fixing to clean my clock."

"Good guess."

"The unis gave Ed their take on what had happened. Man, I was sweating bullets. I appealed to his better nature. I pleaded with the detective. Told him everything. That I saw the man responsible. I was a witness, not the killer. Then I started crying like some snot-nose kid."

"Aww."

"Ed asked how old I was. The unis thought I was unloading some bullshit, but Ed pointed out the blood I had on me was transfer, not spatter, and that the killer who slashed her throat was bound to be covered in spatter."

"Smart guy, and before all the CSI shows, too."

"He told them to bring me down to the station. They took my statement and set me up with an artist. I gave them a good enough description they recognized the guy as a fellow with a rap sheet that stretched from New Orleans to Baton Rouge. Ed saved my ass. The forensics proved him right. I had her blood on me, but the pattern wasn't right for the doer. Later they found trace evidence and connected him to the scene.

"So you weren't really arrested..."

"No, but I came mighty damn close. They held me for forty-eight hours. When Ed found out I didn't have a home, he took me in, sort of on trial at first, then he adopted me."

"I wish I could've known him. I'm sure I would've liked him."

"Hell, he'd have loved you."

"Really?" Her mouth pulled into a pleased smile.

"I love you, so it just figures..." The words. They just sort of spit out on their own. He couldn't take them back. Not that he wanted to.

Caitlin sent him a catlike smile of satisfaction, then bit her bottom lip. "That's another big ditto, big guy." She let out a heavy sigh. "I don't know what we're thinking. Actually, we're not thinking."

"No, Kate-with-a-K, we're feeling. And the two aren't necessarily connected."

"But we're connected, aren't we?"

"Yeah, we are. We can handle it, too. You'll see." And they would. He'd see to it. No matter what it took, he'd keep this woman close to his side and never let her go.

The next day dawned...finally. Caitlin had lost more sleep over Jake LeFevre than she cared to admit, but today was the day she would have another go at Heaton's office and his personal computer.

So much for best-laid plans. When she walked into Accounting, she found Lisette red-eyed and sniffling, attired in a white tutu, complete with ballet shoes.

"H-have you heard...about Ms. Andre?"

Had she heard? "Yes."

"Do they know who did it?"

"I don't think so."

"You went over there yesterday, didn't you? I recognized her address from the newspaper. It was the same as in the note from your husband."

"Yes, I met my husband there."

"You might've seen the killer?"

"I don't think so. We weren't there very long."

A cunning expression crossed the receptionist's face. "Did the police want to talk to you?"

Caitlin nodded. "They talked to both of us."

"Really? What did they ask you? How did they know you were there?"

How indeed?

"I didn't know you were that close to Ms. Andre, Lisette."

"She was always nice to me. Heaton couldn't stand her. I think she was pretty rough on him, especially since his wife is so sick."

"How long has she been ill?"

"For months, nearly a year. Poor woman. I don't know what he'll do when she goes. I don't think he has much of a life outside the office except for visiting her."

"That's a shame." Somehow, she must induce Lisette to leave the office.

"Why don't you have breakfast in the garden room? My treat. Have a caramel latte grande and eat a beignet for both of us."

Lisette glanced around uncomfortably. "I don't know if I should leave."

"I'll catch the phone. Heaton won't be in for another hour. He'll still be at the hospital with his wife."

"You're sure you don't mind?"

"I wouldn't have offered if I minded."

"Well, uh... Thanks, Kate."

As soon as Lisette shut the door behind her, Caitlin booted up her own computer and then eased into Heaton's office. The lock gave her only a couple of second's trouble and she was in. She opened his desk drawer and found his passwords taped in the bottom.

So much for spyware. She'd do this the old-fashioned way. "You make it too easy, Heaton. Now I'm going to find out just what's going on here."

She sat and scanned Heaton's files.

Personal, okay. "Let's see what you owe."

She found enormous hospital bills. Enough to bankrupt Trump, much less a midlevel accountant.

That was reason enough to embezzle, but where were the records that would prove the Rivera Corporation was moving large amounts of drug money through the casino?

Angie's files—that's where she'd find the real scoop. But the police would have already sealed her files...or had they?

As quickly as possible, she copied Heaton's files onto a flash drive. Never know what she might find.

A noise. Someone at the outer door.

Damn. Lisette must have cut her break short. She exited from Heaton's computer just in time. She stood and Heaton appeared in the doorway.

He wore a dejected expression which quickly changed to puzzlement. "Kate?"

"I heard your phone ring. I promised Lisette I'd catch the lines. She was pretty upset, so I told her to take a real break."

His brow furrowed. "I locked my office."

"It wasn't. Otherwise, I wouldn't be in here, would I?"

"No? I must've forgotten. Too much on my mind."

She smiled and slithered past him.

Crap. The flash drive.

Heaton didn't move. In fact, he seemed rooted to the floor.

She turned. "Are you all right?"

"My wife passed away yesterday afternoon."

"What?" That made three deaths in a couple of days. Just like

Bonnie had always said: deaths came in threes.

"Yes, she's out of her pain now."

"I'm so sorry for your loss." She hesitated. How could she hit him with another hard blow when he was already so down? "I hate to have to tell you this now, but have you heard about Ms. Andre?"

Shoulders slumped, he turned, dejection written over his expression. "What about her?"

"She was murdered yesterday."

"Oh." He shrugged. "Guess it had to happen sooner or later."

"What?"

"That woman was evil...a devil. Deserved to die." He walked over to his desk and sat. "Who called?"

"Sorry, they hung up. Didn't leave a message or speak."

He shivered and turned white. He reached for the phone, his hand shaking as if palsied.

"May I get you something? Coffee, water?" Poor man. Blind-sided by two deaths. But how long would that keep him from seeing the flash drive?

He waved her away. "I'll be all right. I just need some time to process it all."

"Why don't you go home? You shouldn't be here today. Lisette and I can handle whatever comes up."

"I just need a minute here, Kate...alone."

"All right. I'll be right outside...if you need anything."

Damn. Damn. Damn.

In her cubicle, she sat poised on the edge of her chair. Her foot seemed to have a will of its own. It tapped constantly as she waited for Heaton to leave.

Finally, she heard him stirring around the office.

Leave. Dammit, leave.

She held her breath and waited.

His office door opened. She breathed a sigh.

"I'll take your advice, Kate. I'm going home."

"Is there anything you need me to do? Have you—uh, made arrangements?"

A glassy-eyed expression of confusion crossed his face.

"Arrangements?" He paused as if he hadn't a clue what she meant. "Oh, yes. Graveside service at St. Louis's Cemetery...on Esplanade. Ten o'clock tomorrow. You're not obligated to attend."

"Do you have any family?"

"No, she was everything. All I had. As I said, you're not required to attend."

"Oh, you poor man." She put her arm around his shoulders. "I wouldn't want to intrude, but you really should have someone there. I'd be happy to—if you don't mind."

"Thank you, Kate. You're very kind."

"Again, I'm so sorry for your loss."

"Thank you."

She walked him to the door when it hit her. Who would mourn her if she died? Thirty-two years and what did she have to show for it?

Only Bonnie would care. Her father would attend her funeral and be grave and mournful. She was barely a blip on his personal radar. But it would make a great photo op. As for Jake, they were barely getting to know each other.

Okay. Heaton's gone. Get the drive.

Luckily, he'd actually forgotten to lock his office this time. She retrieved the flash, slipped it into her jacket pocket and was closing the door when Lisette returned.

"What are you doing in Heaton's office?"

"I was locking it for him. Poor man. He left here so distracted, he forgot. His wife passed away yesterday."

"What?"

"Mrs. Boyle and Ms. Andre, too? What's going on around here?"

"Well, you said Mrs. Boyle'd been sick a long time. Services are tomorrow at ten at St. Louis's cemetery. I think we should go."

Lisette nodded. "I guess we should. He doesn't have anyone else."

"That's what I thought."

"Which St. Louis cemetery? There're three."

"Three? Oh—he said on Esplanade."

"That's number three. It's not far from where I live in the Quarter."

"Why don't I pick you up? We can go together."

Lisette's eyes widened, but she nodded and gave Caitlin the address.

"It's at ten. I'll pick you up at nine-forty if that's okay?"

"Sure. Thanks."

Caitlin went to her cube and slipped the flash drive into her purse. Best work on his files at home where nosy Lisette couldn't pop in and catch her.

Chapter Nineteen

After closing the office at lunchtime, Caitlin headed home. Yes, she thought of the loft as home. Other than the townhouse in Georgetown, she'd never had a home. Playing house with Jake... God, it wasn't playing house. They were agents on an undercover operation. But the closer they became to being a real couple, the greater the risk to the op, as well as to the two of them. As much as she wanted to succeed, could she overlook her growing feelings for Jake and remain focused?

Originally having a family wasn't part of her career plan. Marriage maybe? But children were out of the question. She'd always vowed she wouldn't have children and then hand them over to Bonnie to rear as her father had.

That was before Jake when all she had was her career. And it was more important than anything else.

Until a few days ago, marriage hadn't been part of her plan. Not really. But being around Jake almost twenty-four/seven, she'd grown comfortable. And now he might even have a daughter. And what if they had kids together. Good grief! She must be losing her mind and jumping or rushing to conclusions.

The light ahead of her turned from yellow to red, and she stopped.

Losing focus could endanger both of them.

But how could she not think of his making love to her? The strength of his body as he knelt over her. His gentle, but sure touch when he stroked her breasts and thighs. The way he held her afterward, tenderly enfolded in his arms, his warm breath on her neck as they fell asleep. The memory sent a flush to her cheeks.

A horn honked. "Get a move on, lady!" the driver behind her screamed.

She tromped on the gas pedal and sped forward. She'd lost focus sitting at a stoplight for Pete's sake. How could she stay focused if it came down to their lives on the line? Maybe Jake was right. She couldn't hold her own, much less watch her partner's back.

Still embarrassed over her lapse in focus when she arrived home, she quickly assembled a salad. Because the visitation for Ed was scheduled the next evening Jake wouldn't be home until his evening shift ended. How he would manage to attend the visitation and attend to his duties at the casino she didn't know, but he'd come up with some kind of excuse or trade hours with one of the other men.

Alone in the loft, she'd have plenty of time for scouring Heaton's files, but without Jake's energetic presence, the place always seemed empty. Her footsteps echoed... A surge of loneliness swept over her. How much longer would they have before the operation was complete and they went their separate ways?

At eleven-thirty, Caitlin leaned back and stretched, rolled her head from side to side to straighten the kinks in her neck. The longer she pored over the files from Heaton's hard drive, the more surprises she found.

How stupid was that? His transactions were too easy to track.

Why would Angelique trust someone in her hire to embezzle money for her? Surely, she had better ways. What did she have on Heaton Boyle?

She reached for her bottle of Evian and took a long drink. Over the years, one thing proved true: blackmail was a risky profession and those who practiced it always ran the risk of being eliminated.

Did Heaton get tired of being blackmailed?

Why was she getting sidetracked with petty corporate embezzlement? Her assignment was to uncover the means involved in Rivera Corporation's money laundering scheme. Solving Angelique's murder might or might not be connected to the bigger picture.

She glanced at the computer clock. Eleven thirty-five.

Damn. She hadn't showered yet and Jake would be home soon. In bed and asleep was how she wanted him to find her. She didn't need a repeat of the previous evening's debauchery.

But was it really...debauchery? Such an old-fashioned word, but she'd always been kind of old-fashioned. For Pete's sake, she was a Republican and all that entailed. Somehow, she couldn't imagine anyone in the party doing half the things she'd done with Jake last night.

She'd lost count how many times had Jake made her come.

Whoa. This train of thought was going nowhere fast. Just thinking about him and his wonderful hands and lips sent prickles of sensation to that best un-thought about part of her body.

She jumped up, stripped off her clothes and left them where they lay. She turned on the shower, adjusted the temperature and stepped under the rain shower head. Lathering her body with clean-scented Aloe Vera triple-milled soap, her hands touched her nipples and found that, like the rest of her body, they were still sensitive from their lovemaking. The hot water sluiced down her body and eased all the tender spots along with the muscles in her back and thighs.

Jeez, how wide had she spread her legs anyway? At the apex of her thighs, she touched her most tender area. Her inner muscles clenched as she slid the bar of soap against her labia. Leaning against the cool tile to brace her back, she massaged her clit. Her thigh muscles jittered, still weak from lovemaking nearly all night.

Jake had known exactly how to please her over and over. Why couldn't she just...

The clichés came to mind: go with the flow, take it while you can get it, just take it.

"I could help with that."

A naked and already erect Jake stood in the doorway, smiling.

Caitlin jumped and dropped the soap; it clunked heavily against the shower stall floor. One hand flew upwards and covered her breasts; the other remained lower and covered her pubic area.

"Out of here. Privacy please."

"I'm not blind. You need some help with..." He paused and positively leered at her, before adding, "...your back."

"No. My back's just fine."

"Then you can wash mine."

With a cheeky grin, he stepped right into the shower with her.

"You can wash your own damned back. Get out of here." She shoved him, somewhat ineffectually.

"You're in the shower at the exact time I'm expected home. What else could I think except that you've come to your senses and wanted to be naked and ready for love when I arrived?"

"Smug, aren't you." She kept eyeing his erection. His gaze kept going from her breasts to her eyes.

"Like what you see? It's all yours...if you want it?" His tone was low and sent a warm feral thrill to her lower belly.

She shook her head; her hair fell in her eyes. "N-no."

He reached forward and lifted the damp locks from her face. Without volition, she moaned from the inner muscles contracting between her legs.

"Is that a 'yes'?" He took a step forward, closing the space between them. His jutting penis pressed into her belly. Hot, hard. Just the way she wanted him. God, she wanted him.

His lips were warm and tender on her neck. Another thrill sliced through her and weakened her knees. What power this man had over her. Why couldn't she resist his hands and lips? She groaned, "Y-yes."

He stopped kissing her. "Sorry I interrupted you when I came in, but I can do a better job."

Her breath caught in her throat as her heart pounded in her chest. She gazed up into his eyes and bit her lower lip. "I know you can."

He took her hand in his and placed it against his chest. "See what you do to me, woman. My heart's ready to explode."

She smiled. "I think the explosion will be lower." She touched him and stroked the soft skin of his shaft.

"Careful. Not yet."

He knelt before her and gently opened her lips and licked her. "Mm. I love the taste of you. You're so wet and juicy." His tongue dipped inside and out, then flicked her clit.

A mewling whimper escaped her. Torturing her again, was he? "Please."

He picked her up and she wrapped her legs around his waist. He nudged at her opening. His muscular hands cupped her hips, then he thrust hard and was inside her, stretching and filling her like no one ever had. Her back jarred against the stall with each slow stroke. The shower sprayed water over their heaving bodies, steam filled the stall, water ran in her eyes.

But she could still see the soft brown gaze of the man she loved...the man she loved to fuck...no, she loved him, pure and simple. Never could she share her body with such a loss of abandon with anyone but him.

Each slow stroke tortured her as he slammed into her over and over again, deeper and deeper. Thrust for thrust she matched him until...her body burned, her nipples tightened into sensitive buds, her breasts bobbed, and he buried his face in the valley between them, lapping the moisture collected there.

His strokes quickened, each one ramming her into the shower wall. She rode his hard dick, grasping his shoulders steadying her body for the onslaught. She came. Wave after fiery wave of giddy sensation shuddered through her leaving her weak, limp and gasping for air.

"Oh, chèr," he breathed into her ear. "You are some kind of woman. My woman."

Gently he withdrew and reached for two towels. He wrapped a towel around her head and patted dry her entire body with the other.

"I'm sorry. I'm an idiot," she barely managed to gasp.

"I'm takin' you to bed." True to his words, he picked her up and headed for their bed. "You need a good night's sleep tonight."

"Mm-hm," she murmured against his chest, the chest hairs

tickling her nose. "Have to go to a funeral tomorrow morning."

Jake set Caitlin on the bed and covered her beautiful nakedness with a sheet. "I thought you said the funeral was set for the day after tomorrow."

"Omigod. I forgot to tell you. Heaton Boyle's wife died the same day Angie was murdered. Mrs. Boyle's funeral is tomorrow at ten."

"She did?" Could the death of Boyle's wife have triggered a murderous rage in the timid accountant?

He finished toweling his body and slid between the cool sheets, then snuggled Caitlin in his arms. Poor thing, she was already asleep. God, how he loved her.

No point in thinking like that. They fucked together like a dream. By far she was the most responsive woman he'd ever known. But she was set on advancing in the Bureau. Would she even want marriage or kids, especially an autistic teenage daughter? In every way, except in bed, they were a disaster as a couple.

The bright winter dawn awakened Jake. He yawned, rubbed his eyes, then rolled over and patted Kate on the ass. "Where's the funeral?"

"St. Louis Cemetery, Number three. The one on Esplanade."

"That's number three all right." He pulled her closer, inhaled her fresh scent, wrapping his legs around hers.

Only too aware of his intent, she sat up and grinned. "There's no time for that."

"Are you sure?"

"Absolutely. I'm meeting Lisette, and we're going to the funeral together."

"Poor guy will appreciate it. Although when he's arrested for embezzling, I doubt it'll make much difference."

"I know, but I can't help but feel sorry for him. He seems to be disintegrating before my eyes. He's jumpy. His hair's greasy, overgrowing his collar. Looks like he's sleeping in his clothes—if he's sleeping at all. Not quite clean." She wrinkled her nose.

"His wife just died, Kate."

"I know. Poor man, but he forgets where the shower is?"

"His whole life has fallen apart. Grief can take a lot of different forms."

His lowered tone brought her back to reality. Shame wracked through her; she reached out and touched his shoulder. "Oh— Jake, I'm such an idiot. I wasn't thinking."

"'S'all right. It's a different situation entirely."

"No, it isn't, not really. You've both lost someone who was more important to you than anyone else in the whole world. You lost the only real father you've ever known. Heaton was devoted to his wife. She *was* his life. He could've embezzled some of those funds to pay her medical bills."

"And I'd bet my left ball that Angelique was behind the embezzling. She had to pay for her daughter's school somehow. Besides, I distinctly remember from orientation that Rivera employees have hospital insurance."

Reluctant to leave an active brainstorming session, she suggested, "Of course we do. But his wife was sick for a long time, and she might've reached her lifetime limit. And it depends on the plan he chose. If they had an eighty-twenty plan, that twenty percent could wipe out his life savings in a hurry. That's something I'll look into. But if we find out insurance covered his wife's hospital bills, why would he get involved with Angelique's embezzling? Why wouldn't he just report her? That would be the most ethical path for him."

Jake levered up on his elbow. "Maybe she had something on him."

"Then we need to find out what. Do you think the locals will cooperate if we need access to everything they have on Angelique?"

"Considering I'm the prime suspect in her death, chances of that happening are slim to none." Jake shook his head.

"Maybe if I made the approach?"

She glanced at the clock. Crap. Eight-thirty already. She rose from the bed. "After the funeral, I'll go downtown and talk to the detectives on her case. What are your plans today?"

He grinned and gave her body an up-and-down appreciative glance. How had she become so comfortable with him? She was naked as the day she was born and hadn't even given it a thought until he leered.

"I've been given bereavement time. I need to touch base with the funeral director about Ed's service. Then I thought I'd go to the school."

"Bridgeview?"

"Yeah."

"If you can wait until this afternoon, I'd like to go with you. You don't have to go through all this alone."

His warm brown gaze softened. "Thanks, chèr."

"I wish I hadn't committed to going to Mrs. Boyle's funeral, but honestly I feel like I ought to go.

"It's all right." He caressed her cheek.

Too bad she had to meet Lisette for the funeral. She wouldn't have minded staying in bed a little longer. Jake's six-pack was more than admirable. The sheet couldn't hide his morning woody.

He grinned. "Sorry, but you have this effect on me."

"You're not sorry at all. I'm the one who's sorry, but I'm running late."

After hopping from the bed, she hit the shower and adjusted the water temperature a few degrees cooler than usual. Damn, but memories of their last shower together had her wanting nothing more than to jump his bones until she was cured of his intense sexual pull. Or was that the road to addiction?

No, loving someone and craving his body twenty-four/seven wasn't an addiction, it was normal. The water sluiced down her body, but thoughts of how they'd ever make a relationship, not to mention family, work still nagged at her.

If the girl was actually his, how would she manage an autistic teenager? Of course, he wouldn't desert the child—if she was his—and if they had a chance in hell of making a go of their lives together, his child would of necessity be a major factor.

The real question was: was Caitlin up to the challenge?

Chapter Twenty

The sun shone brightly, glinting off the hood of Caitlin's new rental car, a silver Intrepid, giving the air a dazzling energy that belied the wintry season and making it a fine day for a funeral. She turned into the narrow street and stopped in front of Lisette's apartment building in the French Quarter. The old, balconied building was in dire need of a fresh coat of paint, but luckily it hadn't been destroyed by Katrina. In fact, the Vieux Carré was mainly untouched by the nightmarish storm. The odor of shrimp remoulade or gumbo wafted through her open car window. Someone was already cooking lunch. Her stomach growled, reminding her she'd skipped breakfast.

She spied Lisette attired in black, but the inappropriately large black hat and veil made her co-worker look more like the grieving widow than a mere funeral attendee. Jeez, what was the woman thinking? Was she trying to impress Heaton?

Caitlin's own stylish black suit, subtle silver earrings, and butterfly brooch were far more appropriate for the situation.

Lisette opened the car door and slid into the passenger seat; her short skirt crept up to show some very fat, dimpled knees before it was tugged down.

Hmm. Better lay off the beignets before mine start looking like that.

"Are you ready for this?" Caitlin asked, more to make conversation than anything else.

"No." Lisette's ebony hat and veil shimmered as the woman shook her head. "Poor Heaton. He was so devoted to his wife. I can't imagine how he'll manage without her. He used to be so neat and trim; his wife kept him that way. She's from an old New Orleans family, the De la Vegas, you know? That's why her burial is at the St. Louis 'cause there's an old family vault. The family money's long gone, but she was a lady…a real lady." She sniffed into her black lace handkerchief and emitted a low wail.

Jeez. What had she gotten herself into? If Heaton acted up, it would be bad enough, but expected, but with melodramatic Lisette along, heaven only knew what she would pull.

They parked on the side of the road and walked by a line of tour buses.

Once inside the iron gates of the cemetery, Caitlin marveled at the eerily beautiful scene. Because of the low water table, New Orleans vaults were built above ground. Row after row of sun-bleached stone vaults, many topped by stone or iron crosses, were separated by paved paths. "However will we find Heaton in all these vaults?"

"Mrs. Heaton, right after she was diagnosed, told me the family crypt was in the north corner." Lisette glanced up at the sun and pointed north. "That way."

Caitlin followed, stepping gingerly. Tourists followed their guides and she followed Lisette. The longer she walked, the more the surreal atmosphere became. Some tombs had guttered out candles in front of them—an offering to some voodoo priestess perhaps? She shivered.

They finally reached the north corner. A priest and two mortuary attendants wearing black suits and thin black ties were standing by Heaton.

Poor man. He truly was alone in the world. He appeared more hunched and gaunter than ever. His suit was new—a price tag still hung from the sleeve. Her fingers itched to rip it away. His white shirt collar was half in and half out. Again she wanted to smarten him up a bit.

Lisette stepped forward and whispered in his ear. His eyes, dull with grief and red with weeping, widened for a second. He fumbled with his collar and managed to set it straight. He yanked at the price tag and stuffed it into his pocket.

Caitlin stepped forward and offered her hand. "We're so sorry for your loss. Is there anything we can do?"

He shook his head. "No, nothing. I'll be all right."

The priest gave a brief blessing, and thankfully the service was over.

Heaton managed to hold it together quite bravely until the end. Lisette held his hand through the entire ceremony and started to weep uncontrollably when the crypt was closed.

"She was such a good woman, a true lady. I'm so sorry for you, Heaton," she said, blubbering into a black lace-trimmed handkerchief.

First Heaton's hands began to tremble; next, his shoulders shook as if he had a chill, then he collapsed and would've hit the ground if the two attendants hadn't caught him. One of them whipped out a small ampoule of smelling salts and waved it under Heaton's nose.

The unfortunate man shook his head and opened his eyes. "Wh-what happened?"

Lisette flipped back her long veil, revealing her funereal makeup—nearly white foundation, bright red lipstick and dark, very arched eyebrows. "You fainted, Heaton. You poor dear. I'm going home with you. You shouldn't be alone. You need someone to take care of you." She draped her arms around him and led him from the site.

"I guess you don't need a ride home?" Caitlin called rather half-heartedly after the departing couple. "Guess not."

Who knew Lisette was cemetery shopping for a husband?

Just as well—she'd now have time to check with the local detectives and then meet Jake for the trip to Bridgeview Academy.

Once she was cleared by the desk sergeant, Caitlin found her way to Sergeant Pelletier's desk. The red-faced detective was poring over the morning *Times-Picayune* and sipping coffee from a Styrofoam cup.

"Detective Pelletier."

The detective slowly folded his paper, then finally met her gaze with a glare. "Mawnin', Special Agent Chaney. What can I do you for?"

"I just wondered if you were in the mood to share any intel you might have on the Andre murder?" Caitlin couched her words with a smile. Charming him couldn't hurt and it might just help.

"Now, ma'am—sorry, Agent—here at the NOPD, we're known for our cooperation and desire to—"

"Now I know you like my partner for her murder, but we're in the middle of an important investigation, and I really would appreciate your help. Believe me, I've driven him to distraction and pissed him off more than once. He leaves when he's angry. He doesn't engage."

Pelletier nodded. "First of all, you're his boss—right?"

"I'm in charge of the operation, yes." Where was Pelletier going with his smug questions?

"He'd be pretty stupid to 'engage' his boss." His mouth quirked to one side, but his gaze pinned her. "Appears you find him a little engagin' yourself."

"Our cover is that of a married couple. We've come to know each other in the process. That's why I'm sure you'd want to give me a hand with this tiny little matter." Caitlin took a deep breath. Why was she wasting her breath trying to explain?

Her fingers beat an uneasy tattoo against her thigh, but she kept smiling. "Please don't tell me, my being here is a waste of time."

Pelletier leaned back and rocked back and forth in his chair. "Not a waste of time, as far as I'm concerned." His lopsided grin grew wider and his gaze more pointed. "Your little visit tells me a lot."

Like what?

Keep loading on the charm. It might actually work. "I really would appreciate any updates on the Andre case. Ms. Andre was integral to our money-laundering investigation of the Rivera Corporation. Her death is inconvenient, as well as a personal tragedy for a member of my team."

"Agent Chaney, if we turn up anything related to money laundering, we'll be more than happy to share it with the Bureau. The murder is under local jurisdiction, and don't either one of y'all leave town."

He took a sip of his coffee and retrieved his newspaper.

So much for charm. So much for interdepartmental cooperation.

"Thank you, Sergeant. I knew you'd see things my way." Like hell he had.

She glanced at her watch. Twelve-thirty. Just enough time to meet Jake.

"I'm glad you came," Jake said, covering Caitlin's hand with his. Her presence was a much-needed calming influence.

They drove up to the private school's gate and stopped.

He rolled down the window, smiled pretty for the security camera and said, "Jake LeFevre and Caitlin Chaney to see Ms. Massey."

The wrought-iron gate opened, and he drove through the stone arch. The drive to the main school building was long and narrow. The gnarled branches of tall live oaks on either side of the lane entwined over the lane forming a shady green canopy.

At the far end, the trees gave way to a clearing where an antebellum mansion stood proudly.

Some school.

His tires crunched in the pea gravel drive as he pulled to a stop. As instructed, he walked up the steps and banged the brass knocker against the carved mahogany door.

It opened silently. A penguin of a butler inclined his head ever so slightly. "Ms. Massey awaits you in the library."

They followed the butler through the marble-tile foyer into the library.

Impressive was an understatement. Everything was done in silk brocade. Ms. Massey herself looked as if she'd been cured and tanned, even if her stylish suit was well-cut and worn with an elegant air.

"Mr. LeFevre. Ms. Chaney," she said with a business-like nod.

"Yes." He pulled his credentials from his jacket and allowed the headmistress to examine them carefully. He imagined she did everything carefully.

She motioned for them to be seated. "How may I help you, Agent LeFevre?"

He settled his long frame precariously on the gilt-armed settee. Damn thing must be worth a mint. Caitlin sat next to him, her hand in his. "I'm here about Miss Andre's daughter."

Hands folded primly on the desk, she glanced at him over her half glasses. "And what is the FBI's interest in the child?"

"Miss Andre informed me shortly before her death that Charlotte is my daughter."

She straightened. Her eyes widened, then she pursed her lips. "And what proof is there other than your word?"

"I'm prepared to have my DNA tested against hers. If she's my child, I'm ready to accept full responsibility."

"That's admirable, but I'll require a court order before I can allow any invasive tests."

"It wouldn't have to be invasive. Her hairbrush or toothbrush would contain a sufficient DNA sample for the test."

"And if she is your daughter, what then?"

"I live in DC when I'm not on assignment. I'll look into schools there—special ones—like the one she has here."

"It's not that simple, Agent LeFevre. Charlotte's been here for five years and she's made amazing progress. She's nearly ready to leave us, but she'll always require a somewhat sheltered environment. A consistent one at the very least. How do you expect to care for her? Are you married?"

"No, not yet." He didn't dare glance at Caitlin. Dumping this on her wasn't part of the plan.

"Miss Andre has provided for her child very well financially, but the plan was for Charlotte to live with her mother. That's what we've been working toward for some time. Currently, she's under my guardianship as a ward of the State. There's no provision for releasing Charlotte into the custody of anyone else...father or no. You have no idea about the state bureaucracy you'll be dealing with."

"Believe me, I know all about bureaucracy."

Ms. Massey gave him a tight smile. "I'm sure you do; however, first, let's find out if you are her father, then we'll proceed from there."

"Fine."

The headmistress picked up the phone and punched a button. "Aurelia, bring Charlotte's hairbrush to my office. No, don't clean it. Bring it as it is."

"Thank you, Ms. Massey."

"Charlotte is housed in Magnolia Cottage. It's a ten-minute walk from here."

"I don't suppose I could see her? I wouldn't approach her or anything."

"She's in art class. You may observe her through the two-way mirror."

"Like an interrogation room?"

"Similar. Most parents are content with the term observation room. It's less disruptive for our students."

She led them through the house and outside to a large one-story building whose roof was pierced with multiple skylights. Inside the observation room with his mind awhirl with all the possibilities, he walked over to the window and took a deep breath. "Which one is she?"

"Charlotte is the girl in the corner working on the stone sculpture. When she came to us, she was unfocused and fragile. Now she's a gifted artist."

Charlie, no—Charlotte was better—was a tiny slip of a girl, hair and eyes so dark, he wondered how Angie could've been her mother. The dexterity and strength of her hands as she worked the stone with her chisel amazed him. Such delicacy and strength in one small package.

"Her hair and complexion are like yours," Caitlin said, "but her pale gray eyes are like Angelique's."

"Yes, there's some resemblance, Mr. LeFevre, I can see that, but..." The headmistress paused.

"I know. DNA results first."

"Yes, I'll confer with our attorney, and we'll proceed at that time."

He had forced his gaze from the girl...his daughter?

"Charlotte has made great strides since coming to us. But anyone who gives her a home will need to be educated very quickly. We are happy to do that here."

Could he take a leave of absence from the Bureau? He'd have to if...

"If you are indeed her father, then I will be able to go into the specifics of her problems and her gifts. I'm required to protect her privacy."

"I understand."

He turned for a final glimpse of his maybe daughter. It hit him: she looked like an old picture he had of his mother. God, she had to be his daughter. The responsibility he would likely take on shook him. It wouldn't just be a matter of taking a leave of absence. It would be a vast life change for both of them.

What about Caitlin? He couldn't ask her to take on something that was his responsibility alone. A woman might want to care for another woman's child, but an autistic child? She was a good woman, if somewhat rigid in her approach to life, but it was too much. Way too much.

The thought of spending the rest of his life without her sickened him. Their pretend marriage had become a real partnership...and now it was derailed before it could move to the next level.

DNA. Everything depended on the DNA. Hell. The test was a formality. Gut deep, he knew. Charlotte was his daughter.

Chapter Twenty-one

On the trip back to the loft and acutely aware of Jake's agitation, Caitlin drove while he rambled and gesticulated wildly.

"Yes," he said. "She's mine. I know it. The DNA test will confirm it. You saw her. She's a tiny little thing, but so strong. My daughter's a sculptor. The kid certainly knows her way around a chisel, doesn't she? She's incredible...really."

Keeping her eyes on the road ahead, but determined to play the devil's advocate, Caitlin persevered. "What makes you so sure?"

"She looks just like my mother. I have one photo of my mom—just the two of us—before she ran off with God knows who. Same jet-black hair, skin like ivory."

"Come on, Jake. Be logical. You're getting ahead of yourself. What if you're wrong and the girl isn't yours?"

He clenched his fist and hit his knee. "Charlotte. Her name is Charlotte. If she's not mine, the director of the school is her appointed guardian. But if Charlotte is my daughter, I'll take steps to care for her. I won't abandon her."

"Of course you won't. But how, Jake? How will you manage your career and this gifted but challenged girl? After all, Angelique resorted to embezzlement to provide for her daughter. What will *you* do?" What will *we* do was the unspoken question Caitlin didn't have the courage to ask aloud? Not yet.

"I don't how I'll manage, but I won't run out on her. I know it won't be easy. Ed didn't give up on me. I won't give up on her. I have time to make arrangements. Nothing will change immediately."

"At least Angie thought that far ahead."

"It's a tragedy, and now Charlotte's almost ready to mainstream. She would've been living with her mother."

"But, Jake, it wasn't going to happen. We were already homing in on Angelique as part of our investigation. We already knew she embezzled money to pay for Charlotte's school. Unless she turned State's evidence and gave up her bosses for money laundering, she would've gone to prison. None of her plans and hopes for Charlotte would've come to fruition." Caitlin sighed, but couldn't help wondering what the future held for the young teen

He reached over and touched her knee. "This really puts a major wrinkle in our investigation. Sorry."

His touch unnerved her. She clenched the steering wheel and maneuvered around a slow-moving semi. But he was right about complications and not just about the investigation. If Angelique's daughter was Jake's, their new relationship could suffer if she didn't step up and support him. "We're a team in more ways than one, Jake."

He shook his head. "What we're doing here is different. As a couple, we have choices. *You* have choices. With Charlotte, I don't have a choice. If the roll of the dice says she's my kid, then she's my responsibility for good."

"Somehow we'll manage. You're a good man. I know you'll do the right thing, no matter how the DNA test turns out."

"You just said 'we'll manage.' You didn't sign on to cure my problems, Kate. I appreciate your listening, more than you know, but you have your own career to consider."

"But I've seen her, too, Jake. She's so like you. How could I not care about her?" All right. What was the old saying—in for a penny, in for a pound?

"Neither of us knows what we're getting into."

"Wait until we know for sure one way or another, then we'll do the research," she insisted. "I'll help. I'm a part of this."

"Kate, we're on an undercover operation. All this other..." he waved his hands, "is driving me crazy."

"Short drive, if you ask me," she said pertly in an attempt to pull him back to a modicum of sanity.

"What?"

Rush hour traffic was heavy. She didn't dare take her gaze off the road. Finally, she heard him take a deep breath.

"I get it. I'm obsessing and—"

"You got that right, fella."

"I don't know what I'd do without you right now."

"Frankly I don't either, but you don't have to find out. I'm here for the long haul or at least," she craned her neck and checked her blind spot before changing lanes, "until we get back to the loft."

"We've come a long way, Kate."

"Don't you mean *v* have?" Realizing how egocentric she sounded, she amended, "Just kidding. Of course, we have."

From hatred on sight to lovers and more...but how much more? Was she ready to give up her dream career? Better yet, was she truly up to supporting Jake's plan of taking on his autistic teenage daughter?

"It's good to be home," Caitlin said, glancing around the loft. "It really feels like home, doesn't it?"

Jake's arms went around her, and he nuzzled her neck. "Anywhere you are, chèr, feels like home to me."

She turned to face him, slipped her arms around his neck and gazed into his dark brown eyes. They were full of warmth and glittered with desire. "That has a suspicious sound to me, Agent LeFevre." She tiptoed and gave him a light peck on the cheek.

"Suspicious, how so?"

"Like maybe you're thinking of having your way with me." She twitched her shoulders and rubbed against his broad chest.

"Knew I couldn't fool a smart special agent like you, Chaney. Guilty as charged." He inched her farther into the loft and nodded toward the bed. "There's a great big old bed over there."

"I know. I have a notion about having a little lie-down..." She finished with a southern drawl, "...after our long drive and all."

"Music to my ears. You're a woman after my own heart."

"That was my plan all along," she said with a giggle since absolutely nothing was farther from the truth. As much as she loved being with him, she couldn't always put aside the idea of his having a daughter. If only it were the two of them, it was clear they might actually have a chance of a lasting relationship, but the ramifications of his having a child definitely muddied the Mississippi.

He scooped her up in his arms and carried her the rest of the way.

"You are my heart," he whispered.

"Never doubted it for a moment," she murmured, biting her bottom lip and still hiding her doubts. Here he had a chance at having a family, and she was worried about how it might affect her life. Selfish. That's what she was. Selfish and confused.

He took her sweetly, gently as if for the first time. And when they came, they came together utterly and completely.

While Jake napped, Caitlin eased from the bed and padded over to the desk. She booted up her laptop. What could it hurt to do a little preliminary research on autism? Jake was damned certain Charlotte was his. How would he ever be able to afford the same type of schooling the girl was used to? Angie had resorted to embezzlement and extortion to pay her daughter's tuition. And the FBI sort of frowned on their agents doing the same.

While it was true she could afford the girl's tuition, it remained to be seen if Jake would allow her to contribute to his daughter's schooling. He was proud and stubborn. It would all depend on her powers of persuasion.

She found numerous sources. The longer she read, the more respect she gained for parents of children with any of the Pervasive Perspective Disorders.

Research. Definitely. Autism/Asperger's Syndrome— So much information. How to absorb it all?

Inside a selfish little voice said, "Don't be silly. If she's Jake's daughter, she's his problem."

No, she argued. Not true. If she and Jake had a future together, and it looked like they might, Charlotte would be her opportunity. She refused to call the gifted young woman a problem.

Opportunity was an understatement. Together they could give Jake's daughter a real home with a real family.

But it would mean sacrifices. Was she really prepared to make them? Give up her career plans? Give up showing everyone she had value beyond who her father was?

Wait a minute. She was getting ahead of herself. They didn't know for sure that Jake was the girl's her father or if he even wanted Caitlin in his lifelong term.

And first, there was the wake and funeral to get through before any DNA results would ever come back. One step at a time.

The sun had already sunk below the horizon and there was an unaccustomed nip in the air when Jake and Caitlin pulled into the parking lot at Rotier's. The funeral home occupied a three-story brick house. Square white columns and gingerbread carvings decorated the entrance. Someone's idea of refinement, he supposed.

Caitlin reached over and patted his knee. "Are you going to be okay?"

"Yeah. Mainly it'll be some of Ed's old pals. They'll be here most of the night. Telling stories and raising one in his name every thirty minutes or so."

She gave him a smile that was probably meant to be encouraging. "Sounds like quite a party to me."

"Yeah, that's 'bout it. Might get rowdy 'fore the night's over." He squared his shoulders and sucked in a deep breath. Might as well get it over with.

"So, you're ready?" She raised an eyebrow and unlocked her door.

"Not really, but it's not like I have a choice."

Her clear green eyes were soft with emotion. "I know. But you'll get through it. For what it's worth, I'm here for you."

"It means a lot, Kate. Worth a lot." If she only knew. Here he was a big shot FBI agent and scared to stare death in the face, specifically the death of his father. A good man and a good cop, Ed shouldn't have died alone.

Jake eased from the car and met Kate on the brick walk leading to the front porch. Before he could reach for her, she grabbed his hand and held on tightly. Her warmth and strength radiated through him, maybe even touched his heart. She was a good woman, too. Deserved the best. Better than him, anyway.

Kate, so close by his side, her musky floral perfume assailed his senses. She was career-bound for better things than undercover work. A successful outcome on this op would put her in line for another promotion. She deserved it, and he wouldn't stand in her way.

They climbed the steps and entered the mortuary. "Hoolihan," he said to the solemn greeter.

"Second room on the left."

"Thanks."

Still holding hands with Kate, Jake walked into the visitation room. The carpets were the rich color of wine and thick underfoot. Lighting was subdued and provided by torchieres that flanked either side of the casket. His peripheral vision noted the presence of several older men. But first, he needed to face Ed.

The coffin was left open. According to the funeral director, being able to see the deceased was supposed to help the family and other mourners with closure. Frankly, he would've preferred it closed, but he wouldn't deny Ed's old friends this last chance to see him.

Jake eased forward, dreading the moment when he had no choice but to gaze on his father's still face. Even though Ed's death had been more or less expected, it didn't make it any easier.

His knees buckled for a second, then steadied. Mounted on the left of the casket was an eleven by fourteen photographic portrait which had been taken in his father's prime. Ed stood proudly in his uniform. Now that was the real Ed Hoolihan, the one Jake remembered so well. That was his father, not the shrunken man in a satin-lined coffin with a rosary of black beads in his hands.

He released Kate's hand, then dropped to his knee on the kneeling bench and quickly made the sign of the cross.

Everything was as Ed would have wanted, and he'd have to content himself with having carried out his wishes. He rose, grabbing the back of the pew to steady himself.

"Are you all right?' Kate asked, her gaze watchful and full of concern.

He regained his balance and nodded. "I'm fine." He turned ready to meet his father's colleagues, most of whom he guessed were in their fifties to sixties.

One of them stepped forward, a grizzled man who was seventy if he was a day. He held out his hand. "Jake? You're his boy, the one he took in?"

Jake took the old man's hand. "Yes. Yes, I am."

"Tom Brennen. I just want to say how sorry I am for your loss. Ed was a good cop. I was his first partner when he joined the force."

"He spoke of you often and kindly, sir," Jake said with a smile.

Brennen laughed. "And well he should. He was the most stubborn young officer I ever worked with. And honest as the day is long."

"I certainly appreciate your dropping by. There's a spot of refreshment if you're feeling dry," Jake offered and nodded toward the bar set up at the back of the room.

"Might be a touch on the dry side, now you mention it." He nodded at Caitlin. "Fine looking wife you got there, boy."

Caitlin smiled and glanced lovingly up at Jake. His heart clutched in his chest. If only she were his wife.

"Yes, sir. She's mighty fine." Most of Ed's older friends were retired and wouldn't know anything about his being a murder suspect. Hopefully, Sweeney and Pelletier wouldn't bother to come by and express their sympathies.

The next couple of hours were more of the same. Men offering their condolences and moseying to the back of the room. Caitlin's reassuring presence grounded him. Kept him sane.

Around ten o'clock it was five old men, Jake and Caitlin.

Tom Brennen hoisted a plastic cup with a shot of whiskey. "To Ed Hoolihan, here's hoping you make it to Heaven afore the devil knows you're dead."

Caitlin frowned. "What?"

Jake laughed. "It's an old Irish toast suitable to the occasion."

"Sounds almost like an insult," she whispered.

He laughed. "Not at all."

Brennen downed another sip of whiskey. "Now, Jake, did Ed ever tell you about the time he took two nuns from one motherhouse to their new one in Baton Rouge?"

Jake smiled, knowing his father's old partner was about to tell a funny story, probably exaggerated. "I don't believe he did."

"Is this the start of a joke?" Caitlin leaned forward and asked.

"No, darlin' this story is a true one." Brennen laughed, then cleared his throat. "Seems Ed used to give the local Little Sisters of the Poor a hand now and again. Anyway, they were driving to Baton Rouge, didn't take the Interstate—it was still under construction, you see—Sister Michael and Sister Mary Luke were sitting in the back seat and as they were going through one of the small towns, they got stopped by a train. And you have to understand policemen tend to use more colorful language when amongst themselves. Anyway, they're stopped and waiting and waiting. 'Sure is a long-assed train,' slips out of the good detective's mouth afore he remembers the two sisters in the back seat. He hears the sisters suck in a breath in shock at his raw language. 'Sorry, sisters.' He says, 'I'm not used to such refined company.' 'Faith, detective. It's too late. We've already heard you.' Then they set to giggling like schoolgirls, he said."

Jake and Caitlin both laughed. A funny story anytime, but even funnier after three whiskeys. At least for Jake. Caitlin had already abstained and was nursing a cup of coffee.

Ed's last partner, Bob Grogan, in his early fifties with dimming red hair, slapped his knee and guffawed. "I've got a better one than that."

"Tell us," Jake encouraged Grogan. He'd known Ed such a short time of his life—only sixteen years.

"Ed and I were investigating a robbery-homicide extortion scheme. See, there was this couple from Metairie. They preyed on upscale couples with too much time on their hands, met 'em at swinging parties, then they'd hold one of 'em hostage, usually the husband, and force the wife to withdraw most of the money from their bank account. Got wind of it because one of the wives was a karate expert. She put a hammerlock on her kidnapper and called the police."

"Man, what with AIDS and blackmailing swingers, it just don't pay to play 'round anymore," Brennen said, with a wheezing laugh.

Maybe it was the booze getting to him, but Jake joined in the laughter.

"Anyhow, we traced down a couple who'd placed an ad in a swinger's magazine, found they'd filed a robbery report. We went to see 'em. First, we met a sweet young thing who ID'd herself as the younger sister. Then came in a woman with a face and an attitude like a bulldog's. Then the husband rolled in and declared he didn't know anything about any robbery report." Grogan stopped and chuckled.

"Turns out the husband was swinging with the younger sister. The wife flew into a rage, knocked her sister out and blacked her husband's eye before Ed and I could get her under control. I'm tellin' you that was one pissed-off woman and she would've got away if Ed hadn't grabbed her by her sweatpants and tackled her. Her pants came down and the sight of that dimpled arse still haunts my nightmares. Then she elbowed Ed, blacked his eye, too, all the while screaming about police brutality. 'Lady,' he says, 'if you were the last woman on earth, you'd be safe from me.'"

At the last of the story, Jake was in the middle of swallowing. He coughed and choked. "Good one. Have to remember that." There was so much he'd never heard about Ed's life on the job. Surrounded by Ed's best friends and comforted by Kate, the ache in his heart eased a bit. He'd miss his father for a long time, but in truth, the real Ed had been gone since his line of duty injury and subsequent stroke.

Around one-thirty in the morning with Caitlin's arm around

Jake for support, they staggered to the car. "Wha's on the agenda for tomorrow, chèr?"

Stone-cold sober, Caitlin sighed. "With Heaton on leave, I'll run into the office for a couple of hours, then I'll meet you back home for the funeral. How's that sound?" From all the drinking he'd done at the wake, she wasn't sure he'd sober up in time for the funeral.

"All right with me. You sure you can drive?" he asked. "Wouldn't want to get in trouble with the law."

"I'm fine. Haven't had anything except coffee and bottled water tonight. I can drive."

"Good, 'cause you know what? I can't walk too good. Guess I had too much Irish Whiskey."

"That's a good guess." Her heel caught in the cracked brick walk. She pitched forward, stumbled, but Jake caught her.

"Whoa there. You're s'pposed to be sober."

"It was my shoe." With a grunt, she yanked off her shoe and jerked it from the sidewalk. Holding it in her hand, she tugged on his arm. "Come on. We're almost to the car."

"You're a good woman, Kate-with-a-K," he drawled. "I really didn't like you at first, but you've grown on me. Oh, you had a nice rack and all, but you have to admit you were a little testy."

"I don't know if you remember or not, but you were pretty damned obnoxious yourself."

When they reached the car. Jake leaned back against the passenger door, a bleary smile across his handsome face. She unlocked the door and opened it. "Get in. You can do that much, right?"

Jake took a faltering step and Caitlin nudged him inside. "Fasten your seatbelt."

He reached for it twice and missed, then grinned at her. "Help?"

"You're helpless as a baby," she said. "Just this once."

Once he was belted in, she went around and got in behind the wheel. "You're going to be sorry tomorrow morning. Just you wait."

A loud snore was his only response.

Caitlin smiled. Oh, yeah, he was gonna be sorry.

Chapter Twenty-two

It was seven-thirty when Caitlin managed to drag herself from bed. Jake managed a grunt and rolled over. The air in the room was chilly so she pulled the bed linens over his broad shoulders and left him in peace. She'd call from the office to wake him as soon as she was ready to leave. After showering she donned her single black suit and added a string of pearls, then headed out the door.

During the drive to the office, she planned. No doubt Heaton would remain at home. No one expected him to come to work the day after his wife was buried. She couldn't resist another possible opportunity to get at his computer.

Lisette was already at her desk in relatively normal attire for once, a navy skirt and sweater.

When Caitlin entered, Lisette glanced up with a frown. "I didn't think you'd be here since your father-in-law's funeral is today."

"I'm not staying long," she said and stowed her purse in a drawer, but not before carefully removing the eight-gig flash drive and slipping it into her pocket. "I just wanted to make sure everything was copacetic here."

Lisette sniffed. "I'm perfectly capable of seeing to the office for a day or two."

"Of course you are. I'm just one of those workaholic control freaks. Accountants are like that."

"Heaton came in," Lisette said.

"What?" So much for best-laid plans.

"I think he's losing it. He's very shaky. I already took him a cup of coffee, but he might need something a little stronger."

"I'll check on him," Caitlin offered.

"Control freak."

Caitlin almost missed Lisette's low mutter. "I'm a control freak, so what? I'm still gonna check on him."

So what if it was the day after his wife's funeral? Heaton had come to work. He reached for his cup of coffee, then stopped. His hands shook as if he were palsied. He grabbed his right wrist with his left hand to steady it. Slowly he guided it to the cup. At the very moment, he grasped it, his body shuddered. The cup tipped.

"Damn!" He jumped up, snatching papers out of the way, and tried to keep the spreading puddle of latte from spilling onto the floor.

"Who? What?" He glanced around. He'd heard her voice, laughing, mocking his clumsiness.

"Bitch," he hissed. "You're dead. That lover of yours saw to it before I could. And not a minute too soon. Don't blame him a bit. And now he's headed for hard time and I'm not. Now that sweet little wife of his will go back home to her family."

He sat back down and assembled his papers into some kind of order. "I don't need another accountant in this office, now that you're dead and not leaching money away like river water pouring over a paddle wheel. You dead whore, I hated you. I hated what you made me do."

A rap on the door startled him.

"Mr. Boyle, are you okay?"

The little accountant. "C-come in."

"I thought I heard you in here. Why on earth are you here? You buried your wife only yesterday."

"I-I didn't know what else to do, Kate. I needed..." He shook his head. "I'm sorry about your husband's being arrested. I guess you'll resign and go home to your people. I understand."

Her eyebrows drew together. "My husband was released—and how did you know about it anyway? And if he weren't, I wouldn't be going anywhere. I'd stand by him."

"Yes." He giggled. "You'll stand by your man...like Tammy Wynette." He leaned back and restrained an uncontrollable urge to scream. Released? How could that be?

Little Mrs. Girard leaned over him. "I don't think you're well enough to be at work. Why don't I call you a cab? Do you have friends or neighbors who can stay with you for the rest of the day?"

"N-no, I just need to calm down a bit." He waved her away. "I'll be all right. Just go on—go on."

"All right, if you say so, but I don't like leaving you like this."

He wiped the sweat from his forehead and sucked in a breath. "Very nice of you. Really. And I appreciate your coming to the services. Very nice of you." He motioned to the pile of papers on the desk. "Now, I have work to do."

Caitlin left Boyle to his *work*. The man had fallen apart before her eyes. He hadn't noticed her for a full minute when she opened the door. Muttering to himself? And how had he learned of Jake's arrest? Did Boyle have something to do with Angelique's murder?

In the outer office, she approached her co-worker. "Lisette, why don't you see if you can get him to go home? Close the office for the day."

Apparently offended, Lisette flushed and raised her chin a defiant notch. "Are you ordering me around?"

"No, just making a suggestion, but in the light of Heaton's loss, he'd be better off at home. Don't you think?"

"Well, he shouldn't be here," Lisette agreed.

"And since there's nothing else for me to do here, I'm calling my husband to let him know I'm on my way to pick him up," Caitlin added with a smile. "He's a little under the weather after last night."

"Sounds like it was a good wake."

"Guess so. It was my first Irish wake."

"They tend to be lively—the good ones."

Caitlin nodded her agreement. "Then it was a good one." She

collected her purse, then pulled out her cell phone.

It rang twice, then Jake picked up. "Mmph."

"Get up sleepyhead. I'm on my way."

"Right," he said with a groan. "I'm up...sort of."

Wearing a black suit with charcoal-pinstripes, Jake was waiting when Caitlin pulled to the curb. His coal-black hair was neatly combed, but still wet from his shower.

He entered the car and leaned forward for a quick kiss. "I appreciate your getting me home last night."

"All part of the job," she said with a smile. "How're you feeling?"

"Mother of a headache. Otherwise, I'm good to go."

"Hm. Your color's a little on the pasty side," she said.

"Gee thanks," he said with another groan. "I feel so much better now."

"I thought you would," she said as insincerely as possible, then finished off with a smile. Not that she was trying to make him feel bad. Her banter was more on the order of taking his mind off where they were going.

After the funeral, Caitlin and Jake followed in the mortuary's dark maroon limo behind Ed's casket in the procession to the cemetery. "Is it me or did the Mass seem to last forever?" she asked.

"It was too long." His color was still pale.

"Feeling any better?"

"I could use another cup of coffee."

"I'm afraid asking the driver to leave the procession and stop at Starbucks just isn't done."

He waved away her concern. "I'm all right. I never drink that much. Not since I was a teenager."

Could his addictive personality be taking a new turn? "About that..."

As if reading her mind, he shook his head. "Don't worry. Last night was an exception. Besides, alcohol isn't my problem."

"Oh, yeah. That's what I figured," she said as nonchalantly as possible.

"You've been wonderful, Kate. I really appreciate it—in case I haven't mentioned it."

She smiled. "Partners cover each other's backs. Nice of Alex to come to the funeral, too."

"Yeah, he was covering my nights at the casino. He's a good kid."

"He's not a kid. He's a full-fledged agent."

"Yeah, but he's not world-weary and worn yet." Jake leaned back and shut his eyes.

They reached the entrance to Greenwood Cemetery and the limo slowed, turned into the gate and passed the monument of a Confederate soldier. Jake straightened his back and sucked in a deep breath. "Man, I hate this."

The limo stopped. The chauffeur opened the door and they emerged into the sunlight. The Emerald Society Pipes and Drums were there in their green and gold uniforms.

"Why the bagpipes?" Caitlin asked, hoping to distract Jake. "I know it's customary, but why?" Hand in hand they walked to the spot where Ed would be interred.

"When the Irish immigrated to the States, no one would hire 'em, so they took what they could get. Police department. Fire department. Back then those jobs were the lowest of the low. The Irish and the Scots both played Celtic music with the pipes back in the old country. Now it's customary for any officer who dies in the line of duty. At least that's what Ed told me when I asked him."

She reached for his hand. "You'll get through this. I'm holding on tight and I won't let you go."

"I wouldn't be anything without him. I owe him everything."

"And you're honoring him today exactly the way he wanted. I know he had to be so proud of you."

His reply was tinged with bitterness. "Yeah. But I should've spent more time with him."

From the choked sound of his "yeah", she could almost imagine losing someone dear, like Bonnie, and how she'd feel. As for her mother, she'd never known the woman who gave birth to her. Bonnie was the only mother she'd ever known.

Almost.

Tall, blond Alex wearing a navy suit joined them, then hugged Jake and clapped him on the back. "Sorry, man."

Jake nodded. "Thanks."

Together the three of them walked over to the aboveground tomb where Jake's father would be laid to rest. His casket was draped with the flag of the United States as befitted his death in the line of duty.

Jake squeezed her hand. Sooner or later the circulation would return—at least she hoped it would.

The ceremony was brief and after the priest completed his part, the bagpiper began to play *Amazing Grace*. After the honor guard presented Jake with the folded flag, each mourner stepped forward laid a white rose on the casket, Jake and Alex stepped forward and saluted Ed, one final measure of honor.

The last eerie strains of the hymn faded into the air. Hands sweating, Jake swallowed hard. Kate took his hand and gently led him toward the car.

"This was my first police funeral service," she murmured. "I had no idea it would be so touching and beautiful."

The lump in his throat felt as big as a snooker ball. "Ed was big on tradition, especially when it came to the job."

"I didn't know him, but I'm sure you've done what he would've wanted."

"At least some of the guys he knew were still on the job. I knew they'd come. Couldn't risk a big production since it might draw attention to me as Jake LeFevre when I'm supposed to be someone else."

"Nice service, Jake," Alex said. "He'd be proud." He cleared his throat. "I came in my own car. How about I pick us up some food?"

"Thanks." Caitlin gave Alex a wistful smile. "Chinese?"

Alex nodded, then loped off toward his Intrepid.

Jake's eyes stung with tears he was too macho to shed. "I owe Ed everything, Kate. Everything. My life. My job. He was the only person who saw any good in me...ever loved really me...until you."

"And I do love you," she said, then fell silent.

How had he managed to win her heart...for the time being anyway? But once their operation was over, whatever happened next was a crapshoot.

Chapter Twenty-three

After a leisurely dinner of the best take-out Chinese food she'd ever eaten, Caitlin cleared the table before joining Jake and Alex for coffee in the living area. Jake's mood was more upbeat. Planning a covert op was just the prescription he needed.

"It's time we checked out Ms. Andre's computer, but we need to accomplish it without tipping off the head honchos at Rivera Corp. what we're up to," Jake said.

Alex's expression pulled into a frown. "Well, we're the Feds. Why don't we, just go in and take Miss Andre's computer for evidence? I wouldn't object to a little covert work, but why don't we just use the direct approach?"

Caitlin sat on the sofa and smiled. "The problem is sailing in there would tell them we're interested in her files and in Rivera. We don't want them to know that, yet. We'll get the appropriate warrants, but the mission will be a covert one."

"What do we know about HQ's security?" Jake asked.

"They have a team of three who make hourly rounds of all offices," Alex said. "Each team member covers three floors each in the corporate building. Our approach will coincide with the time the team member exits from the seventh floor."

Caitlin frowned. "And we know the exact time?"

"We have a contact on the cleaning crew who has provided us with the schedule, an ID badge and uniform." Alex grinned. "See I haven't been goofing off while y'all are on your honeymoon. Man. I'm *so* ready for this."

"You're not going in. I am," Jake said.

She stood and set her hands on her hips. "No way! It's too soon. Alex can do it."

Jake clenched his jaw, then sucked in a deep breath. "Look I know you're the boss, but I *need* to do this, Kate. I do." He shot her a pleading expression. "It's a simple in and out."

Was she boss or not? Apparently not when it came to executing a covert op like this one. Was it worth fighting over?

Not really.

"Okay," she said, giving in grudgingly. "But we'll have backup and a surveillance van." She rose from the sofa, stretched her back, then let out a yawn. "Guess I'd better get off my butt and contact the local Bureau office and make nice."

Nice guys, the New Orleans field office—they'd handed over the high tech van after a mere three hour's investigation by the U.S. attorney and the signing of a mountain of paper, and made them seal it with the promise of a first-born child if the said high-tech van wasn't returned in good condition. And another four hours later, a special warrant in hand from the good graces of a judge who wasn't too happy at being interrupted during a chess match, Jake was ready to go. Disguised in a depressing gray uniform, wired up the yin-yang and ready for his covert mission, complete with a mop bucket. He concealed a compact one terabyte external hard drive in his front pocket. He spoke into the mic. "You there, big guy?"

"On point," came Alex's reassuring voice. He and Caitlin were a half block away in the van.

Jake was sure young Alex would've preferred something a little more dramatic, like shooting a grappling hook up to the roof. Coming in with the cleaning crew meant saner heads had prevailed.

Once Jake reached the seventh floor, he eased down the semi-darkened corridor of Rivera Corporation. Now, this was more like it. Riding herd on a spreadsheet wasn't his idea of a covert op.

Might be Kate's, but not his.

He turned left. According to the building specs, the CFO's office was second on the right. He stopped at the door; Angie's nameplate had already been removed. He pulled a set of lock picks from his pocket and inserted them in the knob.

After a manipulation or two, he felt and heard the tumblers click into place.

He eased through the open door and surveyed the room for her computer. Good. The police hadn't taken it. It was a desktop computer—not a laptop. Good thing he had the external hard drive.

He booted up her computer, slid the password decryption program into a disc drive and waited.

A long ten minutes later, all the files were open to his view. He had a choice. It would take too long to go through them all. He pulled the external hard drive from his pocket and connected it to a vacant USB port on the PC. The backup program began automatically.

Now if the process would complete before he was discovered.

"Yeah... Mission accomplished." He disconnected the hard drive and shoved it into his pocket, then shut down the computer.

He stood, glanced around the office space and—

Damn. A small red light flickered in the upper corner. Had he been observed? Luckily, he'd only worked by the light of the computer screen. Was it enough light for someone to make out his face?

Not good. Not at all.

"Gotta get out of here," he said into the mic. "I see a red light flickering to beat the band."

"Just exit the way you came. Slow and steady." Caitlin's measured tone calmed the elephants stomping around his gut.

All he had to do now was get out of the building without getting caught.

He stopped at the door, opened it a crack and checked to the left—clear. Then the right—not!

"Two guards—not one—two!"

Shit.

"We're moving the van closer to your exit point."

"Fucking great. I gotta get outta the office first. Got two guards bearing right toward me."

"Can you take 'em?" Caitlin asked.

"Sure thing—if I were an offensive tackle for the Titans."

Maybe he could blitz them by surprise.

Here goes nothin'.

He held his breath and waited until guard numero uno poked his head into the office.

Jake spun and shoved the mop bucket into the first guard's crotch—mop handle first. It connected with a thud. Down he went with a sick groan.

Sorry, dude. I know you're just doing your job.

The second guard entered and tripped over his partner's crumpled body. "What the fu—?"

A snap kick to the second guard's balls disabled him damn quick. Jake leaped over the two men and sprinted down the hall, rounded the corner to the right and skidded to a halt. Between him and his exit point waited the biggest son of a bitch he'd ever seen.

Caitlin held her breath while Alex eased the van as close to Jake's exit point as he could get without raising suspicion and stopped. "We need to give him a hand. He's cornered." Caitlin checked the magazine in her Glock 22. Hoping she wouldn't need the gun for anything more than intimidation, she stood and reached for the door lever.

"Hold on, mother hen. No point in exposing ourselves. Jake can handle himself. Sounds like he's already taken out two."

"Third incoming," came Jake's voice over the comm. "Armed and dangerous."

"Alex, we have to do something!"

He shook his head. "No. As it is, there's only Jake exposed. We can't interfere."

"Dammit. I'm in charge and I say we proceed."

"No. Just keep your head. You're not Spiderwoman. What're you gonna do? Shinny up the wall? Or maybe charge the information desk with your gun blazing? We can't get in the way. Keep with the mission profile."

Desperation swept through her, sickened her. "Your profile is going to get our team member hurt."

Not just a team member—Jake.

"This isn't a spec ops mission behind enemy lines," Alex said. "You're exaggerating the danger. This is a low-level covert op. He's not in any real danger. The guards aren't going to kill him for a B&E. At worst, he'll be caught, taken into custody, released and sent back to DC."

She sat and drummed her fingers against the console. "I don't see how you can sit here and do nothing." Panic built in her chest. No, it wasn't panic. This was the adrenaline high she hadn't experienced since Quantico. And the training maneuvers there didn't begin to compare with this.

"He'll be all right."

Kate's gaze was glued to the monitor. The bright blue blip was Jake. "He's about ten yards from his exit point, and he's holding position."

Okay, he'd be all right, she told herself. He had to be.

While he walked, Jake kept his face lowered. No need in letting them know who he was unless it was absolutely necessary. Kept his mouth shut, too. The behemoth in front of him had his gun drawn.

"Thought you'd get away with breaking into this building, you son of a bitch?"

What to do? He could always drop cover and tell them he was with the FBI, but then the bad guys would find out the FBI was interested in their operation. And that would blow the entire investigation.

"Against the wall. Spread 'em."

Again, he complied with the guard's instructions, his body

tensed for the first possible opening to escape. "I'm not armed," Jake said, then waited until the guard bent to pat down his legs. He spun and brought his knee up with a sharp crack into the guard's jaw.

The guard grunted and staggered for a second.

Jake followed by jamming an elbow into the guard's ribs.

Nothing gave. Hitting the guard's heavily muscled body was like hitting a steel barge with an overcooked noodle.

The guard recovered and powered a fist into Jake's gut. Down he went, flat on his back. He swallowed back a wave of nausea and kicked both feet into the guard's gut. The guard went down.

Thank God.

Jake scrambled to his feet, scooped the drive back into running back mode and sprinted for the stairs. A quick glance over his shoulder. The guard was already on his feet and lumbering toward him.

Shit.

Helter-skelter, he raced down the longest seven flights of stairs he'd ever seen. His heart pounded in his ears, his breathing ragged but deep. Every sense was alive with adrenaline thrumming through his body, his knees aching like a son of a bitch. And if they didn't require years of arthroscopic surgery, he'd be a stripe-assed monkey. He hit the first floor and glanced around for the side exit he'd seen on the specs.

Door! Yes. He snatched it open.

Closet.

Voices...guards calling to each other. Could it get any worse?.

One more door. Yes! The ripe night air hit him in the face like a wet blanket.

His feet hit the pavement with a thud, and the hard drive still in his pocket. Mission success!

What a rush.

"Location?" he gasped into the mic.

"Quarter block away on your left, moving up now."

He sucked in a deep breath and sped for the dark van. His long strides ate up the distance as he made the last push for the goal line. The van's side door slid open. Caitlin reached out, grabbed his shirt and jerked him inside. At the same time, Alex floored it. The sudden forward movement threw Jake on his knees and into Caitlin's arms.

"Sure am glad to see you guys." He untangled his body from hers, then shrugged off the uniform shirt and Kevlar vest and handed it over to her. "Nice way to end an op," he said. At least he could feel again. Not since he'd received the call about Ed had he felt this alive.

More than a little shaken by Jake's nearness and overwhelmed with relief he was safe and sound, Caitlin straightened her clothes and grinned up at him. "Obviously, but I could've done without being groped."

In the dim light of the van, she watched a seductive smile spread over his tanned face. "Was it as good for you as it was for me?"

"How can you joke when you were nearly caught? I was worried sick."

"Aw, chèr, it was just enough to get my heart pumping."

"Mine certainly was," she said and caressed his cheek. "I don't know what I would've done if anything had happened to you."

"I don't know if you mean to, but you're making a very good argument for why partners shouldn't be—you know."

"Yeah." She let out a deep sigh. She regained her seat and motioned for Jake to do the same. "Now, what did you bring me?"

He faked a half bow from his perch. "My fair lady, I've brought you a wondrous treasure. The not-so-fair Angelique's files transferred to yon hard drive." He handed her the hard drive.

Alex's puzzled voice came from the front. "What the fuck?"

Caitlin whipped around and leaned through the opening. "What's wrong?"

"There's a local LEO behind us with his blue lights on. I've got to pull over."

"Well, you *were* speeding. Take the ticket and be done with it," Jake suggested.

A protracted fifteen minutes later, they were away with only a warning. Caitlin let out a deep sigh. "Now, once again. What do you have?"

"Everything. There was a surveillance camera in her office. I didn't see it until I was finished."

"Did anyone get a look at your face?"

"I kept my head down as soon as I noticed the camera. It was dark in the office, but with the casino's facial recognition software, they might be able to come up with enough points for a match."

Time was running out. She shook her head. "That mustn't happen. Is there any way you can get hold of the tape before they do a comparison?"

Jake shook his head. "If the tape was kept at the casino, yeah, but the corporate offices are a different matter."

"Agree," Caitlin said. "Now they know someone's interested in their late CFO's files, they'll most likely double their guard."

Jake shrugged. "I'll keep my fingers crossed."

"No. I'll go over these files all night long. The sooner we close up this operation, the better—for all of us," she said, then angled her head from side to side to loosen her neck muscles.

Jake slipped his arm around her shoulders. "Need a massage?"

"If we had time, but we don't." Caitlin smiled up at him. "I think the local office would appreciate the return of their precious surveillance van first."

Chapter Twenty-four

After dropping off the van at the New Orleans field office, Jake drove the three of them back to the loft. Caitlin sat beside him, tapping her foot and twitching.

"A little anxious to see what's in the files, are we?" he teased.

Caitlin gave a quick nod. "You know I am. They might even tell us why Angelique was murdered." Drumming her fingers on the dash, she continued, "I don't know why the NOPD hadn't already confiscated her files, although...I have to say I'm very glad they didn't. They certainly aren't anxious to share their intel with us."

"Can't blame 'em," Jake said. "They hate it when the Bureau sweeps in and interferes with one of their cases."

At ease on her home court, Jake noted his Kate was all business.

"I'm setting up the files to share, but we'll do better to split the files. Jake, you do anything that appears personal, and I'll do the financials."

"Okay by me." He sat on his side of the partner desk and booted up his laptop. He frowned at the rows of files filling his screen then glanced at Kate. "Looks like you've hit a gold mine. There's a ton of shit here."

She nodded. "I've already rerun the decryption program. It should take care of most problems we'll run into."

Alex paced from one side of the partner desk to the other.

"What can I do?"

Kate glanced up. "You've already done your part by driving the van and keeping us out of jail. We'll do the rest."

"What am I—chopped liver?" he asked, using an exaggerated Brooklyn accent.

"Not at all." Kate gave Alex a dazzling smile. "This is my thing—numbers and computers."

From his laptop, Jake grinned then gave her a slow wink. "Yeah, numbers make her heart beat faster." He cut her a heated glance. "Don't they?"

Her cheeks flushed a pretty pink. Yeah, numbers might be her specialty, but they didn't compare when it came to her ability to speed up Jake's heart. Not that he was about to make such a sappy admission in front of Alex, who actually looked like he might fold any second.

"Hey, kid, why don't you take a nap? You worked my shift last night and you've been up all day and tonight, too."

"A nap? Now, why didn't I think of that myself?" Alex plopped on the couch and was snoring softly five minutes later.

Jake frowned. One of his files wasn't too cooperative. He ran the decrypt program again.

No luck.

"I've got a folder here. Can't get in."

"And you've already run the decryption software?"

"Twice." He yawned and glanced at his watch. One A.M.

She pursed her lips. God, those lips. If only he could take her to bed—right then. But given the gazillion files they were plowing through, he had a better chance of winning a world-class poker match.

Alex sat up, yawned, cracked his knuckles, then got to his feet. "Here's where I came in, folks. Let me try something. There's always a back door built into the software."

"Wish I could wake up that fast." Jake arched a brow.

Alex shot Jake a Cheshire Cat grin. "I'm young, not old and worn out like you two."

Jake spun his laptop in the younger agent's direction. "Have at it, kid."

A mere five minutes later: "Holy shit, man. You gotta see this." Alex rubbed his eyes. "Honestly, I'm scarred for life." He swiveled the computer back to Jake.

A man and woman entwined, making the beast with two backs. The woman with the long, long legs was Angie—no doubt about it. And the man? Fifties, paunch, sagging butt, and male pattern baldness. Who the hell was he? Damn.

"Kate, we may just have a motive for Angie's murder and her murderer, too."

Eyes widened, she glanced up. "Wh-what did you say?"

"Have a look."

She stood and walked around to watch over his shoulder. "Is that what I think?"

"Oh, yeah."

"I can't imagine Heaton Boyle ever..."

"That's Boyle?"

"I'd know his bald spot anywhere." She reached over his shoulder. "Is there audio? Can you turn it up?"

"No-o-o-o!" Jake and Alex groaned together.

She rolled her eyes at him. "All right. When the hanky-panky is over, I just want to hear if there's any conversation."

"You want to hear the pillow talk? Why are you so interested in what was said? A hidden voyeuristic tendency, perhaps?" He shot her his best evil-creepo leer.

"As gross as it sounds," she said with an exasperated expression. "Heaton Boyle was afraid of Angelique Andre. The man positively cringed every time she breezed into the office. He must've been under duress, and we might be able to ascertain how, if we could hear what they're saying."

"Oh, baby. Oh, baby! Do it to me." Alex's affected falsetto sent a chill through Jake.

"Alex! The woman is dead. Show a little..."

The younger agent dope-smacked his forehead. "Whoops. Sorry."

"If you two can *both* show some maturity. This has to be what

Angelique had on Heaton—the reason he was embezzling. I wouldn't put it past her to seduce the poor man and then use it against him. His wife was dying; he would've done anything to keep her from finding out about his infidelity."

"She had it against him, all right," Jake muttered. He hated seeing what Angie had become. As a young hooker, she'd been honest about what she was. What you saw was what you got with her then, but this...

Unable to stomach watching any longer, he stood. "You want to listen, have at it. I've seen enough. I need some air."

Kate gazed over the laptop, her gaze full of sympathy. "It's okay, Jake. Go on. You've been through a lot in the last few days."

His heart swelled with gratitude for her understanding, he rose, then walked around to her side of the desk. "Thanks, chèr." He leaned over and placed a light kiss on her forehead. "Won't be long."

Minutes later, he strolled down the street with every intention of heading for the nearest bar for a stiff drink.

How was it a woman with Angie's intellectual gifts couldn't overcome her early background?

Damn waste. That's what it was. Could anyone overcome being a teenage prostitute? Had he overcome being a street rat? He liked to think so. Without Ed Hoolihan's intervention, where would he be?

Probably deep in the numbers, drugs, rackets...or worse.

Instead of popping into the bar, Jake turned and strode purposefully back to the loft. In spite of losing his father and the regrettable death of an old love, there were more pressing matters.

Caitlin hit the power button on the coffeemaker then headed back to the computer. She sat and scanned files but stopped when she heard the rattle of Jake's key in the door. So soon? He'd only left—what—five minutes ago?

When he opened the door, she glanced up. "You didn't stay very long. Everything okay?"

"Yeah, just had to walk it off. Sorry for leaving like that."

"Not a problem."

"I'm sorry. Seeing Angie in that video must've hurt."

"Not the way you think." He said and took off his jacket, letting it fall across the counter.

"Right after you left, I started a fresh pot of coffee. Oughta be done soon." She rose and moseyed into the kitchen.

"Great. I could use some." He smiled, then ambled around the island, opened a cupboard and pulled out a clean cup.

The coffee pot finished its gurgling and hissing. She poured a cup for Jake. "Alex? Want some?"

"No, thanks. I'll never get back to sleep if I do."

Jake took a quick swallow from his cup, then inclined his head and kissed her full on the mouth. His lips tasted of strong black coffee and hunger. She melted into his embrace with a moan.

"You're too good for me, Kate."

"Hey, you two. Get a room," Alex said with his hand covering his eyes. "Mom and Dad aren't supposed to do stuff like that in front of the kid."

Jake released her and they both laughed. "This is our room," Jake said with a wide smile. "Go home, Alex. I catch you up tomorrow on what we find."

"Yeah, right." Alex hauled his rangy body from the sofa and ambled to the door. "Night, y'all."

As soon as Alex left, Caitlin snaked her arm around Jake's waist. "Why don't you tell me how it hurt you?"

"She accomplished so much. She was so bright. Why did her life have to end like this?"

Caitlin sighed. She had to tell the truth, even if it hurt him. "Most of it she brought on herself—not that she deserved to be murdered—that's not what I mean." She took a deep breath and continued. "She made choices. And they weren't all good ones. You made choices, too, but you had Ed. Whoever helped pull Angie out of the gutter wasn't as good an influence as Ed."

Jake raised his cup. "Here's to Ed."

She raised her cup and met his gaze. His warm brown eyes were full of regret. It was just too much in too short a time.

"I should've tried to find her. I let her down."

"No, your life was headed in a different direction. You can't go back, Jake. It's not your fault what she became."

"Maybe if I'd just tried..." He shook his head, then pulled her into his arms again.

She sighed. "You know we have work to do?"

He grinned down at her and winked. "That's the reason I came back so soon. Didn't feel right leaving it to you and the kid."

"Then let's get to it. I think we're close to finding something significant. I just feel it in my gut."

"In your gut? Ever-logical Caitlin has a gut feeling? Are you sure?"

She smiled. Heavens, she loved that man. "You wouldn't be teasing me, would you?"

"Another gut feeling? What's this world coming to?" he asked, his dark eyes sparkling with mischief.

The sadness was gone, for the moment anyway. "Yeah, must be a miracle."

By three, they knew everything...almost. The embezzling, blackmail and money laundering. Harris, his boss Rivera, and a mysterious money man in DC whose name they would know as soon as the wiretap warrants came through. "To recap," Caitlin said. "We've pieced most of it together. Carlos Rivera is the honcho at the corporate, and Angelique answered directly to him. Harris ran everything at the casino level. I'm guessing they realized she was cooking the books in her favor, so they killed her or had her killed. Same deal with Terri Thibedoux."

Jake stood, paced, then frowned and sank onto the sofa. "What about Boyle?"

"My opinion—he was too late. He might've been ready to kill her himself. His wife had just died; he had nothing to lose. He saw you come out, headed up there to do the job and found her already dead. He figured you did it."

"Poor bastard probably dropped the dime on me himself."

"That's the most likely scenario."

"You realize this operation could be over in a few days?" he said.

"Oh...I hadn't really thought about it." She took a deep breath and tried to concentrate on the files.

Over in a few days? What was the big rush? Okay, so the government was paying for their faux honeymoon. What would happen then? There'd still be paperwork, trial, testimony, but any chance for real interaction between them would pretty much be over. Isn't that what she wanted in the beginning? Yes, but circumstances had changed.

Jake shrugged. "You should get a big promotion after this. And you deserve it. Fast. Efficient."

"Thanks. Sounds like you're writing my annual eval."

"Your father should be proud. You've proved yourself. Isn't that what you set out to do?"

Wise to his tricks, she let the "father should be proud" crack go by. He was goading her, trying to make her mad. It wouldn't work. "More or less—okay, yes, that was my original agenda, but..."

"But what?"

"I didn't expect to fall in love—with undercover work," she added quickly. What made her say such a stupid thing? There were so many unknowns, plus she wasn't entirely sure how she felt about her future or his.

He grinned. "Is that what you fell in love with, Kate? 'Cause I fell in love with *you*."

"You really mean that?" *Omigod. What now?*

"I do, but I can't make any promises. Once this mission is over, we have different paths. I may be a father. There's all that stuff to sort out."

First, he said he'd fallen in love with her, and now it sounded like he was brushing her off. Okay, two could play that little game.

"It's too soon to make plans, Jake. You don't know anything for certain, and I don't have the least idea what my next assignment will be, either." Okay, that sounded a little on the haughty side.

Fine.

"But you're set for advancement. There's just no way we can work this out. We've had a good time. I'll never forget you. Just remember me the next time I get in trouble with the Bureau and put in a good word for me."

"You love me but this sounds like a good-bye. Just a thanks-for-the-sex kiss-off."

"It is what it is, Kate."

She stiffened. "You're right. Obviously, we made a mistake getting too close. Inevitable in this sort of situation, I guess." No skin off her nose if he wanted to back away from what they'd shared.

Liar. Liar. They'd grown closer than she'd ever imagined they could, much less *would*.

"Where do we go from here?" She choked out the words.

He rose from the sofa and walked around to her side of the desk, then perched on the corner. "Up to you, chèr."

Up to her indeed. She averted her gaze from his dark brown eyes, counted to ten, she said, "Up to me?"

"You're the boss lady. I take my cues from you."

She tried to hide the pain of his casual dismissal. What kind of man told a woman he loved her then was ready to let her go without another word? "Be the first time, but since you've accepted that I'm in charge, I believe it would be easier on us both if we went back to the original arrangement and performed our duties as professionals..." The words hung in her throat, but she persevered. "I-I'm going to bed—alone."

He reached out and caressed her cheek, the rough pads of his fingertips searing her skin. "Gonna miss spooning with you in that big old bed. But you're right."

She stared at the keyboard as if the magic words would appear and right the wrong they'd done to each other. To their hearts and minds.

Full of hurt pride and more than a little disbelief, she rose and pushed back her chair. "I don't think there's anything else to be learned tonight. Once the warrants come through and we find out who the DC moneyman is, we'll take our evidence back to the Bureau."

Easing off the corner of her desk, he snapped a two-finger salute. "Right, boss."

"'Night, Jake." She headed to the bathroom, brushed her teeth and changed into the largest T-shirt known to mankind. Her bed would be cold and lonely without him. God knew she'd just gotten used to having him there.

Was there still a chance? Or was he right about their not having a future? How had it gone from "I love you" to "it is what it is" so wrong, so quickly?

While Kate fiddled around in the bathroom, Jake let out the sofa bed. He'd done the right thing. There wasn't a chance in hell for a future with her. He had too many problems looming, and she deserved better than him.

He heard her go to bed. Heard her body shifting around, trying to get comfortable enough to go to sleep. He punched his pillow into just the right shape.

Gonna be a hell of a long night.

Chapter Twenty-five

Bud Harris entered the CEO's office. The scowl on his boss's face said the meeting might not be a pleasant one. "Carlos, we had an intruder last night."

Carlos Rivera glared over gold-rimmed glasses while he fiddled with a silver pen, turning it end over end. "What did we do with his body?"

"He—uh, got away."

The pen fiddling stopped. Rivera's frown deepened. "How much did he get away with?"

"Money? Nada. He was after Angelique's computer. Sounds like he had some kind of external hard drive. Not sure if he had time to copy her files or not."

"Where are her files now?"

Rivera clenched the pen in his fist. Bud hoped his boss wasn't going to stab him with it. Bearer of bad news and all that.

"Well?"

"Uh, her hard drive's locked in my office safe."

"Any idea who we're looking for?"

"Pretty good. He's a good six-foot or six-one, fast on his feet. The facial recognition software came up positive for one of the new casino security guys."

"First see if anyone's close to him. Question them. No need to be gentle. Find out who he's working for and get rid of him."

"Consider it done."

Later that day, and only twenty minutes late for his shift,

Alex strode into the outer office of Security. He might be late, but there was no point in acting guilty.

He winked at the boss's assistant. "Afternoon, Donna."

"Alex, you're—"

"Yeah, yeah, I know."

"You've got a message." She leafed through the small message sheets and handed him one.

"Thanks, kiddo." He winked again. Donna, who was also the boss's daughter, was definitely out of bounds for hired help like him, but hot she was. And hot was always good.

He glanced at the small sheet.

New development. Meet me at 9:30, Pier 52. J—.

"Did he say anything else?"

Donna shook her head, then patted her blond curls back in place. "Nope."

"Thanks." He shoved the note into his pocket. Jake and his choice of meeting places. Pier Fifty-Two was probably a local hot spot on the docks. And a great place to meet chicks.

Hell! Anywhere in New Orleans was still a great place to meet chicks. Katrina or no, that hadn't changed.

Alex swiped his door key and entered Security.

Bud Harris glared at him. "Thirty minutes late, son."

"Naw, only twenty. I ran into a traffic jam on the bridge. I got no control over the traffic, boss man."

"Alex, if you weren't so highly recommended, your ass would be outta here."

"I'm sorry. I really am. Look, it won't happen again. I'm trying to find a place to live on this side of town, but it's trés expensive— know what I mean?"

The boss's face flushed red. "You little scumbag." Bud pounded his fist on the desk. "You're late and hitting me up for a raise at the same time."

Alex raised his hands in surrender. "Now, man, don't get your blood pressure up. You misread me."

Bud leaned back and roared with laughter. "You got balls, kid. I'll say that for ya."

Close call. Harris was known for his volatile temper. "So we're okay—you and me, boss?"

"Yeah, we're okay. Listen, I need you to pull a double. Hate to ask it, but Billy Bob's wife went into labor. What else can I do?"

"Oh, man, I gotta date. A real doll."

"I need ya, kid. But if you can con someone else into taking it..." He shrugged. "Okay by me."

"Cool."

Luckily Billy Bob's wife was in false labor and already back home. At nine, Alex headed down Tchoupitoulas, then turned south toward the river. The docks couldn't be too damn far. What really bugged him was he hadn't been able to raise Jake on his cell all day. Maybe Jake and Caitlin had shacked up for real. A light misting rain beat down on the car hood. The night air was chill. Damn temperature must've dropped twenty degrees in the last two hours. He shivered. Not a bad way to spend the night, old man. He didn't blame Jake a bit. Caitlin was hot, hot, hot.

He pulled onto the docks. No pickup bar visible. "Damn. Dark as hell too."

Okay. So if his guts yaw-yawed around like he'd had a bad bunch of oysters, that only meant one thing.

Trap.

He slowed his car. The pressure of the Glock 22 in the middle of his back was a comfort, but he'd been in tight situations before. He could handle this.

He eased past the warehouses until his headlights reflected off the number fifty-two. A dark figure eased from the shadows. His face wasn't visible, but his height was right for Jake.

Alex lowered the window. Keeping true to their covers, he called out softly, "Jack? It's Alex." The figure shuffled closer, avoiding the direct beam of the headlights.

Not Jake's easy gait. Reaching behind, he eased the Glock from his belt and held it by his thigh. "Hey, man, what's up?" he bluffed, but his foot jittered on the brake pedal.

Only a moment's warning, the rush of a second figure. He emerged running low from behind Alex's vehicle and *thwack!*

The lights dimmed.

Sometime later, Alex's eyelids flickered. He tried not to move. One by one, he assessed his body parts. Gag. Blindfolded with what felt like duct tape. Hands tied behind. Ankles tied, each to the front legs of a chair.

God. Head ached like a son of a bitch.

"So nice of you to join us, Mr. MacGregor…if that's your name?"

The gag was jerked from his mouth. He tried to swallow his spit. The man's voice was guttural and somehow familiar. Jersey boy? He shrugged. "Can't say much for your welcome. What'd you hit me with—a fuckin' sledgehammer?"

"Let's say I like to be in control of all situations."

"Yeah, well, I'm definitely under control. How 'bout taking off the damn duct tape so I can see who I'm talking to?"

"I don't think so. You're sticking your nose into things that don't concern you, buddy. And you're gonna stop. One of our sources says you've been asking a lot of nosy questions and you're mighty chummy with the new guy, Jack Girard."

"So? We're both new guys. We like to hang together." Alex snickered. "Besides that wife of his is smoking hot. Thought I might have a chance with her." His mind whirled. What source? The little gal in the money cage?

"Bullshit. Start talking or you're gonna wind up somewhere you don't wanna be. What do you know about him?"

"Nothin' much, man. He's just a dude who came to work here after I did. All I know is he used to work at the Bellagio in Vegas."

Soft footsteps. "Now, who do *you* work for?"

"Palais Pontchartrain, a division of the Rivera Corp—"

A powerful backhand nearly snapped his head from his neck. A new trickle of blood oozed from his nose.

"Shit! What'd you do that for? You want specifics? Specifically, I work in Security."

Another backhand snapped his head in the other direction.

Damn. Where was his backup when he needed it? Obviously, Jake was compromised. Maybe Caitlin, too.

"*Who* do you work for?" This time the question was louder and more forceful. His captor was so close, his garlicky breath nearly choked Alex.

"You probably ought to try some mouthwash after dinner. Might get rid of your bad—"

A hard punch to his gut cut off his air. Alex gagged and tried to force his diaphragm to work.

"He's not gonna talk. Kill 'im," a guttural voice said to someone who'd not said a word until now.

"Easy or slow?" The accent was pure *Hee Haw* country.

"Your choice, my man."

A Jersey boy and a hick—he'd walked into their trap like a damn rookie.

The brunt of the week's events weighed heavily on Caitlin's mind. Ed's death, Angie's and even Heaton's wife. Life was precious. Too short to be wasted on arguments over the future. She glanced over at Jake working on his laptop. He was quiet but appeared to be bearing up better. "When do you have to report back to the casino?"

"Tomorrow. Four to midnight." He shifted uneasily as he worked. "I still don't see anything about those wiretap warrants coming through."

"Probably take another twenty-four," she said. So that's how he was handling it. All business. All the time.

"I've set the table for three," she said, then glanced at her watch for about the tenth time. "What's keeping Alex?"

Jake shrugged. "Hell if I know. You know Alex. He's probably 'investigating' with one of the showgirls or one of the dealers."

The doorbell rang. "I'll get it." She grabbed her purse. "It's either Alex or the food."

After paying the delivery boy for the Thai food, she staggered back with the bags. "Hey, there. I could use a hand with these."

"Sorry." He took half the cartons from her when his cell phone rang. He checked the caller ID. "Damn. It's work."

"Think they want you to come in?" Frowning, Caitlin arranged the cartons and chopsticks on the table. The casino had no right calling Jake in the day after his father died. It was too soon. He needed time to decompress. They needed more time together, even if he was silent and way too businesslike for words.

Her foot tapped while he answered his cell.

He disconnected, then shrugged, carefully avoiding her direct gaze. There'd been a lot of that today.

"Gotta go in. Boss won't take no for an answer. Stick around and wait for Alex. If you don't hear from him in an hour, call me, and I'll try to make some excuse and leave."

Not the way she wanted the evening to end at all. Dammit. "Okay. But if you can't get away, do you want me to try and find him?

Jake snatched his jacket from the hook. "Nah, he's probably screwing around somewhere…literally. I still gotta go in and see what the damn emergency is."

"I don't like it." Determined to make eye contact, she strode to the door and placed a hand on his shoulder. He turned with a flash of anger sparking in his dark brown eyes, which she ignored. "You're on bereavement leave. They shouldn't be calling you unless it's to express condolences."

He shut his eyes for a moment. "I don't have a choice. I have to go in and maintain my cover, otherwise, I'd tell 'em all to kiss ass."

"You won't have to put up with the casino or me much longer," she said, then cringed at her whiney tone. "Sorry. That was passive-aggressive, wasn't it? Okay, here's the more direct and adult way—you and I still have plenty to discuss. This isn't—by that I mean we—aren't over yet."

"It's over. *We're* over. And I don't have time right now to get into it again."

"Okay, Jake." She raised her chin a notch. "Just so you know. I've always been a little on the stubborn side."

He gave a quiet snort and the corner of his mouth kicked up. "Tell me about it, chèr."

"Ah-ha! You called me, 'chèr'. You're not over me."

He opened the door, then stared her down. "Not yet, I'm not. Give me time."

Unwavering, she grinned. "I'm not giving up. I warned you."

"Yeah, you're stubborn. Nothin' new 'bout that."

He darted for the elevator. She shut the door and leaned against it with a sigh. Okay, he could go to work. Sooner or later he had to come home, and they *would* work everything out.

And she meant everything.

Caitlin checked her watch. Okay, Alex. One hour and then she'd call Jake.

She sat down at the table. Already she missed Jake's presence—his Jake-ness. She picked at her cashew chicken for a few minutes, then set everything into the fridge. Time seemed to drag, and creepy crawlies started to dance up and down her spine. Goosebumps raised on her arms. She checked the thermostat. Geez, it was only sixty in the loft. She cranked it up another ten degrees. That ought to do it.

She turned on the radio and waited for a weather report. Her goosebumps went away as the loft warmed, but the creepy crawlies had segued into a full-out march. What was it?

"Severe weather conditions for New Orleans. Cold air from a Canadian system pushing far south. Icing conditions already in Baton Rouge and points south. This severe winter weather system expected to reach the New Orleans metropolitan area in less than an hour. Repeat. Severe—"

The apartment's landline phone rang. She switched off the weather radio and snatched up the telephone. "Yes, Alex?"

Silence.

"Who's there?"

"Uh, K-Kate?" A female voice, low and hesitant.

"Yes, who's this?"

"Never mind. Your friends are in an old warehouse at the end of Pier Fifty-Two. They need you."

"Are you sure?"

"Yes—"

"Wait! Don't hang up." But it was too late. The line was dead.

"Damn." She glanced at her watch. Forty minutes since Jake left. She punched in his cell number.

Voice mail.

Why wasn't he answering? Was he in danger, too?

"Jake, it's Kate. About Alex. We need to check the warehouse at the end of Pier Fifty-Two. On my way."

She grabbed the only boots she had, a pair of Ferragamo ankle boots with three-inch heels, and pulled them on. She put on her shoulder holster, checked the Glock's magazine, found it full then slipped a spare into the pocket of her leather jacket. No time to waste. At least she knew where Jake and Alex were...unless it was a setup.

She snatched a third mag...just in case.

Once downstairs, she stepped outside. An icy blast of cold air hit and staggered her. Tiny needles of ice stung her face.

Damn. She'd have to run a block to the parking garage in that mess. She pulled her collar up and headed slipping and sliding into the brisk blowing wind.

Damn designer boots! What she wouldn't have given for a warm pair of UGGs.

Once inside the car, she pulled the city street map and a flashlight from the glove box. Where the heck was Pier Fifty-Two?

Light. It alternated with a dim gray fogginess. Alex struggled to concentrate. He'd drifted in and out of consciousness so many times he couldn't hazard a guess at how long he'd been tied to the most uncomfortable chair in the world. Hands were numb. Feet not much better.

How long did he have before they came back and killed him?

Damn duct tape. Every handyman and serial killer in the

fucking world carried a roll. Couldn't tear it for shit. He tugged against it, but it wouldn't budge. Now he understood how an animal could chew off its own leg to get out of a trap.

"He's awake."

Shit. No two ways about it. He was gonna die. And that sucked big time.

"Why're you snooping around, asking questions?"

"I work for Security for the Rivera Corporation. We're paid to be sneaky."

"Smart guy. Hear that, Stevie? He's a smart guy."

"Yeah, boss. I hear him."

Bad Breath leaned closer. Hell, the garlic alone might just do the job. "You work on the casino side. How come your buddy Girard's been messing around in the Corporate building? None of you got no bid'ness there."

"Why don't you ask him? By the way, seen any signs of the cavalry, Bad Breath? They always show up about now."

"Good try, kid. Think again."

Another backhand across Alex's face rang his chimes—the Big Ben version this time.

"We're ain't gonna screw around all night, kid. This is your last chance."

Alex smiled. "Yeah, you said that before."

"I was the good cop that time. This time...uh-uh."

"Sorry to hear that."

"Tell us about Jack Girard!"

"Already told you all I know."

Time's slipping away. Think dammit. Think.

"Did you hear that? I told you the cavalry was coming. If I were you two, I'd be heading out the back door."

Bad Breath and Stevie laughed.

"Sorry, kid. You're real entertaining, but...what else can I do? I got a job just like you. Ya done yours kinda half-assed 'cause we're on to ya. But we're good at what we do. Tell ya what. I'll make it quick 'cause ya been such a good sport about it."

"Ah, hell, don't do me any favors."

And where the hell was Jake? And the answer? Jake wasn't coming, much less any damn cavalry.

Chapter Twenty-six

Jake strolled into Security and glanced around the observation room. All posts were covered. "What's the deal? I saw Pearson on the floor when I came in. Why do you need me? I'm on bereavement leave."

"Shut the door and sit down, Girard," Harris said.

Jake shut the door but didn't sit. Folding his arms across his chest, he stood his ground. "What's up?"

Harris ignored him and pushed a button. The door behind Jake opened. He turned. Two of Harris's muscle-bound goons stepped into the office.

Shit.

"What's up?" he asked, biding for time.

"Your credentials don't check out. You're being escorted from the premises."

Impossible. "You called me down here in this weather to fire me?"

"That's the size of it, sport."

"I deserve a better explanation."

"One of my contacts at the Bellagio says he never heard of you."

"So what? The Bellagio's a big place. Maybe he didn't know everybody."

"He was a pit boss during the time your resume says you were there. I think he would've known ya."

Harris jerked his head in the direction of the door. "Get 'im outta here. Take him to the warehouse."

Alex regained consciousness. Listened. Nothing. He shook his head and opened his eyes. Under the edges of the duct tape, all he could see was a dark room, the only light was a narrow slit visible beneath the door. He was alone...for the moment anyway...and alive.

Sweat—or was it blood—dripped down his face to his neck. Funny, he'd always known death was possible, in an intellectual sort of way. Now that it was staring him in the face, he didn't feel too fucking intellectual. His gut twisted like a couple of squirrels had taken up residence and were burying their nuts for the winter.

Nothing noble about it. Fear, the worst and lowest kind. Mouth dry as cotton, he tried licking his bruised lips. They were caked with dried blood.

He'd failed. If they knew about him, then the entire mission was compromised. Jake and Caitlin—somehow, he had to warn them.

No point in waiting around to be 'gator bait. A shudder tore through him. He'd heard all about what had been left of Terri Thibedoux.

Think. There had to be something in this storeroom that he could use. *MacGuyver* he wasn't, but a MacGregor he was. Dammit. He was a survivor.

Inch by inch, he worked his chair around the room until he bumped into what he sure as hell hoped was some kind of tool cabinet.

He bent over and repressed a groan. Ribs were bruised. He pulled at the first metal handle with his teeth. Wouldn't budge. The second—it gave a fraction. He pulled again. He might need dentures later, but by God, he'd get the damn drawer open or die trying.

He nudged it open with his chin. Now, if he could just get something between his teeth. They hadn't tied his shoulders to the chair, just his legs. He could bend and hack at the duct tape if he could just find something with a sharp enough edge.

Finally. Something he could use to work on the duct tape—if could just get hold of it. He crouched over the open drawer, nosed around and grabbed a narrow piece of metal with a sharp point on one end—a beer opener—between his teeth. He doubled over and tried to reach the tape on each of his ankles.

Why hadn't he taken up yoga? How was he supposed to know being a contortionist might come in handy? At first, he didn't make much progress, but eventually, he began to appreciate a slight looseness in the binding on his right ankle. By worrying, stretching and scraping against the tough fibrous tape, he loosened it a tad more.

His jaw ached from holding the beer opener, but taking a rest wasn't an option. Without warning the last fiber broke.

One more to go and all he'd have to worry about was his wrists.

Caitlin peered through the fogged car window and rubbed at the condensation with a fast food napkin.

Damn. Was that sleet pinging on the car hood?

Fortunately, she was used to driving in all weather conditions. DC was good for that. She eased around the next corner, and the car fishtailed as a reminder of the slick streets. She held her breath and let off the gas.

"Pier Fifty-Two, where are you?" she hummed. All she needed was to be meandering around the deserted docks in a blankety-blank, almost unheard of, New Orleans ice storm.

Crap, the docks all looked the same. She pulled over to the side and hit the map flash. Okay, she wasn't far off now. Another block, a left and then a quick right. A shiver worried its way up her spine and then down. She shook off the dread gathering in her gut and tried both Jake's and Alex's cell phones.

Nothing.

Scenario? Nothing like the tried and true woman with car trouble in bad weather. That ought to work since it was pretty damned close to the truth. The docks were dark and deserted. And the sleet hitting her windshield was real enough.

Right. No one with any sense was out on a night like this.

Fifty-two. She barely made out the numbers in the glare of her headlights. She slowed and with a sickening slide careened into the side of the warehouse.

Way to go. Nothing like a stealthy approach.

A slit of light appeared...and widened as a door opened.

Damn.

Two men emerged. Both of the hulking variety. Not good.

At least she didn't recognize them, which should mean, if she were on the good side of lucky, they wouldn't recognize her either. She rolled down the window.

"Hey, little lady. You're making a lot of noise. Got a problem?" asked the Southern-accented hulk.

"You could say that. The boss isn't happy with how things are going down here. He sent me to straighten you out."

"What duh fuck?" This from hulk number two.

"Bud wants me to question those two bozos before..." She paused, stalling for time. Did she really want to open the car door and give the two hulks a chance to manhandle her? First, she'd better make sure they were buying her story.

"Since when does duh boss send a woman to do a man's job?" asked the taller of the hulks in a distinct New Jersey accent.

"Since the two of you are muscle, and this takes some finesse. Something which, if I'm not mistaken, neither of you have in abundance."

"Kinda smug, ain't she?" The *Hee Haw* southern boy grinned, and thank heavens, he had all his teeth because an insane urge to giggle hit her. She clenched her jaw and barely managed to hold it at bay. Neither of these stereotypical bad guys was a joke. More like bad news.

"I'd better call the boss," Jersey said, then pulled out his cell phone.

Caitlin held her breath and darted her gaze from side to side scoping out possible escape routes in the vast warren of warehouses.

"Voice mail," he muttered, then shrugged and left a message to verify what the broad was doing there.

She might just get out of this alive if she could just get inside and find Alex and Jake. "Cut the crap," she ordered. More than a little unsure if they were going to follow her lead or knock her in the head, she opened the door and slid her feet out of the car.

"Purty little boots for a night like this." Hee Haw sniggered.

Caitlin clenched her jaw. "Enough with the fashion commentary. Let's get inside and see what I can get out of those two." Okay, so she was betting on Jake and Alex both being inside. So much for backup.

"Neither one of dose guys are talkin'. You're wastin' your time. We should just ice 'em." He motioned upward at the falling sleet and guffawed at his pathetic joke. "Better call the boss anyhow."

Not yet, Jersey. Not yet.

"Nah," Hee Haw said, "Why would any woman be out on a night like this? Ain't fit for polar bears."

"The boss says, *Go*, I go," she said with a shrug, holding back the nausea roiling in her stomach. It was crunch time. All her training wasted if she couldn't pull it off, and Jake would be proved right—she had no business running an undercover operation.

Not that it really mattered. They'd all be dead.

She followed Harris's goons inside. At least they weren't behind her with guns drawn. They'd accepted her as being in charge. For the moment anyway.

Or more likely considering their marginal IQs, they figured a single woman wasn't much of a threat.

Once the last strand of duct tape shredded at his ankles, Alex started working on his wrist restraints. As soon as he freed his hands, he ripped the duct tape from his eyes. The room was pitch black, and he stumbled into the cabinet. He jerked open the rest of the drawers.

Dammit. He needed a weapon in the worst way. A beer opener

wasn't much good against the goons' guns. He rummaged through the contents and slipped what felt like a box cutter into his pocket.

He shivered. Damn. It was getting cold. Sure it was winter, but winter in New Orleans meant rain, sometimes a lot of rain. But if he didn't know better, he'd think it was about to snow.

Nah.

With the cold seeping into his very bones, he eased open the door, blinked while his eyes adjusted to the dim light in the long hall and listened. They must've held him in some sort of storage room.

Right or left? His sense of direction all shot to hell, he slipped into the hall and crouched low.

Time to get his ass out of this shit hole of a warehouse.

A door slammed. Voices.

Damn. He ducked for cover.

Caitlin followed Hee Haw and Jersey Boy through a maze of crates and past a forklift in the corner. "Where are they?" Caitlin demanded.

"We got one of dem in back in a storage room. Other guy's in duh office."

"Which one is closer?" she asked.

"Office."

"Check on the one in the storage room," she ordered Hee Haw.

Divide and conquer. No way could she take on both of them at once. Chuck Norris she wasn't.

"Sure ya don't want me to soften him up some more for ya?"

Some more?

"No! I want him able to talk. Just wait for me." No telling what the goons had already done to Alex—or was it Jake in the storeroom?

Jersey lumbered by another row of crates and took a left. "Office's here." He opened the door and Caitlin walked inside. The office was pretty bare. There was a metal desk, a filing cabinet with a drawer partially opened.

And Jake.

Hands cuffed behind him and calves tied to a chair, his head hung low on his chest which rose and fell with each breath. A quick rush of relief flooded through her. No major damage visible.

She walked over to him, took a handful of his dark hair and jerked his head back. "You! Who do you work for?"

His lids snapped open. Just as she thought—faking.

A half grin quirked the side of his kissable mouth. "Depends on who wants to know."

"Information's going to flow one way, fella. From you to me." Having Jake at her mercy was kind of fun. But back to business. Jersey was looming over her shoulder, and this was no time to think about what she would like to do with Jake at home.

"Thinks he's a tough guy."

She gave Jersey a coy look and fluttered her lashes. "What about you? Are you a tough guy, too?"

He lumbered a step in her direction with a definite leer flickering in his mud-brown eyes. "Yeah. I'll show you after we take care of dis guy."

She had no doubt exactly what he intended to show her. Fat chance.

Whatever she did, she had to be fast and accurate. No way could she risk letting him get hold of her. She took a deep breath and focused all her body's energy for one lethal strike. The fingers of her right hand rigid and—

Snap. Right into his left C2 carotid space. He shook his head for a second and toppled like a tall pine felled by one expert blow of a lumberjack. Whether she'd actually ruptured his carotid sinus remained to be seen, but for the moment he was no longer a problem.

Jake struggled against his bonds. "What the fuck did you just do?"

"I may have killed him...or not." She knelt down and felt in one of Jersey's pockets, then reached over to his other. Had Hee Haw taken the keys with him?

"But what was that thing—that blow?"

"My version of a *dim-mak*." She frowned. No key in either shirt pocket.

"A poison hand strike? That's what that was?"

"Yeah. Never used it before." She reached for Jersey's pants pocket. "Didn't know if it would work. I—"

The door flew open and banged against the wall. "What the fuck?"

She looked up from Jersey's body. Bud Harris stood looming in the doorway, his gun drawn and aimed at her head.

Crap. She snapped up her weapon. "FBI, you're under arrest!"

"Oh, yeah? Looks like I've got the drop on you. Your pal, Jack—whatever his name is—he FBI, too?"

"Damned straight he is." Instinctively she edged away from Jake. One man couldn't cover two people on opposite sides of the room.

"Stay where you are!" He motioned his gun in Jake's direction. "Or I'll shoot your partner."

God, no. She willed her hands not to shake. Jake was right. She had no business...

"Drop it or your partner's a dead man." Harris took a step forward. Damn, the man was as tall as Alex and she was nearly within his reach.

Taking a step back, she shook her head. "And you'll let us live if I do? I don't think so."

"We've got backup, Harris," Jake bluffed. "Don't make things worse for yourself by killing two federal agents."

"Gotta have bodies to prove murder. There won't be enough left of you two to ID. Matter of fact, you might just *never* be found."

"We *found* Terri Thibedoux," Caitlin said, remembering all too well just how little of her was found. A hard shiver ran through her body.

Not that. Chained, left alive in the bayou for the alligators' munching delight.

An expression of pure evil shot from Harris's eyes. "If you had backup, they'd be here by now. Put the gun down, girlie."

"No."

"Put the gun down now, and I'll do you both quick. Gators aren't picky. They won't mind if you're not all that fresh. In fact, that's how they prefer it."

Caitlin's gorge rose. She put her gun down and kicked it toward Harris. He was thin, not a bruising hulk like his henchmen. She could take him…if she could disarm him.

The sound of crates falling and crashing.

Harris turned his head.

Now.

Caitlin rushed forward and slammed her shoulder into Harris's rock-hard belly. Apparently, he was all wiry muscle.

He grunted, but recovered quickly, whirled around and backhanded her with his fist.

Pain exploded in her head. Prickles of light.

"You son of a bitch!" Jake bellowed.

Down she went, landing on her side.

Chapter Twenty-seven

Once the voices had faded away, Alex eased into the warehouse where crates were stacked to the ceiling. But now he heard footsteps headed in his direction. He froze against a crate labeled *Furniture*. All he had was a frigging box cutter. He glanced around for something...anything he could use as a weapon.

In the corner, he spied a forklift.

How hard could driving a forklift be? If warehouse guys could operate it, surely, he could. He eased toward the corner, trying like hell to be quiet, but in the dim light, he caught his foot on a pallet and crashed his knee into the corner of a crate.

"Yeow." Excruciating pain lanced from his shin to his brain. He grabbed his knee and held his breath. Had anyone heard?

Given he'd yelled loud enough to wake the dead, chances were someone had.

Footsteps. Quicker this time.

Alex hobbled toward the forklift and reached it in time to see one of the men come barreling around the corner.

"You, sumbitch. How'd you git out!"

This one had to be Hee Haw. "Yeah, can't keep a good man down. That would be me." He scanned the dashboard. Okay there was a steering wheel, a gear shift thing—was that what operated the lift? —and what appeared to be gas and brake pedals. Doing pretty good so far. Key, where was it?

"You're dead meat, kid," the good ol' boy bellowed and rushed toward him.

Short of throwing the seat cushion at the goon—he reached

under.

Hot damn. The key was under the cushion!

He jammed it into the ignition, fired up the forklift, pushed the pedal to the floorboard and headed straight for said goon.

Hee Haw pulled his gun and Alex ducked, hunkered down behind the steering wheel and kept his foot on the gas.

Ping.

A bullet glanced off the dashboard. Dang, that was close. Close to the gas tank in back, too.

Pop. Pop.

The shots echoed in the warehouse, almost deafening him.

Thud and then a sickening groan.

The lift rocked and almost knocked Alex from the seat.

Damn. The good ol' boy was skewered...all the way through, his face a hideous mask of pain.

Alex backed up the lift, jumped down. Blood ran from Hee Haw's mouth and down the body, pooling in a dark puddle on the floor.

He felt for a pulse. Nothing.

"Shit, man. Why didn't you jump outta the way?" He shuddered. He'd never killed anyone in the line of duty before, and this was one helluva grim way to change that statistic.

Before he could make up his mind whether to try CPR, the sound of raised voices stopped him, one a woman's.

Caitlin? What was she doing here?

Jake wrestled against the cuffs behind his back. Son of a bitch. No way could he shrink his meaty hands and escape from the damn things.

Harris' body language grew more threatening. He loomed over Caitlin's still body. Bastard had backhanded her.

"You conniving little bitch. Think you can ruin my operation here? Think again."

An urge to heave his guts wracked Jake. Caitlin hadn't moved since Harris hit her.

In the distance: *Pop. Pop. Pop.*

Gunfire?

Harris stopped and turned toward the sounds. "Too bad about your friend. At least one of my men is capable of following orders."

Alex? God no. Jake struggled harder against the cuffs. "Leave her alone, you son of a bitch."

Harris did a slow turn and glared. "You—I'll take care of soon enough." A sneer pulled his thin lips into a grimace. "Maybe you'd like to watch?" He laughed. "Maybe not, but I'm not giving you a choice. Take notes or a picture if you want while I taste every inch of this little gal."

"Touch her and you're a fucking dead man."

Harris laughed. "Deadman speaking."

The cuffs bit into his wrists, as a rage, pure and hot built inside him. "Take these damn things off, you coward. Fight me—man-to-man."

"I'm tired of your mouth. Shut it." A back fist whipped across Jake's chops, ringing the bats in his belfry.

His vision blurred. Jake shook his head in a vain attempt to see.

Harris shrugged and turned his attention back to Caitlin. "I didn't hit you that hard. I think you're playing possum." He stood spread-legged with his hands on his hips. "I usually like a little more action when I'm gettin' some, but—"

A blur of feet and legs sent Harris crashing to the floor. He screamed and cradled his balls. Gasping for air, the bastard bawled worse than a loser in a high-stakes poker game.

Caitlin retrieved her weapon with one hand and dipped into Jersey's pants pocket with the other. "One move and I'll cap your sorry butt." No need to worry, he was breathing but still out.

"Catch." She tossed the key in Jake's direction.

He stood, turned his back and caught the key in cupped hands. "Thanks."

"I'm not taking my eyes off this murdering asshole."

"Gonna Mirandize him?" Jake reminded while he managed the cuffs. He slipped them off and rubbed his wrists. "If you can stop playing bad-ass bad cop long enough."

Awareness dawned on her face. "You're under arrest. You have the right..."

He heaved a sigh. What a woman. She'd kicked Harris's ass in less time it took to roll snake eyes. He'd have to re-evaluate whether or not she could hold her own.

After Harris was cuffed and read his rights, Caitlin's mouth dropped open. "But where's Alex? Someone dropped a dime and said you were both here, so here I am."

Lucky to be alive, too. He'd never seen her more beautiful. Her green eyes snapped with fire and excitement. Her red hair was curling in every direction. "God, you're cute when you talk tough."

"Cool it. The tip said you were both being held here." Her eyes widened. "They better not have..."

"Someone mention my name?"

Alex strolled in, his lip swollen and a big shiner discoloring his handsome face, but not too great the worse for wear.

"I heard a god-awful racket and thought I'd better investigate." Alex folded his arms across his chest and leaned against the door jam. "Now, Jake, did you whip Harris' ass all by yourself, or did Caitlin have to rescue you?"

Plastering on a fake grin, Jake muttered, "Wouldn't you like to know?"

"Man, this is one report I can't wait to read."

Jake growled. "Why don't you call the local office to pick up the trash?"

Alex flashed a grin and saluted. "Consider it done." He turned to leave. "Oh, by the way, we need a meat wagon, too."

After Alex left, a tiny smile played about the corners of Jake's mouth. "But you're in charge. I haven't forgotten. You proved you're damn tough. You can be in charge of me any old time you want."

Caitlin let out a sigh. "Being in charge is overrated. All I proved is that I'm not really suited to fieldwork."

Jake staggered back, holding his hand over his heart. "No, I don't believe you. You're damn tough. You saved my ass. What else do you have to prove?"

"No, that's not what I mean. I did the job, but my internal organs were trying to exit through both orifices."

He gave her a wide grin. "Not an uncommon reaction."

"Just listen. I don't have to prove anything to anyone anymore. I guess I just needed to prove it to myself."

"After we debrief at the field office, I'm taking you home. I need to show you how glad I was to see you show up at the warehouse."

"Sounds good to me." And it did. They would work things out, after all.

After a lengthy debrief, he'd promised to take her home and take her home he did Through the sleet and icy winds, Jake drove with Kate snuggled close to his side. He'd never been so proud or glad in all his life when she showed up. Hold her own? Hell, yeah. What a woman; she could whip her weight in wildcats.

"You asleep?" he asked softly.

Her head popped off his shoulder. "No way. I don't know if I'll sleep tonight or not. I'm totally jazzed."

"That's how it is. And I was wrong about you."

"What? Jake LeFevre is admitting he was wrong. Has to be a moment for the record books."

"Be nice."

"I'll be nice. Never fear. I was so scared I would screw everything up and get us all killed."

"Hold on. That's another moment for the record books. SAC Caitlin Chaney admits she was insecure about her abilities."

He pulled up in front of their building. "Go on. I'll park the car."

"Aw, you've come a long way, baby."

He chuckled. "I'm teachable."

"Yeah." She leaned over and kissed him long and hard. Her hand ran up his thigh. He hardened like a shot and let out a groan. "Woman, you're killin' me. Get inside and warm up the sheets."

Okay, maybe he'd had time to reconsider a lot of his insane ideas about how they'd never work out a future together.

They say being close to death could do that.

Chapter Twenty-eight

The sun shone and sparkled on the winter wonderland that was New Orleans. Already the icy trees were dripping as the sun's rays melted. Caitlin looked out the window of the local FBI office, but there was no sunshine in her life. Her heart was darkened with the pain of betrayal. Jake reached for her hand and rubbed his callused thumb across the back of it. She shook her head, still not wanting to believe the evidence before her.

The paperwork was done. The warrants had come through and what they revealed was far worse than her worst nightmare.

The money trail had been exposed. Her father, the Secretary of the Interior, and Carlos Rivera were at the bottom at a money-laundering scheme—one that turned drug money into weapons and funded a rogue terrorist cell in the U.S. A cell dedicated to ensuring that the U.S. would be involved in a "War Against Terrorism" for years to come. Just in time, their investigation had stopped attacks on soft targets all over the United States. Schools. Hospitals. Churches. Temples.

All that remained was waiting to hear of her father's arrest. Harris had already been picked up. Rivera was in the wind, but he'd be located sooner or later.

Case closed...almost.

"How could my father have been so corrupt? Attacking his own country to justify reprisals on our enemies abroad?" She gazed into Jake's warm eyes. Why didn't he turn from her in revulsion? How could he stand to look so lovingly into the eyes of the daughter of a traitor?

His arm snaked around her shoulders. The comfort of this strong man was all she had to hold on to. "Who knows why anyone condones the murder of innocents. I sure as hell couldn't."

"Collateral damage, Jake. That's what they call it."

"He's one sick bastard."

"I can't believe I bear his name. The thought that his DNA makes up half my body sickens me. No matter what I thought I needed to prove...I'll never live down what he's done...or tried to do."

"It's not you. You're your own person. You always were. You're worth ten times a man like your father."

Tears forming, she leaned into his embrace. "Everything I thought he stood for in government, it was all a sham."

The door was flung open.

Alex bounded into the office and banged his fist on the desk. "Have you heard? Harris gets a pass on two murders."

Poor Alex.

He was young in his career...naive.

"In exchange for exposing the entire Rivera Corporation's money laundering scheme and drug contacts and weapons dealers," Jake added. "This shit happens...all too often."

Caitlin couldn't bear to tell Alex about her father's role in the treachery. Not yet. "And Heaton Boyle? Poor slob. Angie had certainly worked him over. His wife's dead." She added, "They say he fell completely apart and confessed everything. And he'll be going to jail for embezzlement. I almost feel sorry for him."

"You do?" Jake arched an eyebrow. "Bastard tried to frame me for Angie's murder."

"Don't be petty. He really thought you did it."

"Only because he was on his way to do the job himself."

Alex stopped pacing and glared at the two of them. "But two women are dead. And Harris gets to live out the rest of his life in Nowhere, Arizona, in reasonable comfort and safety."

Jake scowled. "Maybe. Maybe not. The mob's been known to find a witness or two. He'll always be looking over his shoulder."

"I have half a mind to let someone in Rivera's mob know where he goes."

Jake frowned. "That's one reason none of us will ever know where the U.S. Marshals take him." The frown disappeared, replaced by a somewhat grim smile. "Otherwise, I'd beat you to it."

Caitlin drew up and tried to lighten the mood. Her pain was best shared privately with Jake. "Gentlemen, we're law officers.

I don't want to hear this."

"Chèr, it's going to be all right." His gaze was warm and caring. "Case closed. We're going home. Then we'll see what else Jose has planned for our sorry butts."

Alex shook his head and headed for the door. "I'm on the redeye to DC, and I got a girl I oughta say *adios* to before I go."

She watched the young agent leave. A smile tugged at her mouth. "Obviously he'll be all right."

"What about you? You're all I care about."

"I'll resign. My career in the agency is over."

"Resign? You can't."

She shook her head. "I don't want it anymore. I've proved all I needed to prove."

"Don't do anything rash. Take a night to think it over."

Late the next morning, Jake lay with Kate spooned in his arms. Her warmth seeped into his very soul. They'd been good together in every way—a successful mission...and in bed. Dammit, they were fucking great. She felt so right in his arms. He wasn't sure he could bear leaving her and the loft...their home. But except for packing up the loft, their mission was over. Then they'd still go their separate ways.

Sure as hell, she wouldn't be cuddling up like this once they were back in DC—no, not the ex-Secretary of the Interior's daughter. No matter what her father had done, she'd go back to climbing the career ladder, if not in the agency, then somewhere else in the corporate world, just like his ex had, without a second thought. He'd either be on to his next assignment or...

Well, his future depended on the results of a certain DNA test.

Caitlin wasn't the only one who mattered unless he could work out some kind of arrangement for his daughter. How could he manage undercover assignments and provide a home for Charlotte? Maybe a change in careers...something a little more stable?

Ed had managed.

So would Jake. Somehow.

The phone rang. Caitlin stirred against him but didn't waken. He grabbed it before it could ring again. Damn, it was already a quarter after nine.

"Yeah."

"Mr. LeFevre?"

The voice was female and familiar. "Yes."

"This is Ms. Massey from Charlotte's school."

He sat up. "Yes. Has something happened?"

"The students from her cottage were taking their morning walk, and she was...oh my word, I can barely say it—"

"What?"

"She's been kidnapped."

"Kidnapped? But there's an iron gate with a six-foot fence."

"It was a—I still can't believe it—a helicopter. It landed and two men jumped out, chased Charlotte down and dragged her off. This is so upsetting. Nothing like this has ever happened before. Poor little Charlotte, she was screaming. I don't how she will absorb this. It'll set her back—oh, I have no—"

"Have you called the police?" he snapped to stop her mindless blathering.

"Yes, of course. I called them immediately but given your interest in her and that you're possibly Charlotte's father, I felt it behooved me to let you know."

"Were there identifying marks on the helicopter?"

"Well, it was black—I'm told. Not very big."

He stifled his rage. "No, I mean numbers and call letters."

"I've no idea. The two caretakers were too busy trying to bring the other students under control. When the helicopter approached, the noise was quite loud. The students ran in different directions. The caretakers did their best to keep them together. In normal situations, two can handle the six students easily, but with all the noise, but it was simply impossible."

"I'm sure. All right, thank you. I'll be in touch."

"Will there be a ransom demand? What about the FBI? Should we get them involved?"

"I'll call them immediately."

"Yes, of course. I'd forgotten you're with them. I'll let you go."

He broke the connection and called the local Bureau office. He quickly gave them the few details he had. "I think this is related to our operation here. Harris' boss—Rivera. He'll want to trade the girl for Harris' whereabouts."

"Back off, LeFevre, we'll handle this."

"Hold on. I'll stay here, but I want someone out at the school, just in case they try to contact someone there."

He hung up and sank down on the bed, catching a glimpse of the woman he couldn't live without. Wide-eyed and pale, Kate was awake. "What's happened? Start at the beginning."

He shook his head. "No time. Charlotte's been kidnapped from the school. You man the phone." He ran to the armoire and jerked open the door. "I'm heading out to the school."

She rose quickly and placed a delaying hand on his forearm. "No, you're not! Jake, you have to do this by the book. You can't rush off on your own. You're too close to the situation."

"Like hell! I'm not gonna sit here and wait for the phone to ring."

"You will if I have to knock you in the head and tie you up. And how many times have you told an upset parent to sit tight? This is the one time you'll have to follow the rules. You have to. This girl's life depends on your doing exactly as the agents say. You're too close, and you know I'm right."

He crumpled to the floor. "I know. I know. What am I going to do?"

She knelt beside him and put her arms around him. "I'll help you, Jake. You know I'll do everything I can."

The telephone rang again. Nine-twenty-five. Too soon. No way to trace the call yet. "Yeah?"

"We have something you want." The voice was metallic and almost garbled—mechanically altered. Dammit.

"So?"

"You have something we want: Harris. How about a trade? We've got this young girl—quite a handful she is. The sooner you meet our demands, the happier she'll be."

"I want to talk to her. I need proof that she's all right."

"Get the girl."

Faintly he heard a disturbance and a girl speaking in a halting monotone. "I don't talk on the phone. I'm due in class. I'm late. My schedule is important. I have to keep to it. Talking on the phone isn't part of my schedule."

"Come on. Be nice. Talk to the man if you want to get back to your schedule. You gotta talk to the man."

"Talk to the man," was all she said.

Relief at hearing his daughter's voice surged through him. Then a reality check: he didn't even know what her voice sounded like. "Hi, Charlotte. This is Jake. We're doing everything possible to make sure you get back to your school and your schedule as soon as possible."

"My schedule is very important. My day is ruined. I didn't get my exercise this morning. I need exercise to stay healthy. It's important." His daughter's voice was halting and her tone almost automaton-like.

This young girl, likely his daughter, in the hands of a dirty bastard...

"Yes, and we'll do everything to make sure it doesn't happen again."

"Thank you. I have good manners. Good manners are important."

"Yes, Charlotte, they are, and yours are lovely. Are they treating you all right?"

"Tha's enough," said the male voice—he'd forgotten to use the voice device; Jake could pick out a faint Hispanic accent. "Enough. You've talked to your kid. Now, wait one hour. I call back with instructions. And keep your fucking organization out of it."

Your kid? Jake's heart pounded against his chest wall. His face grew warm.

"What makes you think she's my kid?" he growled into the phone.

"A little blond bird told me before she died. She also told me your real name's LeFevre." The kidnapper broke the connection.

He turned to Kate. "Dammit. Angie actually told somebody else Charlotte was mine. It has to be somebody from the casino. 'A little blond bird told me before she died.' That's what he said."

Kate nodded. "Then that's who murdered Angie."

"He's dealt the cards. Charlotte may be his hole card, but he won't hesitate to kill her if we don't give him what he wants."

"Maybe not. And at least you know she's alive for now." She wrapped her arms around him, and his heart steadied. "It's going to be okay."

"I can't just sit here. Whether she's my daughter or not..." He paced back and forth. "You know as well as I do that the Bureau isn't going to hand over Harris for any reason."

"But they'll pretend to negotiate...to buy time."

"Why isn't that a reassuring option? Too many things can go wrong, Kate."

Before Caitlin could respond, there was a knock at the door. She darted a glance at her watch. Quarter of ten. Jake jumped up and raced to open it. The Feds had come to the rescue. Both men were tall and wore dark suits, white shirts, and dark ties, the typical uniform, neither of whom he'd met when he and Kate had first checked in with the locals.

The blond flashed his I.D. "We're Agents Boudreau and Mendoza. We're here to set up the trap and trace and—"

"—hold my hand? Keep me from interfering?"

The Hispanic agent nodded. "Yes, sir. That's exactly what we're here to do."

By ten, a somber Agent Boudreau announced, "The tap's in place. You know the deal: let it ring twice before answering."

"Yeah. Yeah, I know."

Boudreau stared at Jake; a frown wrinkled his forehead. "You know, you have a real familiar look about you."

"Really?"

"LeFevre? You from here in New Orleans originally?"

"Yeah. What about it?"

"Got a third cousin, still lives in the bayou. You could pass for his twin."

Jake shrugged. "No relatives left I know of."

"Neither side? Lotsa LeFevres back home in Baton Rouge."

"In the bayou? I was born in the city."

"Your *maman*, who was she?"

Jake jumped up and started to pace from one end of the loft to the other. "What's the point of all this chit-chat? My daughter's in the hands of kidnappers and drug dealers, and you want to trace my family tree?"

"Seeing as we're supposed to keep you occupied and out of the way, I thought it might help pass the time."

"I don't know anything about my father's people." Jake took a deep breath. "All I know is my mother came to New Orleans before I was born. When I was two, she married my stepfather. When I was six, she disappeared one night. Stepfather said she ran off with a trumpet player."

"So *his* name was LeFevre?"

"Nope. That was my mom's name. I never knew my father. She told me he was killed over in Nam, and her family kicked her out because they weren't married. That's all I know."

"While you're here you ought to do some research...once your daughter has recovered."

Jake stopped and shrugged the frustration and tension from his shoulders. "I should be a part of this. She'll be upset with everything. You don't understand how she is. I barely do."

"She's autistic, that right?"

"Asperger's Syndrome. High functioning and very talented...and very fragile."

"But not without her problems?"

"Right. I don't know what she's going to make of me. I don't know if her mother told her anything about me. I don't even know if she knows about her mother's death yet." He shook his head. "What I'm going to do...if something happens before I even get a chance to...?"

"You have to step back. We know what we're doing. Let us do our job."

"I *have* to be there."

"Where is there?"

"One of their fucking warehouses...or on one of their gambling boats. Hell! She could be anywhere."

"We already have a lead on the chopper they used."

"Yeah? That's great!"

"One of the kids was fascinated by the numbers on the bottom. It's owned by a subsidiary of Rivera Corp."

"Those sons of bitches. Have you checked out the warehouse at Pier Fifty-Two? That's where they held MacGregor and me."

"Yeah, nothing going on there."

"You have to have something. Look, I can help. Just give me a lead to work on. Anything. Otherwise, I'll go nuts just sitting on my hands."

Caitlin chewed her bottom lip. If she could just do something to help him. Jake paced, running his fingers through his hair, his eyes wild with fear.

With near certainty, Caitlin was sure the girl was his. Bad enough to have a child kidnapped, but one with Charlotte's challenges? Would her problems drive her captors to distraction? How carefully would they handle this girl who needed special attention and patience?

It would be a long day. How would Jake make it through? And what if the worst...?

No. She refused to think the worst. She jumped up. "I've put on a pot of coffee," she told the agents, "and then I'm hitting the company files," she said. "Maybe I'll find something we can use."

But first, she had to get Jake under control. "Sit down. You're driving yourself crazy."

He turned to glare at her, his eyes shining with emotion. "I can't. Don't you understand?"

"I do understand. Now, sit!" Dear heaven, what a hypocrite she was. She wasn't a mother and would never likely be one if she lost Jake.

He sat at the desk and stared at the ceiling. She walked behind him and began massaging his shoulders. "Your muscles are like steel bands. You're going to have a lot of pain if you don't relax." She added quickly, "And I know it's nearly impossible to relax in a situation like this. But you've got to make it through the hours somehow."

Silently he nodded.

Chapter Twenty-nine

The phone rang again at 10:25. Jake jumped at the sound but sucked in a deep breath and waited. That was one...two.

Agent Boudreau nodded.

Jake jerked up the phone. "Yeah?"

"You have twelve hours." The digital voice scrambler again. "You hand over Harris, and the girl will be released."

"The Bureau won't do it. He's being relocated by the Marshal Service. I don't know where. I don't have any way of finding out."

"That's too bad. She's a cute young thing."

Desperation grew and thickened in Jake's throat. "Look, I'll pay you anything for the girl's safety. Anything."

"Don't need money. I want Harris. Surely you see my dilemma."

"Yeah, he's already spilling his guts about your money laundering operation. And his information is so valuable the FBI's willing to overlook a couple of murders and put him in witness protection just to take your operation down."

"I still want him. I'll call back in two hours with details. You'd better have him ready."

"Dammit! He hung up." He glanced over at Agent Boudreau. "Anything?"

The agent shook his head.

Outside Washington, DC.

Derrick Chaney sat in his study. It contained everything vital to his comfortable existence: Napoleon Brandy, furniture covered in the finest Spanish leather, a priceless George III mahogany desk with inlaid marquetry, as well as a commercial-grade shredder. He sighed as the last notes of Mozart's piano concerto in D faded away.

His cell phone sounded a discordant note and spoiled the effect of the lovely concerto.

All day long, a sense of unease had gathered in his gut, and now the number displayed did nothing to reassure him. Better to answer and get the bad news.

"Yes?"

"The feds have Harris, and he's talking."

Ah, the reason for his uneasiness and a disaster looming on the horizon. "What are you going to do about it?"

"I've kidnapped LeFevre's daughter. We can trade one for the other."

"His *daughter*?" Nothing in his file about any family other than his adoptive father."

"Long story. Wanted to warn you."

"The Feds won't ever hand Harris over to you. No matter what they say or bargain."

"Fuck! You think I don't know that? The kid is a diversion."

"What's your plan?"

"We take out Harris when he's transferred from the jail to the Marshals. We have someone on the inside."

"Your inside man needs to take care of him now before he ruins everything. What are you going to do about the kid?"

"Just holding on to the kid until Harris is iced."

"Do whatever you have to do as long as it can't be traced back to me." Derrick broke the connection and took another sip of brandy. Damn LeFevre and his daughter Caitlin. They were too sharp by half. If worse came to worst...

He shook his head. Time enough for that later. He picked up a file and started shredding.

*

By noon, Jake and Caitlin had scanned through the document files. All thoughts of the money laundering op were secondary. Harris' inside intel had taken care of that. For only having been in business three years, Rivera Corporation's holdings were vast. They owned a nice chunk of riverfront property, not as much as Harrah's, but a nice chunk all the same.

At the very least, there were hundreds of places where Charlotte could be held. Office buildings, back rooms in the casino, two new casino boats set to launch in two weeks and even some residential rental properties. But, as was apparent from the first phone call, Charlotte could be noisy when not handled gently.

The site must be remote or deserted, where no one could hear an obstreperous teenager. Of course, they could always shut her up with a gag. But what effect would such an act have on his daughter's fragile psyche? And by now he was damn sure she was his.

He banged his fist on the desk. "Fuck! This is impossible." He jumped up and started pacing between the two agents. "See here, Boudreau, I've got a better chance of hitting a natural ten times running than finding Charlotte in all this mess of computer files."

"We'll find her. It just takes time. You know the drill."

"I don't see how. We don't even know if she's still alive. The last call was too short, I didn't get a chance—"

Caitlin got up from the desk and wrapped her arms around him. "We'll find her. We have to." Her comforting presence meant everything. But even she couldn't understand the blind panic ready to explode in his every thought. He couldn't bear thoughts of what might happen to Charlotte. And he knew all too well what could happen to kids who'd never done anything wrong—kids who would never grow up. Visions of their battered and bloodied bodies left to rot and to the predations of animals flooded his mind.

They'd left poor Terri Thibedoux in the swamp. A shudder ran through his entire body.

A cell phone rang.

A rush of nausea clenched his gut.

"Mine," Boudreau announced, then reached for his cell phone. "Boudreau. The kidnappers want to trade Harris for the girl," he told whoever was on the other end of the line. Jake watched Boudreau nod, his expression remaining grim. "All right. I'll tell them," he said.

"What?" Jake let out a groan. "What's happened?"

"No. Sorry. That was the local SAC. They're transferring Harris to a federal facility at five this afternoon. The U.S. Marshals will then relocate him. No trade."

"Then we have to find her first."

"The police and local agents are searching all the likely sites where she could be held." This from Agent Mendoza, whose dark brown eyes were full of sympathy. He was young; he'd soon learn to hide his feelings.

"It's not enough. I have to do something."

"You have let us do the fieldwork. You have to wait."

"Could you, Mendoza? Could you just sit here and wait?"

"I have a little boy—just two," Mendoza said. "I'd freak. But I hope there'd be a couple of fellow agents to keep me from doing anything stupid."

Jake snatched his coffee mug and heaved it across the room. It shattered against the old brick. The urge to trash the entire room surged through his entire body. His hands, clenched in fists, shook from the effort to hold in his rage.

"Did that help?"

Kate's gentle hand on his shoulder steadied his heart rate. He sucked in a deep breath and then slowly let it out. Couldn't trash the place. She'd kill him.

"No." He turned to her and placed a hand on each side of her face. "You're the only thing that seems to help."

"We're doing everything we can. We'll find her."

"Before it's too late?"

"No other option. We have to," she said gently.

God, he loved this woman. How could he go on without her? Would he have to?

*

Jake paced back and forth. Already 12:25. Damn wonder there was a floor left in the loft. Why hadn't they called? It was time. He glanced at Kate. Her mouth was set in a grim line, her hands clenched at her sides.

The phone rang.

He had an inner moment of relief, but then his gut-wrenching level of panic escalated a quantum leap with the second ring.

Boudreau nodded. Jake tamped down his rage and snatched the receiver. He had to keep his cool and keep them on the line long enough for the trace to go through. "LeFevre."

"Have Harris ready at ten."

"I can't be sure. The Agency won't deal. I'll have to—"

"If you want to see that little girl of yours alive, you'll bring him to me at ten. I'll call specific directions for the handover later. Stay near the phone."

"See here. Why don't you call me on my cell? That way I won't have to stay here in the apartment."

There came the sound of an ugly laugh, then, "No. Too easy to trace. It suits me that you're tied to the apartment. Stay there."

"I want to talk to my daughter again. I need to know if she's okay."

Click.

"Son of a bitch! He's too smart." And Charlotte—was she okay? How were they treating her? He sure as hell wouldn't agree to anything without additional verification.

Agent Boudreau shook his head. "If he's too smart to call you on your cell, he may be using a cloned cell phone himself." He studied the screen. "He won't stay on long enough, so all I can pinpoint is the general area—Riverfront."

"That still leaves a lot of territory to search, and it's where we're already concentrating our efforts," Kate said.

"Rivera didn't get where he is from being stupid," Agent Mendoza said.

"We have to outsmart this guy. Just once, we need the cards to break our way." Desperation settled in Jake's gut. Not since he'd lost twenty thousand on a sure bet had he experienced the gnawing misery of being in a bottomless pit with no fucking ladder in sight.

Jake ran his hands through his hair. "How do people do this?"

Kate crossed the room and put her arms around him. "We'll find her."

Miraculously, her warmth and her encouragement were all that kept him going.

Never one to panic, Carlos Rivera drummed his fingers against the glass-topped desk. With a view of the intercoastal waterway, his hideout was all brushed steel and glass—nothing like the mud-floored hovel in Guatemala where he'd been born. Nor was he inclined to give up the advantages of his present position as head of Rivera Corporation—the multimillion-dollar gambling corporation he'd founded using the seed money he'd made first by selling drugs and then later by gunrunning. Once he had Harris, he'd take his headquarters international.

He held his hands in front of him. They were steady and the nails were well-trimmed and manicured. No dirt there.

He had a good life, supported his family and even supported the economy of the United States of America. He was a good citizen. To lose that now because of two stupid women and a loose-lipped underling—unthinkable.

When would his inside contact report? Twelve thirty-five and still no word. Time was short. And getting shorter.

Bud—what kind of name was Bud? —Harris was spilling his guts to the cops and FBI. But as long as he wasn't around to testify in court, the damage could be controlled.

Salsa music tinkled from his cell phone. "Yeah?"

"The party is at five. Use the back door."

"Right."

The NOPD mole disconnected. No point in long traceable conversations. He punched in another number.

"Yeah."

"Transfer at five o'clock," Rivera said. "Rear entrance main station."

"Got it."

"No mistakes."

"Got it."

Satisfied, he lit a Montecristo cigar and took a puff, then he smiled and leaned back in his chair. It always paid to have a hitman on retainer. All Carlos had to do was keep the girl alive for a while—just in case her papa needed additional verification she was okay. Once Harris was dead, all bets were off.

Charlotte's internal clock told her it was two PM. She forced herself to think of fields of flowers. Each field of thousands of flowers, each field a different color. Her mind settled as she focused on each flower and how it differed from the others. Classes would be over for the day. She'd missed an entire day of classes.

No. Focus on the flowers.

The door opened. She froze and shrank back on the narrow cot.

A new one of *them* walked inside the room. "Hey, *chica*."

"My name's Charlotte Andre. I don't know *Chica*."

He knelt beside her and smiled. He had soft brown eyes and he was closer to her age than the others. "*Chica* is Spanish for girl," he said. "You're a very pretty *chica*. I'm Diego. You should be nice to me."

She straightened. Maybe... "What happened to the other man? He wouldn't let me go back to school. Will you take me back?"

"Maybe later. Are you hungry? I can get you something to eat...if you're a good girl."

Hungry? Her stomach growled. "Yes, I'm a good girl. I'm a good student, too, but I've missed all my classes today."

"Well, there's good and then there's *good*."

Why did the same word sound so different when he said it?

"I only know one kind of good. I'm well-behaved. I have good manners. Manners are important—that's what my teachers say."

"Your teachers are right." He reached to touch her.

She jerked away from his hand. "No! I don't like to be touched."

"Sorry, Carlotta."

"Charlotte. My name is Charlotte." What was wrong with him? Why couldn't he keep her name straight?

"Right. My mother's name was Carlotta. It's a different form of Charlotte."

"Oh." At least his tone was gentle. He didn't yell at her like the others. Still, something in his eyes... A shiver ran up her back and made the hairs on her neck prickle.

Too many distractions.

Focus on the flowers.

It was 2:30 and all day long, Caitlin had scanned files and kept the coffeepot going. The enormity of finding Charlotte was similar to finding the proverbial needle in the haystack. She leaned back from the computer and stretched the aching muscles in her shoulders and neck.

"Anyone for something to eat?"

On the other side of the desk, Jake shook his head. "Not hungry."

"Don't go to any trouble," Agent Boudreau said. "We're fine. We're used to living on coffee."

Caitlin stood. "Bull. My housekeeper Bonnie always said the brain requires energy to work. Protein to make the synapses snap." She picked up the phone and ordered sandwiches from the nearest deli.

"Once it arrives, fellows, help yourselves." She went back to trying to locate the girl. She scanned lists of addresses and checked them with map coordinates, anything to keep from thinking about how Jake would react if they didn't find her in time.

Mendoza's eyes brightened. "Great."

*

After the food was delivered, she stepped back and waited for the stampede to end. A five-minute break would refresh their outlooks and renew their efforts. Even Jake wandered into the kitchen and grabbed a sandwich and cold drink. "Thanks, chèr. I'm sort of hungry after all."

Good sign. His survival instincts were still working.

Someone knocked at the door

"Who is it?"

"It's Alex. Come on. Let me in."

She opened the door. "I thought you—"

The young agent ambled into the loft, a big grin on his face. "I took the red-eye, but when I heard what happened, I twisted Jose's arm a bit. He let me come back. Seems like I can pass for Harris— from a distance. We're the same height. Same hair color. I just don't have his forty-year-old wrinkles. And voila! I'm your official FBI-sanctioned decoy." He spread his arms wide and twirled around.

"A switch?" Caitlin nodded. Alex was spontaneous and good for a laugh, but... "It's a good idea, but damned dangerous."

"It's better than letting some sniper take Harris out."

"But it could be *you* the sniper takes out." Damn the kid. He was too excited, too reckless.

Alex's smile faded; his gaze grew serious. "I wasn't born yesterday. I know the risk, but the risk is greater for Jake's kid. I don't have a family. That fact and my looks make me the perfect decoy." His smile returned. "Besides, I'll be wearing a vest, and you guys are going to pick off any bad guys before they can pull off a headshot. Right?"

Caitlin scanned the four agents sitting in her living room, munching on sandwiches and chips. They looked back at her, their expressions earnest as choirboys.

"Right," the four of them said at once.

"Yeah, right," she agreed, not feeling as reassured as they apparently were. Too many things could go wrong. It was far too personal for Jake. How effective could an agent be when he was very likely that girl's father?

*

At the NOPD stationhouse, Caitlin tightened the straps on Alex's vest. "There," she said, giving him a pat, "you're done." With his hair slicked down like Bud Harris's, Alex could easily pass for Harris from a distance.

He buttoned his shirt over the vest and glanced over at Jake who'd come in with Agents Boudreau and Mendoza. "Why's Jake here? Isn't he supposed to stay at the loft?"

"Mendoza forwarded the landline so that it would ring on Jake's cell phone. He doesn't want to miss anything. Rivera's already proved he won't stay on the phone long enough for a trace, so he might as well be where the action is."

The muscles around Alex's eyes were tense. His Adam's apple bobbed as he swallowed hard.

"Scared?"

He shook his head. "Nah. It's just the adrenaline's already pumping."

"You've got the best backup in the world. I'll be right beside you. Jake will be covering our backs. Relax."

"Yeah, right. That's next on my list of things to do." He pulled at his collar.

"Hands behind your back." Jake placed the cuffs on him, loosely.

"I hate these things. Makes me feel helpless."

"Hush. They're barely fastened. Jake has to make it look good." She patted his shoulder for reassurance. "You'll be fine."

"1650 hours. It's showtime," Jake said, shifting to military time. "The van's in place. Our guys are in place. Everybody, stay sharp."

Once everyone was set, the transfer took place at a pace more rapid than Caitlin could've imagined. Down the back hall, down the steps to the basement and out the back door. It was already getting close to dusk. The alley was lit by one lousy streetlight. No big deal for a sniper with a night scope. Better to make the transfer now than take a chance after dark. She shivered. Her gut heaved, and she knew without a doubt someone was overhead. At least

Jake had her back. And in her book, there was no one better.

Of course, there was someone overhead. There were two agency snipers in position on each end of the alley. She moved in close to Alex. "Keep moving and keep your head down."

Too late.

Alex stumbled and dropped before she even heard the shots. She fell over his body while chaos reigned around her. "Don't you die. So help me, I'll kill you myself if you do."

Jake pulled her off Alex's body and dragged the two of them into the dark van. "Turn me loose! I'm all right." She knelt over Alex's still body. He was covered in blood, but she couldn't find an entry wound. Alex's head was fine, except for the blood. Where was it coming from?

The young agent groaned. "Damn. This hurts like a son of a bitch." He tried to raise up on one elbow. "K-Kate—"

"Be quiet and lie still, Hon. We're taking you to the hospital." She turned to the driver. "Can we get a move on, please! He's going to bleed out."

"Caitlin, you're the one bleeding." Jake reached over and brushed back the hair over her ear. "Here."

"I am?" She shook Jake's hand away and tracked the shallow wound in her scalp. The warmth of her own blood flowed over her fingers. The coppery smell.

Black splotches appeared before her eyes, then green ones. "Ohh." Just before she passed out, she heard the sound of more gunshots.

Chapter Thirty

In the captain's quarters of the *Palais Gulf Queen*, a telephone rang. Carlos shoved up the cuff of his silk shirt glanced at his Rolex. Ten minutes after five. Yes, it was time for his hit man's call. "How was the party?"

"Party's over, boss. Everyone loved their presents. Check your local TV station."

Carlos smiled. "Excellent. I'm very pleased."

Click.

Now time to get rid of that brat. "Diego!"

Diego was a smart kid as well as his nephew, so he'd placed him in the Palais Ponchartrain's security section.

"*Si, Tio* Carlos?"

"It's time to get rid of our troublesome passenger." He took a puff off his Montecristo. "I'll give you a box of these fine Cuban cigars when you're finished. Maybe a little trip out of the country, too."

"How? What do you want me to do with her?"

"Dump the kid overboard. Whatever. I don't give a shit what you do with her." He took another puff. "Just get rid of her."

He waited until Diego was gone, then picked up his phone. Time to update his silent partner. He hit the speed dial and waited for Derrick Chaney to answer.

"Well?"

"Harris is no longer a problem."

"What about the kid?"

"She's being taken care of now."

"Unfortunate."

"It was necessary, and you know it. Besides, once our plans go through, there will be more than a few—"

"That's different," his partner barked in Carlos's ear. "They'll be collateral damage."

"So's this one." The Secretary of the Interior was a pain in the ass but vital to achieving his end game. "You're not losing your nerve now—are you?"

"No. This is what the country needs to wake it up. America needs to stay in this war. This is just a little encouragement."

"Just doing your patriotic duty, Mr. Secretary. I couldn't agree more."

Click.

Carlos set the phone down and rubbed his chin. His silent partner could turn out to be a problem. Maybe he should be eliminated as well. But there was plenty of time for that.

Five minutes later, his uncle's instructions ringing in his ears, Diego moved down the narrow hallway toward the cabin where the lovely young *chica* was locked. He wasn't ready to get rid of her—not before he had a little fun. But he'd have to move her to a more secure place.

He unlocked the door.

Her piercing gray eyes stared at him. "It's you again. Did you bring me something to eat?"

"I'm going to take you to the food. Just come with me." He motioned for her to follow him. "It's not far." He remembered she didn't like to be touched and took care not to touch her. Later it wouldn't matter. No one would hear her down in storage.

He held a finger to his mouth. "We have to be quiet."

She nodded and followed him like an obedient puppy.

Twenty-five minutes after the sniper's attack, Jake could barely

284 | Marie-Nicole Ryan

contain his rage. He strode back and forth in the squad room. "There's a rat in this department. Not that it should surprise anyone. So who is it? Who's the mole?" He banged his fist on Sergeant Pelletier's file laden desk. A cup of coffee spilled, and one stack of files tumbled onto the floor.

Pelletier glared at Jake and coolly wiped up the spreading stain of coffee. "Just calm down, LeFevre. We're already dumping the phone logs. We'll know soon enough." He bent over, reaching for the files, but couldn't reach them for his paunch.

To steady himself, Jake picked up the files and shoved them back on the desk. "And one of you bums let us down—fellow law officers."

"That's enough, Agent LeFevre. We're doin' our best here."

"Whoever it is. You're mine!"

"Relax, man," Pelletier said, "they're both okay."

"Could've been a lot worse. Agent Chaney could've been killed instead of grazed. And there's still a missing child to consider. Don't forget that."

"Jake, it went down like clockwork," Caitlin said, fingering the edge of her bandage. "Our guys grabbed the hitman right after he made his call. I just wish I could do the interrogation."

"And I wish you had let the EMTs take you to the hospital."

"I don't need stitches. My wound is covered. I'm all right. Alex just has a bruised chest."

"What about the phone dumps?" Kate asked, eyeballing Pelletier.

"Any minute," growled the detective.

"Then we'll know who the mole is." Jake took a deep breath. "Time's running out. Now he thinks Harris is no longer a threat, he'll kill her."

"Maybe not," Caitlin said, her eyes bright.

"There's nothing to bargain for."

"Can we leak that it was a decoy shot? That should give her more time and a renewed incentive for Rivera to bargain."

Pelletier nodded. "Yeah, assuming it is Rivera. Maybe we're barking up the wrong tree?"

"I know it's Rivera. As the agent in charge of this operation, I'm authorizing the leak. In fact, a breaking news report would be even better."

"I'll set that up."

"Pelletier! Can we get a TV announcement? Can you set that up? Like pronto."

The detective sergeant reached for the phone, then stopped. "On it...as soon as I bring the Lou up to date," he said and lumbered off in the direction of the lieutenant's office.

"Marci Santora, WDSU News, coming to you live from the New Orleans Police Department. It's five-thirty, and only minutes ago we were summoned to the main station for this announcement from Lieutenant Ralph Cardamen. Now to the Lieutenant."

"Today during a prisoner exchange between the NOPD and the FBI, two undercover FBI agents were injured by sniper fire. One of those agents was a decoy for prisoner Delmar 'Bud' Harris, the executive director of the Palais Ponchartrain casino, who is currently under investigation for a multitude of charges, including RICO violations, money laundering, and murder. Both federal agents have received medical treatment and are expected to make a full recovery. The NOPD's SWAT snipers were able to locate the suspect and take him out before more injuries were incurred."

Carlos Rivera threw the TV remote across the room. "*Bastardo!*"

The girl. His bargaining chip. "Diego!"

The news flash had gone off without a hitch. Jake settled at an empty desk, plagued with questions. Had they done all they could? Was the announcement quick enough? Had Rivera even seen the news?

"Better have some coffee." Sergeant Pelletier set a Styrofoam cup in front of him. The brew was black...and bitter.

"Just what I needed..." Brake fluid with a heavy aftertaste of quinine.

"Maybe you'll like these better." Pelletier dumped the phone record printouts.

Jake snatched them and started scanning the lists, row after row of calls.

By a quarter of six, Jake determined only one call was made within ten minutes after the exchange details were decided. He made note of the number called as well.

"Pelletier." He held up the list. "Let's go talk to your lieutenant."

The detective sergeant nodded and followed him into Lieutenant Cardamen's office. "I have your mole. Sergeant Sweeney made a call at twelve-thirty-five which only lasted fifteen seconds. That's within five minutes after the prisoner exchange time was set. Here's the documentation. That phone number coincides with the last phone call made by Rivera's hitman. I want to question Sweeney. We still have to find Charlotte Andre."

The lieutenant scowled. "Who may or may not be your daughter?"

"That's right. Your announcement may have bought us some time, or it may already be too late. Chances are Sweeney knows something."

The lieutenant nodded. "He's yours. Good luck."

Pelletier walked to the door. "Sweeney!"

The squad assistant looked up from his paperback novel. "He left a couple of minutes ago. Said he needed to take a personal day."

"Call downstairs, Stop him. He's wanted for questioning."

For five stress-filled minutes, Jake all but held his breath until an angry Sergeant Sweeney stomped into the squad room. He glanced from Kate to Jake. "What's this all about?"

"We have a few questions for you, Sarge."

"I'm on my way—" The sergeant's eyes widened, and he glanced around as if looking for an escape route.

"This won't take long." Basically Jake didn't want to embarrass the detective in front of his fellow officers without reason. His gut hunch and evidence were circumstantial so far. Soon he'd know for sure.

He and Kate followed Sweeney into the interrogation room. "Want some coffee?" Kate asked. "Not that I can recommend it."

Sweeney leaned back in the metal chair and folded his arms across his chest. "See here, Agent LeFevre, I've got things to do today."

Playing good cop, Kate asked the first question. "And there's a young girl who's been kidnapped, and we think you know where she is."

"Me? Are you nuts?" His gaze averted to the left. "I'm one of the good guys, remember?"

"You're a mole for Carlos Rivera and you called him at 12;35, right after the exchange time was set. Convince me you're not!" Jake thumped his fist on the metal table.

"I called my wife when we got out of that meeting. That's all."

Jake pulled out his cell phone. "If I call that number now, is she going to answer?"

Sweeney shifted in his chair, his gaze darting back and forth between them, and chewed his bottom lip. His hands clenched and unclenched over and over. Finally. "No." He leaned forward. "See here, I didn't have anything to do with the girl's kidnapping. Yes, I made the call, tipped him to the time of the transfer. I owe the casino ten grand and—"

"And Rivera called in the marker?" Kate asked.

"Yeah. That's what happened. One phone call and I cleared my account."

Jake got in Sweeney's face. "I understand. I've been there, but I never compromised an investigation to pay off a gambling debt."

"You know what it's like? It's a sickness." Sweeney mopped his sweaty forehead with the sleeve of his jacket.

Good. Let the bastard sweat.

Yeah, Jake knew about the lies and cheating. "You're gonna need a new definition for sickness." Jake kicked Sweeney's chair halfway across the room. "If you don't spill the rest of what you know right now."

Panic crossed the detective's face. "I don't know nothin'. I told you I didn't have anything to do with the kidnapping."

"This is your last chance, Sweeney. Where're they keeping my daughter?" He glanced at Kate. Her face was pale. Did she think he was losing control? Maybe he was.

A bead of sweat formed and rolled down Sweeney's five o'clock shadowed face. "Fuck you!"

"You're just lucky you don't have a couple of murder charges hanging over your head. So you need to talk while you still can." Jake got down in Sweeney's face and whispered, "But if that girl has so much as a broken fingernail, I'll beat the stuffing out of you. And if anything really bad happens to her, you won't have to worry about murder charges, I'll kill you myself. Are we clear?"

"Your FBI agent. He was a last-minute swap. I didn't have time to warn them."

"The girl! Where's he keeping the girl?" Jake jerked Sweeney up by his suit lapels and slammed him against the wall.

"I don't know!" Sweeney yelled.

"And I don't believe you. I don't believe you made that phone call just to clear a debt. You're a no-good, low life grinder who blows the money his family needs on craps or blackjack. Which is it, Sweeney? Talk to me."

"C-craps."

"That's good. I really like it when you cooperate." Jake banged the detective's head against the concrete block wall. "Now tell me where my daughter is."

"Jake, stop!" Kate cried, but he was too far gone. He'd pound the information out of Sweeney in a heartbeat.

Sweeney shook his head as if to clear it. "Man, you can't do this. I have rights."

"Do you see anyone coming in here to stop me?" He nodded at Kate. "Even she can't stop me. I can do any damn thing I want. Now talk!" A quick backhand fist to Sweeney's lying face jarred all the way up to Jake's shoulder.

Sweeney's right eye puffed up; he blinked. "Boat. She's on one of their new casino boats. That's all I know—honest to God."

"Which one?" He drew back, ready to give Sweeney a little more encouragement of the painful kind.

"*Palais* something or other. The bigger one. It's fitted with some cabins. They'll take the high rollers on two-day cruises out on the Gulf. "

"You'd better not be lying, you sack of shit." Jake bounded out of the interrogation room, leaving Kate behind to watch the suspect. "Pelletier, pull up the files on Rivera Corp, anything about new casino boats and one with cabins for Gulf cruises."

"I'm already on it." Pelletier's fingers were hunting and pecking over the keyboard.

"Let me do it," Jake said. "I'm faster, and we don't have much time left."

"Sure thing." Pelletier shoved the keyboard in Jake's direction.

Jake hunched over the desk and quickly found a reference to the *Palais Princess* and the *Palais Gulf Queen*. "This has to be it— the *Palais Gulf Queen* moored at their riverfront casino." He turned to Pelletier. "I need the SWAT team for a stealth approach—like thirty minutes ago."

"Done." Pelletier grabbed the phone and started punching numbers.

Jake headed for the door.

"Hold on, cowboy," Pelletier jumped up and yelled. "You're not doing this by your lonesome."

"No, he's not." Kate came up behind him. "I left a uni with Sweeney. "I'm going, too."

He whirled to face her. "No, you're not. You have a fresh head wound, and I don't want anyone—read you—passing out at the worst possible moment in this operation." He set his hands on her shoulders. "You've already proved yourself in the field. This is a risk you don't have to take. Besides, the EMTs said you were to take it easy for twenty-four hours."

"All right, dammit. I'll stay behind...under protest."

"Understood."

*

Six o-clock. Better hurry, if he was going to have his fun. Diego led the pretty little *chica* down six levels into the bowels of the riverboat, taking great care not to spook her. He'd had time to outfit the storage room with a cot and a hidden video camera. He would film his best work and then end it with her death. Snuff films were tremendously popular in some communities, and it would make him a fortune when he sold it over the Internet. After all, he was an entrepreneur. His uncle would approve.

"Here we are." He opened the door and followed her inside, his gaze riveted to her firm little ass as it swayed from side to side under her short plaid skirt.

"This is a long way to go to eat. I don't have to go this far when I'm at school. We have dinner in our cottage. Here we've gone down six levels, and I've taken seven hundred and sixty steps since we left the other...place."

She glanced around the room. "Where's the food? If I'm going to eat, there has to be some food. I'm a good eater. I like most foods, except beans—I hate beans."

"*Chica*, you talk too much."

"Charlotte. My name is Charlotte."

"Yeah, like I keep forgetting. Sorry." She took a deep breath and let it out with a small sigh that brought his attention to her perky little *tetas* which swelled beneath the yellow sweater she wore. His dick hardened instantly, and his balls ached. Man, he wanted to bury himself in that tight little virgin pussy.

But not yet. No, he would force himself to take his time with her. She was young and firm and there were so many ways to find pleasure with her.

His mouth watered and he licked his lips. Such a juicy little thing. He reached forward with one hand to brush away a lock of hair—black as a crow's wing it was—from her face.

She hunched her shoulders, folded her arms across her *tetas*, and backed away from him. "No touching! I don't like to be touched."

"I'll be gentle. We'll get to know each other, and that's what friends do. They touch each other."

"No!" She said it louder this time, like a robot. "If someone tries to touch you and you feel uncomfortable—I've been taught to just say no. I said no."

Freaky. A little conversation went a long way...and so would a little duct tape.

Then no one would hear her screams. No one at all.

Chapter Thirty-one

By six-ten, Jake and the rest of the assault team set up a staging area just beyond the sightline of the *Palais Gulf Queen*. In addition to the NOPD SWAT team, Agents Boudreau and Mendoza were in attendance.

"Thanks." Jake took the Kevlar vest from Agent Mendoza and donned it while surveying the men who were prepared to storm the gambling boat. True to her word, Kate remained behind at the police station under protest. Still, she was one less female in his life to worry about. Dread clutched his heart and squeezed. If a heart attack felt any worse than this...he sure as hell hoped he never had one.

Had the news flash come in time to keep Charlotte safe?

"Too late. Too damn late." Carlos Rivera worked feverishly over a keyboard, transferring funds to his offshore account in the Caymans and deleting files.

Shit. He was no computer geek, and he was bound to forget something. Something that could give him a lifetime residence in a Federal pen. The FBI bastards had played him for a fool. Now Bud Harris would sing like a canary and rat out the organization and his only bargaining chip was already dead.

He punched the ship's P.A. system. "Diego!"

"Diego!"

*

Diego stopped, listened then tore off the final strip of duct tape and fastened her wrists behind her back.

"Diego!"

Damn. Why was *Tio* Carlos bellowing for him on the P.A. system? What could he want now?

He glanced down at the *chica*. Damn. He'd have to wait a little longer for his fun. Tying her up had been a bitch. He looked at the back of his hand and the perfect red impression made by her pretty little teeth.

He walked over to the intercom and hit the buttons for his uncle's office. "What?"

"The girl? Is it done?"

"Why?"

"We need her. Otherwise, we're fucked. Harris is still alive. Our guy shot a decoy."

Diego looked at the hot young thing lying on the cot—eyes wide and full of fear. Should he tell his uncle, he'd disobeyed orders and kept her alive or not? Would he be rewarded for thinking ahead or be tossed overboard for disobeying orders?

Fuck no. No way was he leaving without a taste of freaky chica. "I guess we're fucked then," he told his uncle

"I'm heading to the airport. My plane is waiting. If you're not on board when I get there, you're out of luck, *chico. Comprende*?"

"*Si, Tio* Carlos."

He walked over to her. "Well, *chica*, it's just you and me now."

At 6:20 Carlos hit the speed dial for Secretary Chaney. When the call went to voice mail, he said, "The party's over," the failsafe code for "cover your ass, the Feds are on the way."

No time to delete any additional files. Instead, he clicked on the My Computer icon, selected the C: drive and clicked on format. So what if his action crashed every computer on the network. No point in making it easy.

*

At 6:25 Jake peered over the technician's shoulder. "How many onboard?"

"The heat imaging scanner shows the boat is almost deserted. One up in the upper deck. Here." The tech pointed at the ship's schematic diagram. "There are five more scattered along the deck just below, probably his guards. Access ladders to the uppermost deck are here and here."

The tech squinted at his scanner. "Hm. This is weird."

"What?"

"There're a couple more warm spots down at the lowest level. Now on the diagram, it looks like a storage room, but it might just be an anomaly from the generator or the heating system."

"But the boat's not fully operational yet. Might be a good place to hide an unruly girl."

"I'll take the lower level," Jake said.

"We've got your back," Boudreau and Mendoza said in unison. "Rest of you, take the upper decks. And remember there's a young girl's life at stake."

The assault team sped quietly up the gangplank and through the gangway. Jake, Boudreau, and Mendoza headed for the bowels of the ship. Level after level, they scrambled down the ladders from one deck to the next.

Overhead Jake could hear small arms fire. "They've engaged," he said under his breath as he ran along the passageway. Adrenaline jolted through his body, and his heart hammered as if he'd cleaned out the house. "If we can hear it, chances are whoever's down below can, too."

There were four doors labeled *Storage*. Second from the right or was it the left?

Boudreau shrugged, then pointed at the door on the right. With Mendoza and Boudreau on each side of the door, Jake took the point position and kicked the door open.

A slender Hispanic male spun and aimed his gun—Diego from Security. Jake fired and struck him in the chest. Charlotte lay very still on a cot. Had he already killed her?

Rushing to her side, Jake stopped, bent down and unbound his daughter's cold hands. God. His daughter. He didn't need a DNA test to tell him what he knew down to his very bones.

"Don't be afraid, Charlotte. I'm Jake and I won't let anyone hurt you again. I have to take this tape off your mouth. It might sting, but it won't be bad."

He eased it off. He couldn't bear to rip it off her tender, fragile skin.

The girl glared up at him, her cool gray eyes so like her mother's, but Charlotte's hair and coloring were his. She took a deep breath and wiped her mouth. "Jake. You're the man I talked to on the phone?"

"Yes."

She pulled away from him and tried to straighten her clothes. "Why did they make me talk to you? I don't know your face. I have a very good memory. I'm not supposed to speak to strangers."

"And that's a very good rule, but I'm here to take you back to your school and your schedule."

"You did something to that man—Diego. He's not moving. He wouldn't let me stick to my schedule. It's very important that I keep my schedule. He said he would bring me some food, but he didn't."

He resisted the urge to scoop her up in his arms. According to her teachers, she didn't like being touched. He could only imagine what hell she'd gone through in the last two days. Grabbed, whisked away in a helicopter, all that manhandling...

"Did he hurt you?" he asked as gently as he could, all the while tamping down the rage still roiling through him. Other than a bruise on her cheek and a little mud on the toes of her tennis shoes, she appeared unharmed.

"No." She rubbed the red markings at her wrists. "They interrupted my schedule. I've missed an entire day of my studies. He tied me up. He touched me." Running out of words, she gazed up at him, her gray eyes assessing his intentions. "You have a good face. Your mouth is smiling but your eyes are sad. Why are you sad?"

Such an innocent, but eerily perceptive. "I'm sad you were taken away from where you felt safe, but I'm happy you're safe now."

"Does my mother know?" Charlotte stood. "Will she be waiting for me at school? I haven't seen her in twenty-five days. She works very hard, so I work very hard at school as she does at her job."

Searing pain tore through his chest. Grief tightened the muscles in his throat until he could barely breathe. How could he explain to this child of his that her mother wouldn't be waiting for her...ever?

Caitlin waited at the police station for exactly ten minutes. Enough waiting on the sidelines. Not her cup of tea.

Without telling anyone she simply left the stationhouse, hailed a cab and gave him the address for the docks where Rivera Corp. moored their new riverboats.

Once there, she emerged and paid the driver

"Looks like there's trouble brewing, lady," he said.

"I know." She smiled and gave him a big tip. "That's where I need to be."

She produced her ID badge to the uni who was monitoring the perimeter of the scene, then hot-footed it to the staging area. From the looks of it, the op was already in progress.

"Already in motion?" she asked the SWAT commander.

"Yeah, just a matter of time. They've already taken down some of Rivera's guards, and Rivera himself is in custody. Haven't found the girl yet, but Martinelli on the scanner says they're closing in on her location. At least if that infrared is working right."

"Good. Any injuries on our team?" she asked, anxious for Jake's welfare.

"Minor. Nothing to concern yourself with. Agent LeFevre's fine," he added with a grin.

"Thanks, Commander."

"Say, weren't you supposed to stay at the station?" he asked.

"I stayed...a while, but I couldn't stand it any longer."

"You got a taste for action." He grunted his approval, then listened intently to his headset. "Hold on, small arms fire."

She held her breath. What if Jake...? What if the girl...?

"Okay, that's it. Victim recovered. Last suspect out of commission."

"No wounds for the good guys?" Caitlin fidgeted from one foot to the other.

"Agent LeFevre's bringing the girl out."

She let out a deep sigh of relief. Her knees weakened. She wobbled and nearly collapsed, but the commander caught her and led her over to a weapons case. "Sit still until your head clears, okay?"

She nodded and took a deep breath. While she waited for Jake and the girl to appear on the gangway, her vision blurred. He was okay. All sorts of images had spun through her head when the round of weapons fire had commenced.

Jake dead or dying primarily among them. Or the girl. Jake would never have forgiven himself if she'd been lost in the recovery operation.

"There they are, Agent Chaney."

She glanced toward the riverboat and strained to see. Difficult to make out their figures in the dark—her heart clenched felt as if it were preparing for takeoff.

Dressed in black gear, Jake grinned widely and waved. The girl walked sedately beside him—not touching, but close. From a distance she appeared unharmed, but who knew what could've happened while Rivera's men had her?

Caitlin resisted the urge to run to greet him, hug him, kiss him the way she wanted. No, that might scare the girl even more.

So she waited.

Shivering, Caitlin chewed her bottom lip and watched from a distance while Jake took the girl over to the ambulance to be examined by the EMTs. She saw Charlotte resist their attentions, but it appeared as if Jake was talking to her, soothing her through the experience. She allowed them to place a blanket around her slender shoulders.

Once the medical personnel were satisfied, she had no serious injuries, Jake nodded in Caitlin's direction. Charlotte nodded and walked at Jake's side.

"You're not supposed to be here, Kate," Jake said calmly, but his steely gaze was another matter.

"I was worried about you and Charlotte."

"I don't know you. Why were you worried about me?" Charlotte asked, her pale gray gaze fixed on Caitlin.

"Charlotte," Jake said, "this is Agent Chaney with the FBI. She works with me and her name is Kate. She helped us find you."

The gray stare turned in Jake's direction. "No, you found me. I didn't see her there."

"That's true, but all these people here this evening helped. We worked together as a team."

"A team. Like baseball," she said with a nod. "Thank you. I always say thank you. Manners are important. That's what I've been taught."

The girl spoke haltingly without inflection, but Caitlin's heart was touched by this teenager's sweet face and manner. "You're welcome, Charlotte. I'm so happy you're okay." She arched a brow at Jake, questioning her own statement.

"Yes, she's in good shape. Hungry and cold."

"I need to go back to my school. My schedule is important."

"That's where we're going now, Charlotte," Jake said. "Do you mind if Agent Chaney rides along with us?"

A quizzical expression crossed the girl's face. "Do you want to see my school?"

"I'd love to, Charlotte. Thank you for allowing me to come with you and Jake."

"I like Jake. After he shot the bad men, he didn't make any more loud noises, and he doesn't try to touch me. I don't like to be touched." Her fingers toyed with the collar of her white blouse at the V-neck of a yellow sweater.

Caitlin couldn't help but let out a sigh of relief. Thank God it was all over.

Jake settled Charlotte in the front seat and Caitlin rode in the back. Already she could see a strong connection between Jake and his supposed daughter.

Strong connection or no, there were many struggles ahead. Someone would have to tell this child her mother was dead. And that was the least of the issues Jake would have to deal with.

And what would Caitlin herself have to deal with if this fragile teen was Jake's daughter? At this moment the possibilities seemed insurmountable. Was she even capable of dealing with the girl and all her problems? Would the girl accept her? How long and how difficult would the adjustment be?

Would she have to give up her career?

So many questions and so little time to decide. Once the DNA results came back, matters would kick into high gear if they were a match.

And if they weren't, Jake would be devastated because it was apparent that he'd already bonded with the teen.

An hour later, Jake carefully ushered a calm Charlotte into Ms. Massey's office while Kate remained in the outer office. The less stimulation Charlotte experienced the easier she would be to deal with. The woman glanced up as they entered. Her color brightened and her eyes glistened with tears. She clasped her hands to her chest. "Thank heavens. Are you all right, Charlotte? Did they hurt you?"

"I have a bruise on my left cheek. There's mud on the toes of my shoes. My clothes are wrinkled, and I missed all my classes. I'm sorry, but they wouldn't listen to me when I told them how important keeping my schedule was. I-I couldn't make them understand. I tried."

"I'm sure you did, dear."

"I'm ready to go back to classes now."

The headmistress shot Jake a questioning glance. He gave a slight shake of his head. God. He dreaded what they were about to do. How would this fragile child of his react? How could he console her if she rejected him outright? Why would she accept him? All he was to her was a stranger with a "good face".

"Charlotte, we're going to excuse you from classes for the next week. There are some things—"

"But," Charlotte interrupted quickly. "I need my schedule. I have it all worked out how I can make up for the time I missed."

The older woman rose slowly from her desk. He imagined she dreaded telling Charlotte as much as he.

"Charlotte, you must listen to me for a moment. I have something very important to tell you." She motioned to the sofa in front of the window. "Let's sit over here."

"Yes, ma'am." His daughter walked obediently and sat.

Mrs. Massey sat carefully beside Charlotte. She didn't touch the girl. Instead, she folded her hands in her lap and began. "I don't quite know how to tell you this." She gave Jake another glance, one so full of agony the pain knifed through him as well.

"Just say the words, Mrs. Massey...unless you have forgotten how to talk?"

Still watching the painful tableau, Jake bit the inside of his cheek. Charlotte took things so literally—something to remember.

"That's not it, dear. It's about your mother."

"Yes, I miss my mother. She works very hard to pay for my school. It's been twenty-five days since her last visit."

"Charlotte. Please...your mother has suffered an accident...and I'm so sorry, but she's dead."

His daughter sat straight, her back rigid, but her face was expressionless. "Dead. Definition: Ceased to breathe. No longer alive."

"Yes, that's right."

"She said she'd visit soon." Her eyes widened, and then she looked at the director with a plea in her gray eyes. "She always keeps her word. She does." Charlotte gave a vigorous nod.

"It's not her fault, dear. She can't come. She's gone."

"She never told me this could happen. How could this happen? It's not in my schedule."

"It was an accident—something you can't plan for. If your

mother had a choice, I know she would never have left you. She loved you very much."

The girl began to breathe rapidly. Her gazed darted from the headmistress to Jake.

"Charlotte," the director said firmly. "What did your mother ever tell you about your father?"

"My father?"

The question seemed to ground her. "Yes, he was young and handsome and died before I was born...in an accident. Both my parents died in an accident. Does that mean I'll die in one as well?"

"Not at all, my dear." She stood and picked up the telephone. "Send in Aurelia." She turned to Charlotte. "Now then, Aurelia is going to take you back to your cottage and prepare you some dinner. You need to get some rest, and then we'll discuss what comes next...tomorrow."

Relief rolled through him. At least he wouldn't have to stun his daughter with another piece of news. She'd been through too much already.

Aurelia entered the office and Charlotte stood like any well-mannered child. "Thank you, Mr. LeFevre, for bringing me home—to my school."

He stood out of respect for her innate dignity. "You're very welcome. It was my pleasure."

"I hope to see you again."

"Same here, young lady."

He watched her leave. When the door closed behind her and the housemother, he wiped the sweat from his brow. "Is she all right? I thought she'd—hell, I don't know what I thought."

"It hasn't hit her yet. I know you wanted me to tell her that you were her father. I could see it in your eyes, but until there is official verification of your relationship, I thought it best not."

"No, I understand your reluctance. There's time."

"How much longer will you be in New Orleans? Is your—uh, operation over?"

"Not long, but I won't abandon her. Once it's official, I'll have a lot of arrangements to make."

"In the meantime, there are the funeral arrangements for her mother."

"Uh, yeah, I know. Do you know any details?"

"One moment." In a fluid, elegant movement, she rose from the sofa and crossed the room to her desk. She tapped on her keyboard. "Let me see. I've contacted Ms. Andre's attorney of record—one Philip Armitage. Perhaps you'd like to speak with him and advise him of..." She shrugged. "...you know." She clicked and the printer spewed out a sheet of paper. "Here's his address."

"I will. Thank you for everything. I'll be back in touch."

He stood and rejoined Caitlin in the outer office. She rose quickly. "How'd it go? Charlotte seemed quiet enough when she left."

"She understands the literal definition of the dead, but the reality hasn't hit her."

"Are *you* all right?" Kate slid her arm around his waist and stared at him with shining green eyes.

"So far. So good. That's about all I can say."

"Where to next?"

"I have the address of Angie's lawyer. I'll make an appointment to see him—today if possible."

"I'm going with you...if that's okay?"

"You don't have to."

"Yes, I do. You need me—at least I'm vain enough to think you do."

"You're right. I do." He gazed at her, his chest filling with emotions he couldn't quite express. She was there for him—one hundred percent.

Chapter Thirty-two

Jake and Kate walked into the attorney's private office. Typical lawyer digs with leather upholstery and rows of law books. He was greeted by a short, barrel-chested man with a flushed complexion.

"Philip Armitage." He rose and extended his hand to Jake.

"FBI Special Agent in Charge Caitlin Chaney and Special Agent Jake LeFevre," Caitlin said.

Armitage motioned for Jake to be seated. "What can I do for you, agents?"

Jake swallowed. "We're here about Angelique Andre's funeral arrangements and about her daughter. I believe her daughter, Charlotte, is my child. Angie told me shortly before she was murdered. We were together as teenagers. The timing would be right. DNA tests are in the works, but nothing's definite yet."

Kate leaned forward. "Jake wishes to go on record that he is willing, anxious even, to take responsibility should Charlotte prove to be his daughter."

"I intend to initiate adoption proceedings if that is the case." Jake reached for her hand and entwined their fingers.

The attorney's expression never changed. He sat and laced his fingers across his chest. "Ms. Andre elected cremation, and there will be a memorial service at Haley's Funeral Home tomorrow at one. Regarding her daughter, Ms. Andre never addressed the issue of Charlotte's father in her will, even though I specifically requested she do so. If these DNA tests should prove you are her father, we'll discuss the issue further at that time."

"I understand." Nothing else to do, Jake stood, held out his hand to Kate and left the attorney to the comfort of his leather upholstery. She kept a reassuring grip on his hand as they walked to the elevator.

All the way back to his vehicle, he tried to erase the images of the young Angie from his mind. Stealing time to be together whenever they could get away from her *house*. The streets of the French Quarter had been their playground. Those few times had been never enough to suit them. It had ended with his near arrest for murder. He'd never looked back. Ed took him in and gave him a good home and kept him off the streets. Would things have turned out any differently for Angie if he'd made different choices?

Questions he could never answer, but ones which would plague him for a long time.

Kate nudged him, bringing him back to reality. "You're a million miles away."

"Sorry, there's so much to think about."

"For both of us."

Her words troubled him. Neither of them knew what they were getting into... especially Kate.

The next morning, Jake stood in front of the medicine cabinet, tying his tie. Kate was putzing around in the kitchen. The homey sounds were comfortable. "Angie's memorial service is today."

Kate stood in the doorway and set her coffee cup down on the counter. "I haven't forgotten. I'd like to attend."

"You don't have to."

"I want to go—just to be with you. Do you think they'll allow Charlotte to attend?"

Jake nodded. "Yeah. I called the headmistress while you were in the shower. She thinks it'll help Charlotte accept what's happened."

He leaned his hands on the lavatory and shook his head. "God. I already love that kid so much it scares me. I don't know what I would've done if..."

"It didn't happen. She's okay. And you'll be a great father."

He wrapped and slipped the final end of his tie in place. He turned to face Kate; she straightened his tie and tightened it into place. "Thanks, chèr." He planted a light kiss on the tip of her nose.

"So, it's settled. I'm going."

"Okay, you're going." He grinned. "After all, you're the boss."

Kate gave Jake's hand a quick squeeze for moral support as they walked into the funeral home. The atmosphere was hushed; quiet baroque music played in the background.

"May I assist you?"

"Andre service."

"That would be the Magnolia Room," the mortuary greeter said. "Straight down this hall, then left. First room on the left."

They followed the directions to the Magnolia Room. The gathering was small. Caitlin recognized most of them from the casino and what was left of the corporate staff, but in the corner was Charlotte flanked by the headmistress, tall and elegant, with gray hair pulled back in a smooth chignon, along with the woman she'd seen take Charlotte from the headmistress' office. She was shorter and plump with a café au lait complexion. Both women wore black suits. Jake leaned close and whispered, "That's—uh, Aurelia. She's the house mother for Charlotte's cottage."

Caitlin nodded. "I remember seeing her."

She glanced at Lisette, who had to have come for the entertainment since she was attired in a black lace suit complete with a mantilla. Modern Lady of Spain.

"Hail. Hail, the gang's all here," Caitlin said under her breath.

Jake smiled. "Come on, we need to express our condolences."

Kate glanced around cautiously. "We're surrounded by Rivera employees. Think we should? The operation is over, but..."

"We'll play it by ear."

"Hi, Age—" Charlotte's eyebrows drew together in puzzlement.

"LeFevre," he finished quickly before she could announce his agent status to the entire group of mourners.

"You remember Kate. She helped me find you," he said in an undertone.

The girl turned her cool gray gaze on Caitlin. "Did you know my mother?"

"Yes, and I'm so sorry for your loss."

"I didn't lose her. My mother died in an accident, and her ashes are in that urn. I know exactly where she is." She pointed over her shoulder at the silver urn placed bedside a large framed photo of Angelique. "An accident is something you can't plan or schedule."

"Your mother was very pretty," Caitlin said.

"Yes, I don't look like her. She said I look more like my father. He's dead, too, but I never met him. My mother was going to let me move in with her soon. Now, I don't know where I'll go. Ms. Massey said I could stay at the school, but I want a home...like a normal person." Her bottom lip started trembling; the sheen of tears glistened in her eyes. "I-I want my mother. I want my mother!"

The girl's wail rose, peaked, then fell into sobs, hard sobs that wracked Charlotte's slender frame. Caitlin wanted to gather the girl in her arms and comfort her, but Charlotte didn't like to be touched.

Luckily Aurelia, the cottage housemother, was at Charlotte's side. She spoke softly and soothingly. Caitlin couldn't hear what was said, but the girl soon quieted and sat through the remaining service without another outbreak.

How would he ever deal with his child's grief, if she was his child? Dammit. That DNA report had damn well better come back soon.

Once the service was over, Caitlin walked at Jake's side. An overpowering, heavy scent emanated from all the flowers in the small mortuary chapel. Someone nudged her.

Lisette, her former co-worker, frowned and curled her lip. "I've heard all about you, and I know who you really are. A low-down sneak of an FBI agent. It's your fault Heaton's in jail for embezzling," she hissed. "The Feds shut down the casino. We're all looking for jobs—thanks to you!"

"No, it's *his* fault. Whatever the reason, he embezzled the money. There's a lot you don't know about the rest of it. For what it's worth, I'm sorry about your job." Caitlin turned from Lisette and ran ahead to catch up with Jake. She grabbed his hand and let out a deep sigh. "Finally, the funerals are over. This operation is over."

"How much longer can we stay in the loft?"

"We'll stay until you have the DNA results, then I'll make arrangements with the concierge to have the rental furniture removed. Basically, all we have to do is pack our personal belongings. Whatever food's left in the cupboards I'll donate to a homeless shelter."

Nonchalant words and a concise plan. But the thought of leaving the place—the home—where she'd fallen in love, truly fallen in love for the first time....not so clean and simple.

The next morning after dropping Alex at the airport, Jake returned to the loft with the *Times-Picayune.*

"Mail's on the table," Caitlin called from the kitchen, making coffee and something sweet, too, if his nose wasn't mistaken. "There's something you need to see."

Jake shrugged off his jacket, crossed over to the table and picked up the mail. As soon as he read the return address, his hand started shaking.

Metairie Genetics Laboratory.

He ripped apart the envelope. He read the words, but something was out of sync. The words weren't connecting with his brain. What did it say?

Charlotte was his daughter. His child. Yes.

Relief flooded through him. His and Angie's fevered and brief times together had produced the lovely but challenged young girl he'd met only the week before.

"Well?" Caitlin's soft voice brought him back to the present.

"She's mine."

She sat on the arm of the sofa; her hand rested on his shoulder. "What will happen now?"

"Right now, she's a ward of the state. I'll notify the school and then the attorney that I'm proceeding with the adoption. At least Angie thought far enough ahead to see that her estate was in order."

"But what will you do? Where will she live? Who will care for her when you're on assignment?"

"That's something I still have to figure out. All I know is once I met her, I was sure she was mine. I felt a connection..." He shook his head. How could he explain the sadness and disappointment in himself? His throat ached with the effort it took to suppress those feelings. She hadn't signed on for anything like this. He didn't even have a right to ask. He had to give up and let Kate go.

Kate smiled, then said, "We could..."

"What? We could what?"

"There's a superb school outside DC. I checked into it this morning while you were taking Alex to the airport."

His heart swelled with emotion. "Thank you for all the trouble you've gone to, but will the state of Louisiana allow me...?"

"The adoption should only be a formality since you can prove you're her biological father and her only living relative. We can't just let the impersonal State of Louisiana take care of her. She needs someone who loves her. She needs a family, Jake. She needs *us*."

He gazed into Kate's green eyes—eyes that shimmered with unshed tears. Her heart was as big as Ed Hoolihan's, and how he loved her for the offer.

"I can't let you do it." There, he'd finally said it.

"And just why not? Together we can do anything. Hasn't this mission shown you that?"

"It's too much. You have a great career ahead of you. The last thing in the world you need is being tied down with another woman's teenage daughter. Need I add, a daughter with unique challenges?"

"Don't you want me...to help give your daughter a home?"

"Look, if things were different if it was just the two of us, but that's not how it is. I've decided to take a leave of absence until I get things settled here."

"What if I don't *want* to continue with the FBI? What if I've proved all I need to prove? This daughter of yours needs both of us, Jake. You're her father, but she needs a mother, too. And even if I didn't have a mother of my own, I had the most wonderful substitute in the world."

Jake grinned. "Bonnie."

"Yes, my Bon-bon. That's what I used to call her. She loved me, defended me against my father even when he threatened to fire her every other day."

"Are you sure about this?"

"Never been more certain about anything in my life."

"You'd do this for a girl who has no tie to you, whose mother was...?"

"Blood doesn't matter. You already feel something for her, and I do, too."

"Really?"

"We'll make it a family tradition. Ed adopted you. We'll adopt Charlotte."

"Are you asking me to marry you, Kate?"

"No, I'm *telling* you. I'm still in charge."

"Oh, chèr. Are you ever?"

"Well?"

"We need to keep at least one tradition. I'm gonna need to see you get down on your knee for this marriage proposal."

"Me? Well we're not a traditional couple, are we? And I'm still in charge."

He grinned. "That's why you're the one who's going down on bended knee." He loved teasing her.

"All right."

She knelt down, but as she did, so did he. He took her soft, gentle hands in his roughened ones. "You are the most maddening woman I've ever known, and I love you and your open-heart. If you will do me the honor of becoming my wife, I will love and protect you forever."

Tears welled in the most beautiful green eyes he'd ever seen. "Oh, Jake. You are the most maddening man in the world, but I will marry you. Yes, I will."

"Where's my ring?" he asked with a wide grin.

Kate's expression went from a wide, beaming smile to furrowed brows and a frown. "Hm. Your ring? Aren't you carrying this unconventional proposal a little too far?"

He leaned forward and kissed the tip of her nose. "Maybe I am at that." He reached into his pocket and pulled out a small blue box.

Caitlin's mouth dropped at the sight of the Tiffany blue box. Any woman worth the name knew what the small box held.

"You just happen to carry around an engagement ring all the time?"

"Believe in being prepared, chèr. I had a hell of a time getting them to send me this little token, but I finally convinced them."

"Omigod. I mean..."

"For once in your life, words fail you, and you haven't even opened the damn thing yet."

"You're right. Let me see!" It came out as a squeal, but she didn't care. This was a very girly moment, the best she'd ever known. She bit her lips until Jake opened the box and revealed a perfect white, three-carat diamond, Princess setting in platinum.

Her left hand shook as he took it in his strong hand and eased the ring onto her third finger. She held it up and let it flash in the light. She swallowed hard. "It's gorgeous. I've never seen such a... But it's way too expensive... You shouldn't have spent this much. I'd have been happy with a gold band as long as it was from you."

"I can return it," he said flatly and reached for her hand.

"No!" She snatched her hand away, wrapped her arms around his neck and hugged him. "I know you're kidding. It's beautiful and so are you."

His eyes were warm and full of love and good humor. "So, that's all I get for my trouble? A hug and a compliment?"

"Oh, no. You are going to get *so* much more. And whether or not you'll be able to walk tomorrow morning is another issue entirely." She growled into his ear. "I'm gonna have my way with you, and it starts now."

Jake picked her up in his arms and carried her to the bed, then set her down softly. "Yes, it starts now."

Chapter Thirty-three

Jake paced from the living area and back to the kitchen table. He snatched up the coffee mug and drained the last drop of coffee. The strong taste of chicory suited him just fine. It was a New Orleans thing; he'd grown up on the stuff.

"Aren't you ready yet?" he yelled at Kate who was taking her damn sweet time in the bathroom. "Need some help?"

"Not likely. I'll be ready in a minute."

Fingers drumming against the table, he grabbed up the newspaper and read the headlines. *Federal Agents Nab Rivera Corp. Execs*. "Hey, we made the newspaper." He read further. "Local FBI agents—great, give them all the credit."

The next paragraph... "Shit," he muttered. Kate's father was named in the money laundering scheme and was under investigation, and according to an unnamed source, his arrest was imminent. Not that it was a surprise. Kate herself had traced the drug money trail back to her father. But they would have to put it in the paper today of all days. He quickly refolded the newspaper and left it beside his cup.

"Ta-dah!" Kate sauntered into the kitchen and twirled for his approval. She was in her impress-the-world suit of navy blue. Her hair was its natural shade of red again and styled in a sleeker version of the tousled do she'd sported throughout their undercover op.

"So, do I pass muster?"

Her green eyes sparkled—that was all he cared about.

"Sure 'nuff, chèr. You look great. Charlotte will love you. I'm just worried about how she's going to react when she meets me again."

Kate leaned forward, brushed his hair off his forehead and kissed him lightly. "Don't worry. She'll love you the way I do." Arms crossed, she stood back and gave him the once over, then flicked a piece of lint off his lapel. "You're perfect."

He shook his head. "Far from it."

Doubts plagued him during the drive to Bridgeview. Doubt about his ability to guide this special child of his to a happy and productive life. Doubt about his ability to deal with her special needs. Doubt about overwhelming her with a new family and a new school.

Kate reached over and patted his knee. "It'll be all right. You can do this...we can do this.

He forced his hands to relax on the steering wheel. "Yeah, sure."

The manicured grounds of the school came into view, and he gripped the wheel tighter. Screw up—that's what he was. What he'd always been until Ed.

Thank God for Ed Hoolihan's intervention so long ago, and thank God for the woman riding by his side. None of this would be possible without her open heart and loving nature. "I love you."

She smiled at him, and his breath caught in his chest. It seemed as if his heart filled with all the love he knew she possessed. Damn. He was one lucky son of a bitch.

Jake and Kate were shown into Ms. Massey's office. The headmistress rose from her desk and held out her hand in greeting to him and Kate in turn. "I'm so glad we're resolving Charlotte's future in this fashion. For all intents and purposes, it's an ideal arrangement for her. Her biological father and...Agent Chaney?"

"Ms. Massey, Caitlin is my fiancée. We plan to give Charlotte a very stable and loving home."

"Agent Chaney." The headmistress smiled and nodded. "I hope

you understand about Charlotte's special needs." With a graceful movement, she motioned for them to be seated.

Kate sat, then leaned forward. "Yes, I'm well aware of Charlotte's gifts and the challenges ahead. I've done as much research as possible. We've located a wonderful school in DC for her until she's completely ready to live with us full time."

"Yes, research is one thing, but the reality of living with a child with Asperger's Syndrome is something else." Mrs. Massey returned to her seat.

"I know, but we're determined to do everything humanly possible to give her a good life and home."

"Hold on. I'm still here," Jake interjected. "What else has Charlotte been told about me?"

"We've prepared her as much as possible. She's been told her biological father has been located and that she will meet him today. The rest is up to you. Don't expect too much."

"As long as she doesn't scream in horror and run from the room, that'll be good enough."

Mrs. Massey gave him a polite smile. "Indeed." She punched a button on her desk console. "We're ready for Charlotte and Aurelia."

Jake drummed his fingers on the chair arm, the sound reverberating in the subdued, almost tomblike atmosphere of the office. He tried to stop but couldn't.

"Mr. LeFevre, being nervous is only natural. This is a life-changing moment for all of you."

"Thanks for not adding to the pressure," he quipped before he thought better of it.

Kate's hand on his knee was the only thing that kept him halfway sane. Where was his daughter coming from—outer Siberia?

But then, too soon, the office door opened, and his daughter entered with her caregiver, Aurelia.

"You're the agent who rescued me. Why are you here?" She gazed up at Aurelia. "I'm supposed to meet my real father, aren't I? It's exactly eleven-ten, and that's when my schedule says I'm to meet him."

"Yes, honey, and now why don't you let this good man explain why he's here."

Jake swallowed. Damn. He might as well have rolled snake eyes seven times in a row, his throat was so dry. He stood slowly. He already knew not to make sudden movements or touch her, although he desperately wanted to take her in his arms and tell her he would take care of her, love her for the rest of his life.

"I'm Jake LeFevre, Charlotte. And yes, I'm the agent who rescued you when you were kidnapped. Your mother and I were friends when we were just a little older than you are now."

The quizzical expression in her pale gray eyes didn't alter.

"We were very close friends, but I was homeless and just a little older than you are when a very good man, a cop, adopted me. I didn't know your mother was going to have you. Even though I was just a kid, I would never have abandoned your mother. I didn't know she'd had a baby until she told me shortly before she passed away."

"Dead. She's dead," she said flatly.

"Yes, that's right."

Shit. Would he be able to get through to her or not?

"I want to give you a home with me and," he nodded in Kate's direction, "Caitlin. She's my fiancée."

"Fiancée. That means you're going to get married." Her reactions remained flat with monotone responses.

"Yes, it does." He sucked in a deep breath. Might as well wager the whole wad and go for broke. He continued, careful to keep his tone soft and non-threatening. "We want you to live with us when you're ready to leave the school."

"I was supposed to live with my mother. But she died." His daughter glanced at her caregiver. "What should I do? What if he— my father—dies, too? Where would I go then?"

"You don't have to worry about that, honey. Your father's not going to die for a very long time."

Aurelia's soft southern voice was soothing. The woman seemed to have a calming effect on his daughter. Maybe...

"No. I have to know the contingencies. My mother didn't plan on dying. She would have told me if she had." She eyeballed him. Except for her gray eyes, she looked so much like his mother it was eerie.

"Are you going to die the way she did? Someone killed her. You're an FBI agent—isn't that a dangerous job?"

Damn. His daughter was relentless. "It can be, but there are things I can do at the agency that doesn't involve fieldwork—that's what we call the—uh, dangerous work."

Charlotte turned to Mrs. Massey. "I know him. He's the one who rescued me. There's something about him. He doesn't make me upset. Like I get sometimes—you know?"

"Yes, Charlotte, I know."

"What about my school?"

Kate spoke before he could. "We've found you a wonderful school, much like this one, but closer to where we'll be living."

Thank God for Kate. His daughter's unwavering attention was overwhelming. What had he gotten all of them into? Surely taking his daughter home wasn't the wrong thing. Why was doing the right thing always so damn hard?

"But you won't be there long," Kate continued.

"How long?"

"Long enough for your father and me to settle in our home and for the two of us to educate ourselves on...on your condition and how we can be the best parents for you."

Charlotte shook her head. "I don't like change. I have to have a schedule."

"That's one of the things we'll be learning," Jake said. "We'll learn about your schedule. We'll have a studio just for your art." He glanced at Aurelia and hoped she could see the unspoken plea in his heart. Could they take this wonderful woman with them? Even if it was just for a short time?

"When?" This bald question from his daughter.

"Soon. The school says they will take you anytime in the next month." How Caitlin managed to get the school to take her mid-term and ahead of the waiting list, he really didn't want to know.

Her political connections probably. No doubt those same connections would dry up pretty damn quick now that it was general knowledge that her father was a corrupt crook.

"'Soon' is an adverb, but it isn't specific. I need to know exactly." Damn if she didn't pull a smartphone from the pocket of her skirt. "I'll add the date to the calendar." She gazed at him waiting for his response.

Jake calculated in his head, one day to pack up their personal items from the condo, paperwork all done, uh...

"Wednesday morning at ten," Kate said. "We'll pick you up. It takes thirty minutes to get to the airport from here. That gives us two hours to go through the safety checks. Our flight is at twelve-thirty."

Charlotte quickly entered the information into her cell phone. "Good. You're very specific and organized. I like you." She turned to Jake. "Your fiancée is efficient. Is that why you chose her?"

A smile tugged at his lips. "That's only one of *many* reasons I chose her."

Not deterred by his smile, she tapped on another app. "And the others? I'd like to list them. My records are always complete."

He reached for Kate's hand. "She's the love of my life and puts up with all my idiosyncrasies." Before his daughter could ask for a list of those, he quickly added, "I'm sure Kate will fill you in on all my faults later."

"Idiosyncrasies aren't always faults. They are—"

"Charlotte," Mrs. Massey interrupted. "It's time for your art class. You will have sufficient time in the coming days to get to know your father, but it's best if you keep to your schedule while you remain with us."

"Yes, you're right." Charlotte nodded. "Good-bye. I will be ready on Wednesday at ten-twenty-five which allows five minutes for error." Without another word she turned and left the room with Aurelia following close behind her.

Jake let out a low groan and wiped the sweat from his brow. "I think she'll make a hell of an interrogator someday."

Kate rose from her chair. "Thank you for all your efforts with

Charlotte. There's just one thing... I don't know if I should even ask, but is there any way Aurelia could come with Charlotte? They seem so close, and it would ease the transition. We'll pay her handsomely."

"That would be up to Aurelia. I'll put the proposition before her and let you know."

"Thank you."

Once they were outside the school, Jake raked his fingers through his hair. "Have you lost your mind? We can't possibly be ready to take her with us on Wednesday. Today's Monday, for Pete's sake."

"Jake, Jake, Jake." She shook her head and rolled her eyes. "Of course we can. Just leave it to me."

Leave it to her? And why not? The woman he loved could whip her weight in poker chips, rescue his sorry ass from the bad guys, order the best take-out food in town, and then screw him until he didn't know his dick from a pool cue.

Leave it to her? You bet he would.

Epilogue

Four months later

Six-thirty. Caitlin couldn't wait any longer. Her hands shook as she opened the box and read the specific directions. She'd already read them the night before, but she didn't want to make any mistakes. She had to know.

Jake was still in bed sound asleep in their bed on the second floor, as were Charlotte and Aurelia in their private apartment on the newly renovated third floor of the townhouse.

The smell of freshly brewed coffee reached the second floor which meant Bonnie was up and moving around in the kitchen. The same Bonnie who suspected Caitlin was expecting.

All right here we go.

She pulled out the stick and peed on it, then checked her watch, noting the time. After the required minutes had passed, she took a deep breath and picked it up.

A definite blue plus sign. Pregnant.

She carried a new life within her body, a life borne of their frenzied, tender and frequently wild lovemaking.

Suddenly the realization she was no longer in control swamped her like a storm surge. She was committed—even more than the simple ceremony had committed her to Jake and his daughter. This child would depend on her body for sustenance for the next eight months, and then look to her for everything...home, shelter, guidance and most of all love for the rest of his or her life.

A life sentence.

She wouldn't fail this baby of hers, not like her father had failed her. No shame would tarnish this child's life. Her hand instinctively cradled her lower abdomen. She smiled, but her heart ached with a touch of sadness. Caitlin's mother would never know her grandchild, but there were plenty of people who would love this little life, and one of them was in the next room.

She walked back into the bedroom. Jake was still asleep.

No. He turned over and smiled sleepily at her. "What has you up so early?"

She scooted under the covers and snuggled under the covers against his warmth and morning woody. "I have some news."

"That's nice." He kissed her neck, cupped her breasts in his strong hands, and tweaked her nipples. "I have something for you, too."

"Mm, yes, I can tell." She brushed his dark hair from his eyes. "We're going to have to add a room to the house."

Puzzlement wrinkled his brow. "But we're almost through converting the basement gym into Charlotte's studio."

"We are, but..." She paused to tease him and give him a second or two to guess her real meaning.

"My brain's not firing yet." He gave a low sensual growl. "I just need some coffee...or some loving from my wife." He nudged her belly with his erection, and she melted into a warm pool of need, but she persevered.

"A nursery, darling. We're going to need a nursery in about seven and a half months."

Jake's brows rose, and a smile broke across his entire face. He hugged her so tightly she couldn't breathe.

"I love you so much, chèr. I can't believe it. I'm the happiest man in the world."

"How could we have known our first meeting in Jose's office would end like this?

"You were such an upright and uptight witch."

He nibbled a trail of kisses from her ear to her throat. Her nipples tightened into points of pleasure and she gave a low moan. "And you were such a jerk."

"I was." His hand slipped underneath her gown and dipped into her damp folds.

"I remember." She parted her thighs and reached for his cock and rubbed the head up and down her slit. "Come here."

He levered onto his elbows and paused. "Is it all right? Now—I mean—"

"Yes," she hissed. Already wet, she was more than ready for him. She wrapped her legs around his waist and arched upward to meet his first strong thrust. Their fingers entwined above her head, they moved together in burning thrust after thrust until her orgasm exploded in waves of fire.

Jake increased the pace of his driving thrusts and finally groaned as he came in a sudden rush of pleasure. He sank into the sweet warmth of her body and arms. "I love you, chèr," he gasped. "You've given me so much, more love than I ever thought possible."

Beneath him, she breathed in ragged gasps. "At least I've proved one thing. I can hold my own—my own husband and soon our baby." She cradled his face in her hands. "I love you so much. You and Charlotte and our baby are all I'll ever need."

"No regrets? You've given up your career...everything for me."

"Regrets? You've given me love...a family...a real life. No. For the first time in my life, I don't have any regrets...or anything to prove."

About the Author

Marie-Nicole Ryan was born in a small western Kentucky town, but after college and marriage, she said "Goodbye" to small-town life. After spending three years as an army wife, she landed in Nashville, TN, where she spent several decades working as an R.N. and case manager. Finally, in 2002, she achieved her lifelong dream of becoming a published author.

She loves all lawmen and detectives and writes erotic historical western romance and contemporary romantic suspense. TOO GOOD TO BE TRUE, won a 2008 EPPIE for erotic romantic suspense. In addition, her mystery/suspense novel, ONE TOO MANY, was a 2009 EPPIE Finalist.

She returned to her old hometown in western Kentucky in 2010. When she's not slaving away at her current work in progress, you might find her walking her dog Cassie, a Sheltie rescue, or at the Y. But you won't ever find her on an airplane. No, not ever.

She's a former member of Romance Writers of America® To learn more about Marie-Nicole Ryan, please visit her web site at marienicoleryan.com. To keep up with her latest releases, news, and contests, send an email to Marie-NicoleRyanNews-subscribe@yahoo.com_Or you may follow her on:
Facebook: http://facebook.com/marienicoleryan.author
Twitter: @MarieNicoleRyan

Read on for an excerpt from the next book in the FBI Guys series, *Broken Promises*.

BROKEN PROMISES

FBI Guys 2

© 2011 Marie-Nicole Ryan

Chapter One

The phone rang.

"Just ignore it," she whispered and pressed her lips and body against his.

It rang again.

Alex shuddered awake. To an empty bed and no sign of a woman. Hell, he'd dreamed about Bette again. An unwelcome reminder he'd been too busy to check on her since they'd gone their separate ways. He groaned and reached for the phone. "MacGregor."

"It's Bette. You have to come home."

Was her tone a touch on the hysterical side? That was Bette's voice, all right. "No can do. Things are about to break on this case—"

"No, you don't understand. Listen to me. You have to come home. Your sister is *missing*."

He sat up and rubbed the sleep from his eyes. A never-quite-forgotten dread jarred his gut and spiked his heart rate. He squinted at the clock. Four. And not a sign of dawn.

"What do you mean she's missing? Where's Brad?" Brad was his sister's husband. Why wasn't he calling?

"He's in New York for a seminar." A note of rising panic was clear in her voice, as well as more than a hint of her Jersey-girl accent.

"Hold on. Take a deep breath. Start at the beginning. What makes you think she's missing?"

"I left her alone in the office last night. Just as we were leaving, someone pulled in and said his cat was ill. She told me to go on home, that she'd take a look at the cat, and then head on to the emergency clinic. Last night, she was supposed to be on call, but the clinic assistant called me after trying Jackie's cell and home phones." She took a couple of gulping breaths. "Omigod, Alex, she never showed up. She's gone—like, vanished into thin air. Someone took her!"

"Okay, maybe she had car trouble and her cell phone was dead," he suggested, trying to think of less ominous reasons for his sister's being out of touch.

"No, she keeps her phone charged during office hours. Something's happened. I just know it. I shouldn't have left her alone with him."

"Why did you?" An accusatory tone crept into his voice, even if Canandaigua wasn't nearly as dangerous as Chicago.

"I thought it was someone she knew. I mean, I heard her laugh when they went inside."

A nightmare. A freaking nightmare. Why couldn't he still be dreaming? "Have you called the police?"

"Yes. They're trying to find Brad at his hotel."

"Where's Cody?" His five-year-old nephew must be terrified to learn his mother was missing if he'd even been told.

"He had a sleepover last night at the Crandalls'. What should I do? Should I pick him up? Take him to kindergarten or wait until Brad gets home?"

He could almost hear Bette wringing her hands. "Call the Crandalls. Tell them what's happened. Have them send Cody to school. The locals will want to talk to Brad." The husband or significant other was always the first suspect in a woman's disappearance. "I'll catch the next flight to Buffalo. No, wait. First, I have to let my boss know what's going on." Asking for personal leave while he was ass-deep in a serial killer case could stall his career with the Bureau for years. Talk about kissing his dream job on the Violent Crimes Task Force good-bye.

Couldn't be helped. No question about it. No way could he endure losing his sister the way he'd lost his brother Andy. His identical twin.

"I'm sorry, Alex." Bette's voice quivered, sounding clogged with tears. "I know you're busy, but I just didn't know who else to call. The sheriff's deputy didn't seem too alarmed. The jerk acted like she was probably stepping out while Brad was out of town. I haven't known her all that long, but I know she'd never run around. And she'd *never* miss her turn at the emergency clinic."

"You're right." Trying to clear his head, he stood and yawned until his jaw popped. "Hang tight. I'll call you as soon as I'm on the ground."

He rang off, shook his head, shrugged into a shirt, and tugged on a pair of jeans. He snatched up the go-bag he kept packed. An FBI agent could conceivably be sent anywhere on a moment's notice. Being prepared wasn't just for the Boy Scouts. He called a cab. Since this was personal, he'd be on his own for transport and—

Crap! He hadn't called the Special Agent in Charge.

He called and awakened the SAC. By the time he finished giving the SAC a sit-rep, he was downstairs in time to meet the cab as it pulled to the curb.

Still, on the phone, he nodded and tossed his go-bag into the backseat. "O'Hare," he told the cabbie and slid inside. "Yes, sir," he continued with his SAC. "I know it's inconvenient. Yes, I realize I can't function in an official capacity, even if the locals call in the Bureau."

While he rode to the airport, he used his iPhone to purchase a ticket on the next flight to Buffalo.

The SAC was understanding but made it clear Alex would be replaced on the VCTF if his situation wasn't resolved in forty-eight hours.

Forty-eight short hours to find his sister.

But forty-eight hours was a long time to avoid getting involved with one sexy Bette Smithson. Dark chocolate doe's eyes. Dark brown hair, thick and silky as a waterfall. No matter how much he'd itched to get tangled up in the sheets with her last New Year's Eve, he'd remained a gentleman.

Damn. Who the hell cared about being a gentleman nowadays? No one he knew.

And what'd he done? He'd kissed her *adios*, put her on the plane to Buffalo, and forgot all about her.

Almost.

That one heated—and unfortunately unforgettable—kiss had been a mistake, all right. He'd promised he'd call. And he hadn't. Now he'd be forced to face the woman who plagued his dreams. Dreams like he hadn't experienced since he was a horny teen.

Bette set aside the phone and balled her fists. Good-guy hero Double-O was on the way. He'd find Jackie before anyone hurt her...if they hadn't already. Dammit. Things like this weren't supposed to happen. Not to someone as good and kind as her boss. After all, Jackie was as much a friend as a boss. When Bette had landed on Jackie's doorstep, she'd welcomed Bette with open arms and given her a job and a place to live.

Still, there must be something she could do before Alex arrived, which probably wouldn't be for another two or three hours. And only if his flight connected just right.

Not like New Year's Day, when she'd flown from Nashville to Buffalo. Jackie's husband had braved the ice and snow, picking up Bette at the airport. At least in June, the roads were clear, making Alex's drive from Buffalo a breeze.

Calling Alex took every ounce of courage she possessed and shook her to the core. Bette wouldn't have called him, not in a million years, if not for Jackie. In spite of their brief night together—where nothing actually happened, thank you very much—it seemed they had a connection. At the airport, he promised to call soon. And then he kissed her. Kissed her good, like call-your-best-girlfriend-and-tell-her-all-about-it good.

Guess Special Agent MacGregor was just too busy with his new job to keep his promises. Hell. He wasn't the first man to disappoint her. Not by a long shot.

Still, none of that mattered. Not really. Not when his sister was missing and maybe already dead. And it was Bette's fault.

I should've stayed with her.

But, hell, this was Canandaigua. Upstate New York, for Pete's sake. Nothing much ever happened here. People didn't lock their doors, except maybe in the summertime when the small rural town was flooded with tourists.

Lined with summerhouses, Canandaigua Lake's ice-blue waters drew boaters and water-skiers. The perfect climate and the hills above the lake were ideal for growing grapes, which made the Finger Lakes area the New York version of Napa Valley. In addition, there were a million and one places to go and things to do, from antiques to boutiques to one-of-a-kind potteries. And for a small town, Canandaigua boasted some very fine eating establishments. Very fine indeed.

Yet in the middle of all this idyllic beauty, Jackie Stinnett had vanished as surely and silently as the early morning mist on Canandaigua Lake.